THE

SCEPTRED ISLE CLUB

John Le Brun novels by Brent Monahan

The Jekyl Island Club (Book 1)

The Manhattan Island Clubs (Book 3)

The St. Simons Island Club (Book 4)

available now

The St. Lucia Island Club (Book 5)

new release for Fall 2016

THE SCEPTRED ISLE CLUB

A JOHN LE BRUN NOVEL

by

Brent Monahan

Turner Publishing Company
424 Church Street • Suite 2240 • Nashville, Tennessee 37219
445 Park Avenue • 9th Floor • New York, New York 10022

www.turnerpublishing.com

The Sceptred Isle Club, A Novel

Cover design: Maddie Cothren
Book design: Glen Edelstein

Library of Congress Cataloging-in-Publication Data

Names: Monahan, Brent, 1948-
Title: The Sceptred Isle Club / by Brent Monahan.
Description: Nashville, TN : Turner Publishing Company, [2016] | ©2002 | Series: A John Le Brun novel ; book 2
Identifiers: LCCN 2015035663| ISBN 9781681621135 (softcover) | ISBN 9781681620329 (hardcover)
Subjects: LCSH: Le Brun, John (Fictitious character)--Fiction. | Sheriffs--England--London--Fiction. | Men--Societies and clubs--Fiction. | Murder--Investigation--Fiction. | Americans--England--Fiction. | GSAFD: Historical fiction. | Mystery fiction.
Classification: LCC PS3563.O5158 S28 2016 | DDC 813/.54--dc23
LC record available at http://lccn.loc.gov/2015035663

Printed in the United States of America
15 14 13 12 11 10 9 8 7 6 5 4 3 2 1

For

Rosemarie Monahan

who loved mysteries

PROLOGUE

Wednesday, October 18, 1905

TIMOTHY BURKE WALKED UNDER the enormous clock in London's King's Cross Station. The clock's hands indicated 10:32. He had arrived two minutes late, which he knew would be a problem. He swept the waiting room with his eyes. He had expected the place to be largely deserted at such a late hour, but travelers and employees alike plodded in and out. As he had been instructed, he moved to an empty bench close by the clock that had another empty bench directly behind it.

Burke had with him a shoe box tied up with string. He set it on the floor behind his feet and opened a copy of *The Strand Magazine.* He scanned the paragraphs of a detective story with no interest. Presently, he heard the rustling of a newspaper behind him.

"If you're late here, how dependable will you be on Saturday?" asked the holder of the newspaper. The words, spoken in a forceful whisper, gave the voice an androgynous, almost ghostlike quality.

"I came here by foot and misjudged the walk," Burke defended, holding up his magazine so no one would see his lips moving, assuming the newspaper holder was doing the same behind him.

"Perhaps you should ride less and walk more."

He guided the shoe box as far back as he could with his heel.

Inside it, cushioned in crumpled newspaper, lay two Belgian-made Galand service revolvers. They were a poor choice of weapon for killing beyond twenty feet, but more than adequate for the close-in slaughter the recipient intended. "There won't be any trouble on Saturday," Burke said in firm, measured tones.

"There had better not be. You must have everything assembled well in advance."

"I know. I've already got my ticket for the train."

"Have you purchased a whistle?"

"I have."

"The safety of the one we both love hangs in the balance."

"I am well aware of that. You really don't have to lecture me," Burke said.

"You got all day Saturday *and* Sunday off?"

"Yes. Cost me two crowns for the favor. Speaking of money, I'll need some, for the guns, the lodging, my food, the train, the—"

"Jesus Christ, don't you put anything aside?"

"With what you stand to make, you're taking *me* up on a few bob?"

"Anything I make is an indirect result. If someone were able to suddenly shift the Thames ten miles south of London, they wouldn't produce the effect we're about to. We shall change the history of the British Empire on Saturday, young man. I should think you'd be willing to contribute a few shillings up front."

"I'm risking my bloody life," defended Burke through clenched teeth.

"So am I. When I get up, I'll leave a ten pound note under the bench."

Burke heard the newspaper close.

"And, Timothy?" the voice said. "Don't forget the bottle to collect the blood."

ONE

Wednesday, October 18, 1905

"YOU ARE SITTING WITH one of the world's best detectives," Geoffrey Moore declared to the other guests at the dinner table.

The beaming smile his promoter offered John Le Brun was halfheartedly returned. In the six years of their acquaintance, John had come to admire Moore for several characteristics. The Englishman's compulsion to fill silences with speech was not one of them. One such silence had punctuated the conversation at the captain's table aboard the *Empress*, but only for a moment.

"I'm just a simple sheriff from Georgia," Le Brun asserted, to ten sets of widened eyes. "My friend likes to brag on me."

"And well I should," Moore insisted. He was seated at the bottom end of the table for twelve, directly opposite white-bearded Captain Reginald Winslow. John sat to Moore's immediate right, making it easy for the Englishman to focus past his scowl. "He solved a murder at the most exclusive men's club in America. Have you heard of The Jekyl Island Club?"

Two heads nodded. Four shook no. The rest perched on their necks unmoved, as if they belonged to waxwork dummies.

"It lies off the coast of Georgia, and its members are the wealthiest in America," Moore shared. "Membership is strictly limited to one hundred, but that handful controls one-sixth of the entire country's wealth. The Vanderbilts, Rockefellers, Goulds. What's more, Mr. Le Brun solved the case while President McKinley was visiting. Saved the life of J. P. Morgan as a bonus."

"My, my," said the woman seated directly across from Le Brun, arching a respectful eyebrow. She had been introduced as Alice Lamb. She looked to be about thirty and seemed to come from money. Peacock feathers and tortoise combs adorned her curly brown hair. She wore an evening dress of black satin with cut velvet motifs and rhinestone details, trimmed with Chantilly lace. The bodice was cut low so that an impressive rope of pearls could rest upon her flawless white neck and upper chest. For added effect, she raised her right hand and covered the lowest arc of the necklace, as if to suppress her thumping heart. "It would seem that you are too modest, Sheriff Le Brun."

John noted the slight slur in her voice from overindulgence in champagne. "No. Too lucky."

The group laughed dutifully, guessing there was humor somewhere in Le Brun's reply.

"The only luck he had was that Joseph Pulitzer is also a member," Moore bulled on. "The newspaperman was able to help Mr. Le Brun deduce that the club's physician, of all people, was the murderer."

"Oh, yes. Pulitzer is a genius," a woman named Davenport seated close to the captain asserted. Not at all embarrassed at having stolen Le Brun's thunder, she asked him, "How long ago was this?"

"Six years," John replied.

"And how was it that we didn't hear about such an incident?" her bookish-looking female traveling companion inquired.

"For the same reason that these folk chose an island a thousand miles from New York," John answered. "They don't like the rest of the world knowin' about their affairs."

"Wintering resort, is it?" Alice's husband asked. Raymond Lamb looked not much older than his wife. His evening dress was impeccable, his dark hair pomaded with brilliantine. He sat as erect as if he had a lightning rod for a backbone.

"That's correct," John replied. He rearranged the snapping fresh linen napkin on his lap.

"A true wilderness from civilization. I expect you picked up your skills from the College of Hard Knocks," Lamb said, through a smarmy smile.

"I had plans to attend university, but a long war intervened," John replied, with a stare that dared Lamb to make light of the War of the Succession. The man declined. "Which university did you attend?"

"Columbia," Lamb announced with overloud pride, his eyes roaming the table to collect the looks of admiration.

"Fine school. And what have you done with such excellent education, Mr. Lamb?"

Lamb's elbows rested on the edge of the table. He made a tent of his hands and smiled over it. "Oh, I've dabbled in several businesses. Real estate, mostly."

John studied the man's soft hands and perfectly manicured fingernails. *Not the dirt variety of real estate*, he thought. *He will never drown in sweat.*

The conversation shifted resolutely to the precipitous climb in the price of Manhattan property, as if everyone had believed Geoffrey Moore was indeed exaggerating and glad to be done with the tale of the super-rich and murder. John was relieved to be dismissed as a topic of conversation. He glanced slowly around the grand dining room, with its twelve tables and one hundred and forty first-class passengers, all as well behaved as children at their first high tea. Every night, a different set of first-class passengers was bestowed the honor of sitting with the ship's captain. John felt more comfortable with the group he and Moore had assembled during the first day's voyage: an elderly couple from Washington, D.C. and a pair of businessmen from Atlanta. Everyone else they met came from the North or from England, and their words eventually betrayed their condescension at John's sun-worn looks and his accent. He had been told the crossing on the *Empress* from New York City to Southampton, England, averaged six days and twenty hours, and between the supercilious passengers and the limitless seas, it would not end a moment too soon.

The chamber ensemble returned from their break, launching into a Parisian can-can energetic enough to mask the words at the captain's end of the table. John figured the music would make him all that much safer. Then Mrs. Davenport spoke.

"Every time I visit England, I go to Canterbury. Do you plan to duplicate the Shire Reeve's pilgrimage, Sheriff Le Brun?"

"I'm not sure yet, ma'am," he returned. "I might could."

Mrs. Davenport and her companion nodded as one.

John redirected his gaze in time to witness Raymond Lamb whispering something in his wife's ear. Looking straight at John, she laughed. Her fork had been raised almost to her mouth. As her body quivered with giddy mirth, the morsel of beef tenderloin on its tines lost a dollop of bechamel sauce. It landed squarely on the largest pearls of her necklace.

With a gallant flourish, Le Brun daubed his napkin into his water glass and offered it to the woman. Her husband reached out first, acknowledged his thanks with a curt nod, and proceeded to clean the necklace bead by bead.

Geoffrey Moore touched his companion lightly on his sleeve and, with lids lowered to signal the barb to come, said in a stage whisper that could be heard halfway down the table, "Some people should lay off the sauce."

The *Empress* was not one of the new Cunard Line leviathans such as the *Ivernia* or *Saxonia,* which were called "express steamers" and both of which made the Liverpool-to-Boston crossing in less than five days. The *Empress* had been launched fully seventeen years earlier and offered passage at a relative bargain. Geoffrey Moore had chosen the ship not for economy, however, but rather because it was to leave New York City only sixteen hours after he and John had arrived there from Georgia. If they had delayed in New York for even three more days, Moore had declared, unique opportunities would be missed in London. Thus, an extra thirty hours on the high seas had to be endured by John Le Brun, who was a dedicated landlubber.

John moved to the upper deck's sturdy portside rail and clamped his fingers around it. Every night before sleeping, he perambulated the ship, ostensibly for an evening constitutional but in fact to reassure himself that the lifeboats still hung from their davits.

The stars were hard, untwinkling pinpricks of light beyond the cold North Atlantic air. Among them, the moon hung so still that it seemed hammered to the heavens. In contrast, its beams danced tirelessly upon the restless, rolling sea. John had looked at more water in the past four days than he had ever imagined existed. When he thought about the fact that three miles of ocean lay directly beneath the ship's keel, he felt a bit unbalanced. The planking under his feet, however, felt remarkably solid. He marveled at how smoothly the passenger liner cut through the rough surface of the deep.

Daunting as the crossing was to Le Brun, the landing would inaugurate the greatest challenge of his life. This was John's great Voyage of Discovery. As far as Geoffrey Moore was concerned, the trip to England was a mere holiday for his friend. While John had been talking about it for five years, he had not been able to get away until his retirement at the age of fifty-eight. Geoffrey had been let in on the fact that a bit of investment knowledge stolen from J. P. Morgan during the solution of the Jekyl Island Club murders had allowed the ex-sheriff to retire early. He had not been made privy to the fact that John could have indulged in a trip to England and France at any time in the past five years. Yet John had delayed, postponed, bided. After he retired on the first day of July in 1905, he could reasonably have been in England a week later. Yet, he continued to temporize, electing to wait until Moore's next visit to Brunswick and to arrive in England at the side of the well-traveled, well-educated Englishman. Moore was Le Brun's unwitting buttress, the city mouse leading the country mouse.

Born in 1847, Jean-Chrétien Le Brun (as he had been christened) was like an intricately crafted chronograph inside a deceptively simple housing. He was third-generation American, from more or less pure French extraction. His heritage had been partially from royalty fleeing the French Revolution. Any vestiges of education and refinement that emigrated with them, however, soon vanished. His family had lived among the south Georgia Golden Isles for all of those generations, owning large stretches of land from which a good living could be extracted but from which it was difficult to grow rich. John had been raised as a Sea Isle cotton farmer but had more intellectual curiosity than his relatives. Virtually any book he could lay his hands on was read. Eager to discuss the knowledge he learned and to add his own speculation, he became an annoyance to his parents, siblings, cousins, aunts, and uncles. Not that they were not appreciative and in awe of their kinsman. In fact, by 1860 it had been decided within the family that their surplus money must be pooled, to send their brightest son up to the College of William and Mary.

Then Lincoln had been elected, and the South had seceded. The War of Northern Aggression forever put an end to John's dreams. As one of their most precious commodities, the family had held him back from the fighting against his will until November of 1864. He was one of many youths whom Jefferson Davis sadly referred to as "grinding our seed corn." He was wounded in March of 1865 and recovered but slowly. After John became well enough to attend university, there was no money to support him. The economy had been wrecked. Every time it rallied, a depression would descend on the Golden Isles. John had no choice but to return to the soil beside his less intellectually adept and curious cousins.

The bitterness of defeat and the despair of opportunity caused John to retreat into himself, a private man who could only be drawn out with difficulty. An insightful, young woman named Claire Caulaincourt had seen through John's quiet exterior and married him. She was clever if uneducated, and she had been delighted to act as an insightful sounding board. She alone made the simple life on Jekyll Island tolerable, until she had died of one of the periodic yellow fever epidemics that swept through the Georgia lowlands. She had been carrying what would have been their first child. The twin losses stole his courage to risk such an intimate relationship again. In the years following, several understanding women took from him as much as he was willing to give. None of them was a woman of breeding or high education.

Soon after his wife died, John gave up farming and moved across the water to the mainland town of Brunswick. At first, he worked as a handyman. Occasionally, he earned money when an extra deputy was needed. In time, his natural gifts for enforcing the law were noted by the town fathers, and he was promoted for sheriff. His service record in the war and his wounding further guaranteed his election. Partly because John had served as such a successful law officer, Brunswick had grown into a peaceful and safe resort city. The outside world seeped in. From time to time, John found a learned vacationer, whom he would drain of knowledge with vampire-like intent. An inventor of internal combustion machinery, a published poetess, two professors, several physicians, and a militant abortion rights advocate were but a few of the passing parade whom John befriended and interviewed. From a naturalist photographer who had journeyed to Brunswick to capture images of the marshes of Glynn, he had learned chess. It had become his great passion. The influx of vacationers allowed a theater and an opera house to thrive in Brunswick. Through frequent attendance, John had been exposed to the most profound and artistic investigations of the human condition. His disquiet grew.

Sharp analytical skills, a keen eye and a near-photographic memory suited John ideally for investigative work. He had indeed solved several difficult crimes in his first years as sheriff, but nothing in his life had compared to solving the murders at the fabulous Jekyl Island Club. From that moment on, a mantle of celebrity had been draped around his shoulders. From that moment, too, the hunger for validation began to consume him. His success with crime-solving suggested an extraordinary intelligence, but he could never know from his limited vantage point in provincial Brunswick whether he was merely the one-eyed man in the land of the blind and the Jekyl Island Club solution a fluke. Only considerable exposure within a concentration of intelligentsia would satisfy him that he could have been someone of greatness had fate only been kinder. Over the years, Geoffrey Moore had assured him again and again that London was the hub of the learned world. He promised to introduce his American friend to great and accomplished persons on a daily fare. There was no war or depression to thwart him.

The long-delayed Voyage of Discovery would be a grand, self-imposed test. If he passed to his own satisfaction, John had decided he must reinvent himself and transform his life. He was not yet sixty. With luck, he had perhaps a score of years ahead of him. Only a few friends held him to Brunswick. He had to find out if he would be happier in a one-room apartment near libraries, museums, and theaters than on his quiet acre in Brunswick. But first he had to see if he truly belonged.

John reflected on the evening's table conversation. When he had used the phrase "wish book,"a few eyebrows had furrowed, and he remembered that those in the North called them "mail order catalogues." Clearly, the Southern penchant for softening expressed desires by saying "might could" instead of "perhaps" invoked derision in some Yankees. John was not about to allow himself to be judged by the likes of Raymond or Alice Lamb. But how much should he worry about his accent and Southernisms presenting baffles through which his true intelligence might be obscured to worthy judges? Regardless, the black beast of self-doubt had been conquered, and he was finally on his way. *But,* he asked himself, *to what?*

As he gazed down into the dark waters, John remembered a phrase from Oscar Wilde's *Lady Windemere's Fan:* In this world there are only two tragedies. One is not getting what one wants, and the other is getting it.

TWO

Thursday, October 19, 1905

HIS FROCK COAT NEEDED pressing already. John studied it with dismay in the stateroom's full-length mirror before inspecting the heavily starched wing-tip collar, the cravat, the high-cut vest, the pin-striped woolen trousers. Geoffrey had warned him that he would need "two sets of formal togs." There was nothing to be done but purchase a second set of evening clothes. Moore, of course, had his own bespoke tailor in Savile Row, but he had assured John that a passable imitation could be had quickly at Harrods, Dickins and Jones, or any other of the half dozen better department stores.

Le Brun considered the body beneath the suit. At least he looked good, relatively speaking. A little more than a year ago, his stomach had become quite finicky. He had been obliged to cut back on meats, sauces, whiskey, and wine. Between that and an increased regimen of walking, he had shed some twenty pounds and was not more than ten over his ideal weight. Even the ancient war wound under his right shoulder had begun to feel better. If these improvements were only a brief respite before the final spiral into ill health, John was happy to enjoy them. One had to count every blessing at fifty-eight.

John had just finished knotting his bow tie when the door resounded from a pair of sharp knocks. When he answered it, he found himself confronted by Captain Winslow. Another man stood farther back in the corridor, wearing a uniform as dark as Winslow's was white and with less piping, insignias, and ribbons.

"Yes, Captain?" Le Brun said, noting how ill at ease the officer looked.

"I'm afraid we have need of your skills as a detective, Sheriff Le Brun. A pearl necklace is missing from the ship's safe."

"Whose necklace?"

"Mrs. Lamb's."

"How interestin'!" John remarked, casting his mind back to supper the previous evening. "Nothin' else missin'?"

"Not that we can determine," said the second man.

"This is Mr. Whitechurch, our chief purser," Winslow introduced. The second man stepped forward and offered a curt bow. His eyes were huge and baleful, and his cheeks were drawn from the tension of the underlying muscles. "May we show you?"

"Certainly." John patted his pocket to be sure he had his room key. He was led to the purser's anteroom, which lay just to the right of the first-class dining salon's main doors. Directly across the corridor were placed two tufted red velvet benches, flanked by potted palms. Passenger access to the purser's anteroom was blocked by a massive walnut counter, upon which passengers placed their most valuable belongings and received in exchange a cardstock receipt of their deposit. A note of each deposit and withdrawal, its hour and date were noted in a large ledger book that remained fixed on the counter.

John was first shown that the safe was in perfect condition, with no sign of forcing. Then the ledger book was put in front of him. It indicated the deposit of the pearls the previous evening at 21:43 hours.

"I saw the pearls on Mrs. Lamb last night," John said.

"I as well," Captain Winslow agreed.

"Who was on duty to receive them?" John asked.

"I was," Whitechurch replied. He reached under the counter and produced a black lacquered box, about five by seven inches. "I watched her put the necklace in this." He opened the box, revealing black velvet cushioning. "I personally transferred it into the safe. Just half an hour ago, Mr. and Mrs. Lamb appeared and asked me for the necklace. I almost always take dinner duty. When Mrs. Lamb opened the box, there was nothing inside but the cloth and the bill of sale." He lifted the velvet to reveal a folded piece of paper.

John took the bill and looked at the numbers written on it. He whistled softly. "That's about two months' salary for me." He replaced the paper. "How many people have a key to the safe?"

"Four," Winslow supplied. "Mr. Whitechurch, his two assistants, and myself."

"No master or duplicate key exists anywhere else on the ship?"

"No, sir."

"And do these four keys ever leave your persons?"

"They do not. I can vouch for Mr. Whitechurch and Mr. Rawlings, one of his assistants. The other is relatively new. He seems honest enough. But perhaps we should begin by searching his bunk and footlocker."

"You may certainly do that. But I've seen diamond chokers and tiaras on some of the ladies that beggared those pearls. If the thief were one of the staff with a key and content to steal only one item, he'd likely have gone after somethin' better. Let's think about another possibility." John lifted the lacquered box and felt its weight. "Let me ask you a few questions, Mr. Whitechurch. Has Mrs. Lamb taken her necklace out of the safe every evenin'?"

"Yes, sir. Just before she dined."

"Did she always return it directly afterward?"

"According to my recollection and this ledger."

"Cast your mind back to last evenin', a few minutes before you stuck this box back in the safe. Was there anythin' special or different you noted about Mr. or Mrs. Lamb's actions?"

The purser's eyes drifted downward in thought. "Let's see." They fixed on Le Brun again. "The previous three nights, they came directly out of the dining salon to me. Last night, they went over and sat on one of those benches."

"Alone?"

"No. The little man who gave me all the trouble was sitting, too. Not on the same bench, but over there."

"Who was 'the little man'?" Le Brun asked.

Whitechurch consulted the ledger book. "His name is Jacob Stone. He's a dealer in jewelry and coins. He had taken one of his cases out. To show a prospective buyer, he said."

"Were he and the Lambs talkin' to each other?" asked Le Brun.

"Not that I saw. He isn't even a first-class passenger." After having pronounced "fuhst-clahss pahsunjuh," Whitechurch sniffed softly.

"But they all got off their benches at the same time and came over to you," Le Brun stated.

"That's right, along with . . ." The chief purser again consulted his ledger. ". . . Mrs. Forbes."

"Quite a rush," John remarked.

"It's like that," Whitechurch shared. "An entire table will leave the salon together, and three or four persons arrive at once."

"Mrs. Lamb arrived at the counter first, and the little man pushed himself in front of Mrs. Forbes," John said.

"How did you know that?" the purser asked.

"Deduction," the captain interrupted. "He looked at the order of deposits on the ledger."

"Oh, I didn't need the ledger," Le Brun told them both. "Please go on, Mr. Whitechurch."

"I fetched her box and watched her put her necklace in it." The purser's eyes went suddenly wide, and his hairline receded a fraction in his surprise.

John smiled at the purser's sudden epiphany and, before the man could say more, asked, "What did Mr. Stone do at that moment?"

"I had fetched the case that held his coins at the same time I got Mrs. Lamb's box." The man's eyes took on a faraway stare as he relived the moments in his memory; his voice softened. "He refilled it in a hurry and shoved it at me. I failed to get a good grip, and the case fell on the floor. Mr. Stone passed a few rude remarks and demanded that we account for each coin immediately."

"And Mrs. Lamb and Mrs. Forbes were also demandin' to be taken care of," John pursued.

"Exactly!"

"Am I to understand that while Mr. Whitechurch was gathering coins off the floor, Mrs. Lamb removed the necklace from the box?" Captain Winslow asked.

"Either her or Mr. Lamb," the sheriff said. "The other one's job was to get in Mrs. Forbes's way so she couldn't see what was goin' on." He handed the captain the lacquer box. "Pretty heavy for just a necklace, and I'm sure for a reason. No one . . . even an experienced purser such as Mr. Whitechurch . . . could tell the difference between it empty or with a string of pearls in it. And even if Mr. Whitechurch might have considered that he left the box unguarded for just a few seconds, the presence of Mr. Stone and Mrs. Forbes at the counter as witnesses would have reassured him. The fallin' coins are too convenient. What's more, Mr. Lamb probably couldn't have shielded the views of both Mrs. Forbes and Mr. Stone. Your rude little man was in on it."

The captain said, "When the Lambs are at luncheon, we should enter their stateroom."

"You won't find the necklace," John asserted. "Not with Mr. Stone either. There must be a thousand places on this ship they could hide such a small thing."

"Then what are we to say to the Lambs?" Winslow asked. "They are ranting as if they had actually been robbed, doing considerable damage to this company's reputation."

John shrugged. "You can't do much about that just now, I'm afraid. Assure them that they will be compensated if the necklace is not found."

Winslow's face reddened. He opened his mouth to say more.

"There you are, John!" Geoffrey Moore approached at a good clip.

"I shall write down a plan," Le Brun said in a quick, low voice before joining his friend. "This *will* be resolved to your satisfaction."

THREE

Friday, October 20, 1905

JACOB STONE GRINNED at his luck. Raymond and Alice Lamb were nowhere in sight. His luggage had been at the head of the line set out by the stewards. He looked down the other end of the huge Southampton customs building. Early morning sunlight streamed down through clerestory windows in hard white shafts. Even the salt-seaweed scent of the docks smelled good to him.

For just a moment, Jacob toyed with the notion of not meeting his fellow swindlers at the Grand Hotel in London and nipping off with the money he owed for their pearls. But despite the husband's pampered looks, Raymond was more wolf than lamb, and he would make Stone sorry back in New York. Besides, there would be other ocean voyages to Europe, with other lines, and who knew how many times he and the Lambs could work the scam in coming years.

The customs agent nodded for Stone to move forward. A pleasant steward helped him move his belongings to the counter.

"Papers, sir," the agent said. "Here for business or pleasure?"

"Business."

"Your profession?"

"Jewelry and coin wholesaler. Here's my license and the papers to bring gold into the country."

The agent scanned the inventory of items and compared them to the precious items inside Jacob Stone's three cases.

"Three pearl necklaces," the agent recited, comparing words with commodities.

"Right."

"New or used?"

"New." The little man resisted the compulsion to grin again. Despite what he had declared, the case had held only two necklaces when he left New York City. Naturally, no customs agent there was interested in what he took out.

"Very good, sir. Follow the steward." Stone repacked his precious display cases and hurried after the young man lugging his two valises.

"I'm bound for London, boy," Stone called. "Waterloo Station."

The steward gave no indication of having heard. In fact, as soon as he passed through a set of doors, he made a hard left.

"Hey, where are you going?" Stone called out, lengthening his stride. The steward ignored him.

Just as Stone was about to touch the young man on the shoulder, he spotted four men walking in his direction, four sets of eyes leveled on him. He recognized only one: the captain of the *Empress.* Stone's footsteps faltered. Then he remembered how perfectly they had pulled off the scam and affixed his best bluff face.

The tallest of the group withdrew a badge from his coat pocket and flashed it at Stone. "Customs police, Mr. Stone. Be so kind as to come with us."

"What's this about?" Stone demanded.

"The theft of a pearl necklace."

"What?"

"This way, if you please."

"I don't please at all, brother."

Ignoring the response and not bothering with introductions, the tall man made an about-face that indicated military service and headed for a nearby door. Stone could smell copper on the man closest to him as well. Then there was the captain. The fourth man was the shortest. He had a southern French face, with a pronounced, slightly hooked nose, heavy brows, weathered and permanently tanned skin, and dark hair liberally peppered with gray. Stone thought that he might have seen the man onboard the *Empress.*

The group entered a cluttered office. An expanse of space had been cleared on the desk closest to the door.

"Would you mind opening your cases there, sir?" the customs officer asked.

"Aside from the time we're wasting, not at all."

Stone opened last the case with the three pearl necklaces. He fished into his billfold and took out the declared inventory, passing it to the officer. "What you see before you I brought over myself. Three on the list; three in the case."

"You may only have departed the States with two," the French-looking man declared, with a Deep South accent, "or you may even had had some poor imitation set that you threw overboard, but you did not start out with these three necklaces."

"And who are you?" Stone requested.

"I sat across from Mrs. Lamb at dinner three nights ago." Le Brun picked up one of the necklaces and spread the individual pearls apart, examining the string. He put the first strand back into the case and withdrew the second. "The same night she dropped bechamel sauce onto it." He repeated his actions, spreading the beads one by one. This time, he smiled. "Her husband did a satisfactory job of cleanin' the pearls, but I saw that he was also rubbin' the sauce into the string between them." He held up the necklace for inspection. "And here is the result."

Jacob Stone's eyes went wide. He attempted to recover, grunting an approximation of annoyance. "Those yellow marks could be anything."

"But you just told the customs agent that all the necklaces are new. What would a new necklace be doin' with food stains?" Le Brun countered.

"We will hold you while we have the stains looked at under a microscope," the customs agent declared.

"And by that time, the Lambs will have left Southampton," John Le Brun told the jeweler. "We figure they approached you with the idea. Or would you rather bear the guilt alone?"

THE TRAIN WAS MOVING at high speed, but not swiftly enough for John Le Brun. All those clacking miles with nothing to do but gaze out the window had Geoffrey Moore filling silences with a vengeance. The first hour he described with the detail of a Baedeker's guidebook the places John should visit in London: the British Museum, Crystal Palace, Westminster Abbey, St. Paul's Cathedral, the Zoo, Hyde and Regents Parks, the many public and private art galleries, and, with his highest recommendation, Madame Tussaud's waxworks.

As they rolled nearer to the capital city, Moore hoisted his gold watch from his vest pocket and peered at it with a scowl. "We've lost this day for any touring, despite our early docking. Blasted petty criminals. But I suppose the time you spent was well worth it, seeing as how you'll be the line's guest on the voyage home, eh?"

John nodded amiably.

"'A penny saved is a penny earned,' as Benjamin Franklin wrote."

"I'll be able to afford another few days," John granted.

"A few days? More like a week. And now you can invest in a truly splendid second set of formal togs. None of the clubs will allow you to dine without them."

"Clubs?" John exclaimed.

Geoffrey answered the near-bark with a lynx-eyed smile. "Naturally. Where do you think these lectures and meetings will take place?"

"You know my opinion of clubs, Geoffrey."

Moore certainly did. At least once during each of his six visits to Brunswick, his friend Le Brun managed to growl out a tirade against social organizations.

Geoffrey knew that Le Brun was by his nature an independent thinker and a lone wolf, but he also suspected that John's vocal antipathy to clubs arose from his exclusion from the ones he secretly admired. Le Brun was a Catholic in a Protestant-dominated town, not a member of the rich or landed, and had not attended an institution of higher learning. High on Moore's agenda for John's holiday was to drag him into clubs he was sure to admire and obliquely to convince him that such organizations indeed had merit.

Geoffrey reached for his portmanteau and opened it. "I do indeed know your opinion. But the gentleman's club is the center of London society." He withdrew several telegrams and fliers and spread them out. "It's been that way since Shakespeare's time. In fact, the Bard was a member of the first recorded one, held in the Mermaid Tavern. You wouldn't object to belonging to a club with Will Shakespeare as charter member, would you?"

"Depends," John replied, unwilling to lose the battle at the first volley.

"And what if Beaumont, Donne, and Fletcher were members as well?"

John shrugged.

Moore shook his head in amusement. "You haunt the Oglethorpe Hotel in search of chess players, don't you? Well, English clubs began as places for like minds to meet, eat, drink, and play. Not long afterward, there arose houses that sold coffee, tea, or chocolate. In that era, naturally, these were all exotic imports and very dear. You had to be someone of means to frequent such establishments. As with the actors and writers of the previous age, this commonality gave them a reason to congregate. During the day they might be exchanging promissory notes and trading checks on each other's banks. Or taking cargo space on another merchant's ships and underwriting maritime insurance. By night, the action changed to gossip, politics, and gambling."

"You never said that our evenin's would be spent at clubs," John said.

"Didn't I? Well, all of them won't be. For example, this very night we'll attend one of Maeve Godwin's fortnightly Friday soirees. You remember I've spoken of Trent Godwin, our solicitor?"

John crossed his arms and lowered his chin to his chest. "You think I haven't read about your English gentlemen's clubs? Your own Jonathan Swift called them 'the common rendezvous of infamous sharpers and noble cullies.' "

"Swift was a cynic," Moore dismissed. "He was talking about White's. It was *the* Tory stronghold until the Carlton Club opened. One practically must inherit membership. The wait is eighteen years, and unless you're of the right family you're bound to be blackballed. We say 'pilled,' actually. At most clubs, nomination takes place once a month, around midnight. It can be vicious. Gladstone's Home Rule proposition nearly split Brook's right down the middle." In an apostrophe voice, he added, "Home Rule is giving Ireland the right to govern themselves. Their own parliament and so forth."

"I know what 'Home Rule' is," John said.

"Of course you do. You know everything there is to know about us. This whole trip is a pointless redundancy."

John ignored the rebuke. "And what happened at Brook's?"

"Well, one side favored Home Rule and was trying to swell the membership with like minds. The other side tried to do the same. The upshot was that practically everyone nominated was being blackballed. It was finally up to Lord Granville . . . now there was a great statesman . . . to deliver a speech pleading for one place in London where gentlemen could truly be gentlemen and set their differences aside. From then on, the politics were less heated."

Le Brun declined to offer even a token grunt to indicate that he was still listening. From his point of view, Moore was off in his own world, wearing an expression of serene joy on his face that John had only seen in medieval paintings of saints. Knowing John's low opinion of clubs, Geoffrey had limited his discussion of them over the years, but John knew just the same that they were a mania with the man. He had, in fact, become tedious in pumping the Brunswick native for news about the Jekyl Island Club.

"Brook's membership act quite snooty," Geoffrey rattled on, like a locomotive whose governor had gotten stuck. "For example, no one who isn't a member is allowed past a tiny anteroom off the entrance. Even a gentleman's solicitor isn't welcome inside. The clubs I have membership in are more liberal. But, in fact, Brook's is the bastion of Whiggery."

"Of what?" John asked.

"Those men traditionally more liberal in their politics. As opposed to the Tories, the rank conservatives."

"Why didn't you just say 'Whig' in the first place? So, you're a Whig?"

"Certainly not. A Tory, as my father before me and his father before him."

"But didn't you just say that the clubs you have membership in are more liberal?"

Moore sighed. "Only compared to the old White's and the Carlton Club. Perhaps it's best if you don't try to understand,

John. It's like me trying to understand your Mugwumps and Know Nothings."

"Political clubs. They're high in my circles of club hell, but you've got even worse. You admitted at the start of all this prattle that London clubs are thinly-veiled gamblin' parlors," John baited.

"I did nothing of the sort! At one time, perhaps. At Brook's, Charles Fox once played faro for twenty-two straight hours and lost one thousand guineas. But that was back in the wild days. Brook's was founded as a young men's club, you see. Most had visited Italy and called themselves 'Macaronis.' At least they brought back some good recipes with them. Many of the clubs have excellent chefs. None of mine, mind you. The Sceptred Isle has particularly poor fare," Moore shared, "but the one thing that can be said of all the clubs is the price is right. Meals are served at or near cost. Why, I dined at the Athenæum just before leaving for the States, and the cost was only three shillings, eight pence! And no tipping is allowed." Moore punctuated his incredible news with raised eyebrows.

"How do you manage to keep waiters?" John had to ask.

Moore looked as if he'd been slapped. "Well, they enjoy the proximity to class and greatness, don't you see? We shall definitely visit the Athenæum. You *know* you've arrived when you secure membership. My father was a member, but I wasn't allowed in until seven years after joining his firm. My article in *Import Quarterly* secured the matter." Castle & Moore was a seventy-two-year-old firm importing cotton, hemp, indigo, and other dye ingredients from the New World. Geoffrey had apprenticed with his father for five years and then had become the main New World agent for the company, traveling across the Atlantic twice a year.

"You'll love the Athenæum," Moore stated emphatically. "I'm sure its heritage of writer members will impress you. Sir Richard Burton and Macaulay used to work in the Writer's

Corner. Enormous library. Trollope, Matthew Arnold, and Dickens were also members. You like Dickens."

"He's my favorite author."

"Then you should know he had memberships in Garrick's Club and the Arts Club as well. Isn't it possible that there's something about clubs that you've missed?"

"I doubt it. It must be a national mania," John judged. "Why did Dickens jump from club to club?"

"He didn't. He held memberships simultaneously. Men tend to join as many as they can afford, to increase their circulation and connections. I'm a member of three myself. There are about two hundred clubs in London right now."

John found the number frankly astonishing. "Surely, you're countin' female clubs as well."

"No indeed. The class of club I refer to has nothing to do with women. Women have a need for their own private nest; men need a place to bond with each other." Moore broke into a broad grin. "And to get away from the women and their broods. In fact, some of the clubs even provide lodging. All these conveniences allow well-off bachelors to avoid marriage into their thirties. You'll soon see, John, that it really is the most civilized invention of the most civilized city of the most civilized nation in the world. The lecture I've asked you to deliver on your experiences during your Civil War will be at the Sceptred Isle Club, because it was formed around history enthusiasts." He held up one of his fliers. "You've professed such interest in the conquest of the North Pole. Where do you suppose that lecture will be held?"

"It should be held at the Royal Geographical Society."

Moore shook the flier in front of Le Brun. "No. At a club."

"You're Shanghain' me to your damned clubs," John fumed.

"You know the Sceptred Isle is where you'll deliver your lecture," Moore added, evenly. "Where do you think you'll get the surprise I promised you?"

"I know . . . at a club."

Moore looked down at the papers in his case. "Oh Lord! I thought I'd finished this report. Please excuse me, John."

"With pleasure."

John glanced out the window. Buildings appeared with increasing frequency, and isolated farmhouses and outbuildings were replaced by joined homes and businesses.

"We'll reach Waterloo Station within the half hour," Moore announced, without looking up from his papers.

JOHN USED THE ENSUING stretch of silence to study the evolving scene beyond the window. The buildings closed in upon each other until they became solid masses, block after unrelieved block, segmented only by roadways. The structures, whether of stone, brick, or wood, became increasingly dilapidated. The people in the streets grew increasingly dirty and ragged. He saw tottering chimneys, sagging rooftops, windowless wall after windowless wall. Among the many shabby, gray figures receding from his view, he was particularly struck by a pair of little girls pretending to ride a horse lying dead in the street, its ribs protruding under its mangy hide. He estimated that they had traveled at least ten miles into what seemed to be one continuous city.

"Is this London?" John asked.

Moore gave a fleeting glance at the cityscape. "It wasn't fifty years ago, but since the train and the Underground, the city's spread out and swallowed dozens of villages. This is the bottom end of Lambeth, I believe. Waterloo isn't far now."

John continued to stare at the mottled mass of misery crowding up against the tracks. He had never witnessed so many grown men loitering idly. He had read often about the phenomenon of modern inventions halving the number of workers needed on farms, in mills, in mines. This was the consequence.

The unemployed fled into cities, hoping to find work in the thousands of sweated shops, in construction, in the on- and off-loading of commodities. But there was not enough work to go around, and because of the high supply of workers, those who did get jobs had to take them for near-starvation wages. He was glad he had served as sheriff of prosperous Brunswick, Georgia, instead of a place like Lambeth, where people had so little to lose and would therefore risk so much more. He was also glad he had been born in the first half of the nineteenth century. *Surely,* he thought, *this new century will be a hard one for the common man.*

They detrained at Waterloo Station in the midst of great bustle. When they worked their way outside, John noted that approximately every fifth vehicle was motorized. Moore paid to have John's three suitcases and his own valises plus steamer trunk loaded into a truck but insisted that he and his traveling companion take an open-topped landau.

The first thing that John noted was the smell. Ammonia and methane from horse excrement mixed with the acrid stink of coal soot. The second thing was the London skyline. Since Waterloo Station was close to the Thames River, an open view of the great city appeared almost immediately. John looked upon a mammoth man-made panorama with a myriad of architectural styles, much of it made from dark materials. He had viewed the glittering New York City skyline from across its main river, the Hudson, the evening they arrived at the Hoboken train terminal. He had also experienced it the following morning from the canyon streets of Wall Street before being whisked to the passenger ship pier. In those few hours, however, the awesome verticality of Lady Liberty's city and its clean, light colors had impressed him as no sight ever had. Even on first views, there was no ignoring pronounced differences between the premier commercial cities of the Old and New Worlds.

Moore delivered explicit directions as to the sequence of streets the driver must take to bring them to his home. "There's never a second chance to make a first impression," the importer told his guest.

They crossed the Thames by Waterloo Bridge. Moore pointed to the southwest. "There's Cleopatra's Needle," he said. "It's actually much older than Cleo. About fourteen hundred years older, in fact. It was a gift of Egypt as homage to the Empire."

What interested John more than the pink granite obelisk was the activity on the river. Lightermen scurried like ants as they moved cargoes onto wharves which they had earlier off-loaded downstream from ocean-going ships into small barges. Amazing to John was that, despite the frenzy of their labor and the relative warmth of the day, they all wore vests and jackets. The typical "uniform" also seemed to include a white handkerchief tied around the neck and a pork-pie cap. John spied enough ivory tusks in one passing barge to have exterminated several elephant herds.

The landau took a left turn onto the Strand and passed Charing Cross Station, the horse's shod hooves ringing against the granite street settes, the street itself throbbing from the rumble of an Underground train. They passed in front of an arresting statue of General Gordon, who was killed while attempting to maintain British control over the Sudan. The bronze officer sat athwart a camel, wearing a fez as comfortably as he had a top hat in his own land. Three Chinese gentlemen passed in front of the statue, all wearing silk Mandarin clothing.

A short block after, they were in Trafalgar Square. There, an army of workmen labored at erecting reviewing stands, positioning thick garlands of greens, and securing what looked to be a dozen guy wires stretching from the base nearly to the top of the 170-foot monument to both Lord Nelson and to the maritime victory that had given Great Britain a century of dominance upon the seven seas.

"We'll be here tomorrow for the festivities," Moore promised. "Trafalgar Day is always an important London holiday, but tomorrow is the centenary of that brilliant triumph."

They made a quick left turn, onto Whitehall. A building

two city blocks long and eight stories high in some places filled their right-hand view. That the gargantuan structure was quite new was confirmed to John, along with the facts that it housed the Foreign Office, the Home Office, the Colonial Office, and the India Office. The great pseudo-Italian palazzo was, in fact, the heart of the British Empire. Down a set of its steps walked several Indian men, dressed in western suits but each wearing a turban.

Le Brun understood that none of what he saw since leaving Waterloo Station had been by chance. Despite knowing his country's many shortcomings, John was a proud American and not at all shy of telling any foreigner, Geoffrey Moore included, that he expected the United States would soon emerge as the dominant world power. This had always rankled the importer and resulted in several amiable but forceful discussions of the relative mights and destinies of their respective homelands. Now Moore was attempting to trump all previous arguments by letting his city speak for itself. To prove John's surmise, the landau passed yet another memorial. This one, at the confluence of Knightsbridge and Brompton Roads, depicted mounted and Indian-helmeted Field Marshall Hugh Rose, conqueror of India and Syria. The carriage swung around it, then made three lefts, doubling back to arrive at Moore's home.

The large, three-story townhouse lay well within the fashionable district known as Belgravia. What John had always suspected was now borne out: Geoffrey Moore was extremely well off.

Daphne Moore and her daughters, Phyllis and Myrtle, emerged from the townhouse as the taxi men transferred the luggage to the sidewalk. Considering that Geoffrey had been gone for eight weeks, John had expected a rush of silk and lace and an explosion of affection. Instead, the three women waited with tepid smiles at the top of the townhouse's front steps, expecting the family patriarch to climb to them. Each, in turn, planted a pristine kiss on Geoffrey's cheek. John's intuition had him doubting it was his presence that had turned their greetings more formal than usual.

Moore beckoned John to climb the wide steps. "Daphne, Phyllis, Myrtle—this is the amazing Mr. John Le Brun about whom I have told you so much."

John received similarly restrained emotion from their combined reception. The daughters, whom John knew to be sixteen and fourteen, spoke with precisely their mother's clipped tone and nasal inflections.

Just as John entered the large foyer, a pair of golden retrievers skittered across the marble floor and leapt up against his chest.

"Charlotte! Emily! Down!" Moore commanded. The dogs obeyed only after a few forceful shoves from John.

Moore was in the process of apologizing when the elder daughter, Myrtle, took his hand and shook it several times. "Father, there's a super gown at Worth's for my coming out, and unless we rush there I'm afraid someone else will—"

"My God, Myrtle!" exclaimed the younger daughter with disgust. "Can't you even let Father into the door?"

"Oh, shut up, you!" her sister snapped.

One of the dogs began sniffing at John's crotch. Moore pulled her back and called for his manservant to put down the luggage he was transporting and move the dogs to the pantry.

"Do I assault Father with *my* need for a wardrobe closet?" Phyllis resumed. "Daddy, they have one at Altheim's that precisely matches my bed, even to the floral decoupage. The sale ends—"

"You don't want me spending beyond the normal budget while you're gone, Geoffrey," his wife reminded him at the same time, "but special needs do arise. A household simply cannot stop operating for six or seven weeks."

Moore shot Le Brun another apologetic look and dipped his head in the direction of the front parlor. "Make yourself comfortable, John. I'll be back in a moment."

The three women followed Moore to the back of the house, whence uninterrupted pleading and cajoling could be heard. John settled into a heavily padded armchair and looked about the room. He recognized it as a belle example of the Victorian Age, which had officially ended in 1901 with the death of the queen but which lived on here. Moldings were huge. French floral wallpaper covered the walls, and much of its pattern was hidden by heavy cloth draperies and craze-surfaced oil paintings in overlarge and hideously ornate gilt frames. The dark-stained mahogany furniture was equally large and protected by doilies and antimacassars. Burgundy red, tufted velvet covered the chairs and sofas, a double layer of carpeting covered the floor, and every free horizontal space was covered with a knickknack, paperweight, photograph frame, vase, candlestick, porcelain dish, or framed mirror. The best homes of Brunswick, Georgia, had similar rooms. John had generally only been invited into them following burglaries. It was all too stuffed and stuffy for his taste. He much preferred the simplicity of everyday Colonial period furnishings.

From the back of the house, the exchanges became more strident and loud, liked a trio of Wagner's Valkyries. Only during unison inhalations could Geoffrey's placating voice be discerned. From having heard Moore's wistful remarks about the joys of travel and how young men could forestall marriage because of clubs, John was sure that his friend contributed equally to a cycle of discord. John scowled. His face pinched also from the room's oily dog odor. *I am trapped among all of Moore's bitches,* he thought grimly. The London leg of his vacation would be far less relaxing than he had anticipated.

John's host appeared, holding two crystal tumblers filled with whiskey and ice. He presented one. "It's always an uproar when I first return," he explained through a forced smile. "It calms down quickly." As if to belie his words, the teenagers' voices echoed from upstairs, angry and shrill.

John cleared his throat and coughed for effect. "You never mentioned that you kept your dogs inside the house."

"Didn't I? Is there a problem?"

"I'm afraid so. I have an allergy to dog dander," John lied. "In the South, we don't allow our animals in the house. I might have to refuse your very kind offer of lodgin' and move to a hotel. It's no problem. I have the extra money now, thanks to the ship company."

Geoffrey's mouth turned down. "I'm very sorry, John. Perhaps we can arrange some other gratis lodging. Can you endure the afternoon?"

"Certainly. My allergy builds up over time."

"Then why don't you go up to our guest bedroom and lie down? The dogs aren't allowed upstairs. You'll have a respite at the Godwin's party. No better way to introduce you to London than through some of its more interesting inhabitants. We'll leave at about eight then."

The muffled arguing continued upstairs.

"I'm very comfortable right here for now," John said, saluting Moore with his drink.

EXCEPT FOR A SIMILAR architectural scale of grandeur, the Godwin townhouse could not have been a greater study in opposites from the Moore home. It lay on the northwest verge of the Mayfair district, close by Marble Arch. Its floors were of highly polished light oak, with no carpeting. The walls were painted either matte white or sorrel gray. Instead of oil paintings of bucolic landscapes, they had a collage work by Klimt and numerous posters by Mucha and Toulouse-Lautrec, hung inside sleek metal frames. At the four corners of the living room, bronze or brass statues sat on high marble pedestals. John noted that all of the wall pieces and statues were of women, with most of them naked or in states of undress. The Nouveau furniture followed function with form, lightly lacquered to allow the beauty of the wood to shine through. A heavy cotton fabric covered several of the chairs and sofas, with simple botanical designs in light colors.

Superfluous decorations were all but nonexistent, except for three vases on the living room's simple, white fireplace mantelpiece. They were each filled with fresh flowers. The first was in an iridescent peacock design of *favrile* glass; the second featured the figure of a woman in low relief and alive with deep, translucent colors. The last was of stylized high grasses waving in the wind, executed in several shades of green. Several Art Nouveau lamps lit the entry foyer and dining room, but the main attraction of electrical illumination was a magnificent chandelier hanging dead center from the living room ceiling. Its twenty-four small bulbs had been blown into the shapes of flower blossoms, and around their glowing beauty swirled leaves, stems, and tendrils of brass. John noted that the one commonality between the Godwin and Moore homes was the number of filled bookcases.

Although he would not have been comfortable living in such a place, John liked it very much. He had read about such radical changes in lifestyle and even seen several drawings in magazines, but he had never personally experienced them. He reminded himself that any Voyage of Discovery would present exotic ports, and that a true mark of intelligence was the ability to adjust quickly to new situations. He inhaled a fortifying breath.

John had arrived in Geoffrey and Daphne Moore's tow, fashionably late. Trent Godwin had stood at the far end of the foyer with two other men. All three wore formal dinner dress. Trent was the most sartorially splendid. His jacket was of the finest black silk. His patent leather pumps shone like black mirrors. All three also wore beards and mustaches. Since touching ground at Southampton, John had noted that most Englishmen no longer cultivated beards, although a goodly number still sported mustaches. Trent appeared resolutely conservative Old

School. He and another of the men puffed on cigarettes with a furious energy, as if their smoky exclamation points could make their pronouncements more irrefutable.

"There they are," Geoffrey said. "The triumvirate of Godwin, Penfield, and Bushnell. Man for man, among the most powerful law firms in London."

"I thought you said a business suit would be all right," John whispered self-consciously to Geoffrey.

"It is. Very much so, I assure you." Geoffrey led John from the middle of the foyer. While he introduced the American to the group and vice versa, as if by pre-arrangement the string trio beyond the back end of the wide hallway began bowing an American ragtime tune.

"So good of you to accept our invitation," Trent Godwin said, with genuine enthusiasm. "Geoffrey has often praised you as an independent thinker among a race of such men. We're just now discussing how to ensure this country experiences evolution, not revolution. We don't want another France and its Robespierre and Napoleon."

"Notions of socialism and communism, scarin' the status quo?" John asked.

All the heads in the tight circle nodded gravely.

"I believe gradualism is the best course," Trent declared. He blinked, as he had a dozen times since John was introduced to him. At first, John thought a speck was irritating his eye, but as time went on he understood it to be a nervous habit. "There's plenty to give the lower classes before we turn over the keys to the factories. Everyone should be entitled to a minimal level of food, health care, and education."

" 'Give' isn't the right word, Trent," one of his partners said. "They must come halfway to us, be willing to *earn* their increases in society. Do you agree, Mr. Le Brun?"

Having been candidly asked, John expounded at length on his political and social views. He commented on the arrogance he had overheard from the mouths of American millionaires in the Jekyl Island Club and how his country's citizens were beginning to take these robber barons to task, investigating and breaking their trusts and monopolies. He expressed his view that no man should be able to earn more than ten times the lowest-paid worker's salary for the same day of earnest work. He admitted, however, that his proposal contained a dilemma; the self-interest of capitalism would be stifled by imposed limitations on earnings. He kept a sharp eye on the faces of the men in the group, watching for the first signs of offense. There were none.

After a few minutes of expounding, John invited reaction. The group enthusiastically challenged and picked at some of John's contentions. He, in turn, with Socratic method, forced them to concede he was right. While he listened to more conservative points of view than his own, John noted that Geoffrey had been correct: The crowd indeed sported all manner of fashion. Among the most daring was a woman wearing a liberty dress whose simple lines and delicate embroideries contrasted sharply with several hooped and stayed French gowns on display. She looked directly at John and headed toward the pack of men.

Trent said, "John Le Brun of Brunswick, Georgia, meet your hostess, Maeve Godwin."

"The champion among sheriffs and chess players!" Maeve exclaimed. She offered her hand and, before John could bestow a kiss, gave his hand a firm, strong shake. Her smile was easy and broad, formed of straight teeth and generous lips. Her blue eyes flashed with intelligence. She was a tall, big-boned woman without being heavy, handsome without being beautiful. She had a bird's nest of auburn hair piled high on her head and freckles splashed across every inch of skin the sun had kissed. John guessed her to be in her late forties. "Geoffrey has told us so many interesting things about you, Mr. Le Brun."

"I will labor not to disappoint," John replied.

"Please do not! We don't intend to sit in judgment on you," she said, as if reading his mind. "Be yourself." She tugged John from the group. "Excuse us, gentlemen."

"Don't feel that you have to stay to the bitter end, old chap," Trent called to him. "I never do . . . and I'm the host!"

Despite what sounded to John like a high-class English accent, the woman looked as Irish as a Celtic cross. "Maeve is an Irish name, isn't it?" he asked.

"Some say Middle English. I was born in Londonderry. Lived for years in Belfast. Irish but Orange through and through. Can I interest you in food?"

While John chatted with his hostess and sampled hors d'oeuvres, a younger woman glided up beside them. At first, all he could see were her eyes. *Claire's eyes,* John said to himself. *That impossible blue flecked with violet.* Old heart scars burst open.

John forced himself to concentrate on the young woman's other features. She had enough of Maeve Godwin's structure to suggest close relation, but for each plain feature of the older woman this one substituted that of a Gibson girl. She had the same unusual height and, in fact, looked athletic, but her waist was much narrower and her bosom more pronounced. Her skin was creamy and smooth. *Much finer pores than Claire. Never felt a semi-tropical sun.* Her hair was chestnut, wavy, and allowed to hang low on her shoulders, sinfully luxuriant from the oils of youth. *Claire cut hers so much shorter. Couldn't stand the heat of it on her neck.* Her smile was the same beguiling feature as that owned by her mother. John estimated that she was barely into her twenties. Pleased whenever he could be unpredictable and contrary, John made it a habit to give young beauties the most cursory of glances. In this case, he had to look away before her eyes totally captured him. By sheer force of will, he returned his attention to the older woman.

Through John's expression, Maeve became aware of the

beauty's presence. "John Le Brun, this is my daughter, Veronica."

"A pleasure, Miss," John said, careful to return his focus immediately to the mother.

"I'm not a Miss," she said, through a naughty smile. "There's nothing amiss about me."

"So I noticed," John relented, which clearly pleased her.

"You're that sheriff who's solved so many difficult cases," Veronica stated in a challenging tone. "When Geoffrey told us about you, I pictured a nasty, uncouth bear . . . not a distinguished-looking gentleman. May I introduce him in the back of the house, Maeve?"

Mrs. Godwin arched an eyebrow. "Be good, girl."

"I'm always good." Veronica lifted her elbow for the crook of John's arm. As they started off, she said, "We enjoy throwing together people with different backgrounds and attitudes in our little soirees."

"And I was supposed to be the bear uncaged among lions and tigers," John assumed.

"We didn't know you were coming, matter of fact," Veronica said, executing a turn into the dining room with a ballerina's grace and causing her skirt to billow around her. "But we're glad you're here. I'm sure you've already gleaned our method just by looking at our guests. That gentleman over there is W. H. Davies." She nodded at a man dressed in clean corduroy trousers, a flannel shirt, and a gold brocade vest. He had a boot on one foot; the other leg ended with a wooden peg. He was short and dark, with coarse skin, and eyes like a pair of stewed prunes.

"We all come into this world dressed the same," John observed. "We should worry less about style and more about whether it's doin' a good job keepin' us warm, cool, or dry."

"Exactly," Veronica agreed. "I shall give you credit when I quote you."

"Thank you. And what does Mr. Davies do?" John inquired.

"He's a prodigiously gifted poet who wanders the countryside.

He has a book of his works out . . . *The Soul's Destroyer.*"

"Do tell."

"Our guests tend to be more artistic than political. My mother is no Lady Nevill. I'm sorry. She's the daughter of Lord Orford. Lady Lansdowne and the Duchess of Buccleuch also throw lavish parties crowded with policy makers. Unfortunately, a woman must be of nobility to affect politics in England."

"Not in the ancient sense of the word," John replied. " 'Polis' meant 'the people,' and the arts can have a tremendous effect upon the masses. Every politician knows the masses can't be ignored. There was an opera written about seventy years ago that dealt with an Italian revolt against the Spanish leaders in Naples. When it was performed in Brussels, it sparked a Belgian revolt against the Dutch."

"Really?"

"You can look it up."

Veronica's eyebrows rose in amazement. "Goodness! Are you a devoté of opera?"

"No," Le Brun said flatly. "I favor operetta a lot more. Especially Gilbert and Sullivan. But I read an opera history once. The point is that by cultivatin' artists you *can* have an influence over politics, Miss Godwin."

"I believe you. And call me Veronica." When she smiled, dimples formed in her rosy cheeks.

"If it pleases you." Because of her looks, John had been predisposed to dislike her. Experience with other women of like physical beauty had him expecting unapologetic ignorance or at least a self-limiting narcissism, but so far he was delightfully disappointed.

"And I shall call you John, if you don't mind. I've thought of going into the theater. Until recently, it was considered vulgar and nothing for a lady. But ever since women like Sarah Bernhardt and Lillie Langtry, there's no more stigma attached. Now that you remind me of the political power of theater, perhaps

I'll pursue the craft seriously."

"You have presence already," John could not resist admitting.

Veronica suddenly assumed a plaintive look and launched into one of the speeches from Shakespeare's *Romeo and Juliet.* When she finished, she waited for John's critique.

"You would make a most beguilin' Juliet, Miss Veronica."

"Thank you."

"Hello." A horse-faced woman in a mock-medieval gown suddenly loomed in front of Veronica and John.

"Lavinia Dunwoody, this is Mr. John Le Brun, of Georgia, in the States."

"Oh, how lovely! Do you own a plantation, Mr. Le Brun?"

"My plantation is exactly one acre, ma'am. I raise vegetables, not cotton or tobacco, and I have a chicken coop and a couple of bee hives." John expected a look of disgust.

"How wonderful!" the woman exclaimed with genuine enthusiasm, taking John completely by surprise. She stretched out her arm and reeled in a man John supposed was her husband. "Victor, you must hear this. This gentleman is living the life we envy. Chickens, vegetables, and bees!"

As soon as Veronica could, she extracted John from the woman's control. "Lavinia's family has been in London for ten generations. This is the latest craze, owning a rustic farm in Surrey or Kent. Some are actually doing it . . . with disastrous results. But failed experiments are to be expected and applauded. These are tumultuous times. London is the great billboard of the Empire, showing how change can happen. We're casting off the drab mantle of Victorian convention and experimenting with new freedoms."

John noted privately that casting off convention in the Godwin household did not extend to racial liberalities; every guest was Caucasian.

After introducing John around, Veronica strolled him into a corner and fairly monopolized him herself. She spoke with enthusiasm of the general enlightenment that had arisen out of the English laws enacted almost two generations back, ensuring an elementary education to every citizen. Book and magazine reading had increased tenfold in the past decade. Ideas were traded like physical commodities. Politics was every man's passion. Socialism found flesh in a thousand activities, clubs, and parties.

"A wise man once said, 'It is not enough to acquire wisdom; one must use it,'" John shared.

"Precisely!" Veronica had set her hand familiarly on John's wrist, and now she gave it a squeeze. "Talk about using it? There's sexual freedom, too. Most of Mayfair is rather staid, but you should hear what goes on in Bloomsbury," she said with widening eyes, in a half whisper. "They don't just *talk* about penises and vaginas, copulation and buggering."

"Goodness gracious," John exhaled. "I didn't use those words even with my wife."

"She's dead?"

"Yes."

"Recently?"

"No. A long time ago."

"I'm sorry nonetheless." Veronica's eyes unfocused to infinity. "I'm quite enthusiastic about sex, but I'm not at all interested in being anyone's wife. I follow Hamlet's words: 'I say we shall have no more marriages.'"

"What about if you have children?" John asked, struggling to accommodate such liberal thinking.

"What if I do?" Veronica shot back. "I'll have enough trouble caring for them; I can't have a man bothering me to be his wife at the same time." She opened the glass-doored cabinet beside her and indicated two books from its crammed shelves. "If you wish to review the sources of my credo, here they are: Ibsen's *A Doll's House* and H. G. Wells's *Wheels of Chance.*"

"I'll consider them," John told her. Just as he was feeling overwhelmed by the young woman's forceful opinions, Geoffrey

Moore came to his rescue.

"I told Trent and Maeve about your dilemma with our dogs, and they're happy to give you lodging here."

The proxied offer caught John off guard. "I couldn't impose on strangers."

"They're no longer strangers," Moore argued. "In fact, Trent feels a mystic kinship with you. I told him about how you had lost your young wife and unborn son to yellow fever. He lost *his* young wife and eight-year-old son to an influenza epidemic in 1890."

"I'm sorry to hear that."

"He also admires your mind. He just remarked to me that you have clearly thought long and hard about the issues you discussed with him and his partners. They're impressed by your depth of knowledge."

"How flatterin'."

Geoffrey waggled his uplifted finger. "In fact, he said, 'Mr. Le Brun clearly has a deep keel. I imagine when confronted by huge waves, he neither plunges foolishly headlong into them nor runs from them, but cuts through them at a smart angle.'"
John broke into an unaccustomed broad smile. Away from the narrow-mindedness of Brunswick, he was being accepted by people of quality. "I'm not a nautical man," he said, "but I like the metaphor." He looked at Veronica, hoping she would second the invitation, but she was at the moment staring at the group over which her mother held sway.

"Then it's settled," Geoffrey decided. "You said your lungs can stand the dogs for one night. Tomorrow, we'll meet Trent at our club and bring along your luggage. He wants to spend more time with you."

John looked around at the unaccustomed splendor. "Well . . . if he personally assures me it's all right," he relented.

Veronica excused herself to join her mother.

Geoffrey said, "Let me tell Daphne about your change of plans. I won't be but a minute." He hastened back into the living room, leaving John standing in the dining room. John drifted back toward the kitchen. Before he reached the entryway, he heard something that stopped him dead.

"I heard the whole story from Geoffrey . . . several times," a man said in a high-class accent. "It's very clear what happened. Joseph Pulitzer has at his disposal the best fact-finding staff in the Americas. He set them to work on the various suspects, and in short order they came up with the physician. When they all return to New York, this fellow takes the credit. Let's be serious; what hayseed sheriff from the swamps of Georgia could possibly solve such a complex murder? His accent alone tells the whole tale."

"That's Herbert Hyde," Maeve said softly, from over John's shoulder. "He's the part of the horse that goes over the fence last. Pay no attention to him. I, for one, am going to feel a great deal safer with such an accomplished law officer under our roof."

"Thank you, ma'am," John replied. "But I'm just an ordinary citizen now. Happily retired."

"Nonetheless," Maeve said. She patted John's shoulder and moved into the kitchen. John listened to her attack everything from Hyde's manhood to his tie without once mentioning Le Brun.

One win; one loss, John said to himself.

A moment later, Geoffrey returned and led John away to a makeshift bar set up in the dining room. A Negro barman dressed in a uniform that harkened back a hundred years was pouring drinks.

"And as an added treat, you get to spend more time with Veronica. She's quite a free spirit, eh?" Moore said, glancing at her over his shoulder.

"I applaud different ways of seein' life," John said, "especially if people show me what they mean in a plain way."

"She'll show you all right," Moore said. "Just give her half a chance."

John accepted a whiskey from the bartender. Another liveried man stood under the entry arch to the room, apparently just waiting for direction. "They seem to have so many servants," he observed. "Are they not expensive?"

"*English* servants are," Geoffrey answered. "Daphne and I feel we can only afford Mrs. Rainsford as our cook and her daughter as our maid full-time. The rest of our staff is part-time. The Godwins have a husband and wife team who live in an apartment above their carriage house." Moore nodded at the white-haired, superior-looking man. "He's their butler-cum-chauffeur; she's their cook. They also have a maid Monday to Friday during the day. This man serving drinks is just for the night. Anyone can fill a house with Caribbean or African servants. Or Irish. But good English folk are becoming increasingly dear. Drink up, old friend; you're on holiday!"

ON THE RIDE BACK to the Moore home, Daphne filled Geoffrey's ear with her need to upgrade the artwork in their home. After listening to her drone on about it for several minutes, John made an offhand remark on the beauty of the Godwin house.

"Do you really think so? I think it's a museum of modernism," Mrs. Godwin said, with more than a tinge of disapproval in her voice. "Thousands and thousands of pounds for one-of-a-kind pieces. Art is one thing, but furniture's another. Department stores or regular shops are not good enough for her. Oh, no! If she's going to spend that kind of money, she should at least buy some works of Englishmen, instead of so many French and Germans. I tell you, I'm certainly glad I'm not their maid. One slip dusting a vase, and there goes three months' salary."

"I agree with John. Their house is quite impressive," Geoffrey opined.

Daphne glowered at her partner. "I think it's being different to be different. And to show off."

"What was that Trent said about not stayin' at his own party?" John asked.

"Oh, he has very little tolerance for social events," Geoffrey said. "He usually takes a cab home early from balls and outside parties. Sometimes leaves before the last acts of plays, ballet, and opera. And he actually does retire early from his own parties."

"Because they're really *Maeve's* parties," Daphne imparted archly.

Looking at the couple from across the carriage interior, John admitted, "They do seem to have their peculiar traits. I've never met a family quite like the Godwins."

"Trent's your basic John Bull," Daphne observed. "But Maeve and Veronica are three steps ahead of avant-garde. They even had Emmeline Pankhurst and her daughters to one of their soirees."

"Women rabid about getting the vote," Geoffrey told John.

"Veronica told me their parties aren't political," John reported.

"Not for lack of trying," Geoffrey countered. "The truth is, they're both natural rabble rousers. Change for the sake of change, seems to me."

"I don't quite see Mr. and Mrs. Godwin together," John said.

"Chalk and cheese," said Daphne.

"Excuse me?" John said.

"It's an expression we use when referring to an unmatched couple," Geoffrey explained. "Trent's first wife was as conservative as he. That was a marriage of minds and temperaments. When he lost her, he vowed he'd never marry again."

"And we were sure he meant it after a decade of romances

with no altar," Daphne interjected.

Geoffrey nodded. "But then he begins dating this woman newly arrived from Belfast, and after just six months he announces he'll marry her. That was a little more than four years ago."

"And it's not like he seemed any more smitten by her than half a dozen others before her," Mrs. Moore observed. "But *chacun a son gout, n'est-ce pas, M'sieur Le Brun?*"

"*Vraiment, Madame,*" John agreed. "*Vraiment.*"

FOUR

Saturday, October 21, 1905

JOHN LE BRUN'S FIRST FULL day in London began at Harrods, which was to London what Macy's was to New York City and Bon Marché to Paris. He was fitted with a respectable set of frock-coated evening wear and promised it would be ready by Tuesday afternoon. From there, he and Geoffrey Moore hurried to Trafalgar Square for the celebration of all that nineteenth century British imperialism meant. The crowds were massive but orderly. It was not in the English nature to disobey the patrolling bobbies, whose bullet-shaped helmets rose above the milling throng. Banners, candies, stick toys, fish and chips, hot sausages, and lemonade were hawked from little carts. The everyday London street-sellers, which Geoffrey assured him numbered in the thousands, sold tarts, ices and strawberry cream, mince pies, heart cakes, Chelsea buns, muffins, and crumpets. Men perched protecting hands on their precious pints of beer and ale. Politicians from reviewing stands and crackpots with soapboxes harangued whomever would listen. The disturbed pigeons circled above, dropping their annoyance on unsuspecting revelers.

At the center of the gathered thousands, like a huge pivot point for the world empire, stood Nelson's column. Its reliefs, formed from the melted cannons of ships captured at Trafalgar, and Landseer's four lordly lions at the corners of its base, were festooned with floral tributes. A crisp breeze made a huge Union Jack snap proudly below Nelson's feet. Twenty-eight flags hung from two of the guy wires John had noted the previous day.

They took a position at the southwest corner of the activities. A few minutes later, Maeve Godwin walked up to them, surrounded by five other equally stylishly-dressed women. She introduced them one by one to John and Geoffrey and announced that they were the heart of her charity ball committee. Before John could politely inquire about the ball, Maeve pointed to the column and asked, "You know what the flags spell out?"

" 'England expects every man to do his duty?' " Le Brun guessed.

"Naturally he'd know," Moore stated. "He knows more about British history than any other American I've met."

"I simply read," John said.

"He knows J. P. Morgan and Joseph Pulitzer, the newspaperman," Maeve announced proudly to her cronies, as if he were a precious possession.

"Truly?" asked one of the women.

"Yes," John admitted. "But I'm not asked to their poker games." The group tittered and giggled.

"Well, we must be off to the Westminster Palace," said Mrs. Godwin. "We just had to see this, to be able to say we were part of the celebration, no matter how briefly. But duty calls."

The ladies excused themselves and followed Maeve, like so many chicks, in a southward direction away from the crowds.

"Are those women members of royalty?" John asked Geoffrey.

Geoffrey laughed. "No. Why do you ask that?"

"They're going to Westminster Palace."

"The Westminster Palace *Hotel.*"

"Ah."

"They may not be royalty, but they've all got husbands who earn royal livings. Every one of them makes more than Trent, but Maeve has taken charge of the group nonetheless. I told her we'd be here at this time, and she asked me to stand on this corner, so she could show you off."

"By the time you get through as my advance man," John remarked, "they'll be havin' me pose for a figure in Madame Tussaud's."

"I'm afraid you'd have to solve a horrid *British* crime," Geoffrey answered. "Then they'd consider your likeness in their criminals gallery. You might have a whack at the Jack the Ripper murders. They've never been solved."

"That's all right. I'm retired and on holiday."

They listened to His Majesty's Royal Marine Band play two of Edward Elgar's *Pomp and Circumstance* marches, followed by a rousing version of *Rule, Britannia!* They left early, so that they could find a seat at a local restaurant and lunched at Scott's, near Piccadilly. Geoffrey gulped down his food, and as soon as John had finished they hurried on to the British Museum. Moore conducted his tour as would an historian rather than an art lover, lecturing how the collection began with the collection of Sir Hans Sloane, how Lord Elgin had spirited the marble high reliefs from the ruins of the Parthenon, and how British archeological teams were busy raiding half a dozen countries for their ancient treasures. What struck John most about the place had nothing to do with its collections but rather that the rich and the poor were enjoying it equally, with the poor showing every bit as much appreciation and manners. Among the number was a Levantine family and a group of Africans in tribal dress, whose faces were decorated with raised tattoos.

In the late afternoon they gawked at the Tower of London, and John received a lengthy treatise on its history since Roman times. On the ride back to the Moore house, Geoffrey pointed out several places of interest that John must visit by himself. He apologized that, between the demands of his firm and his women, he could spare little time beyond this day.

JOHN NAPPED FROM FIVE-THIRTY to six-thirty, in preparation for what he expected to be a long evening. He knew that all the sites Moore had shown him were prelude in the importer's mind to the clubland tour he would conduct tonight. He had been making preparatory remarks throughout the day, such as advising John to wear comfortable shoes because they would be parading no fewer than ten blocks. At the end of the march, John would be trundled out as Geoffrey's prize and made to dredge up unhappy remembrances from the War between the States for an hour or so. To minimize John's grousing, Geoffrey kept promising a surprise that he was sure to enjoy.

The cabman, whom Moore evidently hired on a regular basis, let them out at Piccadilly Circus and drove on to the Sceptred Isle Club with John's luggage. The two men immediately began walking south-southeast on Lower Regent Street, under a cloud-streaked sky changing rapidly from gold to red above the perpetual smog belching from a hundred thousand coal chimneys. After avoiding a pair of brassy beggars, they passed the Raleigh Club, the Junior United Service Club, the Pall Mall Club, and the United Service Club, each housed behind an impressive façade. They crossed Regent's Street and headed toward a beautiful, white, three-story building in the Grecian style, under which cornice ran a copy of the same

Parthenon frieze John had admired in the British Museum. This was Geoffrey Moore's beloved Athenæum Club.

"It only costs thirty guineas for entry and six more guineas a year to sustain one's membership," Moore told John, "but it takes blood, sweat, and tears to get in . . . unless you're a very high member of the government, a bishop, or an archbishop. They can be elected immediately without waiting for the normal balloting." He nodded at the servant who opened the front door. "Harshaw."

"Good evening, Mr. Moore," the man said, causing Moore to steal a look for John's approbation. They stepped inside. "What do you think, John?" he encouraged.

Le Brun acknowledged that the central hall was grand indeed. It had a barreled and coffered ceiling supported by eight columns. Far back from the door, twenty-four wide steps ran straight up to the first landing before breaking left and right. The image of their mythological patroness of wisdom, Pallas Athena, looked down benevolently from several places upon the members.

"Now remember," Geoffrey coached, "it is not called the dining room but rather the coffee room, and what you would call the lounge is the morning room."

"And it's not the crapper but the lavatory," John said, in a singsong pattern, "and it's not the elevator but the lift, and the members aren't pigeon-toed; they have club feet."

"I hope you're having fun."

"The most I've had all day, Geoffrey."

They turned to the right and stood at the entrance to the morning room, with its green leather armchairs. Members glanced up briefly. Two acknowledged Moore with slight nods of their heads.

"Sorry you're not allowed in most of these rooms," Moore apologized. They crossed the entrance hallway to the pale-green-walled coffee room and peered in at handsomely designed gas lamps hung above groups of tables that sat from two to ten. Servants applied finishing touches to the tables for the dinner meal.

Upon ascending the stairs, on what Moore called the first floor, John was shown the one-hundred-foot-long drawing room, with its paired sets of pillars supporting an ultrahigh ceiling, its enormous mirrors, its eleven vaulting windows, its bookcases topped by busts, and its many groupings of leather chairs and sofas. They peeked into the West library, where cards were played, and the North library, which was used for large assemblages.

As they continued on, Geoffrey said, "Now you shall see what I consider the heart of this club."

"The bar," John quipped.

"There is no bar," Moore replied, incapable of joking. "If you thought you saw books in other rooms, wait until you see the South library."

With toes balanced on the threshold, John leaned into a large room. It was crammed from floor to ceiling with books, running so high against the walls that a suspended iron walkway had to be built, accessed by a spiral staircase. Desks were arranged below.

"Absolute silence is required," Moore said in a whisper. "That's Writer's Corner. And there's Charles Dickens's chair."

A seated figure turned to face the whispering with an annoyed expression.

"Sir Arthur!" Moore exclaimed. "I hoped I'd find you here." He crooked his finger several times.

The man's countenance softened. He rose and set down his opened book on the leather chair. John noted that he was about five foot nine or a bit taller. He was undoubtedly English, but his face had some features John considered German. It was full and fair, with a strong brow and arching eyebrows. His hair was trimmed short. He wore no sideburns. The hairline receded sharply from each temple and began high on his forehead, but it did not seem to be thinning.

He had a walrus mustache, waxed at both tips. As he approached, John thought that he embodied the English phrase "stout fellow." He carried perhaps fifteen extra pounds, but it was added to a powerful musculature and skeleton. He looked to be a very fit forty-five.

"Sheriff John Le Brun," Geoffrey said with a flourish in his voice, "this is Sir Arthur Conan Doyle."

Doyle made a shooing gesture with his hand. "Forget the title, Geoffrey. I only accepted it for my mother and my wife."

"Arthur received it for meritorious service during the Boer War," Geoffrey bragged on Sir Arthur's behalf.

"Went as a senior physician, not a soldier," Doyle said with patent disappointment. "Spent the time fighting typhoid, not the Dutch. So you're the brilliant detective Geoffrey has regaled London about."

"I'm retired," John said. "And I only did detective work because my little city couldn't afford a real one."

"He's too modest by half," Moore affirmed. He swung his head to address John. "Have I mentioned Arthur's done real detective work as well?"

"You have."

Geoffrey chose to ignore the opportunity for silence. "He once found a man who had withdrawn his entire bank balance and vanished."

Doyle shrugged modestly. "He was last seen near Paddington Station after eleven P.M. I suggested to the police that there were only a few trains running at that hour and that they should have him looked for in the cities of those trains' destination. He was found in Edinburgh. It seems as if people think I have a direct line to a real Sherlock Holmes."

"I remember when the Marquess of Anglesey called you in over the theft of her family jewels," said Moore. "Never a dull moment, eh?"

"Rarely."

Moore beamed like Lewis Carroll's Cheshire Cat from his

place between two of his heroes. "This is the surprise I promised. We stopped by here specifically to pick up Arthur. He's coming to hear your lecture."

"I'm honored," said John.

"So what are you up to, Arthur?" Geoffrey asked, nodding into the library.

"A little research for my syndicate." He faced Le Brun. "We're trying to recover the *Grosvenor.* It was an East India ship. Sank off South Africa in 1782, with the spoils of the sacking of Delhi. Maharajahs' jewels, lots of gold bullion."

"Sounds right out of your story, *The Sign of the Four,*" John said.

"Oh, have you read that?" Conan Doyle asked, showing most of his teeth in his pleasure.

"Yes, indeed. I enjoyed it and *A Study in Scarlet* very much." John hoped that the discussion would not go beyond the only two Sherlock Holmes mysteries he had read. He seldom indulged in fiction. His tastes ran more to biographies, histories, and science. To prevent the anticipated question, he added, "I got a war wound in my shoulder, just like your Dr. Watson." Unlike the fictional Watson, whose wound had migrated from shoulder in the first novella to leg in the second, Le Brun's had stayed put. John tactfully avoided mentioning the inconsistency.

"I'm sorry to hear that," commiserated Doyle. "Still bothering you?"

"Not much anymore."

"That's good. Well, I'm gratified you enjoy my detective stories," Doyle said. "Especially after hearing from Mr. Moore your ingenious solution to the Jekyl Island Club murder. I particularly enjoyed how you contrived to get aboard Mr. Morgan's yacht. You should solicit a competent writer to turn it into a book."

"I'm afraid it would fail upon the nature of my personality," John said. "Unlike Mr. Holmes, I am not a colorful person. How did you invent such a character?"

Doyle smiled. "I didn't. Not much of him anyway. I rather assembled him from several flesh-and-blood characters I've met along life's journey. My chief model was one of my professors at medical school. University of Edinburgh. A chap named Joe Bell. It was his contention that a good physician should base his diagnosis not only on symptoms of the disease but on the patient's occupation and character."

"And he did this through observation?" John asked.

"Through not just sight but smell, sound, and touch. For example, a woman he had never seen before came into the examination room at the free clinic where we trained. She had arrived with a little boy. He looked her over for a few moments and asked her several seemingly pointless questions. Directly, he pronounced that she was from Fife, had traveled on foot over a particular road, had dropped off an older child on the way, that she was right-handed, and worked in a linoleum factory."

"The town he identified by her accent, and she probably had a contact skin disease on her workin' hand," John guessed.

"Absolutely correct," Doyle said.

"But how did he know about the road and the older child?"

"A certain color clay on her boot and the fact that she carried a child's coat too large for the toddler."

John nodded.

Sir Arthur leaned against the hallway wall. "Of course, my detective can be even more clever because I work backwards. I develop the motive, then the opportunity, then the execution and the clues."

As the author spoke, John was looking, listening, and smelling, picking up clues as efficiently as Doyle's professor had. He noted that the man had his arms folded, which suggested that he felt somewhat defensive of the accomplished detective in front of him. He wore a wedding ring. He dressed in a business suit cut a bit too large, indicating that he had either recently lost weight or else preferred comfort to stylishness. There was no detectable liquor on his breath, but John's generous nose caught another scent. "I dealt with a bit more than a dozen murders in my career," John said as he observed, "and most of the time the motives were clear: liquor or a powerful passion. No plannin'. Swift and sloppy killin'. Only a few times was there that famous malice aforethought, but those were the ones that proved the challenge. I can't recall bein' blessed with many clues . . . at least no real ones."

"I'd love to hear about some of your cases in detail," Doyle allowed. "Perhaps lunch one day this week."

"It would be a pleasure," John said.

Doyle uncrossed his arms and raised a forefinger. "Just give me two minutes to finish my research. Meet you downstairs." He bounded back into the South library.

"I hope you're up for a brisk walk," Geoffrey told John as they began to retrace their route. "Arthur takes every opportunity for exercise he can."

John insinuated his index finger between his celluloid collar and his neck and attempted to stretch the instrument of torture. "That's fine. He lives outside the city."

"Are you guessing?" asked Moore.

"Yes. I noted he has a five o'clock shadow. Almost all the men at last night's party and the ones I've passed in your club here shave in the evenin' before goin' out. It would be more difficult for Mr. Doyle if he lived in the country."

"Well, he does. He lives in Hindhead. It's just a few miles from Haslemere, which is on the same rail line we took up from Southampton. Are you attempting to rival Sherlock Holmes?"

Le Brun gave up on the collar. "I'm not such a fool. I will wager, however, that he has a mistress in London."

Moore exhaled his amazement. "How the deuce did you know that?"

John started walking toward the grand staircase. "He has the faint scent of a woman's perfume on him. I'm not that familiar with fragrances to tell how expensive it is, but it smelled rich to me."

Moore looked around, to be sure no one was behind them on the stairs. "Don't dare mention this to anyone. Arthur thinks it's still a secret. She's not a real mistress as I understand it. Mostly, they arrange to meet at the same functions. There may be private trysts as well, but knowing Arthur's character it must only be on the order of hand holding and strolling."

"And some huggin' and kissin'," John added, with one eyebrow cocked.

"Evidently. Those who've watched them together say they're very much in love. His wife, Louise, has been dying of tuberculosis for the longest time. They were thrown together by her brother's death. Arthur was the attending physician. Felt guilty about contributing to her loss. All the wrong reasons for marriage. She's a terrible burden on him. I mean he's fond of her and very loyal, but Jean is apparently his soul mate. He'll marry her after a suitable mourning period, I'm sure."

"How long has this been goin' on?"

They came to the bottom of the staircase. Moore signaled for their coats and hats. "Can't say. I've known about it for four years."

By the time they were bundled, Conan Doyle was descending the stairs. John put himself between the author and the importer as they left the building. "How long have you been a member of the Athenæum Club, Mr. Doyle?"

"Since 1901. My uncle was a member back in the, uh, seventies. Used to invite me to luncheon. In fact, in December of '83 he died of apoplexy inside its hallowed walls."

"Goodness!" Moore exclaimed. "I'd never heard that."

"Imagine!" Doyle said in a breathy, mocking tone. "Something the club's fishwife hasn't heard. I'm also a member of the Authors' and Reform Clubs," Doyle informed Le Brun as they walked down Pall Mall Street.

John observed, "You said you were educated in Edinburgh. You still have the remains of a Scottish accent. But the name 'Doyle' is Irish. Are you Roman Catholic?"

"I was raised as such, but I'm agnostic," Doyle said. "What about you?"

"Oh, I call myself a Catholic, but I'm seldom found inside a church. I've read the Bible a couple times. No longer feel a need for a priest's intercession or interpretation. Talk with God directly when I need to. When you say agnostic—"

"And here's the Travellers Club," Geoffrey announced in an overloud voice. "You have to have traveled at least five hundred miles from London to qualify."

"I believe that's our cue to restrict our conversation to socially acceptable subjects," John said.

"I believe you're right," Doyle echoed.

WITH CONAN COYLE ESTABLISHING the quick pace, the three men soon reached the limit of Pall Mall Street and turned right onto St. James. The Sceptred Isle Club stood on the block between King and Ryder Streets, just above the Junior Army and Navy Club. Only a block beyond lay the Elysian fields of Clubland: Brooks's, Boodle's and White's. In comparison to the Athenæum and most other club façades John had seen on the long U they had walked, Geoffrey's favorite was quite unprepossessing. It had obviously been built as a grand townhouse in the early nineteenth century. It was mostly faced in brick, with granite quoins and an inscribed arched marble entrance to give it some character. John judged that it could not have been wider than fifty feet. Entry was gained by climbing four steps from the sidewalk. He could see a pair of tiny, barred cellar windows as he looked over the stair rail, but no light shone through them. The house rose two stories above, and a total of nine windows glowed invitingly.

Immediately after they entered the club, Sir Arthur lagged behind, to speak with a friend he called Bertie.

"Are you deliberately trying to get me in Dutch with a member of my own club, questioning him on his faith?" Geoffrey accused, as angry as John had ever seen him. "A very famous and influential member, I might add."

John linked his hands behind his back and rocked on the balls of his feet as he gave the Sceptred Isle's entry hallway a good look. "Not at all. I just wanted to see how much cachet all your braggin' on my behalf gives me."

"Well... I hope you found out and are satisfied," Geoffrey fumed. He dispelled his anger with a low harrumph. "So, here we are. The home of the historian. Intimate but complete. Servants to provide for all needs, but none of the headaches one has in one's own house. No screaming women. A couple of rooms to smoke in without guilt. A private room to play cards in once a week. Let me show you."

The staircase arrangement was similar to that of the Athenæum but on a simpler scale. At the break where it divided left and right, instead of a pseudo-Grecian statue bracketed by columns, it displayed in inset and gilt lettering the quotation from Shakespeare's *King Richard II* that gave the name to the club.

The second floor consisted of a library, a meeting room, a billiard room (with a bar and where smoking was allowed), and the manager's office and bedroom. By the time they had finished touring the floor, Geoffrey had four times repeated to members his introductory speech about "the detective from Brunswick, Georgia, who solved the Jekyl Island Club murder and probably saved J. P. Morgan's life." John retained his equanimity, telling himself it was the price paid for Moore's gracious hospitality. If the man scored some points from borrowed glory, it was no loss to him. From one of the exchanges, he learned that Moore was the current Member Recording Secretary.

Downstairs, one corner of the morning room had been set aside for chess, since half a dozen members were devoted players. John was shown the marble chess boards and the brass and pewter pieces, but no one played at the moment. The room was not particularly opulent. The Georgian had been in two private parlors in Brunswick as large and as well decorated. As Geoffrey had told him often, the Sceptred Isle Club's reputation was built on its membership, not on its facility.

John's opinion of the membership of both clubs he had visited was that it was staid to the point of brittleness. Even the young men seemed old, as if they should be caked in dust. If they were having fun, it eluded John's keen observations. He decided that the rest of the world could not imitate clubland precisely because it was a phenomenon unique to the very proper and dignified British.

As they exited the morning room and reunited with Conan Doyle, Trent Godwin came bounding up one of the sets of stairs that led to the cellar. He did not slow his pace as he neared the three men but offered a quick smile and an explanation for not stopping.

"Evening, gents. I'm up forty quid. Should have visited the loo half an hour ago."

John watched him disappear down the opposite stairs. He turned to Geoffrey. "He just came up, and now he goes down?"

"Yes, well, that's the price the gamblers pay for having their private room. The lavatory is on the other side of the cellar. Many of the members don't approve of gambling, so we stuck the den of iniquity as far away as possible with it still being in the building. It has its own outside door, and the players usually come and go that way. But nature does call. If they didn't come up these stairs and go down those, they'd have to walk through the pantry, the dish room, and the kitchen. Not good form, y'know."

A passing member gave John a quizzical look.

"I'm the celebrated sheriff from Georgia who solved the Jekyl Island Club murder and saved J. P. Morgan," John called out. The man's expression brightened, and he flashed the thumbs-up sign as he shambled away.

"You mock me," Geoffrey said.

"You set yourself up for mockery," Doyle interjected.

"It might have been smart to put the rest room on the same side of the buildin' as the gamblin' room, don't you think?" John observed.

Moore smirked. "Might have, except both are afterthoughts. This house was built before indoor plumbing."

"And how many members do you have?" John asked, having seen fewer than twenty during his tour and thinking the number was small for a Saturday night.

"It's a very restricted club ... by design," Moore said, lifting his chin high as he looked at the fiction writer. "One hundred forty-one on the rolls. One hundred twenty-six paid their dues last year. Ninety-six drop by at least once a month, and I should hazard that sixty would regard this as their main club. That's why I say the dining is so poor. It's not just that we can't afford the best chef but also that we don't seat enough at luncheon or dinner to be able to offer a large menu. One special dish per meal, I'm afraid. We're dining lightly before John's lecture. Won't you join us, Sir Arthur?"

"Oh, perhaps just a bowl of soup. I had a big lunch."

"Very well." Moore ushered the men toward the coffee room entrance, where the maître d'-cum-waiter stood at attention. "Of course for you the menu will all be new," he told John.

"Good evening, gentlemen," the servant said with a broad but hard smile. "I have your reservation."

Moore said, "Bernard, this is Mr. John Le Brun." Despite John's outright rebuke, he yet again delivered his sentences praising John and tying the ex-sheriff's name to those of J. P. Morgan and, for added effect, Joseph Pulitzer.

"We are honored to have you visit the Sceptred Isle Club, sir," Bernard said.

"And I'm sure you recognize Sir Arthur Conan Doyle."

"Who would not?" the servant said with aplomb. "Welcome, Sir Arthur. If you will—"

All words, all motions throughout the club stopped at the muffled yet distinct cracks of pistol fire. They sounded in a rapid group of three, followed by three more which were each spaced by a pair of seconds. By the time the last of the reports had echoed off the club walls, there was no doubt they came from the cellar and more specifically from the area of the gambling room.

"Gunfire!" Doyle exclaimed, as if it could be something else.

In answer, John reached into his jacket pocket and withdrew his two-shot derringer. He was the first of a rush of men to reach the cellar stairs and descend. When he reached the bottom step, he found two men in kitchen uniforms making frantic motions at a door angled in the wall directly opposite. The one with the chef's cap twisted a non-responsive doorknob with both hands. The other's right shoulder had just rebounded off the solid oak door. The chef called through the door.

"Malcolm! What's happened? Open up!"

The mixed odors of cigar and cigarette smoke and gunpowder poured into the narrow hallway from under the door and over a partially-opened transom window. As the kitchen assistant threw himself vainly against the door once more, John tugged his watch out of its pocket and glanced at its hands. He re-vested the watch.

"Kindly step back," John called out, in a tone that belied the pleasantry of his words. The moment the staff member cleared the door, John brought his right foot up and delivered a powerful kick, parallel with the knob. Hardware groaned. The door shuddered but held. He kicked again. This time the door sprang inward with a shrieking of metal and an explosive snapping of wood. Several men exclaimed behind him. The door rebounded against the inner wall. John caught the knob on its flight back. He took one step into the room, weapon raised, and drank in the scene.

A blue-white haze swirled through the gaming room like an animated shroud. It was not thick enough to cover the scene of slaughter. A card table dominated the room from its center. The entire space was a rough square some sixteen feet on a side. Four chairs surrounded the table; a fifth and sixth were suspended on chair rail pegs in the far wall. The chair opposite the table from where John stood had been toppled. The corner formed of the far side wall and the wall with the shattered door held a built-in cupboard which was used to store cards, poker chips, various liquor bottles, drinking glasses, and plates. It had one wide drawer which lay three-quarters open. The only other piece of furniture in the room was a coat tree, upon which hung two full-length woolen coats and a top hat. Between the suspended chairs was a second door. It stood barely opened. This door had a small window at eye level, with a spring-loaded slide mechanism that normally kept the window shuttered. The retracted bolt above the doorknob looked formidable and was fully intact.

Above the outer door lay another transom window, slightly open. Other than the two doors, the room had no access. Those expanses of wall not occupied by doors or furniture were decorated with framed print scenes from Hogarth's *The Rake's Progress.*

A fixture with twin electric light bulbs hanging three feet above the center of the table provided the total illumination. Cards, poker chips, two billfolds, a handkerchief, two ashtrays with cigar stubs and cigarette butts, and two plates with half-eaten sandwiches lay scattered across the table, under the lights' yellow glare. A pair of spectacles sat upside down on the table in front of the chair nearest John. The only motion other than the smoke was the dripping of red liquids from the tabletop. One rivulet came from an upended glass flute losing the last drops of wine. The red stream flowed over a pair of hearts before plunging into a pool on the wooden floor. A second stream of red, a little lighter in color but thicker, ran across the table from a destroyed human head.

In all, four men lay still in the room. The one with his posterior to the inside door was splayed out on his chair, arms hanging to either side, head thrown back to reveal a large bullet hole just above the bridge of his nose. Only the weight and position of the table prevented the body from collapsing to the floor. The corpse's white dress shirt was sprayed with blood and gore belonging to the man directly opposite. This man had been shot in the back of the head and lay face down in an expanding pool of his blood.

Lying propped against the far wall, behind the hinges of the outer door, lay the butler. He had two bullet wounds in his face. He lay in a disjointed heap like a marionette whose strings had been cut, his left leg under him at a grotesque angle. A top hat lay balanced against one thigh. John noted the dark shape of a fourth body, lying face down on the floor, partway under the table. His overturned chair and the one opposite and still upright stood out from the table at little distances.

All this was absorbed by the ex-sheriff in the space of two breaths. He pivoted and faced the hallway, where a throng of men pressed forward from the stairs for a look.

"Jesus, Mary, and Joseph!" the chef exhaled, his eyes huge.

"Call the police!" John commanded, simultaneously pushing the chef back into the hallway. "Where's Dr. Doyle?"

"Here." The beefy man pressed forward.

"Please attend to these men." John found Geoffrey Moore inches from his face. "You stand guard. Let no one else in here, includin' yourself."

Moore, who was hyperventilating, nodded. John turned the club member's face from the carnage. A moment later, the ex-lawman was picking his way carefully across the open floor to the back door. He nudged it open with the tip of his derringer and rushed into the night.

The building that housed the Sceptred Isle Club was less deep than its neighbors, so that an alcove was formed, with an alleyway beyond it. John dashed forward into the alley, glancing first left, then right. Because the house lay in the middle of the block, the alley stretched several hundred feet in either direction. The alley lay empty and quiet.

John looked behind him to the left and made out another, smaller alley, running parallel with the length of the club. It ascended one foot for each run of ten. He sprinted up it as fast as his fifty-eight-year-old legs would move and burst onto the sidewalk of St. James Street. The street was sparsely peopled. On the sidewalk to his right, a pair of lovers were locked in a kiss. Beyond them, a light, four-wheeled carriage made a right turn at the nearest corner and disappeared from view. To his left, three formally-dressed gentlemen were alighting from a boxy carriage. Beyond them, a hansom cab approached at a slow trot. John extracted his watch and again consulted it.

The lovers were still locked in a hot embrace when John strode up close to their sides. Their rumpled and coarse clothing put them out of place on the thoroughfare of the upper crust.

John cleared his throat softly. When that failed to redirect their attention, he said, "Excuse me. Did either of you happen to see anyone come out of that alley?" He dipped his head toward the narrow opening.

The woman shook her head.

The man swallowed his annoyance with some difficulty. "Me neither." He looked up and down the street and seemed surprised.

"Somethin' wrong?" John asked.

"There was a phaeton 'ere a minute ago. Somebody might 'ave got in."

Le Brun thought of the conveyance rounding the corner. "Is a phaeton a four-wheeled, closed carriage?"

" 'as right."

"Did you get a look at the driver?"

The man's annoyance reappeared. "Look, old man, we were busy. Still are." He swung his arm around his girlfriend and guided her away.

John opened his mouth to speak but reconsidered. He gave the area one more sweep of the eye, then returned to the side alley. Three-quarters of the way to its far end, a small window lay in the club's wall. It was positioned low, so that Le Brun could have kicked out its panes with his knee. The casement-style window had two squares of semi-opaque glass. John knelt and attempted to raise the lower half by curling his fingers under the top rail. It would not come up.

John returned to the alcove with stealth. He heard nothing suspicious and saw no movement. By now his eyes had adjusted to the darkness. He speculated that in some earlier era the space might have been a garden. The ground was now completely bricked over. The club and the two adjoining buildings stored their garbage and ash bins there. John trod out to the larger alley. He studied it in the faint light that poured out of nearby windows. It was made of solid cobblestone, a surface that would yield no prints on a night where the damp had yet to set in. On the opposite side of the alley, a brick wall rose eight feet, high enough to discourage all but the most athletic from climbing over it. The wall was punctuated every hundred feet or so by formidable iron gates. John tested the gates nearest the club and found all of them locked. He did the same with the doors on the adjoining buildings, with the same result. Although sounds of the city crept in, the immediate area was silent as a crypt.

When John opened the gaming room's outer door and stepped back inside, he found Conan Doyle with his coat off, kneeling near the prone body. He looked up at John.

"All dead."

John sighed. "We have a sayin' for somethin' like this: 'Shootin' fish in a barrel.'"

"Quite apt," said Conan Doyle.

"I was in there not five minutes ago." Trent Godwin's voice came from the inner doorway, where he stood just beyond Geoffrey Moore's outstretched arms. His expression mingled horror and disbelief, and his eyes blinked like twin semaphore lamps. Other men's faces crowded in on either side of his.

Le Brun moved forward to cut off their view. "Geoffrey, have the police been called?"

"Scotland Yard has been summoned."

"Good. Please close the door and send everyone upstairs, includin' the kitchen staff. Remind them that the police will not look favorably on anyone who leaves."

John pushed on the ruined inner door as Geoffrey pulled so that, together, they managed to jam it closed. Then John crossed the room and shut the outer door. As he passed Doyle, he noted that the man's breathing was regular and his hands easy at his sides. But his eyes blazed. John knew exactly how he felt, because he felt the same. Between them passed the tacit knowledge that they were men totally galvanized by the ultimate of crimes.

"Have you ever come upon murder so soon after its commission, Mr. Le Brun?" Doyle asked.

"Never. I've also never had a doctor of medicine and student of crime so near at hand either. Let us see what we can do together to assist the police before they arrive. What conclusions have you drawn?"

"The first is that the person was known to the butler and judged safe to admit. Clearly, from the little window and the dead bolt on that door, the members feared robbery." He waited until John had nodded. "This trusted person began shooting the second he passed through the door. The gun was of large caliber. At least .38 I'd say."

"A hand gun," John interjected.

"Yes, of course. A rifle would be difficult to maneuver in such tight surroundings." Doyle crossed to the body nearest the back door. "This one was despatched first. Direct line of fire. Didn't even have time to turn to see who the butler had let in." Doyle brushed a lock of his hair off his forehead. "The butler was next. A swift shot, to prevent him from reacting and using the door to shove the killer back outside. The shot, however, is across the killer's body, assuming he's right-handed. It passes through the philtrum . . . He squatted and pointed to the hole just below the butler's nose ". . . and, because of the butler's angle, out his left cheek just anterior to his ear. Not enough to kill the man but enough to knock him to the floor."

Doyle stood again. "Next victim is this fellow across the table. Now that the first chap's head has been blown forward onto the table, the line of fire is clear for a killing shot." The author made a gun of his raised thumb, pointed index and curved remaining fingers and aimed at the man slumped back on his chair. "I'd say the victim had just enough time to rise halfway from the chair when he took the single slug. Good shot even this close, to calculate for his movement and still get him between the eyes. From this point, the order of the other shots probably can't be determined."

"Perhaps they can," John said, slowly circling the table. "Provided there was only one shooter and he or she entered through the outer door."

Le Brun's words had Doyle's brows furrowing.

John stood above the butler. "The spread of shots was three together, a space of perhaps two seconds, the fourth, two more seconds, the fifth, then another few seconds and the sixth and final shot. If we build upon your plausible beginning, the butler would have been knocked down and instinctively, through his shock, have attempted to rise." John pointed to the higher of two circular holes in the wall behind the butler. Both holes were surrounded by blood, but the upper one had only speckles while the lower trailed a long red smear. "This would be the one that exited his cheek." His finger drifted down. "He rose to this point and was shot in the chest. The bullet seemed to miss all bone and exit in one piece. The man collapsed, with his leg under him."

"The leg couldn't have ended up there otherwise," Doyle agreed. "Now, the killer—or killers—must only murder one more."

"Who is by this time cowerin' under the table. This requires the killer a few moments to find a clear shot, one that will at least immobilize the last man. The sixth shot guarantees his death."

"Literally in one ear and out the other," Doyle reported, with no intent at levity. "If I were in this fellow's place, I would have overturned the table and shoved it with all my might against the killer."

Le Brun smiled. "Can you be so sure? Would you still have such presence of mind with men dyin' all around you?"

Doyle smiled back. "Trust me. It will be interesting to compare the bullets."

John came up very close to the face of the man sprawled back on his chair. "Are you agreein' there might have been more than one killer?"

"If not, more than one revolver. Even if there was only one murderer, no sane man would expect to make a clean kill with each shot. There might have been as many as seven men here if the chairs are any indication, and anyone who could get the butler to open the door would have known that. I touched nothing but each man's neck."

"Yes, that's good. One killer or two, there don't seem to be any of those wonderful clues your Mr. Holmes makes so much of."

"I agree. Quickly in and out. Nothing apparently dropped. Little touched. No footprints. I'm glad I'm not looking at this alone," said Doyle.

Low conversation came from the hallway. John moved to the inner door and yanked it open. Trent Godwin sat on the staircase's third step, pulling the crotch of his trousers up and down. He looked at Le Brun and said, "I was just telling Geoffrey that when I heard the shots I was urinating. I was so rattled that I wet myself. That's why I was the last one here. Afraid I couldn't towel all of it out."

Le Brun looked down. Godwin's gray trouser had only the faintest circle near the bottom of his fly.

"Would you be able to look at your friends?" John asked.

"Are they all dead?"

"Yes."

"Lord!" Godwin rose as if a yoke sat upon his shoulders. "I'll try." He gave Geoffrey Moore a weary look and entered the room.

"Look over here, Mr. Godwin," John commanded from next to the cupboard. "Is this where the money was kept?"

"Yes. We each bought as much as one thousand pounds in chips. That's . . . that *was* the nightly limit." His gaze wandered, and he uttered a pathetic groan. "An entire continent of my world has vanished, gentlemen. But for luck or God's grace, I would have been lying right there beside them. Eddie, Hugh, Ralph. My closest friends gone in an instant. And poor Malcolm, too. What monster could do such a thing?"

Le Brun studied Godwin's eyes and posture. "We'll find out. Which one is Hugh?"

Godwin pointed to the slumped figure. "Hugh Wilbye."

"What was his occupation?" asked Le Brun.

"Occupation? Real estate developer. Owned several blocks of London. A hotel, two theaters, shops."

"He was an M.P. as well," commented Doyle.

"Member of Parliament?" John checked.

"That's right."

"So was Ralph," Godwin said, grimacing at the corpse under the table. "He owned several tanneries, here in London and elsewhere."

"And the third?"

Godwin's gaze shifted to the facedown corpse. "Edward Ravenscroft. Railroads and Underground."

"No political position?" Le Brun asked.

"No. Of our seven players, just those two served in government. But the club has six M.P.s in all: four commons, two lords."

Le Brun's lower lip protruded and his eyebrows elevated at the news. "I'm amazed that Geoffrey had somehow omitted such an impressive fact."

"The killer knew right where to go for the money," Doyle remarked.

"Not an astonishin' clue," John countered. "There is no other place in the room not open to direct view."

"True." Watching where he set his feet, Doyle neared the table. "And then he went for the billfolds. Mr. Wilbye first, as the easiest."

Godwin studied the billfold directly in front of the body. "Yes, that's Hugh's. May I smoke?"

"I think it best you don't," said Doyle.

"By this time, the cooks are shoutin' outside the door," Le Brun stated. "Only seconds remain to safely steal one more wallet. Mr. Ravenscroft is lifted up by the hair, I suspect, but there is blood everywhere. A handkerchief is used to get his billfold." He nodded at the second, blood-smeared wallet lying on the table. "My guess is that the police will find the money still inside. Too much mess and too little time."

"But whose handkerchief is it?" Doyle asked.

Le Brun picked up an unblemished playing card and gently poked at the crumpled and blood-soaked handkerchief. He exposed stitching that had barely been visible. "H. W."

"Hugh had a habit of wrapping his billfold," Godwin revealed.

He was breathing rapidly and shallowly. The muscles of his throat began to work. "I'm afraid I must leave the room, gentlemen."

"By all means," John said, rushing to open the door. "You've been a great help. Go sit on the steps and put your head down close to your knees."

Godwin fled the room.

Le Brun forced the door shut and put himself close to Doyle. He spoke in tones inaudible beyond the room. "In spite of the evidence and our mutual conclusions, we must eliminate all other possibilities."

"Naturally. What are you thinking?" Doyle asked.

"There are two doors into this room. The cook's helper could have knocked to retrieve those plates."

"But the butler is on the opposite side of the room," Doyle protested, "Furthermore, the wounds on—"

"If we find the money and the revolver in the pantry," John interrupted, "I assure you you'd be able to explain this scene. If these murders were done from the inside, time demands that both cook and helper must have worked as one. Two guns used, one finishin' off the victims as the other cleaned out the cupboard. They would have locked the inside door behind them on the way out. Split second timin' would have been necessary."

"Absolutely. They were in the hallway when you came down. How long was that?"

"Not twenty seconds."

"Then they couldn't have hidden the weapons or the money more than a few feet from this room."

John produced his watch a third time and studied it. "Which is why we can eliminate them before the police arrive." He opened the inside door. Moore stood above the seated Godwin.

"How are you doin'?" John asked the lawyer.

Godwin exhaled forcefully. "I've done better."

"You'll be fine. Just sit there. Geoffrey, would you please accompany Mr. Doyle and me?"

"Certainly."

Le Brun explained to his friend their purpose as they methodically searched the kitchen, pantry, and dish storage room, with John using the handle end of a wooden stirring spoon to explore the open flour and sugar tins.

"Well, it's nice to know the staff is guiltless," Geoffrey commented with a degree of sarcasm, when the last nook had been scoured.

"At least of murder with a gun," John replied. "I have yet to taste their cookin'."

"There is another possibility that we must explore," Doyle said. "Would you gentlemen do me a favor and accompany me into the lavatory?"

"They couldn't have hidden anything in there," Geoffrey said. "Trent was—" He touched Doyle's shoulder, slowing his progress. "You don't suspect Trent, do you?" he said, incredulously.

"Except for the people I could see during the shooting, I suspect the world," Doyle replied, bulling through the kitchen door that led to a small hallway. "That's how murders are solved, Geoffrey." He held the door for the other two men to precede him. "You saw him come racing up from that room not moments before everyone else was killed. Just luck was it?"

"But what motive could Trent possibly have?" Geoffrey protested.

"Let's explore opportunity first," Le Brun contributed. "Then motive."

Across from the base of the staircase Trent had earlier descended lay a door. John opened it, saw the sink, and entered. One of the members stood inside, buttoning his fly.

"Sorry," John said, holding the door for the man's departure.

"You should have knocked. Do you know who that was?" Geoffrey asked as he entered the room with Doyle directly behind.

"Yes. A much-relieved member." Smiling at his own humor, John opened the door to the private stall that enclosed the toilet. A magazine rack had been fixed to the wall opposite the fixture. Doyle entered the space and examined it, then lowered the commode lid and stepped onto it. He felt around the top side of the tank which had been installed within a foot of the ceiling.

"Nothin', eh?" John asked, peeking in.

"Nothing." Doyle hopped down.

John pointed to the window. "Little wonder I couldn't raise it from the outside. Looks like it's latched."

"The window? Of course it is," Geoffrey called into the stall. "We've talked of installing bars as well, to prevent burglary."

Doyle swung back the latch and tugged. "Or maybe re-latched." The window went up with only the slightest complaint. Doyle put his face up close to the sill.

"So, you also suspected Trent?" Moore asked John.

"I saw a window," John replied. "I had no idea it was to the rest room. But as it might serve as ingress and egress, I am not disallowin' Mr. Doyle's suspicion. Lookin' for threads?" John inquired, watching the author.

"For any clue that would make this monstrous act solvable."

Moore grunted his displeasure from the area of the sink. "Surely you don't think Trent Godwin came up the stairs as an alibi, came down here, climbed out the window, raced around the alley to kill his friends, and then came back this way?"

"I could get through here twice if sufficiently motivated," Doyle remarked.

Moore turned on the water and began washing his hands. "That's absurd, Arthur! Where's the gun and the money?"

"I don't know."

"And why would Malcolm let him in the back door?"

"Why would he not?" Doyle asked.

"Because he went out the other door." Moore closed the spigot. "You two are wasting precious time on the most absurd suspicions."

"Are you telling the detective who solved the Jekyl Island Club murder how to investigate a crime?" Doyle chided, exiting the room.

"Don't forget the part about savin' J. P. Morgan's life," John added, waggling a forefinger at Geoffrey as he emerged from the stall. "And are you simultaneously questionin' the author of the world's most famous detective . . . and a successful detective in his own right, by your own admission? Nice wallpaper in here. Would you make a bit of room, Geoffrey; I need to wash my hands as well."

WHEN LE BRUN, Conan Doyle, and Moore returned to the opposite side of the cellar, they found the club manager standing outside the gambling room speaking with a policeman. Two men in suits stood inside the room, sketching and scribbling into notebooks. One noticed them and tapped the other on the shoulder. The second one, who was a handsome but overweight man with a startlingly white beard, squinted. His grim expression changed to pleasure. He hurried forward.

"Sir Arthur!" he exclaimed, his hand offered.

"Inspector Cooper, is it?" Conan Doyle said.

"Yes. Bob Cooper. How flattering that you remember me. Mr. Roundsville told us you were down here investigating."

"I'm only observing," Doyle told him. "But by chance we have a celebrated American detective with us."

Inspector Cooper looked at Doyle's companion. "Is that so?"

"Sheriff John Le Brun." Doyle shot a quick glance at Moore. "He once saved J. P. Morgan's life."

For once, Le Brun did not protest.

Cooper held out his hand again. "How wonderful! Have you already solved this horrible crime?

"I'm afraid not," John said. "Not *yet,* leastways."

As he drank in the scene, Cooper's upper lip pulled back from his gritted teeth. "I know we're only five years into it, but this has to rank as London's crime of the century. Two M.P.'s killed. Parliament will be howling for a solution."

Roundsville, the club manager, was rubbing both temples simultaneously. "I understand fellows from Fleet Street are outside the building already."

John knew that Fleet Street was to London newspapers what Wall Street was to New York finance.

"We'll soon be lumped in with Jack the Ripper," Roundsville lamented, still massaging his head. "What a calamity for the club!"

"Not necessarily," Cooper countered. "You'd be surprised how even the worst publicity can have positive outcomes. However, this disaster might fall like an ax on the Yard's neck. Let's continue, if you please. We have no witnesses and no suspects."

"That's right," the manager confirmed.

"Well, that's a pity."

"I believe Sheriff Le Brun and I have the best perspective, Inspector," Doyle said, shepherding Cooper back into the gaming room. He gave a beckoning look to Le Brun over his shoulder.

"You're much better with words, Sir Arthur," John said. "Go ahead. I want to do some measurin'."

John asked the manager if he would see that the stairs and the central hallway could be cleared and was told that it would be little trouble. A squadron of policemen and detectives occupied the morning and coffee rooms, Roundsville informed, interviewing every man who had been in the club at the time of the shootings. John confirmed that this was indeed the situation when he took himself back to where he stood when the first shot was fired. He again lifted his watch from its pocket and waited patiently until the second hand swung to the twelve.

"Bang, bang, bang," he said softly to himself, the first of a series of motions that simulated as closely as John could his progress from dining room entrance, down the stairs, into the gaming room, and eventually outside to the sidewalk in front of the club. Standing at the curb of St. James Street, he snapped the lid shut on his watch but did not put it away. Instead, he held it with one hand and tapped out a tattoo like a horse's canter on its surface as he thought. He pivoted slowly, regarding every object on the street. Five times as many people filled the sidewalk as had the first time John emerged from the alley. Half paraded innocently by, wondering what the other half were doing milling excitedly in front of the elegant townhouse. Two of the men came rushing up to him. He smelled the newsprint from yards away.

"Are you part of the investigation inside?" one asked Le Brun.

"Now, would somebody who sounded like me belong in that buildin'?" he asked.

The other man eyed him suspiciously. "You didn't answer his question, Yank."

John stared up at the hazy night sky. "I didn't, did I? Excuse me." He retraced his steps.

John walked to the back alley with the two reporters following at a distance. This time he ranged farther from the club's rear alcove, eyes roving to and fro, up and down.

"Who are you, Yank?" the bolder of the two challenged.

"Be careful who you call a Yank, you ignorant Limie," John replied. He cocked his head. "Sounds like a commotion out on the street."

Whatever the fortuitous event on St. James Street, it was sufficient to send the two men trotting back up the alley. John and the Brunswick press had always had good relations. When the sheriff had needed them to stay quiet about an investigation, they had obliged for guaranteed favors down the road. The two cocky London reporters reminded John of how completely without influence he was in this foreign city. He muttered at the thought. The slaughter inside the Sceptred Isle Club was precisely the sort of situation that made John feel most alive and useful, but he knew he was about to be pushed aside. Despite all of Geoffrey's bragging, he was a nobody in the capital of the world's greatest empire. Then, suddenly, he remembered that that was as it should be. He was retired from all law enforcement, on both sides of the Atlantic.

John looked up at the heavens and shook his head. "You do have a sense of humor, don't you?"

John watched the dark shape of a man gradually sharpen into a policeman as the figure walked up the alley from King Street. The bobby seemed in no great hurry until he spied John.

"What's your business, sir?" the bobby called out, showing the night stick in his right hand.

"I'm helpin' a might with the murders," John answered.

The bobby stopped dead. "What murders?"

"This is your beat, isn't it, Officer?" John said. In the dim light, he could not read the expression on the man's face.

"Yes. What murders?"

John dipped his head. "Four men dead in the Sceptred Isle Club."

"My God!"

John judged the man to be in his late thirties, but at the news he sprinted like an Olympic runner. He was tall and quite thin and made good use of his long legs. John followed him back to the club at an unhurried pace. By the time he returned to the gaming room, Inspector Cooper had already engaged the bobby in conversation. The plainclothesman had one foot crossed over and balanced on the tip of his shoe and one hand dug into his trouser pocket. Le Brun noted that the bobby was fooled by the carefully constructed casualness.

"Sheriff Le Brun," Cooper said, "this is Officer Jeremy Buttons. He's had this beat for a little more than a year."

"That's right, sir. I know all the men of this gaming group and the other two groups that use the room," Buttons volunteered.

"And I'm sure you've seen the kind of money they wager," Cooper continued.

"Absolutely." His wide-set, watery eyes rolled. "Wads that could choke a horse."

"I'm sure you've seen the money when they peel off a pound as a tip, eh? I understand that you and few of the other lads who patrol clubland often accompany the men to cabs," Cooper went on.

Buttons' proper, ramrod stance relaxed a fraction. "Right. But I never accept tips. Plenty of unsavory characters also know about the kind of money carried around here. One of the blighters must have made a move tonight."

"But how could they get inside, Officer?" Cooper asked, maintaining his casual façade. "The door wasn't forced, and, as you know, it has a peephole for the butler . . . precisely to prevent such a calamity."

Buttons's eyelids batted up and down several times. He scratched the side of his neck and shifted his weight, but he offered no more than a shrug as his reply.

"Have you been let inside in the past, Mr. Buttons?" Cooper asked, smiling.

Buttons's head reared back, finally understanding the full implication of Cooper's line of questions. "Once," he said softly, when he had recovered. "It's a pity I was blocks away when this happened. I mean, I don't *know* when it happened, but it must have been some time ago. I do my beat like clockwork. Rob Sheinkopf, the gentleman who owns the book shop across from the Royal Academy, was closing up ten minutes ago. He was just commenting how I'm like Big Ben."

"Have you seen any suspicious characters followin' you and notin' the time?" Le Brun asked.

"No, sir. Can't say as I have."

"Well, best you be back on your beat," Cooper dismissed him.

"I feel just awful about this," Buttons averred, staring at the collection of bodies.

"Yes, we all do." Cooper guided the policeman to the back door. "Thank you, Officer." He closed the door behind the man and regarded Le Brun. "His head was dotted with perspiration."

"He did run in here," John informed. "And this sort of scene'll bring the sweat to most men's brows."

"I suppose," Cooper granted.

"I believe he'll be leakin' juices for the rest of the night now that you've spoken to him," John remarked.

Cooper cocked an eyebrow. "And you would have been more oblique, I take it?"

John held up his hands. "Just a matter of styles, Inspector. I'm retired."

"But we would be very grateful if you would consult on the case," came the voice of the club manager from the inner door.

"You were here at the time of the crime, and you are obviously a neutral but skilled observer."

John tried not to look interested. "I'm on vacation," he protested weakly.

"When I say 'grateful,' Mr. Le Brun, I mean that we would compensate you for your time. Within reason, of course," Roundsville added. "We are not a rich club, but we are intent on having our reputation preserved."

John looked at the inspector. "Would your offices allow this?"

Cooper did not look happy. He glanced at Arthur Conan Doyle, who stood near the manager, and released a weary smile. "Yes. In London, we allow consulting detectives."

John found himself quietly elated. "I accept."

"That's brilliant!" Roundsville exclaimed. "Before you finish your deposition to the detectives, Mr. Le Brun, I wonder if you'd come up to my office?"

BEFORE HE KNEW where he was going, John had followed William Roundsville through his small office and directly into his bedroom. Although large, the manager's living space had neither its own bathroom nor closet. To one side stood a pair of armoires. Across from the wrought-iron bed stood a wall of bookcases. Reading materials constituted a majority of the man's belongings. John felt an instantaneous kinship.

"I'm sorry your lecture was prevented, Mr. Le Brun," Roundsville said.

"Just as well. I'm not much of a public speaker."

"That may be, but I intuit that you are an excellent detective." The manager turned to one of the shelves and lifted a stereopticon. Beneath it lay a folio-sized magazine. "If you protect the club, you protect me. This is my life." He gave a half-hearted shrug. "It may not be much in some eyes, but it fulfills me. I make many fine men happy and provide them comfort in a harsh world. I'm good at what I do, and I'm appreciated."

"Your sentiments are laudable," John offered.

Roundsville nodded his gratitude. He flipped back the magazine's pages and exposed some dozen opticon image cards. His face reddened. "I also had an ulterior motive in hiring you. As we speak, this club is being minutely perused for a gun and gambling money. There is no way for me to spirit anything out. But you are above reproach." He handed Le Brun the cards. "I need you to keep my reputation unsullied."

John found himself staring at the naked figure of a voluptuous female. Her pose left nothing to his imagination. He riffled quickly through the other eleven cards. He had seen worse in his day. At least there were no naked men in *flagrante delicto* sharing the images.

John put himself down in a nearby rocking chair. "You have good taste in women."

"The problem is that I *have* no steady woman," Roundsville replied. "The laws of the club prevent my bringing a female up here. If I wanted to marry, I'd have to give up this job. These fantasy females provide me . . . a necessary solace."

"I've been a bachelor for twenty-two years," John shared. "I completely understand."

"So good of you."

John held out his hand. "Might I borrow your opticon for a moment?"

Roundsville hastened to hand over the instrument. As he did, he glanced at the top figure. "She's my favorite. Quite callipygian, don't you think?"

The woman's buttocks were even more beautiful in three dimensions. "In a word, yes." John handed back the stereopticon. "You want me to stick these in my coat pocket and waltz out with them."

"Please. Then, if you could return them later in the week, I'd be ever so grateful."

"I wonder if you'd do me a favor in return, Mr. Roundsville."

"If it's in my power," the manager said, his face no longer rugose.

"Honestly, do you find my accent annoyin'?"

"Do you find the accents of Englishmen annoying in your home town?"

"No."

"Then why should I? I understand you perfectly."

"And what if I used a word such as 'mosey' in place of 'drift along' or said, 'You can hear her three fields off' to indicate a loudmouthed woman?"

"I'd say that the more colorful and vivid a language is, the better. Language is merely a tool, and it's owned by no one. Don't be cowed by the prigs and pedants who seek to use the King's English to build themselves up by tearing others down. I had to stop myself from laughing out loud when you said the patrolman would be leaking juices all night. It's precisely what he'll be doing."

John got up from the rocking chair and tucked the photographs gently into his jacket pocket. "Thank you, Mr. Roundsville. I shall take very good care of your ladies."

JOHN INHALED DEEPLY. "This vehicle smells new."

"Ah, the leather," Trent Godwin replied. "I think it's because my chauffeur just worked neat's-foot oil into the seats. We've actually had the car for six months."

"It's very nice," John admired. Trent sat facing him, catercornered. Each man had one of John's valises on the seat beside him.

"Yes, tires are such an improvement over iron-rimmed carriage wheels," Trent judged.

John began to yawn and quickly covered his mouth. "Excuse me.

"It's been a long day," the lawyer agreed. "Perhaps the

longest of my life. It must be nearing midnight. At least we determined pretty well that the weapon hadn't been left in the area. And that the killing wasn't done by the kitchen staff."

John merely nodded.

Trent looked out his window at the passing cityscape, the sidewalks still lit by gas where they were. "But you haven't eliminated me. You and Conan Doyle."

"Geoffrey did you no favor by telling you that."

"He's a loyal person . . . and an incorrigible gossip."

"You're right," John said. "You haven't been eliminated. Sir Arthur put forth the suspicion, and I had to admit your steppin' out of the room when you did was a strange if blessed coincidence." Before John and Trent had departed the club, Doyle had drawn the ex-sheriff aside and offered two theories, both with Godwin as the main villain. The first had him getting to the back door from inside the room, unlocking it himself and letting in an armed accomplice, who then held the other men in place while Trent slipped out of the inner door to establish his alibi. The second, by far the more complex, had Godwin crawling out the rest room window and getting the butler to let him in from the outside. Doyle's second scenario also required an accomplice, to carry off the guns and money. When John had mentioned the waiting coach on St. James Street, Doyle had waved John's suspicion away, as he found it hard to believe a man as smart as Godwin would risk involving more than one accomplice. When John mentioned that a hitching post stood at the spot, Doyle modified his scenario, having the single accomplice untie the reins and drive off. Doyle's last words to Le Brun had been to exhort him to keep Doyle informed of his every action and thought. Whether they liked it or not, Scotland Yard had to contend with two non-official detectives on the case.

"And yet I'm assuming I can't be high on your list," Trent said. "Otherwise, you wouldn't be coming home with me."

"On the contrary," John said, candidly, "I'm the kind who would follow a lion into his den to see who he had for breakfast. However, if you want to help prove your innocence, givin' me the run of your home is a good start."

Godwin kicked off his shoes and put his feet up on the seat opposite, bookending Le Brun's luggage. "I should have known even before Geoffrey opened his mouth. Doyle came up to me while you were otherwise engaged and asked me several questions."

"Such as?"

"Did I associate with the dead players outside of the club, and did we do things together with our wives."

Le Brun nodded. "He was workin' on motive. Perhaps you'd found out one of them was sleepin' with your wife."

Godwin's laugh came out like a bark. "Or perhaps that I had been caught sleeping with *his* wife. But if something like that were true, why would I shoot *four* men?"

"To cloud the issue," John replied. "Like a magician misdirectin' the audience with patter and flame, wavin' and pointin'."

"What a monstrous idea. I see how you two could believe I might remotely have been able to pull it off. But I assure you if I lose sleep tonight, it won't be over your suspicion. I have much greater worries weighing me down. I'm the solicitor for two of the murdered men. As you'd guess, they have huge estates. I only hope I can sleep. Thinking how close I came to being murdered myself makes my skin crawl." Godwin's shoulders crept up against his neck. He shook his head several times.

The man looked genuinely shaken and distraught to the ex-sheriff, but John knew that some of the world's best actors used their talents strictly off stages. Moreover, in his experience, a disproportionate number of such characters were lawyers.

"You do understand that the person or persons who killed your friends had to have been recognized by the butler?" John asked. He realized he had put on his spectacles when writing out his deposition for the detectives and had neglected to take them off. He removed them and ran their glass surfaces across his lapel.

Godwin winced at the thought, simultaneously blinking furiously. "Yes. That makes it all the more grotesque. Yet another reason I won't sleep tonight. Even if I could remember every person I'd ever seen him let in and wrote them down, there's been a score of nights I wasn't there. The person could easily have been a friend or relative of one of the other men. I mean, there are a total of seven men who play in the Saturday night game."

John longed to ease out of his shoes as well but was loathe to take the liberty on such short acquaintance. "Who are the other three?"

"Terrance Blight is a banker. He's away on extended holiday in Italy with his family. My firm received a telegram from him just yesterday. Caleb Boulton has mills. Holds several large uniform contracts for the military and other government services. He's in India on business. Nahum Attwater owns warehouses. He went down to Brighton yesterday to close on a building. I expect he'll be back Monday night at the latest."

"I heard Geoffrey say that other groups use the same room on two other nights," said Le Brun.

"That's right. Monday and Wednesday. That puts the list of possibilities up in the dozens."

John stowed his spectacles in their spring-loaded case. He closed his eyes and rolled his head around on his neck in a slow, clockwise circle. "Thank the Lord Scotland Yard can throw ranks of men at the problem."

Godwin made a throaty humming noise of agreement. "It won't be just the Sceptred Isle Club and the government that puts pressure on them. Every club in London will be fearing a similar incident until the monster is caught."

"Well, I've only promised to devote two days to it," John said. "By that time, things grow so cold that the kind of investigatin' I do won't be worth much. I mean, I *am* on vacation and retired."

"Whatever you can do is appreciated." Trent laughed softly, compelling John to open his eyes. "Did you really save J. P. Morgan's life?"

"In an indirect way, I suppose I did. Did Geoffrey also tell you that the Jekyl Island Club murderer got away?"

Trent cast his mind back. The story clearly had not meant enough to him to fully register. "I believe so."

"I had a new deputy at the time. Bright young man. I had foolishly assumed that he understood my wishes, and he let the murderer escape."

With John telling the tale instead of Geoffrey, Trent seemed at last interested. "Who was it?"

"The club physician, of all people. A very well-mannered gentleman from Johns Hopkins Medical School. Selflessly dedicated to saving lives . . . except for one instance. It seemed that, years before when the doctor was but a child, several of the club members had combined forces to destroy his father's business and had driven the man to suicide."

"It was revenge then."

"Pure and simple."

"Well, I can't see the motive for our murders being anything but greed," said Godwin. "The seven of us all have different businesses, different competitors, don't really socialize much outside of the club."

Le Brun leaned forward, happy to have the survivor talking. "What do y'all have in common beyond gamblin' . . . at least the four of you who were playing in the room tonight?"

Godwin shrugged. "Membership in the club, of course. A love of British history? The irony is that we don't even play high-stakes cards."

John's eyes rolled. "You're pullin' my leg."

"No, truly. There are several other clubs that could have been hit where the person would have gotten away with much more."

"Is the limit not a thousand pounds per bankroll?"

"Exactly. No one is allowed to purchase more chips than that in a single night. We're all wealthy men, but we do have varying resources. This prevents the richer from overwhelming the hands with huge raises. Truth be known, we're all more or less equally skilled and lucky. It's a rare night when someone goes home more than a hundred pounds up or down."

"I see."

"So, the killer couldn't have gotten away with more than five thousand pounds, including what was stolen from Hugh's billfold. Perhaps not even as much as four thousand."

"I'm still not comfortable with your currency," John admitted. "What would that be in dollars?"

"I'll make it even easier than that," Trent said. "Five thousand pounds is about what an expert clerk would earn in nine or ten years. Hardly worth killing four men over."

"From your perspective," John said. "I've known men who would gladly burn down an orphanage for a bottle of whiskey."

"But who among the people Malcolm would have let through the door?" Trent asked.

John threw up his hands. "If you find you can't sleep, keep askin' yourself that question, over and over."

Trent snapped his fingers. "That's why a richer club wasn't selected; it comes down to opportunity." Before John could reply, Trent glanced out the window as the car slowed. "We're home. Home, sweet, home."

VERONICA ARRIVED AT THE Godwin home only a minute after John and Trent. She was wrapped inside a black velvet evening cape. Behind her, an equally beautiful young woman came through the front door. Veronica's companion had straight blond hair, large brown eyes, and an elegantly long neck.

"Ta-da! I'm home!" Veronica called, bringing John and Trent down the hallway from the back of the house. "Trent, you remember Millie?"

"Yes, of course. Good evening."

"Mr. Godwin," the young lady said in a demure tone.

"And this is our house guest, Mr. John Le Brun. John, Miss Millicent Saint Albans."

John executed a crisp bow. "Charmed, Miss."

Veronica turned and raced up the stairs, calling down as she climbed, "I won't be but a hemidemisemiquaver."

Trent plodded into his study, leaving John alone with Miss Saint Albans.

"Have you ever seen the opera *Norma*?" she asked John.

"Can't say I have."

Her doe eyes darted back and forth, taking in the foyer, hallway, and living room. "It stinks. At least Veronica and I think so. The other girls liked it a bit." Suddenly, her attention fixed hard on him. "You must be very special," she declared. Her bold, appraising gaze was unexpected from a woman her age. "Veronica's taken quite a fancy to you."

"As have I to her."

The corner of Millicent's mouth curled into something wicked. "Then make the most of it." She winked.

John felt an inner heat rise from his chest and face. Millicent retreated two steps without taking her eyes off him. Veronica bounded down the stairs with unflagging energy. She carried a fox stole.

"I'll lend this to you to one condition," Veronica said, holding the stole out of reach.

"What's that?"

"That you treat Austin better."

"That pimply-faced twit?"

"He isn't a twit at all. And his pimples will clear up someday soon. You'd find him ever so smart and interesting if you gave him a chance."

"Why don't *you* treat him nice if you like him so much?"

"Because he likes you. And besides, I do treat him nicely."

Millicent jumped up suddenly and snatched the stole from Veronica's hand. "I'll think about it." She tossed the stole over her shoulder and headed for the door. As she opened it, she said to John, "Remember what I said. Lah!" Then she was gone.

"What was that about?" Veronica asked.

"I'm sure I don't know," John answered.

"Well, you look terribly grim after a night at the clubs," Veronica judged.

"I should. Four men were shot dead at the Sceptred Isle."

Veronica's large eyes became even larger. "No! How *awful.*"

"All friends of your stepfather's. In fact, he narrowly escaped death himself."

"His gambling group?"

"Yes. Apparently, a robbery. You should go in and comfort him," John encouraged.

"I shall. My God!" The seemingly bottomless gaiety had drained in a rush from the girl-woman. She swallowed hard. "Excuse me," she said in a low voice, and sidestepped past John, heading for the study.

THE FURNISHINGS IN John's guest room were spare but handsome. The armoire and desk reflected an Art Nouveau style, as did the stained-glass electric lamp. The double bed was of an earlier period but tastefully fashioned of solid brass. John took off his jacket, set it over the back of a chair, and began the tedious process of unpacking and arranging his clothing.

With no warning sounds, Veronica appeared in the open doorway.

"Hello again," John said when he noticed her watching him. "How is Trent?"

"I think he's in a kind of delayed shock. He's speaking very slowly and quietly."

"He's lucky to be alive," John replied.

"So he tells me. Terrible. Is it all right for him to be drinking?"

"I think it's only natural."

"Well, he's refilling his courage from a bottle. I feel awful for you as well. What a thing to happen during your holiday."

"I'm all right." John drew himself up a little straighter.

"Are you?" Veronica moved with assured quickness into the room, swung the cape she still wore from her shoulders, and tossed it on the bed. Claire's eyes settled on him. "I'll bet you're just being a typical male, damned if you'll admit even mass murder can get to you." Veronica had more than one face for the world. The simple frock she had worn for the previous night's party had been replaced by a black gown shot with silver thread, its dropped epaulette sleeves suspended on her arms by some defiance of gravity, so that her beautiful upper arms and shoulders were exposed. Much of her upper chest was as well, except where a large diamond depended from a delicate golden chain just above the upper swells of her bosom. "I have a sure-fire test to see just how all right you are."

"What's that?"

"Sit down here on the edge of the bed." Veronica sat as she spoke and patted the bed beside her. "Come on; I won't bite you. Face the door."

John obeyed, feeling as if a secret part of him were just awakening from a long hibernation. He anticipated her fingers on his shoulders but was still not able to keep himself from jumping slightly.

"You're not all right at all," Veronica judged. "You're like coiled steel." Her fingers dug through his shirt into his skin. "Hmm! If I were blindfolded, I'd guess that these were the muscles of a thirty-year-old man. No soft city fellow here." Her voice had grown quiet and mellifluous.

John let out a deep sigh. "I guess I was more tense than I thought. You look even more beautiful tonight than last night."

"Why, thank you, sir. I was at the theater with Millie and several other girlfriends. Actually, two theaters: the divine and the ridiculous. First, we went to see *Norma* at Covent Garden, but it was so depressing and poorly sung that we left after the first act. That was the ridiculous one. Then we went to the cinematograph. I adore moving pictures. Have you seen them?"

"A few times. My hometown, Brunswick, is a resort. Whatever entertainment is the rage, we get it right quick."

"Did you enjoy them?"

"I did."

"Perhaps you and I could go Monday night."

John laughed.

"What?" Veronica wanted to know, as she kneaded his muscles with increasing vigor.

"I'm sure you have much better things to do than chaperone an old man around London."

Veronica stopped massaging. "I see no old man." She leaned in toward John's ear and softly said, "I'll tell you a secret if you promise to keep it to yourself."

The part of John that had been long dormant was now almost fully awake. "What?"

Veronica's mouth came even closer to John's ear. "I have a 'thing' for certain older men. Not because they're older, but because they're more interesting. More attentive. More capable of appreciating a woman for all her parts, not just her beauty. And I'm particularly attracted to very smart men who are assured enough not to have to impress me with their intelligence."

John cleared his throat. "That's quite a secret."

Veronica eased back from his ear and began massaging him again. "That's not the secret. The secret is that I've had affairs with three men over fifty. One of them propositioned me right where you and I met last night."

"I hope he wasn't married."

"Not that night anyway. His wife spends a great deal of time in Exeter. When she's in London, he's married."

"Is this new morality accepted in Mayfair?"

"No. But it's common in parts of Bloomsbury. I refuse to be a prisoner of geography."

It took John a moment to absorb the shock of her words. "Might I ask how old you are, Miss Veronica?"

"Twenty-one. But please don't think I'm a common harlot. I've only slept with half a dozen men in all."

The stairs creaked slightly, causing John to start from the bed. A moment later, when Trent appeared, John was picking up his shoes and depositing them in the bottom of the armoire.

"Hello, Trent," Veronica said, with a breezy tone.

"Mr. Le Brun has had a harrowing evening," Trent said in answer, his voice low and even. "Shall we let him get to sleep?"

Veronica bounced off the bed and headed for John's jacket. "I'm helping John with his belongings." She took it over to the armoire and purposely brushed her hip against John's. John moved quickly for an unopened suitcase near the bed.

"I'm sure he wants to put away his own things."

Veronica hung up the jacket. "Fine." She grabbed her cape and made for the door. "Good night, John."

"Good night, Miss Veronica," John answered, turning in time to see the young woman disappear into the hallway, forcing Trent to step back.

Trent watched her for a moment, looked at John, opened his mouth but reconsidered. "Are you sure you won't have a nightcap?" he offered.

"No. I'll sleep just fine, thanks."

Trent nodded. "Then good night to you." He pulled the door completely closed.

Because of all the clothing he had packed, John began to run out of room in the armoire. He took two of his vests and swung them onto the closet's highest shelf. As he did, his fingers brushed several items. He stood on his tiptoes and inched them forward until he could drag them down. He found himself holding two books. One was Trollope's novel, *The Duke's Children.* The facts of publication indicated it had been published twenty-five years earlier. The second was a Bible. John thumbed through this as well and found himself in I Machabees. John had long since given up regular attendance of Mass, but he knew a Roman Catholic Bible when he saw one. He knew that this particular book was not part of the Protestant canon. Geoffrey Moore had told him that the Godwins were nominally Episcopalian. Moreover, Maeve Godwin had professed to being Orange Irish, which John knew meant Protestant. Thus it was with knitted brows that John flipped to the front of the Bible and found a family tree that included Maeve Meany married to a Graeme Meany and the two of them having a daughter Veronica. As with many forebears, Mr. Meany's death date had been recorded beside that of his birth. He had died in late September of 1900. Apparently, upon his death, Maeve had decided fairly quickly to migrate from Northern Ireland to London. John did not need to spend more time in London to know the low esteem placed on the Irish by the English. He could not blame the woman for lying about her religion.

Maeve's reinvention of the truth took second position to another discrepancy John noted from the family-tree page. According to this Bible, Veronica had been born in 1883. She was not, in fact, twenty-one but several months into her twenty-second year. John shook his head in bewilderment. He knew that women universally lied about their ages, but he would not until this moment have thought that they started lying so early.

If I'd have known she was so old, he thought wryly to himself as he returned to Bible to its hiding place, *I might have taken her up on her proposition.*

JOHN HAD BEEN SHOWN the very modern second-floor bathroom earlier in the evening. Once he had stowed all his belongings and changed for bed, he opened his door and ventured into the hallway, toothbrush and tooth powder in hand. On the way, he saw that a pair of trousers hung over a wooden clothes butler near the top of the stairs. He recognized them as those worn by Trent that evening. After assuring himself that he was unobserved, he lifted the trousers from the rack and pressed the crotch to his face. The distinctive tang of urine invaded his nostrils. He replaced the pants and continued into the bathroom.

Returning to his room, John put away his toiletries and faced the chamber's center, orienting himself for a moment in anticipation of total darkness. He twisted off the electric lights, took a step forward, and saw a flash of light in his right eye. He paused and turned his head. He saw the flash again. He had had the same experience onboard the ship twice, when he was in dark places. Both times he had attributed it to some errant reflection from glass or a mirror. But in this room the windows were curtained and there were no mirrors. The eye felt fine. He had had no trouble seeing, no headaches. Yet something was definitely wrong.

"Wonderful," John said to himself as he scudded carefully to the bed. His vacation was rapidly becoming much more eventful than he had ever expected.

FIVE

Sunday, October 22, 1905

ASIDE FROM THE NORMAL two-thirty visit to the bathroom that his prostate demanded, John slept soundly despite his tumultuous Saturday. He awoke at 8:00 A.M., blessing the shades that had kept the room so dark. Since retiring, he had been gradually rising later and later, but this hour was comparative decadence for him. He dressed befitting a Sunday in an elite section of London and took himself downstairs. While he was dressing, the front door knocker had periodically sounded. It did again, but more sharply, as John reached the foyer.

"Just ignore it," Veronica called from the living room. "It's a reporter."

"A damned rude reporter," John replied. He yanked open the door and found himself facing a man in his late twenties, sporting a bowler hat and a striped suit. The man held a note pad and pencil in his left hand.

"Mr. Godwin?" he said.

Le Brun fixed his stare on the man's left shoulder with such intent that the reporter swung his neck and eyes to see the cause. John reached out with his thumb and forefinger and pinched hard where a nerve lay exposed between the neck and trapezius muscle. The reporter crumpled from the pain, and John followed him down, still gripping.

"Just as I thought," John said, staring intently at the contorted face. "A suit filled with hot air." He straightened up, leaving the man on his knees. "This is the Lord's day. I suggest you find a church rather than botherin' good citizens. Otherwise, you might be visitin' a hospital."

John swung the door closed. It shut with a bang.

"Goodness, how forceful!" Veronica remarked. "We shall have to keep you around here all the time."

John entered the living room, where he found Veronica seated on a cushion in the parlor with sections of a newspaper spread around her. "I thought the British were scrupulous in their manners."

"Not the press. Look!" she said, holding up the first section's front page. In very large type, it read MASS MURDER IN ST. JAMES CLUB. "Trent is mentioned several times and so is Sir Arthur Conan Doyle, but you're not in here."

"I shouldn't be. I'm only consultin'," he replied.

"But Conan Doyle isn't even doing that."

"Yes, but he's an international figure." John looked down into the long-familiar, wide-opened violet-blue eyes. In comparison to her outfit and make-up the night before, Veronica was a virtual vestal virgin. Her white pinafore dress was multi-layered, cut to show her figure but with decorum. It spread around her like full-blown rose petals. The dress had subtle pink piping, and her hair was pulled back by a matching pink ribbon.

"Did you sleep well?" she asked, handing him the section.

"I did, thank you."

"Hungry?"

"Famished. I never got dinner."

Veronica began straightening up the newspapers. "Well, thank goodness you've risen. I loathe dining alone. Trent went out an hour ago."

"He did? Consarn it! I wanted him to arrange interviews today with the families of the dead men."

"Perhaps he can help you in the afternoon. He's at his office, working on the legal papers of two of them."

John crossed to one of the front windows and looked out. The reporter had left. "Where's your mother?"

"She's still not up. She was in meetings most of the day yesterday with her committee. They're throwing a charity ball this coming Friday."

"So I heard . . . from her own lips, in fact."

"Really? Where was that?"

"Down at the Trafalgar Day celebrations."

"She took time for festivities, then?"

"Along with her committee."

"I'll wager they weren't there long. They've been consumed by last-minute details. I suppose it was the hundred year anniversary that drew them there."

"You don't share your mother's charitable efforts?" John asked.

"Oh, when she inveigles me into them. Generally, I'm busy being selfish. It's expected in people my age."

"I recollect. Vaguely."

"Are you starting with that old man nonsense again? Desist! My charitable days will arrive soon enough, I expect." She stood and smoothed down her dress. "Come! Alice must be tired of holding breakfast for us." She led the way into the sun-lit dining room, whose bay window looked out on a planting of trees and bushes and a mulched bed that surely held flowers in the spring and summer.

"What sort of charity is it?" John asked.

"'The Mayfair Mothers for Cleanliness,'" Veronica announced, with the look of amusement that John realized was so common to her. "Stuffy name but a good cause. They raise money to fund what are called 'cleansing stations' for the poor. Many of their homes still don't have running water or, if they do, they don't have bathtubs. The stations provide places to bathe and remove their lice. This one is on Finch Street in Stepney."

John studied the blush on Veronica's cheeks. He had wondered on Friday night if the color had been artfully applied makeup. Now he could see that it was not. Moreover, if she practiced pinching her cheeks every so often to bring up color, as numerous ingenues did, he had been with her for enough minutes to watch them fade. They remained resolutely pink, the hue of the famous English rosebud complexion, even if she was Irish. *As if she needs rosy cheeks,* John thought. Apparently Mother Nature, having bestowed so many beauties on her, wanted to learn what the limits could be.

"Stepney, I take it, is not the garden spot of London," John said, refocusing on Veronica's eyes.

"No, indeed. Mother actually invented this event three years ago. The first year it only attracted seventy-five. This year will be more than two hundred. It's not like the balls during the Season, but she makes sure it has its own charm and draw."

"What's the Season?"

"The height of the London social calendar. First of May through end of July. It's the good weather, when everything happens. It starts with the Private View at the Royal Academy, which signals a glut of dinner parties and balls. The queen's ball had seven hundred attendees, I'm told. The more public events . . . although not for the poor or common man . . . begin with Covent Garden and the Royal Military Tournament. My favorite's the flower show in Temple Gardens. I adore flowers! Later, there's the Fourth at Eton, polo at Hurlingham, and horses at Ascot, Epsom, and

Henley. I've been to Epsom. What a bore! Everyone's there to be seen. They're so afraid of committing a social gaff that they hardly move. It's like viewing a cemetery with everyone popped out of the ground."

John laughed heartily, which caused Veronica to laugh as well.

"Toward the end of the Season are the cricket matches between Oxford and Cambridge and Eton and Harrow. This has also always been the time when the debutantes are presented at court. You know: marriage fodder."

"And how does your mother make her ball popular durin' the off-season?" John asked.

"She hires the most *de nouveau* music groups. The newest dances are taught by professional instructors. And the fancy dress themes are more lively than the upper crust's. This year, the theme is the American nineteenth century. We'll be taught square dancing!"

"Sounds like a laudable undertakin'," John said.

Veronica laughed again. He noted how her voice went up and down the soprano scale, like tinkling garden bells.

"Don't you think?" John asked.

"No. I'm laughing at your turn of phrase so soon after my cemetery remark. Especially since you dropped the 'g' in 'undertaking'."

John shrugged good-naturedly. "You won't hear the King's English from me."

"Perhaps you should try it." When John guffawed lightly, she added, "No, really."

The cook entered the dining room. John half-rose from his chair and made a little bow.

"Good morning, sir. I remember you from the night of the last party," the woman said. She appeared to be in her early sixties, was plump, and iron-haired. Her cheeks were mapped with tiny red veins. She had a pug nose and rather close-set eyes, but her smile was warm and welcoming. Her teeth were so perfect that John assumed they were false.

"This is Mr. Le Brun, Alice. John, this is Mrs. Comfort," Veronica introduced. She turned to the house guest. "Would you prefer coffee or tea?"

"Good mornin', Mrs. Comfort. Whatever's easier."

"An assortment of teas, then," the young woman decided. "And fry up a rasher of bacon as well. Mr. Le Brun took no dinner last night."

While the water boiled and the bacon fried, Alice produced an artfully arranged plate of fresh fruits, a bowl of thick, yellow-white cream, and a large dish with lumpy-shaped biscuits.

"Scones," Veronica told the staring guest. "We have them with clotted cream, but only on Sundays. Far too fattening for regular fare."

They talked about the murders and how the facts compared with the report in the newspaper. John indulged in blueberries, wedges of orange, two scones, and a moderate helping of cream. Presented with the sunny room, the beautiful creature sitting across from him, and the food, life was beginning to feel more like a vacation than his daunting Voyage of Discovery. Then Veronica returned to her crusade.

"In London, people are strongly judged by the way they speak," she informed him. "Folk from a backward part of England speak with an accent like yours. Certain people will simply not give you respect, and that could hinder your investigation and affect your holiday. Someone with your intelligence could modify his speech 'when in Rome,' as it were."

John snapped his fingers. "Just like that."

"It's not as difficult as you might fear. The secret is simply to pronounce everything just under the tip of your nose." She dipped her forefinger into the clotted cream and lifted a dollop to her lips, licking the digit clean while keeping her eyes fixed on her intended pupil.

Rather than taking offense, John was glad that Veronica had made the undiplomatic suggestion. He felt himself heating up under the collar, thought he might actually blush, and hoped she would assume it was because of her words. He knew it was not just the provocative remarks of her friend, Millicent, nor the young woman's convention-crushing advances the previous night that had him fantasizing. He was well aware that seventy percent of the American male population failed to live to his age. That and the closed door of retirement pointed like mile markers to the steeply declining, inevitable path that ended at the abyss. What she offered beyond her embraces was a last grab at the brass ring of Youth, a validation in its twilight of an enigmatic and perverse charisma that had once drawn women to John but had faded in the last decade. And then there was the temptation to recapture his most treasured past, by putting his face so close to hers that all he could see were those familiar eyes. But even as he envisioned her in his bed, he knew just as surely that he would not let it happen. The reasons were myriad, beginning with respect for his hosts.

"I would feel ridiculous," he confessed.

"Oh, please! Just try," she begged.

John rolled his eyes. "All right." He drew in a fortifying breath and touched his forefinger beneath his nose. "I say, Gwendolyn, do you suppose we shall have fog the entire fortnight?"

Veronica giggled. "Perhaps you're right in staying natural." She tilted her head in the direction of the kitchen. "Can you see what time it is?"

The Godwin home seemed to have outlawed time, as only the leisure rich could afford to. Other than the grandmother clock just inside the front foyer, the only timepiece in the house was a black walnut wall-mounted Regulator fixed on the kitchen wall opposite the portal that separated it from the dining room. John had no doubt that it had been placed there for the servants.

"Nine-thirty precisely," John answered.

Veronica expelled a bit of air. "There's not much to do early on a Sunday morning. One can go to church, take a stroll, a canter, or a motorcar ride. We could venture out into the countryside."

"I assume Scotland Yard is open even on Sunday mornin's," John said. He had noted her earlier remark about his not being included in the newspaper's account of the murder investigations. From that, he assumed Trent had told her he had been engaged to represent the Sceptred Isle Club's interests. Nevertheless, he restated his involvement and told her he needed to coordinate with the police.

Veronica pushed back from the table. "Let's go now."

"You needn't trouble yourself. I'll get a cab."

"Don't be ridiculous. Alice's husband, Hugh, will drive us." Veronica dropped her napkin onto the table and headed for the front of the townhouse. "It's what he's paid for."

THE DAY WAS A BIT COOL and damp but felt invigorating to John. When he left the motorcar at the Thames Embankment with Veronica on his elbow, he felt as fit as he had in years. Whatever the flashes in his eye portended, he certainly had no complaint at the moment. The woman made him feel alive, and the investigation demanded his skills. His stride lengthened, and the tall and athletic Veronica kept with him step for step.

As they strolled under a large archway and past ornate wrought iron gates, Veronica explained that this was actually New Scotland Yard. It had replaced an outgrown warren of buildings located on a plot of land given to the Scottish kings for their required annual homage trip to London. She also knew that the two lower stories, faced in granite, were originally built to house the National Opera, a failed venture. The upper stories were of redbrick.

"If you could see my little police station," John said, "you'd die laughin'."

"It's the men who matter in police work, not the buildings," Veronica observed.

They were directed to Inspector Cooper's office and found themselves stepping around piles of records.

"So much for having more space," Veronica remarked. When they located Cooper's name on a plaque in the hallway, a passing gentleman told them, "He's working the late shift this week. Was here until about four A.M. over those gentlemen's-club murders."

"That's what we're here about," John said.

"Then you'll want to see me," a voice called from an office across the hall.

When they followed the voice, they found themselves facing a man who bore a striking resemblance to George V, the reigning king's son. He wore a white high collar without tie and a vest with every hole buttoned. The hair on his crown was greased back, and a walrus mustache curved beyond his neat beard. John judged that he could not be older than forty. He wore no jewelry and had no ring on his wedding finger. If he had thought to remain seated, his mind was quickly changed by the sight of Veronica Godwin. He fairly sprang from his chair and came around the fortification of his large desk, which had no papers on it other than the few in his "in" and "out" baskets.

"Chief Inspector Tibbles, at your service! May I help you?"

"You may," Veronica confirmed, since the inspector's gaze was at the moment riveted on her face. She introduced herself as Trent Godwin's daughter and then introduced "Sheriff John Le Brun, of Atlanta, Georgia." John made no effort to correct her.

"I expected you might show today," Tibbles said to the American. Considering the enormity of the crime and the fact that he was on Sunday duty, Tibbles seemed far too happy to John. His mood was explained a moment later. "You'll be relieved, I'm sure, to hear that the case seems to be solved."

"Really?" John responded, unable to disguise his surprise.

"Not an hour ago, in fact. Inspector Cooper suspected the

local Uniform policeman. He sent a detail directly to watch the man's house through the night. Just after dawn, we searched the property. Found forty-one hundred pounds hidden in a hole underneath a birdbath in his garden."

"Really?" John said. "A metal birdbath?"

"It was made of stone, actually."

"Even worse. What would inspire anyone to look under such a heavy, immobile object?"

"It's my understanding that it had been replaced slightly askew."

"Was this garden accessible to someone off the street?" John asked.

Tibbles's smile slipped. "Why do you ask?"

"Because I met the man. To tell you the truth, Officer Buttons came off less guilty than anyone else I met last night."

Tibbles's brows beetled. "But who would kill four men and hide a small fortune just to pin the robbery on a bobby?"

"How much was stolen?" Veronica asked, leaving Tibbles's question hanging.

John repeated Trent's reasoning that the killer could not have gotten away with appreciably more than was found under the birdbath.

"The only way that would make sense," said Tibbles, "would be if the robbery were secondary to the murders themselves."

"I've been thinking that," Le Brun revealed. "What, besides membership in the club and their common penchant for gamblin', did all the men have in common?"

"No thread that anyone could reveal to our investigators."

"Perhaps only one man was the target," Veronica suggested. "What a wonderful way to obfuscate the real intent!"

Her words, echoes of his own to Trent in the car, made John wonder how detailed her discussion had been that morning with her stepfather.

"Horrid thought," Tibbles said.

"I assume Officer Buttons is pleadin' innocence," John said.

"Ninety-nine percent of those we apprehend plead innocence," Tibbles returned.

"Were large-caliber revolvers found with the money?"

"Revolvers? No."

"Nor elsewhere on the property."

"That's correct." Tibbles retreated behind his desk and snatched up a form, which he handed over to Le Brun. "Our case is not airtight. But how many are? Officer Buttons certainly had the opportunity. You were there when Inspector Cooper spoke with the man." He tapped his forefinger on a paragraph on the form. "Buttons admitted that he had been inside the room."

"Just once, he said."

"He also admitted that he knew the kind of money they wagered."

"May I sit?" Veronica asked.

Tibbles winced slightly. "Of course. My apologies." He started again around the desk.

"No need, Inspector," Veronica said, pulling out the chair. "I only require permission, not help." She sat.

John added, "The officer also told us that he had been elsewhere when the crime was committed. He mentioned a book shopkeeper who could corroborate."

Tibbles had picked up a pen and was twirling it back and forth between thumb and forefinger. "Naturally, we're checking on his story. He is, after all, an officer of the law. We want to give him every chance to exonerate himself. He'll have to have more than one such witness to get him off, though."

"I trust you won't relax your vigilance while you prove his innocence," John said, "such as searchin' inside the club and outside in the immediate area for a brace of matchin' revolvers."

"That's been done to our satisfaction," Tibbles warranted. "Nothing was found. And we are interviewing the families of the dead men. Primarily to ascertain a link with the bobby, but also to suggest other suspects who might stand out."

"You mentioned weapons in the plural before," Veronica said to John. "Why?"

"I'll tell you later. Chief Inspector Tibbles understands, and I don't want to bore him." Before Tibbles could react, he added, "I know the press and members of your Parliament are howlin' for a solution, but we all agree that justice is more important."

The smile that came to Tibbles's face was cloying. "Absolutely. I'm sure the Sceptred Isle Club has hired you precisely to see that justice is done."

"I've only agreed to serve them for two days. I'm retired and on vacation. From my look and sound, some folk might not be inclined to assist me. I wonder if I might impose for a note on official letterhead; a 'To whom it may concern,' statin' that Scotland Yard knows I'm workin' on the Sceptred Isle Club's behalf."

"I can arrange that." Tibbles swung his obsequious smile on Veronica. "Is there anything I can do for you, Miss Godwin?"

"Not a thing."

AS SOON AS they were again under sky and sun, Veronica said, "I didn't find him particularly reassuring. Any man who keeps his desk that clean wants a quick solution."

John chuckled. "Let's hope I cast enough doubt back there to keep the investigation open."

"You made it quite clear you consider the bobby innocent. What *do* you think happened last night?"

"The most likely possibility is that two persons, at least one of whom was known to the butler, were admitted through the back door. They killed the men, robbed the cash pot, had only enough time to rob Mr. Wilbye, and fled with the money up the side alley to St. James Street, where they drove away in a closed, four-wheeled carriage."

"Did you see such a carriage?"

"I caught a glimpse just as it was turnin' the corner."

Veronica nodded several times. "I wonder if they questioned the bobby about it."

"They've probably dismissed its presence as coincidence."

"But how do you explain the money under the birdbath?"

"In one of two ways: Either there was much more money on Mr. Wilbye than your stepfather knew, and he was the target of the robbery, or else money was not the motivatin' factor." Le Brun lifted his hand in a traffic-holding gesture. "At least not the money in the room."

"You mean it could have been done by a person who stands to inherit a fortune from one of the players?"

"That's a good 'such as'."

"Yet someone able to afford to plant thousands of pounds under a birdbath to throw the blame on the beat policeman."

"Right again."

The Godwin car idled half a block from the New Scotland Yard. As they strolled toward it, Veronica said, "I have an appointment to go riding in Hyde Park in forty minutes. Would you care to join me?"

John enjoyed his mental picture of Veronica's figure in a smart riding habit, astride a mount. The notion of her riding sidesaddle never occurred to him. "I get all the ridin' I need at home, thank you. I thought I'd take a leisurely walk over in Lambeth."

"Lambeth? There's little there but slums."

"Exactly. Anyone can tour the British Museum. I want to get a three-dimensional feel for London."

Veronica reached for the car's door handle. "You are a fascinating man, John Le Brun. Can we run you across the river?"

"No. I noticed the Underground is just ahead."

"Very good. Oh! You know Trent's at his office. Maeve's out all afternoon doing her charity work. The help have off from noon until seven tomorrow morning. They usually visit relatives out of town. If you should arrive home and none of us is there, you'll find a key to the back door hidden under a rock at the bottom of the stairs. Ta-ta!"

Le Brun watched appreciatively as Veronica insinuated herself into the vehicle. As it pulled from the curb, she blew him a coquettish kiss.

NEVER HAVING EXPERIENCED a subway system, John was anxious to travel in the original prototype. He followed the signs to Embankment Station and began to descend. He had had no concept that the trains ran so far beneath the streets. "More like the Underworld than the Underground," he quipped to a man who was hobbling down the seemingly interminable steps. The man started at the unaccustomed impertinence of being addressed by a total stranger. He nodded and paused, waiting for John to put distance between them.

After several wrong turns and a missed connection, John found himself exiting Vauxhall Station. He walked away from the Thames into the heart of misery. The streets were filled with manure, litter, and other forms of waste. Paint was at a premium. Soot, rot, and mold held sway. Vermin were bold. Cracks and crevices went unpatched; walls leaned; broken and whole windows alike were sweatered in grime. Soap, tooth powder, and new clothing were rare commodities. Women escaped their hovels in alley gossip sessions; men cursed, smoked, griped, and joked in street-corner huddles. Ignorance and resentment hung on their shoulders as invisible cloaks. A sanitation truck passed by, wetting the street with water that the truck's signs declared undrinkable. This did not prevent the children from running among its streams, in their boisterous habit of wringing entertainment from every unusual occurrence.

John longed to pause and engage some of the men in words, to find out what and how they thought. The looks he received, however, forbade conversation. Clean, in a suit, and in their neighborhood on a Sunday, he had to be a copper or some religious do-gooder. Only the small children approached him, begging for money. He gave them the coins he had but could not rid himself of their bold attacks on his pockets until he turned the cloth out and proved he had no more. He kept track of several tall landmarks as he worked his way east and then north, so that he could navigate back from purgatory. No matter how many blocks he walked, no matter the direction, drab human hovels stretched out to the horizon.

After almost two hours of wandering, John turned toward the river and Westminster's Big Ben tower. A gathering of institutional-looking buildings loomed ahead. He spotted a sign that indicated they formed Lambeth Hospital. He turned a corner, found himself regarding a well-dressed man speaking to a pair of nurses, and realized this was the murderer who had eluded him on Jekyl Island.

Dr. Thomas Russell faced toward the building and was intent on delivering instructions, so that John was able to master his shock, step around him, and continue past without being noticed. The ex-sheriff walked to the end of the block and found a recessed door for concealment.

When the young Johns Hopkins surgeon serving as seasonal physician for the Jekyl Island Club had stolen a skiff and disappeared into the vast marshes that lay to the west of the island, Le Brun had honestly not known whether he had succumbed to wild creatures and the forces of nature or whether he had managed to best every adversity, including the human dragnet John had set out. For certain, if it were the latter, John would have wagered a month's salary that the English-born Russell had escaped to Bermuda, the Bahamas, South Africa, or Australia. That he would return to his birthplace in spite of knowing that Jupiter Morgan would have him hunted to the ends of the earth showed both his nerve and his cunning.

Russell separated himself from the nurses and walked in John's direction, a doctor's black satchel swinging from his right hand and a small briefcase from his left. John hurried out of hiding and got himself well ahead. There were simply too few people on the sidewalks for him to follow for any length of time without being noticed. In his experience, no one ever became nervous about someone well in front of them. He came to broad Kennington Lane and found an alcove for concealment. He watched Russell cross the thoroughfare and head south on Kennington Park Road. John had walked this stretch earlier in the day and knew that an Underground station lay ahead. He crossed to the opposite side of the street and hung well back, waiting for Russell to disappear down the "tube" before breaking into a run to close the gap. He timed his entry to the train platform with the noise of the approaching train. As Russell passed through the car door, Le Brun was right behind him. He followed the physician to his seat and put himself down beside him. Russell never bothered to see who his seatmate was.

"Back to *savin'* lives, I see," John remarked, touching the doctor's satchel with one hand while reaching into his coat pocket with the other.

The doctor looked at Le Brun and jumped an inch off the seat.

John showed the two-shot derringer in the palm of his hand. "Keep your seat. What station do you normally get off at?"

"Goodge Street."

"How long 'til we reach Goodge Street?"

"Seven or eight minutes." The physician glowered at his old nemesis. "Have you been on Morgan's payroll all these years, Sheriff Le Brun?"

John laughed. "I never took a cent from the bastard. Not directly anyway. As a matter of fact, while tryin' to expose you, I uncovered somethin' on him that made what he did to your father look like a benediction. I traded it for a promise he'd give up the search for you."

The fugitive's eyes betrayed his continued mistrust. "Why would you do that?"

"Because he, least of all, had a right to judge you."

"And you want me to believe you happened on me by luck today?"

"More like fate, Dr. Russell."

"My name is Saye now," the man said.

"Ah, yes! Your father's name." Russell was the name of the family who had adopted the boy after his father committed suicide when financially ruined by a Morgan-controlled syndicate.

"I am doing my best to repay any debt I owe to society," Saye affirmed, the muscles of his jaw and throat standing out with tension. "In fact, I just came from charity work at Lambeth Hospital."

"I know. That's where I first spotted you." John was not about to debate the man's indebtedness to the law. Saye would only respond that the ultrarich men he had murdered either made the laws or else paid lawyers and judges to pervert them for their own ends. His victims were, in their own subtle ways, mass murderers. The question was whether or not it was justifiable to punish men above the law with methods equally above the law. John had fallen asleep several nights debating if he would have done the same in the doctor's place. Now that he was retired, he no longer suffered the dilemma of having to ignore his sworn duty. He was not, however, above blackmailing Saye into helping him solve another case. "Forget about what you owe the law," John said. "You owe me, for betrayin' my friendship."

"You honestly aren't going to turn me in?"

"Have you murdered anyone in the past six years?"

Saye's face relaxed. Sensing reprieve, he managed a wan smile. "Not even on the operating table."

"That's good enough for me."

Saye continued to search Le Brun's face for ulterior motives. "You'll pardon me if I don't say, 'It's good to see you,' but you're looking well."

John repocketed his weapon. "Thank you. I'm in London on vacation. Just recently retired from the law."

"Splendid!" Saye winced at his insincere exuberance. "What *do* you want from me?"

"Perhaps nothin'. Perhaps a great deal. By amazin' circumstance, I find myself investigatin' another set of murders at an exclusive club."

"The Sceptred Isle!" Saye exclaimed. "I read about it in this morning's paper."

John briefly described his relationship with Geoffrey Moore and his presence in the club during the shootings. "My intuition tells me it's a complex case," he concluded. "I don't know who to trust, and I have no friends in London other than men who are club members. I may require you simply as another pair of eyes."

"I certainly owe you that much," the physician allowed.

"But I mean at *any* time of the night or day."

"I understand."

"Do you have a business card with you?"

"Two, in fact. And I can always be reached at one of the telephone numbers. My main practice is at University College Hospital, close by my home." Saye dug the cards out of his briefcase and handed them over. "This number is for my home. I'm married now, to a wonderful woman named Julia. Have two beautiful children as well. A girl, three, and a boy, just six months." He beamed. "I'm a model citizen."

He looked every bit the part to John. He had put on weight in the six-and-a-half years since Le Brun met him. Even then, the doctor was the image of civilized benignity. John's experience was that natural-born killers often had a dangerous look about them. Ones pushed to kill sometimes took on the look. But Thomas Russell né Saye had never looked anything but the true gentle man. He had taught Le Brun the valuable lesson that virtually any human being was capable of murder—even cold-blooded, calculated murder—if sufficiently provoked.

For the remainder of the ride, the doctor spoke of operating on the poor, how their malnutrition and hopeless attitudes made recovery all the more difficult. "Believe it or not, many of the indigent Negroes I attended at Johns Hopkins were in better spirits," he said. "This is my station."

"I might as well get off here as anywhere else," John decided.

"Well, you're very near the British Museum. It's open a few hours on Sunday afternoons," Saye suggested.

John thanked him as they exited the train, not bothering to say he'd already had that tour.

As they climbed the steps to the surface, Saye said, "I'd like to invite you into my house, but I wouldn't know how to explain you. My wife knows I grew up in the States, but she knows nothing of Johns Hopkins or my stint at the Jekyl Island Club."

"Quite all right," John allowed.

As they came onto the street, Saye said, "A good deal of this area were slums until recently. The London County Council thinks that by tearing them down and putting up what they call model dwellings estates, they're righting old wrongs. The fact is, most of the time the poorest flee to another poor section, increasing the crowding. They can't afford the new housing, even on subsidy. Of course, as they crowd closer together, diseases spread all the faster. I serve one day a month for the LCC, helping to inspect neighborhoods and trying to prevent outbreaks."

"There are no simple answers," John commented.

"I suppose. But the rich keep getting richer, and that can't be helping the poor. If they don't watch out, there'll be a revolution. It happened in France; it's certain to happen in Russia. Perhaps Germany as well." Saye snickered. "Of course, we'd have to do it in orderly lines in England."

Le Brun laughed along to be polite. He looked around. "What your council didn't knock down still looks neat and clean."

"Not by chance. This is Bloomsbury. I'm one of perhaps a hundred well-to-do families that have moved in in the last decade. The university, the hospital, and the museum act as magnets and anchors. Some of us are socialists, some egalitarians, some culturalists, some humanitarians, but we're all dedicated to improving the lives of everyone in Bloomsbury, by example and by the infusion of our capital. It seems to be working. Well, I'm just down this way." Saye set down his briefcase and offered his hand. "Thank you, Mr. Le Brun, for not judging. Do call on me if I can be of service."

"Depend on it, Doctor," John said.

EVEN DURING THE short subway ride he had shared with Dr. Saye, the air had grown more chill. A temperature inversion had settled over the city, turning the damp air into fog. John noted that it was grayer than the fogs in Brunswick, no doubt owing to the vast amounts of smoke particles suspended in the London air. He watched with interest as it transformed the look of the city, flattening shapes and robbing colors, eventually masking all but the block on which he walked. He was growing weary, and his relatively new shoes had begun to hurt around the heels and toes. He plodded westward nonetheless, stopping often, staring into closed shop windows, appreciating the passing parade of pedestrians, watching umbrellas appear as if by magic. He was particularly struck by the city's many domed buildings, especially those on corners. Also, though the safety bicycle had grown quite popular in Georgia, it was clearly more than a sporting fad here; it served as the transportation for all those who had walked five years earlier. In the middle of one block he came upon a bicycle shop and saw that a new one could be had for as little as five pounds. As he hadn't eaten since breakfast, he found himself a pub that served cold mutton stew and warm beer and contented himself with listening to the melodic accents of Marylebone English while he took unhurried bites.

WHEN JOHN EMERGED at last from the pub, he decided he was too stiff and sore to continue on foot. He hailed a cab, took it as far as Marble Arch, and walked the rest of the way south to the Godwin townhouse. By the time he arrived, the late afternoon and the fog had combined to produce an unusual darkness. He hunted the key to the back door and entered. He felt uncomfortable alone in the place, like a thief. The grandeur and size of the house contributed to his feeling. He imagined looking at it as might one of the myriad denizens he had seen in Lambeth, imagined their mixed awe and anger. He thought how the Thames was not merely a river but a chasm. He trudged upstairs to rest.

Three-quarters of an hour later, the front door opened and closed. John put on his jacket and went down. Trent stood in the parlor with a filled cognac snifter in one hand and a cigarette in the other, looking as if he had weathered a long military campaign. Dark crescents underscored dull but quick-blinking eyes. His shoulders sagged.

"Evening, John. Not here but two days, and you get to see a London 'pea soup,' eh?"

"It's pretty thick out there, all right."

"Have you heard they solved the case?" he asked without especial enthusiasm.

"That's what Inspector Tibbles of Scotland Yard told me this mornin'," John replied.

"You don't believe the bobby's guilty?"

"No."

Godwin nudged his attaché case out of the center of the foyer with his foot. "I'm not convinced either. Which means I'm still on your list."

John shrugged in oblique agreement. "And while they waste time with the poor policeman, the trail grows colder. I wonder if you might introduce me to the families of the murdered men, so I can—"

Godwin shook his head. "They were already interviewed by the police this morning for the same reason. I spent part of my afternoon with Lavinia Wilbye and the rest with Augusta Ravenscroft, sorting out business, wills, bequests, insurance, trusts. I'm sure they're in no mood to entertain a foreign detective for a third round. No offense intended."

"None taken. Even if it means findin' their loved ones' killer?"

Trent took a long drag on his cigarette and stubbed it out in an ashtray that sat on the foyer console table. He pinched the bridge of his nose, then spread his fingers across his lowered eyelids. "I tell you what—"

The front door opened. Maeve Godwin entered, looking as harried and drained as her husband. "Good evening, Mr. Le Brun. Next year, Trent, remind me of today if I consider the charity chairmanship again."

"It sounds like a wonderful thing you're doin', Mrs. Godwin," John offered.

"I wish I could do more, actually," she replied, hanging her wrap in the foyer closet. "You would think half a dozen women of leisure could arrange a ball amongst them, but there are so *many* niddling details. For example, yesterday afternoon the events manager at the Westminster Palace tells us we can't get the flowers we want. Something about a quarantined ship stuck in Calais. Which leaves four days to locate five hundred flowers that match the tablecloths. I have been out all day trying to speak with flower mongers, but what can you expect on a Sunday? And, on top of that, the weather is beastly."

"Go put up your feet, dear," Trent advised. "I was just about to suggest to John that we go out for dinner. Nothing fancy."

"I'm too exhausted to eat," Maeve lamented, plopping herself down in one of the parlor chairs and staring at her feet. "Besides, I had a big lunch at Frascati's."

John was about to mention his mutton stew when Trent said, "Well, I for one am famished. Had some oyster crackers for lunch. I was going to use the meal to fill John in on everyone I can remember from the Wilbye, Homer, and Ravenscroft families who has ever come to the club's back door."

"It would help a great deal," John encouraged.

Trent seemed to have restoked his boiler. "Then by all means let's head over to the Sceptred Isle Club. We'll catch the latest scuttlebutt and thrash out a list. And tomorrow, I'll arrange to have you interview the ones you find interesting."

"I'm lying down for a spell," Maeve announced.

John told Trent that he would change his clothes. He followed Maeve upstairs. In spite of his eagerness to interview his host, he could not make himself dress quickly. His swollen feet fit too snugly in his dress shoes. His collar would not close over the stay. He took his bow tie in hand without enthusiasm.

A crack of gunfire outside and an explosion of glass roused Le Brun from his lethargy. He sprang to one of the windows. The fog pressed against the panes like gray gauze, obscuring everything beyond the middle of Green Street. John dug his derringer out of his daytime jacket and rushed downstairs. He found Trent with his back hugging the span of wall between foyer and parlor. Blood streamed from his forehead and right cheek. He wore spectacles for the first time in John's presence, and the right lens was crazed. He regarded John with wild eyes and gasping chest.

"Someone just shot at me! Through the window!" He pointed into the parlor.

"I'm calling the police," Maeve announced, right behind John. She rounded the banister into the hallway as soon as he cleared the bottom of the staircase.

John strode past the cowering lawyer and threw open the front door, chancing a quick peek outside before darting back behind the protection of thick oak door paneling. He chanced a second, longer look. The fog-shrouded street lay empty to the limits of his vision. He came around the door.

"Don't go out there, John!" Trent warned. "He might mistake you for me."

"I'm all right." John descended the four steps to the sidewalk. The moment his shoes hit the pavement, he pivoted to look at the shattered window, then darted to the far limit of the Godwin property frontage, where bushes of varying heights lined the entrance to the driveway. He knelt and pushed the branches aside. Finding nothing, he darted down the drive a few steps, reconsidered, and turned back to the street, moving erratically, like a bloodhound that has lost the scent. He returned to the front steps, put his hand inside the nearby rain downspout, then tried in vain to pull out the grate that covered the stoop weep vent.

A hansom cab came down the street as John was searching. The horse's iron shoes signaled its approach before the vehicle could be seen. John watched it ease to a halt and noted the driver standing at its rear, top hat pulled to his ears and a muffler wound around his lower face against the chill, damp air. John's attention was quickly diverted to the figure emerging from the open cab. Veronica paused and focused on Le Brun.

"John! What are you doing?"

"We've had a shootin'."

"What? One moment." She handed up a coin to the driver and descended to the street with some difficulty, because of the form-fitting nature of her long skirt. "A shooting you say?"

John pointed to the ruined window. "Your stepfather was nearly killed."

Veronica glanced down the street from where the cab had just come. "That might explain the strange man I just saw."

The cab man cracked his whip. The cab jolted smartly away.

"What did you see?" John asked.

"An older man, I'm sure. He was trotting up the sidewalk, but his movement was rather arthritic. He had his right hand shoved into his coat and his left holding onto his hat, as if he didn't want me to see his face."

"Did you see his hair?"

"No. The bowler covered it."

"His dress?"

"Just a suit. Very dark. Probably black. Couldn't make out the cut or quality." Veronica had a woolen shawl around her shoulders and, over one shoulder, a long strap attached to a large handbag.

"Let's go inside," John said.

When they entered the parlor, they found Maeve ministering to Trent, who had dissolved into a limp mass on one of the plush chairs. She daubed at his face with a cloth, every few moments wetting it anew from a bottle of medicinal alcohol. Veronica let her purse down on the floor and moved swiftly to close the parlor curtains, masking the room from the street.

"Careful of the glass," John cautioned. Shards of twinkling window glass and the remnants of Trent's dropped snifter fanned out across much of the polished oak floor.

"Look what the stupid creature did to my chandelier!" Maeve ranted, with eyes that positively burned. John first noted that one of the fixture's electric blossom lights had blown away, then saw the path of destruction through the forest of brass leaves.

"But Trent is safe," Veronica said with force. "That's all that matters."

Maeve kept her incandescent gaze fixed on the chandelier. "You're right. That's what's important."

"Looks like the same size hole as at the club," John remarked, looking at the black circle in the wall plaster just below the crown molding. He swung his gaze back to Trent.

"Did you see anyone?"

"Just the faintest figure of a man standing out in the street," Godwin replied. "Couldn't even judge his size. Could have been a large youth for all I know. I thought he had raised his hand to wave at me. I had put my reading glasses on, which makes it difficult to focus on anything at a distance. I leaned forward for a better look when a bullet came whizzing by my ear like an enraged hornet."

"Was he right- or left-handed?"

"Right. That much I'm sure of."

"Please don't put your hands on the chair, dear," Maeve instructed.

"I thought I'd been struck by part of the bullet," the lawyer continued, "but it must have been pieces of glass hitting me. Damned good thing I had on my reading glasses!"

"Is it your habit to look out the windows in the evenin'?" John asked.

"Actually, it is. I like to see what's happening on the block as I sip my cognac. I never realized what a habit it is; couldn't see anything tonight, and yet there I was. You believe it was someone who knows my patterns?"

"It's possible. Knockin' on the door would only make sense if the person were willin' to kill everyone in the house."

Trent grunted. "After killing four already, that may have been the plan."

"Be glad of the fog," John said. "What made him so hard to see made you equally hard to sight on."

"That, and my leaning forward." Trent shook his head. "Ironic. I suppose this means that I was actually the target last night."

"Unless you're the missin' piece of a set," John said.

"A set of what?"

"Precisely. *You* must answer that."

"Oh, now look!" Maeve exclaimed peevishly. "You've gotten blood on the chair, even after I asked you to be careful."

"I *didn't* touch the chair," Godwin defended. "It dripped. It's only a chair. Have some pity, won't you?"

Maeve straightened up. "Let's go up to the bathroom. Tile can be cleaned more easily than fabric."

As the couple moved to the stairs, Veronica said, "The police should be here at any moment. I'll wait outside and see they don't miss the house." She pirouetted as lightly as a sylph from a corps de ballet and exited the townhouse.

The moment the front door closed, John rushed to Veronica's purse and thrust his hand into its depths, looking for a gun. Satisfied there was none, he returned the purse to its place and investigated first the umbrella stand behind the front door and then the foyer closet. The police wagon pulled up precisely as he finished.

SHORTLY AFTER THE Uniform Police arrived on Green Street, Inspector Cooper appeared. He interviewed each of the Godwins privately, saving Le Brun for last. He ushered the ex-sheriff into the study, gestured to Trent's high-backed desk chair, and closed the door behind him. The smell of his cherry pipe tobacco became stronger in the enclosed area.

"Tibbles told me you don't believe Officer Buttons is guilty," Cooper began without formal pleasantries.

"And this event would support me, don't you agree?"

A crooked smile animated Cooper's stolid face. "You made a remark to Tibbles about two revolvers. Why couldn't Buttons have worked with an accomplice? He gets the butler to open the back door and shoots the first two men. Then, sure that his accomplice can handle the other two, he dashes away to create his alibi. The second man actually does the robbery."

"It's possible," John said. "But I only mentioned two guns because it would be folly to attempt to kill five or six men . . .

as there well might have been in that room . . . with six bullets. One person could have used two guns."

"But you admit it is *possible* that Buttons could have done it with an accomplice."

"Remotely. But you're about to tell why it's not."

Cooper pulled the room's other chair in front of the door and sat. He spoke in a softer tone. "We now have two shopkeepers vouching for Buttons's whereabouts around the time of the massacre. He would have needed either a motorcar or closed carriage in both directions to have made the plan work. We doubt that he would have risked moving around his beat so curiously."

"Then who do you suspect?"

Cooper leaned closer. "We spoke to Geoffrey Moore. He said *you* and Sir Arthur suspect Trent Godwin."

"Mr. Doyle definitely does. Let's say I haven't yet been able to remove him absolutely from suspicion. However, this attack would argue otherwise, don't you think?"

"Not if it's unrelated. Perhaps someone who hates him. Let's say this attacker saw Godwin's name in this morning's paper and decided to use the club murders to disguise his revenge."

"How likely is that?"

Cooper shrugged. "What about if Godwin staged this attack himself, to kill your suspicions and ours?"

"This man is a highly successful lawyer," Le Brun said. "Such a man would deem it too risky with me and his wife upstairs to have cut his face, put on a pair of spectacles he had previously shattered, dashed outside, fired the shot, and run back inside. From pistol report to when I found him with his back against the foyer wall was not more than fourteen seconds."

"Fourteen, you say?" Cooper asked, with amused surprise. "Not fifteen?"

"No. Possibly as few as twelve."

"I'll take your word for it," Cooper said. "But if he were criminally insane, he might just have risked it."

"Except for three things."

"How he could dispose of the weapon in fourteen seconds," Cooper supplied.

"That's right. I went outside directly and checked every reasonable hidin' place within fifty feet. Nothin'. Same with the hall closet and the umbrella stand. Unless the man can make a loaded revolver disappear into thin air, I don't see how he could have staged it alone."

"You said 'three things,'" Cooper prompted.

"He was supposedly sippin' cognac at the time the bullet was fired. The sounds of glass shatterin' were all together. The bullet that broke the window was clearly shot from the street. He would have needed to break the snifter inside before the window was shot."

"He could have broken it long beforehand, just as you suggested with his spectacles."

"But how would he have gotten the cognac all over the floor?"

"With another vessel."

"But, again, it takes too much time: gettin' the thing from the kitchen, transferrin' the cognac, bringin' it back to the kitchen, rinsing it out, dryin' and storin' it. Washin' the snifter I saw him drinkin' from as well. All too complicated. In my experience, the simple answer is nearly always the right one."

"And the third?"

"What happened here wouldn't have happened if the motive for the killin's at the club was purely robbery. The patrolman now sits in jail. The patrolman's accomplice would have no reason to shoot Godwin. Godwin knows that. Then what is he stagin' a charade for?"

Cooper sat up straight. "So, you've dismissed Mr. Godwin."

Now Le Brun smiled. "Unless *he* is the one with the accomplice."

"Trying to silence him, you mean?"

"No. Workin' with him."

Cooper shook his head as if to clear out all the mental dead ends they had already discarded. "On what?"

"That remains to be learned. Veronica Godwin arrived by carriage about a minute after the gunshot. You've no doubt gotten her story about the mysterious man."

"Made up, do you think?"

"Are you askin' if she's Trent's accomplice?"

"Yes."

John wriggled up his nose and shook his head. "She *and* the cab man? Three were not necessary last night. Therefore, for reasons of safety, three would not be used. But consider Veronica alone tonight. It's highly unlikely she could find a cab so quickly after firin' the gun. She hasn't changed her clothes since the shootin'. Do you think she could have hidden a .38 revolver in that blouse or under that skirt?"

Cooper gave a salacious smile. "No."

"Well, it was not in her purse. That was in my view from the moment she entered the house, and I checked it as soon as she left the room. Furthermore, I know she was at the theater last night durin' the murders. You'd better follow up on her mystery man."

Cooper threw up his hands in frustration. "With that scant description?" He stood and replaced his chair. "My head is about to explode. The only thing I can say with some degree of certainty is: If it isn't Officer Buttons, then more than four thousand pounds were planted to frame him. That means somebody is playing a very high stakes game. However, we have no clue what that game is. Perhaps, with that slide rule you have for a brain, you'll think of something."

"I shall try my best, Inspector," Le Brun said.

VERONICA FOUND JOHN in the parlor, flipping through one of the magazines to which the family subscribed.

"I feel so badly that we're ruining your holiday," she confided.

"Don't. I'm managin' to have a fine time. And I must admit that I'd love to be part of solvin' this crime."

"But must you starve because of it? If you're waiting for Trent to get off the telephone, you may faint from hunger," she said. "He'll be calling his partners and friends until he's thoroughly worked this evening out of his system. I suspect that part of him is thrilled about last night and this," she confided. "He longs to be involved in adventurous and forbidden things, but he's from such a straitlaced family. That's the reason he's a dry, old lawyer."

John closed the magazine. "Is there anythin' to eat in the icebox?"

"Alice shops first thing Monday. Probably not a great deal. Let's see."

They investigated together and found a bunch of grapes, a wedge of cheese, and several slabs of ham. Veronica went down into the cellar and emerged with a bottle of German white wine. As John opened it, she said, "Geoffrey tells me you're a wizard chess player."

"I hold my own," John allowed.

"What say we while the time in a game until Trent appears," she suggested.

"Have you played Geoffrey?"

"Yes. Once. I beat him."

"Then, by all means. He's no slouch."

Veronica rearranged the food and set a wooden chessboard in the middle of the dining room table. The pieces were of ebony and ivory. John expected her to take one of each in her hands, hide them behind her back, and allow him to choose for white. Instead, she gave him a pout.

"You've no doubt been playing since before I was born."

"Not that long, actually."

"Well, everyone knows that men's minds are better adapted for math, music, and chess than women's, so you should give me the advantage."

"I yield to the strength of your argument."

Veronica arched a brow. "You mean to my indirect flattery." She withdrew the white pieces from the box and handed the box across to John.

"Callin' me old is flattery?"

"No. My second assault."

"Ah." John slipped a grape into his mouth.

"Did you find what you were looking for in Lambeth?" Veronica asked.

"And more. A great number of your countrymen, accordin' to the faces and accents."

"Even more in Southwark, the district to the immediate east. I recently read that there are some 60,000 native-born Irish in London and about 435,000 born here. The British could have fed the Irish during the potato famines, but they chose to let them starve. The ones who escaped to London were taken in as Joseph's people into Egypt. The choice was death or slavery. Generations later, it's hardly better."

"Present company excepted."

Veronica placed her queen last. "Very true." She looked Le Brun hard in the eyes. "Play your best game, John. I cannot abide being patronized."

"I never play but to win," John replied.

"Good! If I last twenty moves with you, I'll call myself clever." She moved her queen's pawn to the fourth square, already a statement of unorthodox play.

John countered with king's knight to his bishop three, preventing further advance of the bold pawn. Veronica's queen's bishop pawn went out to the fourth rank. John saw the queen's gambit developing. Now he understood Veronica's demand to go first; she needed the extra move to grab the center successfully. John moved the queen's pawn to queen four, as traditional logic prescribed. Veronica's queen immediately moved up to queen three.

"And you think you can last twenty moves paradin' your queen this early?" John asked.

"We shall see."

John took the available pawn with his pawn. A moment later, Veronica killed it with her queen. John protected his king and worked on control of the center with queen's knight to bishop three. For the first time in their acquaintance, Veronica displayed what seemed to him impetuousness and ill-considered thinking.

Veronica's eyes roamed the board. "So many pieces to move, but only one move at a time," she lamented.

"That's the game's great beauty," John replied. "Anyone can overwhelm a foe. In fact, that's the aim in real warfare. One of the most successful generals of the war I fought in was Nathan Bedford Forrest. He said, 'The key to winnin' battles is to get there the fustest with the mostest.' "

"Then we shall rely on cunning," Veronica said. She moved her king's knight to bishop three, finally putting a lesser back-row piece in play and simultaneously protecting her pawn in the center.

John licked his lips and gave his opponent a little smile. If using the queen early was her forte, he would deny her her game. He pushed his queen out to the fourth rank and expected her to retreat and lose the advantage of development.

Without consideration, Veronica took the black queen. An instant later, her queen had been taken by John's knight. It would be a game of lesser players.

"Who taught you to play?" John asked.

"Me sainted mither," the chestnut-haired beauty replied, lapsing into a heavy Irish accent. "She thinks like a man. But I don't necessarily mean that as a compliment."

"I understand."

Veronica moved her king's pawn up two squares. It was an aggressive move that forced him to relocate his knight, but neither was John bothered. He responded by moving the threatened knight over to queen's knight five, which was a strong play for him anyway, threatening her king and rook with but one more advance. The trundling out of her queen had cost her the time to move her king's bishop and allow for the protection of castling.

"Did you know that my mother has the right to vote in local elections?"

"That's good."

"But not the right to run for local office."

"That's not good."

Veronica had seen the knight's threat. She moved her king to queen one. "Don't patronize me *off* the board either."

"I wasn't."

"Then you believe what your Declaration of Independence says about all men being created equal . . . including women?"

Ordinarily, John would have been annoyed at a partner who spoke so often, but he had her trapped on her home row so well that he indulged her questions. "I believe the founding fathers meant the word 'equal' to apply to treatment under man's laws and in God's lovin' eyes. They knew as well as you and I that a blind child will not run a race equal to a sighted child."

Since Veronica had moved her king onto the queen's home square, John moved his freed bishop down to knight five to put pressure on the diagonal. Veronica advanced her pawn to queen five, threatening one of John's knights. John took her knight with his bishop, staring the king down at two paces. Veronica gave the whole board a survey, then riposted by taking the bishop with her pawn.

"Are you ordinarily so blood-thirsty?" Veronica asked.

"You started it."

"Did I? What do *you* think about giving women the right to vote in all elections?"

John eased back in his seat. The young woman's offense was not restricted to the chessboard. "I don't believe it should be a right for man or woman. It should be earned."

"How?"

"By service to one's country, and by bein' able to answer

simple questions about its laws, its government, and the people runnin' for office."

"Then you do believe informed women should have equal voting rights."

"If they earn them. You've made ten moves. You'll never get your twenty if you don't concentrate," he chided.

"If I let you concentrate," Veronica said through a smile, "I'll never win." But then she was quiet.

John held the advantage, but Veronica was never caught totally off guard. John paid for every piece taken but one. By the thirty-second move, each side was left with a king and one rook. John, however, had four pawns to Veronica's three, and her king was left out in the center of the board, with John having a patently better chance of promoting one pawn to a queen.

Veronica toppled her king.

"You went much farther than twenty moves," John praised.

"It means I could have won," Veronica replied, darkly. "I'm even better at overwhelming."

John thought he knew what she meant.

SIX

Monday, October 23, 1905

TRENT HAD EMERGED FROM his study at quarter to eleven, announcing that none of his friends could think of a solution to the puzzle of the two shooting incidents. Feeling the weight of the two days upon him, John suggested that they sleep on the problem. Everyone retired to their bedrooms by eleven. John lay under the cool, newly-changed sheets, listening to the stillness. His mind worked as methodically as it had at the chess game, examining the facts, searching for connections, extrapolating. Just after the grandmother clock in the foyer chimed out midnight, his doorknob turned slowly. Then the door eased inward, inch by inch. John reached to the bedside table for his weapon. He set it back down when he recognized the silhouette.

Veronica slipped into the room and shut the door behind her. Even though his eyes had long since accustomed themselves to the dark, Veronica all but disappeared as she moved against the inside wall. John's hearing tracked her until finally she came around the far side of the bed and was back-lit by street lamp light filtering through one of the windows. He watched her reach up to her shoulders and slip off her diaphanous nightgown. The mattress dipped slightly as she eased onto it.

"I know you're awake," Veronica whispered. "I came to you last night, but you were snoring away. Now you're barely breathing."

"Veronica—"

A soft hand pressed against John's mouth. "Shh! We have to be very quiet. Their bed is against the same wall as yours. Last night when I hung up your jacket, I felt something in the pocket. I couldn't resist my curiosity and stole in here this afternoon. I thought you said you were an old man. Naughty boy."

John removed her hand from his lips. "Those photographs belong to the manager of the Sceptred Isle Club," he whispered. "It's a complicated story."

"I'll just bet." Veronica wriggled more fully onto the bed. "Whatever the story, they serve a useful purpose. Since we can't turn on a light, picture the girl with the Japanese fan. My figure is most like hers."

"We really—"

Veronica rolled herself atop John and pressed her lips to his.

John had never felt such soft lips. Nor had a woman ever smelled as good as this one did. It was as natural to her as a scent to a rose. Her hair cascaded down and hid their faces. Even as he struggled to find dismissing words, he knew he was too smitten, too selfish to stop her.

"Kiss my neck," she whispered.

John's mouth went to her neck, tentatively. She moved her head slightly, so that his hesitant lips glided over her warm flesh. He could feel the pulse of her carotid artery.

"Touch me."

John was about to obey when a knock rattled the bedroom door.

Veronica slipped from the bed like mercury and disappeared under it.

The rapping grew slightly louder.

"Come in," John invited, rising from the bed and hoping that his nightshirt would disguise the evidence of his arousal.

The door opened. Trent's figure nearly filled the frame. John braced himself for an awkward scene. He grabbed his robe from the foot of the bed and swiftly stabbed his arms into it.

"Yes, Trent?"

"I couldn't sleep." His voice had an excited edge. "Just as well. I believe I've finally found the key to the case!"

"That's great." John cinched in his robe sash and took a step toward his host, cutting off his entry into the bedroom. "Let's talk downstairs, so we don't wake the ladies."

"Yes, of course."

TRENT CHOSE THE dining room table for his revelation. John noted that he bore three scabbed-over gashes from the flying glass, none of which John expected would cause permanent damage.

"I kept thinking about you saying I was part of a set," Trent began. "The problem was the right set didn't include every man in the room. Well, certainly not the butler, but also not Ralph Homer. He wasn't part of the tontine."

"I hope you're about to tell me what a tontine is."

"Oh. Certainly. There was a banker named Lorenzo Tonti. Must have been Italian, but I believe he worked in Paris. Anyway, he came up with a scheme that acted as a kind of life insurance policy. A number of people contribute to a pool, you see, either all at once or over time. In one version, they begin drawing out dividends after a certain period, adding the money of those who died prematurely along with the interest. There is another form. Let's say that ten men get together and each put in a one-time amount of a thousand pounds.

Only the last survivor gets the entire pot which, depending on how long the penultimate man lives, could easily double."

"A tontine is bettin' on others' death," John summarized.

Trent shrugged. "Life *is* the biggest gamble, John. It's nice if *somebody* capitalizes on living through the 'heartaches and the thousand natural shocks that flesh is heir to.' Besides, those who live longest spend the most and have the greatest need to win."

"And you and the other men in your gamblin' circle were part of the second type of tontine."

"The second type, yes. All of us several years ago, but not all of us now. The group has changed. That's why I didn't associate it with the murders. I, Hugh, and Eddie were part. Ralph wasn't. Nor poor Malcolm."

"How many men originally?" asked John.

"There were seven of us, and we created it seven years ago."

"Whose idea was it?"

"Rodney Miller. He was the oldest among our original group. We used to chide him whenever he lost, saying his mind was going, on account of old age. He was sixty at the time. His response was that his grandfather had died at ninety-one, and his father was still vital at eighty-four. He suggested the tontine and the high fee as a sort of 'put up or shut up,' since he proclaimed he would outlive us all. Died two years later, as it turned out. Stepped in front of a streetcar. Otherwise, he damned well might have won."

John looked at the ghostly reflections of himself and Trent in the dining room's black bay windows. "All right. He's dead. Two others died Saturday night. Who else has died?"

"Dickie Stanton and Harry Naylor. Dickie had a heart attack. They found him slumped over his desk. He worked too much." Godwin rolled his eyes. "I should talk. By his measure, I should have keeled over at thirty-five."

"How old was he?"

"Fifty-four."

"And Mr. Naylor?"

"Stupid, unnecessary death. Ruptured gall bladder. He'd been helping his manservant move heavy furniture, so when the organ went bad he thought it was pulled back muscles. Kept pooh-poohing his pain until it was too late. By the time they opened him up, the thing was in pieces. Died of peritonitis." Trent's face screwed up in memory. "Beastly death. He was only forty-eight."

"So that leaves you and who else?"

"Nahum Attwater. You remember, I said he's down in Brighton closing on a warehouse."

"I do. The other two players in your group, the ones in India and Italy, weren't members of the tontine?"

"No. They joined Saturday's Sordid Sinners—that's what we playfully called the group—only a few years ago. Too late to join the tontine."

After so much time working without a tangible clue, John was electrified by the information. He rose from his chair, swung around it, and gripped its back. "Is Mr. Attwater havin' financial troubles?" he asked.

Trent scratched his ear. "He's a bit strapped, naturally."

"Why do you say 'naturally'?"

"You see, with all the new inventions—the telegraph and telephone, trains, and faster steamships, the nature of warehousing has changed over the past twenty years. Used to be that stock arrived once or twice a year, and you could make a killing holding it. Now, when inventory starts to run low, someone sends a telegram halfway around the world. Three weeks later, the exact amount needed arrives. Nahum's had to consolidate. Shut down two warehouses in London in the past four years. The only way he can stay even is by economies of scale. He's been buying or building outlying warehouses and creating a network. Also capitalizing on the increasing demands for more varieties and freshness in food and flowers and shifting to cold storage."

"He's no doubt laid out a great deal of capital to accomplish this," John expanded.

Godwin smirked. "I can see where you're going. But, believe me, Nahum Attwater still earns among the top two or three percent of the population. He doesn't confide in me on such matters, but I'm sure he's let a bank share much of his outlays. He's a prudent man. And he certainly wouldn't stoop to killing his closest friends for the amount in the tontine."

"How much is that?"

Trent's eyelids batted more rapidly than usual. "Miller goaded us into putting in the maximum amount we could possibly lose in a month's gambling."

"Four thousand pounds, then."

"Precisely."

"That's twenty-eight thousand pounds!" John marveled. "With interest over seven years, that must have grown to around . . . thirty-five thousand."

"That's right," Trent agreed, coolly.

"And you told me that five thousand pounds would keep a middle-class family nicely for nine or ten years. This pool is more than a *lifetime's* earnings for a successful clerk!"

"However, it's about what Nahum would net in a year."

"So, you want me to dismiss Nahum Attwater as a suspect. Then if the motive for the murders *is* this tontine," John said, patiently, "the only other person it could implicate is you."

"Not at all."

"Then who?"

"Nahum's son, Lionel." Trent folded his arms across his chest. "Bad baggage all around. If he didn't resemble Nahum, I'd say his wife had a tryst with the dustman. Rude bugger. Never had the slightest inclination toward studies or work. Always overspent his allowance when he was young. Once, he capitalized on the fact that they'd hired a new girl and stole a few pieces of Mrs. Attwater's jewelry. Of course, the Attwaters couldn't admit the obvious, so the poor girl got sacked. He's devoted to the high life. Three years back, he got a publican's daughter pregnant and was forced to marry her."

"Is he an only child?"

"No. Nahum has two daughters." Trent pointed at John. "And *that's* why I know he's the one behind all this. Do you have a son?" Suddenly, Trent remembered Geoffrey Moore's tale of the death of John's wife from yellow fever and the fact that she was carrying a boy. His hand flew to his mouth. "My God! I'm dreadfully sorry."

"It's all right," John said. "It's late, and we're exhausted."

"We share such a similar tragedy, I don't know how it could have slipped my mind."

"It's all right," John repeated.

"But I'm sure you understand how it is when you've spent a lifetime building up a business. You want to leave it to a son; you want him to be responsible, so it will survive after you're gone. Getting that pub girl pregnant was the last straw. He changed his will. I executed the codicil for him. Virtually cut Lionel out." His forefinger went up again, this time vertically. "But, you see, since the tontine was not truly an asset, it isn't mentioned in the will. Lionel must know that . . . and that he's still the primary beneficiary."

John stepped back from the chair. He realized that great relief should have begun buoying him, since he evidently needed to waste no more of his vacation. But his inner pressure was not bleeding off.

Precisely what he felt he could not name, but whatever it was still had him pulsing. The ex-sheriff ignored the feeling and thumped the top of the chair with the flats of both hands. "There it is. Simple as rememberin'."

"Have I solved it, do you think?" Trent beamed. "And I even recall that Lionel showed up twice at the club's back door when we were gambling. Malcolm wouldn't have forgotten him; he was drunk as a lord both times I saw him. Looking for money!"

"Let's telephone the police and have him picked up," John said.

Trent lost his grin. "How can I do that to Nahum?"

"How?" John exclaimed loudly, forgetting the hour in his excitement. "Because the only way he'll claim that money is by killin' you *and* his father."

Trent still did not look convinced. "Then again, it's going to be hard to track him down. He and the wife leave the child with her mother. On weekends, they carouse around the whole city. Almost never come home. Not that they're much better during the week. He works in his father's main warehouse but usually shows up late and hung over. Sometimes doesn't even bother to show up."

"He must be apprehended nonetheless," John insisted. Suddenly, his face lost its rigor. He stared at Trent Godwin slack-jawed.

"What?"

"If Lionel Attwater spends his last farthings on liquor, where would he get more than four thousand pounds from?"

"What four . . ." Trent paused. His eyes showed his understanding.

"Everythin' hangs together except the money under the birdbath."

"In my excitement, I'd completely forgotten about that," Trent admitted.

"And your infectious excitement nearly made *me* forget." John wondered if a subconscious memory of the problem was what had kept him uneasy. Before he could give it more thought, Trent was speaking.

"Perhaps the policeman is innocent of *this* crime but. . ." The lawyer realized the thinness of the straw he was grasping at and let the suggestion drop with a vigorous shake of his head. He knew the amount found was simply too close to what he said had existed in the Sceptred Isle Club's gambling room.

"Might Mr. Attwater have returned from Brighton by now?" John asked.

"Quite possible," Trent replied.

"I assume he has a telephone in his house."

Trent stared at John aghast. "You want me to telephone his residence after midnight?"

John gestured for his host to get out of his seat. "I know proper form is very important in England, but this is a matter of life and death. Let's risk it."

They moved to Trent's study. He found the Attwater number in his appointment notebook and rang up the operator. He held the earpiece up so that John might listen as well. The connection rang for long seconds. Finally, an unexpectedly animated voice answered.

"Attwater residence."

"Jonathan, is that you?" Trent asked.

"Yes. Who is this?"

"It's Trent Godwin."

"Oh, Mr. Godwin. Is this about Mr. Attwater?" the edgy voice asked.

"Yes. Can I assume he hasn't returned from Brighton?"

"That's correct. The entire staff is on tenterhooks here. We had an unannounced visit from a Scotland Yard inspector not three hours ago. He asked all kinds of questions about Mr. Attwater, but I'm sure we didn't have the answers he wanted."

"Looked disappointed, did he?"

"Yes, sir."

"Is his name Cooper?"

"That's right, sir. How did you know?"

"He visited us tonight as well."

"About the Sceptred Isle Club murders."

"Just so."

"As long as he was here, I told him we all wished he'd find Mr. Attwater quickly. We're very afraid some mischief may have come to him, what with these murders at the club. It's not like the master to say he'll be home on a Sunday, not come home, *and* also not let us know."

"Didn't he leave for Brighton on Friday?"

"Yes, sir. Friday noon."

"Ask if he went by himself," John prompted.

When Trent obliged, the servant replied, "Yes, indeed. All by himself."

"Have you seen Lionel in the past day or so?"

"No, sir. I sent the chauffeur over to his house twice, but he wasn't there either time."

"What hotel did Mr. Attwater say he was staying at?"

"The Metropole."

"I'll make inquiries first thing in the morning," Trent promised.

"Ever so grateful, sir," said Jonathan. "Please do keep us informed."

"I shall."

As soon as Trent hung up the telephone, John asked, "Does Mr. Attwater walk with a limp?"

"Yes, he does. Due to a polo accident." Trent's eyes narrowed. "You're referring to Veronica's mystery man."

"Could be the older Attwater," John said.

"Or a wily son imitating his father."

"Inspector Cooper might not know about your tontine, but he certainly did pick up on the fact that Mr. Attwater was not at the game Saturday night."

"Do you think he'll agree with my thinking about Lionel?"

"He seems a competent law officer. If I were him, the younger Attwater would sure become my main focus. Perhaps the four thousand dollars will be the truly difficult part of this case," John said. He opened the study door. "At any rate, I believe we may have made real progress, thanks to you. How far away is Brighton?"

"Fifty miles. An hour and a half by train."

"Would you be able to go with me first thing tomorrow?"

Trent replaced the telephone precisely where it had been on his desk. "I thought we'd just make telephone inquiries."

"Depending on what's happened, it would be much better to be in Brighton," John argued. "You heard what the butler said. And the only way Lionel gets his hands on the tontine money is by killin' his father as well. He won't do that until he's sure you're dead. If he's careless, he may assume the bullet he put through your window killed you."

"I *did* fall to the floor very quickly."

"In that case, his next victim will be his father. Perhaps he contrived some scheme to hold the old man in Brighton for a few more days. Tomorrow, once the evidence has been established that Nahum outlasted you, he's free to do him in."

"I suppose you're right." Trent sighed. "Perhaps I *should* go with you, no matter what the truth of all this is. I've narrowly escaped being killed twice in London of late. A change of scene might be best for my health. But I must return by five, to pay my respects to Mrs. Homer." His lips pressed together hard. "Someone must pay for this."

As the men exited the study, Maeve turned into the hallway from the stairs. She was wrapped in a silk robe and had her arms hidden in its large sleeves, in the attitude of a Mandarin lord.

"I woke up, found you missing, and became worried," she said to Trent.

"Sorry. But I think I may have hit upon the answer to the murders . . . and being shot at tonight as well!"

"Really?" Maeve said.

"You recall I once mentioned a tontine I belonged to?"

Maeve's brow furrowed. "Was that the bet on life your group made some years back?"

"Exactly. Before we were married."

Maeve's face made a sea change. "Is it over that, then?"

"We think so."

"That certainly makes more sense than the poor policeman."

"Only myself and Nahum Attwater are left of the group now," Trent said.

"And Nahum was conspicuous by his absence," said his wife. She snapped her fingers. "And that man in the fog had Nahum's limp."

"Or feigned it," John interjected.

"Veronica told the inspector about it," Maeve said. "Nahum Attwater. It's difficult for me to imagine he'd be involved in this."

"For me as well." Trent cinched in his robe sash. "We're going down to Brighton tomorrow, to look for him."

"Really? Does your schedule permit?"

"I'll make it," Trent replied.

Maeve turned back toward the stairs. "I hope you or *someone* resolves this quickly. It's sure to cast a pall on the charity ball, one way or the other." She glanced at the grandmother clock. "It's twelve-forty. Are you coming to bed?"

Trent rolled his eyes at John. "Yes, dear."

When Mrs. Godwin had disappeared, John said in a low voice. "You didn't mention Lionel Attwater to her."

"You're right. That was on purpose. Maeve has been known to let slip things I've spoken to her in strict confidence. That group of hers are like fishwives. If I mentioned Lionel, it could be all over London by tomorrow night. The little hooligan might slip clean away."

"I see."

Trent yawned. "Well, I think I can finally sleep. What say we return to the comfort of our beds?"

WHEN JOHN ENTERED his room, it was empty. He climbed back under the covers, wondering if the determined Veronica would pay another visit. While he waited, sleep ambushed him.

SEVEN

Monday, October 23, 1905

TRENT HAD SLEPT FOR almost an hour after boarding an early train to Brighton. John had his eyes closed and rested in a semiconscious twilight until the morning light grew bright enough to pierce his eyelids. Between periodic rises and falls of his heavy lids, he viewed with mild interest the passing countryside. His view was momentarily interrupted by the foundation of a bridge.

"Ninety-nine bridges and five tunnels," Trent remarked in an offhand manner, with no preamble. "This was one of the earliest railroads in England, and quite an engineering feat for its time."

"Do you travel down to Brighton often?" John asked.

"Not especially. I know it well because my specialty in historic research is the southern coast of England. Cornwall to Canterbury, as it were. That's how I happened to join the Sceptred Isle Club, actually."

He was glad Trent had finally decided to talk. Ever since hearing Maeve's and Veronica's views on women's liberation and other liberal subjects, John had wanted to probe the master of the house for his thoughts. Although he desired to learn more about the subjects, he mainly wanted to know how divergent the reputed conservative's views were from those of his women. If they were quite different, he was curious to learn what, then, held the family together. He decided to test his host's willingness to change the subject.

"I was chewin' on what Miss Veronica said about women's rights in England," John began. "I wondered what you thought."

Trent uttered a little moan. "Oh, please. Not that. My mind is too agitated by all this violence. I'd much rather speak about something with no opinions. Have you no interest in our coastal history?"

"I do indeed," John relented, believing he had the first part of his answer.

Trent was quiet for a few moments. Then he caught a quick breath and said, "Do you know a Dr. Russell?"

The question went through Le Brun like scalding coffee. He wondered if Trent had suddenly decided to change subjects himself and how he knew of John's relationship to the fugitive from Jekyl Island.

"I should say 'Do you know *of* a Dr. Russell,'" Trent corrected. "He's famous all over Europe."

"Famous for what?" John evaded.

Trent smiled and blinked several times. "Therein lies the tale. For centuries, Brighton was just a little fishing village. Always one storm away from extinction. Then, around 1750, a book was published that turned the town around. Its subject was the excellent effect that sea water produces on human glands, both if drunk and bathed in. The author was a Dr. Richard Russell."

"Richard Russell," John repeated, trusting that this coincidence of professions and last names was unknown by his companion.

Trent reached into his trouser pocket and produced a multipurpose pocketknife. He flipped open the file and began grooming his nails, which, John noticed, shone as if they had been polished. "He practiced in Lewes. Just over those hills to our left. He sent his patients nine miles to Brighton. The town picked right up on the opportunity. Began building what they called chariots. Looked like gypsy wagons that they would have horses push into the water, so the customers wouldn't have to wade out against the waves. Even had professional dunkers. The book was published in other languages, and suddenly people from the continent were paying pilgrimages to Brighton, not willing to bathe anywhere but where Dr. Russell had produced his miraculous cures."

"I've read that Brighton became a second seat of royalty for a time," John said. "I suppose that's the reason."

"It did become a second seat. The Regent to the throne, George IV, loathed London royal life and carved out his own principality in Brighton. He and the Dukes of Gloucester, York, and Cumberland. I'm not sure they bathed, though. Middle and upper class from all over England were drawn to such powerful magnets. By that time there were two inns in operation: the Old Ship and the Castle. Within a few years, however, the beachfront was transformed. And it went right on transforming.

"The third impetus was the invention taking us to Brighton right now. Before the train, the journey was hard and expensive. Especially in the famous muds of Sussex. Suddenly, however, Brighton was within the access of all but the poorest." He patted the seat beside him. "Quite a democratizing invention."

"The train made my hometown of Brunswick as well," John said.

"I can understand. And there's another coincidence. The

east side of Brighton is called Lewes Town, and the right side is called Brunswick Town."

"I should feel right at home then," John said.

JOHN DID NOT FEEL at all at home. Brighton dwarfed Brunswick. He had pictured something intimate and homely, with narrow lanes alternating garden plots and small cottages. Instead, it was a good-sized city. Trent informed him that it had almost one hundred thousand residents and was swelled with one hundred thousand visitors in the high season, which had just begun the week before. As Geoffrey had done in London, Trent secured an open-topped landau and arranged for a circuitous route to Nahum Attwater's hotel, showing John some of Brighton's highlights. He was particularly struck by the many rows of identical houses. Blocks of the city displayed a pleasing uniformity such as John had never seen in the States. The prevailing style was Regency, which created a distinct grandeur. Some were in brick, but many were faced in Roman cement, which gave the illusion of having been fashioned in granite or marble. Many had verandas with iron trellis work projecting from the upper floors and multicolored awnings made of zinc. The effect reminded John of New Orleans. The monotony of the city's inner streets was broken by squares or circuses with meticulously cared-for lawns, shrubs, and flower beds. John noted, however, that iron fences with locked gates reserved enjoyment for eyes only. His sharp eyes also noted that behind the many rows of beautiful houses squatted squalid shacks. In this regard, the city was like London; the dwelling places of those who served were not far from their masters.

The carriage headed east for several blocks and then due south, so that eventually they came upon the broad road running parallel with the sea. They turned west and passed an architectural extravaganza such as John had never seen, a huge building of towers, minarets, fretwork, latticing, domes, and window shapes that John knew to be Asian.

"This is Prince George's Royal Pavilion," Godwin announced. "Started as a stable and grew into a palace. The façade wasn't done as Indian to begin either. That happened along the way. And much of the interior is Chinese. The hodgepodge of an empire. Like many of our royalty, I'm afraid it's fallen on hard times." John noted that it did indeed require repairs and paint.

"I must spend some time down here," John said. Beyond the Pavilion, he could see pile upon pile of sea-facing hotels and grand residences, such as he had only seen before in photographs of the French Riviera. It was almost enough to draw his attention from the solution of the murders. "I've promised myself that I will only spend two days on this case."

"So you said," Trent remarked, with a slight smile and half-lowered lids.

THE REDBRICK METROPOLE HOTEL, a recent addition to the city, lay in the heart of the elite district of Brighton. When John and Trent entered it, business was brisk. Neither staff nor guest attention lingered on them. They were just two more well-dressed gentlemen moving among the columns and the potted palms of the enormous vestibule. Trent strode up to the main desk and asked to see the manager, who was referred to as Mr. Nye.

"We understand that Nahum Attwater is staying at your establishment," Trent said to the crisply-dressed manager, who had appeared from an oak door with the light-footed élan of a matinee idol making a first entrance on the stage.

"I'm afraid we do not divulge information about our guests," Nye replied in clipped, cool tones.

From the man's supercilious look, John had anticipated the answer. His hand was already in his coat pocket before

Nye finished speaking. He produced the official document from Scotland Yard and opened it with a sharp snap of his wrist. It had the desired effect. The manager's eyebrows crept perceptibly higher with each sentence read.

"Yes, sir. Mr. Attwater has been a guest on several occasions, for both business and pleasure. I do believe he's with us now." Mr. Nye consulted the guest book. "I'm correct."

Another staff member who had been hovering and eavesdropping excused himself and drew Nye aside, speaking to him in low tones. Nye returned to the desk.

"I am told that Mr. Attwater arrived on Friday afternoon. He dined with us Saturday morning. Since then, he has not been seen. For the past two nights, his bed has not been slept in, although his belongings are still in the room."

"Might we see the room?"

Nye offered his widest smile. "I'm afraid that's impossible, sir. Not without Mr. Attwater's permission. The privacy of our guests supersedes even a letter such as you possess. If you obtain a document to search from a local magis—"

"That's all right." John had been folding his letter while the man spoke and returned it to his pocket. "We'll take your word on the condition of the room. Let's go, Mr. Godwin."

Godwin followed Le Brun without demur down an interior hallway that led out the side of the building. When they came to a staircase, John turned and began to climb.

"I suppose you aren't taking their word after all," Trent said, falling in behind.

"No, indeed."

"How do you know what room is his?"

"A simple matter of readin' upside down. The room number was recorded next to the name."

John stopped in front of Room 205. "If you'll act as lookout, this shouldn't take but a moment," he told his companion. He reached into his trouser pocket and produced a ring of keys.

He selected one, inserted it into the door lock, and made a few deft manipulations. The door opened. John entered.

"That was an amazing display," Trent remarked. "I'm glad I have nothing hidden behind doors at home."

"I would never insult a host in such a manner," John replied.

"Even one suspected of murder?"

"Indeed. Very nice room," John observed. "Spacious and clean. Good view. Wedgewood bowls. Thick towels."

As the manager had divulged, the bed was made and undisturbed. Attwater had his toiletries neatly laid out. A suit, shirt, and tie hung in the armoire. The amount of clothing there and in the drawers indicated that the businessman did not intend to stay long.

"Two things are not here," John said.

Trent stood just inside the door, out of the way of the ex-lawman's search. "What?"

"Shoes and personal papers."

"He could think like me," Trent suggested. "When I'm gone from home, unless the weather is particularly foul, I take only the shoes I wear. Saves a great deal of weight."

"But he must have had documents concernin' his reason for bein' in Brighton," John said. "In fact, I would expect that he had an attaché case or somethin' on that order."

"You're right. He was here on important business."

John picked up a folded copy of the Friday edition of the *London Times* that lay on the bedside table. "Doesn't look like he got too far into his day here on Saturday. Perhaps he hightailed it back to London, to carry off a mass murder."

"I don't believe it," Trent declared.

"And likewise was not here on Sunday but perhaps fixin' to finish off the one man he had missed," John added, fixing his gaze on the lawyer. "Every man has his secrets. Perhaps Mr. Attwater's were far darker than you could have guessed." For this, Trent had no retort. John got down on his knees and looked under the bed. "Just once in this investigation, I'd like to have one of those Sherlock Holmes-type clues peekin' out from somewhere," he complained. He groaned slightly as he stood and looked down at his trouser knees. "Remarkable. No dust or sand on the carpet. In a seaside town! Let's go back down and demand more information."

NYE WAS AGAIN SUMMONED. Once again, he erected his insincere smile.

"I want to see a summary of Mr. Attwater's charges, please," said John.

"I'm afraid—"

"That's the third time you've said you were afraid, Mr. Nye," John broke in, "and I'm glad of it. You can hear that I'm not from around these parts. So you'll pardon me if I'm not as polite as y'all. Did you not read in the letter I handed you a few minutes ago that this has to do with the Sceptred Isle Club murders? Surely, Brighton is close enough to London that you have heard of this infamy? You can save yourself and your hotel a passel of trouble if you'll just give me the little I require. Otherwise, I'll get on the telephone and talk with Chief Inspector Tibbles of Scotland Yard, and he will call your city's chief inspector, and *he* will come over here all annoyed and order you to do whatever I ask, and out of pure spite I will take up your entire day askin' for every kind of picayune minutia. Have I made my foreign self clear enough?"

The manager's head bobbed back and forth from the combination of unaccustomed direct attack and Deep South English. He looked as if he were about to be overcome by apoplexy. As John finished, he drew himself up and pursed his lips. "What is it that you want, specifically?"

"I want his account to date, and while I look it over you can inquire as to what any of your staff might have seen of Mr. Attwater on Saturday and Sunday. Particularly of anyone with whom he consorted. This would include women of easy virtue. I assure you I am not here to sit in judgment on the gentleman's moral character, but I do need to know as much about his activities in Brighton as I possibly can."

"Yes, sir," the manager said.

"Thank you." John pivoted, hesitated, and returned to the desk. "I really do like your hotel. I want to return to Brighton in a few days as a tourist, and I might could want to stay here."

"We'll see what we can do," Nye said, through his plaster-cast smile.

"I don't know what's surprised me more this morning . . . your amazing ring of keys or your forceful style," said Trent when the manager had walked out of earshot. "This is high season in Brighton. Your chance of getting a room in this hotel was unlikely. Now it's nil."

"You're probably right."

"Was this your usual manner in your hometown?"

"Rarely. Most people already knew my personality and that I'd get what I wanted, one way or another. Is that the usual manner of your service class?"

Trent laughed. "Often as not."

A minute later, John and Trent were studying Attwater's running bill. The last item recorded was breakfast on Saturday morning. John led the way to the dining room. He found the maître d'. The tall, barrel-chested man moved like he had recently been starched.

"Do you know a Mr. Nahum Attwater?" John asked.

"No, sir."

"Accordin' to his bill, he ate breakfast with you this past Saturday."

"If you say so, sir."

"Orange slices. Cherry crépes. Coffee."

"That had to be Saturday or the previous Wednesday," the man replied.

"Why is that?"

"For one thing, we only serve certain dishes when fresh ingredients are available. Cherries have not been good for some time previous to last week. For another, we alternate our menu. Our guests usually stay a week, so we try not to serve any dish more often than twice in seven days. I know we served cherry crépes this past Saturday and the previous Wednesday."

A twinkle lit John's eye. "You certainly know your business. I might just return and sample those cherry crépes."

"Tomorrow, sir."

"I do so love British precision," John quipped as he and Trent left the dining room.

The running bill indicated that Attwater had apparently not dined in the hotel on Friday night. He had had his shoes shined that evening, however. He had also sent a telegram.

"Can we get a copy of the telegram?" Trent asked.

John shook his head. "If we need that, Scotland Yard will have to ask directly. I've had run-ins with telegraph companies before. It's like tryin' to wrestle a fish out of an alligator's mouth."

ON THE CARRIAGE RIDE back to Brighton's train station, John thought about Veronica. She had come into his thoughts several times on the train as well. When he was a young man, his father had told him, "If you can count a lifetime's true friends on one hand and a great love on one finger, you should consider yourself lucky." John had had both, yet he did not consider himself lucky regarding love. He had when he had married Claire. He knew she was more than he deserved, because she was a better person than he and had worked so much harder at the relationship. She had seen through his gruff and contrary exterior and his profound bitterness after the lost war, had stuck with him to the point when she knew he feared losing her, then demanded little by little that he sand the rough edges, work on his temper, look for the good side of people, give a damn what others thought. What had hooked him in the first place and held them together through the tough early going was their great passion for each other. The pure bliss defied John's ability to describe it. In fact, the dazzle of it lasted far longer than the ever-skeptical Le Brun had expected. As it inevitably faded, it was replaced by a love that only time, sharing, caring, and compromise could create. He had anticipated another burst of passion in the birth of his first child. And then they were both gone to yellow fever. For a long time after, it had been easy to hide out on Jekyll Island (which was its spelling before the club came) and mourn in peace. But by the time he left the island and decided he was owed another blinding passion as payment for his losses, he had grown older. Even though he had been made a much better man by his wife, he no longer had youth and promise to attract the slim and supple young women's attention. There had been three older, experienced women who had shared John's bed over the past fifteen years, but each had had divided affections, using him as he did them. All three relationships were social contracts, understandings that followed long periods of familiarity and far too calculated to aspire to wild passion. Nothing like Veronica had ever happened to him. It was insane. The stuff of fantasy. Certainly nothing that could last. But when it came to pure passion, he could not imagine anything more stirring.

Trent did not believe that a determined and dogged ex-lawman such as John Le Brun would give up on a case after two days. But Trent did not know that the only greater passion for the American than pursuing justice had literally climbed into his bed. John resolved to work like a demon on the murders, right up until late Monday evening. The next day, he would pick up his new formal wear from Harrods and, if Miss Veronica was still serious in pursuing an affair, would move himself into a swank London hotel and let her do with him whatever she wished. He did not expect the murders' resolution to extend into Tuesday. While they had waited for the train at Victoria Station, John had asked Trent a few questions about his friend, Attwater. It seemed that, in spite of his wastrel ways, the son Lionel had been supported through three years of college. Now, according to Trent, he was on the payroll but not earning his keep. Both Nahum Attwater's daughters had been married within the past three years. Trent had guessed the weddings each cost about two thousand pounds, with substantial dowries added on. Perhaps the warehouse business was even harder than Trent imagined. All told, Attwater could easily have found himself needing thirty thousand pounds within a short period of time, to prevent his little empire from collapsing. John knew that, just as in affairs of the heart the wife is the last to know, with affairs of business, professional associates seldom had warnings when their seemingly secure friend went bankrupt. A man who had known nothing but wealth and comfort all his life might indeed be driven to murder at the prospect of poverty. The answer lay in the tontine and Nahum Attwater's financial needs, John felt, and the sooner he could help prove it, the sooner he could put himself back in Veronica's way.

"What?" Trent asked.

"I didn't say anything," John replied.

"Yes, you did. You said 'Yep' like you'd just made up your mind."

"Oh, I decided to come down here again for sure," John lied.

"Better have a room engaged first," warned the lawyer. "You could be roaming the streets this time of year."

"I will." John rose slightly from his seat. "Driver, let us out here!"

John had spotted a commercial real estate office, just a block south of the Italianate front of the train station. By a degree of luck, it was the firm which Nahum Attwater had engaged to conclude his purchase of a warehouse. The contract had been signed late Friday afternoon, the firm's owner told them after reading John's official letter. He gave them directions to the place which, as John had surmised, could not be far from the station.

Before starting off again, the pair entered a quaint sidewalk restaurant. It was almost noon, and they each had had nothing but a buttered roll and coffee for breakfast. Trent ordered a salad Niçoise, and John echoed him. They dined under a sky filled with woolly clouds, like sheep grazing in a vast blue meadow. During the meal and afterward when they ordered from a curbside vendor hokey pokey, which was the local name for hard ice cream, Trent resumed his history of the city. People from several nationalities and all classes strolled by. Despite all the diversions, John kept the back of his brain working to solve the riddle of the murders. He had other vacation priorities.

Following lunch they walked several blocks, into a mass of commercial structures that paralleled the railroad's house tracks.

"Tell me how many warehouses Mr. Attwater owns and where they are," John said.

"He has an old one in the City that's used for non-perishables. His main one—where his offices are—is four or five miles down river in East Ham. As the steamships grew larger, the old docks couldn't accommodate them, you see. Then he has satellite warehouses in Cambridge, Northampton, Swindon, and now Brighton."

"And he has no partners?"

"No. He owns them all outright. Why?"

"We might have learned something about his finances from partners, especially if they're anxious to have their fears confirmed."

When they found the right warehouse, they saw that it was at least several decades old. Its dull brown bricks needed repointing. Farther up the tracks stood newer warehouses. John pointed them out, questioning Attwater's reasoning.

"It was the size that attracted Nahum," Trent explained. "This one also had a section for cold storage which could easily be enlarged. The original owner didn't have the capital to modernize."

They found the office door locked. After circling the building once and calling out for a watchman, they decided the place was completely unoccupied. They went to the large double front doors, which were suspended on overhead rollers. The doors were secured by a sturdy chain whose links disappeared between the two steel-sheathed doors.

"Now, don't that look peculiar," John said, cocking his head as he stared at the chain. "You take the handle on that side, and let's see how far apart we can get these doors."

Between muscle and determination, together they separated the doors some four inches. As they did, a length of the chain that had been inside dropped into the opening, exposing a good-sized padlock.

"The last person must have exited out one of the other doors," Trent hazarded.

John declined reply but rather put one eye to the space between the doors. He waited for his iris to adjust to the darkness within.

"Can you see anything?" Trent asked.

"I believe I'm lookin' at a corpse," John answered, focusing on a horizontal and completely still trouser leg and shoe at the left limit of his view.

"Let me see." Trent replaced John at the door, twisting his head to one side and then the other, attempting to wrestle the doors apart another inch. "My God! You're right. Either that or someone is injured or dead drunk. Hey, you in there! If you're hurt, move your legs!"

"How can we fetch a policeman quickly?" John asked.

"They have a booth at the station. I'll run over there." Trent started away at with a loping stride.

John considered using his tools to pick the padlock, in the remote likelihood that the man inside was only injured and in need of immediate aid. The thought of all the trouble he could get himself into in a foreign country, however, stopped him. Instead, he took himself around to the side of the building, careful to stay on the brick walkway. As he went, surveying the ground for footprints, he noted a discarded packet of chewing tobacco. He snatched it up and determined from the embedded grime that it had lain there for some time. He crumpled it up and carried it over to a metal drum that served as a refuse container. Before dropping the paper, he examined the contents of the drum. Most of it was sawdust, bits of cut lumber, and bent nails. An empty ink bottle balanced on one of the pieces of lumber. Clucking at the continued lack of clues, he took himself to the back of the building and mounted the delivery platform. His hope had been that he could crawl through the ice block delivery chute, but an expanse of heavy-gauge metal covered it and could not be budged. He descended again to the ground and continued his second perambulation of the warehouse. The sun climbing the October sky beat through the clouds with sufficient strength to make John too warm in his tweed jacket. He slipped it off.

When he rounded the cranny to the front of the warehouse, John met with a surprise. Standing beside the lawyer was not only a Brighton policeman but also Chief Inspector Tibbles.

"You are indeed serious about solving this case, Mr. Le Brun," Tibbles said in greeting.

"Good day, Chief Inspector."

"Talking with Mr. Godwin here, it seems we've both come to the same conclusion following last night's attempt on his life. And now we have a body inside the missing Mr. Attwater's warehouse?"

"Looks that way."

Tibbles strode up to the door, put his eye to it, murmured something inaudible, then gave the chain an inspection. "Mr. Godwin tells me you have a way with locks."

"Skills of my old profession," said John.

"We'd be obliged if you gave us a demonstration." Tibbles stepped back.

"We both walked up to the station booth at the same moment," Trent told John as the ex-sheriff took out his ring of keys and lock-picking tools.

"Perhaps luck is with us today," John replied, smiling at the expectant group. He turned to the lock and had it off within less than a minute. Tibbles and the policeman, who Tibbles had introduced as Patrolman Gilbert, yanked the doors back, allowing sunlight to wash across the dusty and distressed floor planking.

Tibbles entered first, swinging his head from side to side, advancing one slow step after the other. John followed, with Trent coming directly behind him. The patrolman waited outside.

Tibbles paused, looking straight down. He had ventured some ten feet into the warehouse. He took one step to his left and knelt, then gestured for his companions to focus on the floor. A single padlock key lay there, attached to a large steel ring. Tibbles handed the key to Le Brun, who returned to the padlock and fitted it with no trouble. At the same time, the Scotland Yard inspector and the lawyer continued to advance on the body.

Trent took in a large breath and exhaled forcefully. "That's Nahum Attwater."

John approached the body. Nahum Attwater looked exactly the fifty-five years Trent had reported him to be. His hair had gone halfway to gray. He was of average build, neither thin nor heavy, and, although it was difficult to judge with him supine, he looked to be about five-foot-nine. John noted the revolver just to the right of the man's right hand. He recognized the weapon as a service-type pistol of secondary quality, manufactured in large quantities in Belgium and easy to secure. A semicircle the same diameter as the muzzle of the gun had been freshly dug into the gray planking, exposing fresh wood, indicating that the gun had fallen some distance. On the gun were flecks of dried blood. Attwater's right temple had a dark bullet hole in it, with the telltale powder burn marks of a shooting at point-blank range. The head was turned to its left side, mercifully disguising the exit wound. A pool of blood had spread from under the head. Small rodent tracks in blood came and went from the area. John saw that the man's suit was a very dark charcoal, nearly black, as Veronica had said the man in the fog had worn. Also, as she had described, a bowler hat lay overturned at a distance from the man's head. John squatted near Attwater's feet and satisfied himself that one of the shoes bore the wear mark of a man who limps and favors the strong leg.

"His case is up here," Trent called out, indicating the top of a landing.

"Don't touch it," Tibbles said. He was, at that moment, kneeling on the corpse's left side and lifting the head. "Oh, dear. Some of the local beasties have been making a meal of him already." With difficulty, he bent open the fingers of the corpse's left hand. "Hello." He held up a torn piece of white paper, read it, and said, "Here's a neat ribbon to tie it together."

"A confession?" John asked.

Tibbles handed him the paper. "Indeed."

The quality of the paper indicated expensive stationery. The piece was approximately one-third of a sheet, neatly ripped as if the paper had been folded back and forth many times before tearing. John held it up to the light and saw the watermark, indicating that it had come from the bottom third. He read the words: *I am sorry. Please forgive me. Nahum Attwater.*

"Mighty brief confession," John said.

Tibbles stood. "Looks like he was more specific and then decided to tear off that part and just leave the last words."

"Then where's the other piece?" John asked.

"Could be anywhere. We'll look for it."

John rocked back and forth on his heels. "I think if he had

written more on the top of the paper, he'd have changed his mind at the last second. Otherwise, he would have used a whole fresh sheet. Should be in here somewhere."

"Perhaps, but if he took the trouble to tear it off, he obviously didn't want it read. He probably set it on fire. At most, we'll find a cinder." Tibbles held out his hand for the paper. When he had it, he went to Attwater's attaché case, opened it, and began sifting through the contents. It contained various documents, including the paperwork for the warehouse, the man's personal calendar, his contact book, several pieces of correspondence, a printed train schedule, and a few blank sheets of his stationery. While Tibbles examined the schedule, John picked up one of the pieces of expensive blank paper and took it into the sunlight.

Tibbles uttered a noise that was half laugh and half exclamation of triumph. "He's got the late weekend trains from London to Brighton circled."

"This is the same as the note's written on," John verified to the inspector.

"With his embossed letterhead on the top. Neater all the time," crowed Tibbles.

"That lets Officer Buttons off the hook," John remarked, presenting the barb with a poker face.

"He was released last evening," Tibbles reported. He returned his attention to the note. "An inquiry will no doubt reveal Attwater had a pressing need for ready money. He saw the tontine as the obvious solution."

John glanced at Trent.

"I told him on the way over here," Godwin explained.

Tibbles nodded. "I came down here without that information, but I'm very glad to have it now. He uses his business trip to Brighton as the excuse to be out of town during the Sceptred Isle Club massacre. The truth is he's not more than two hours from the club, but 'away' is a mental thing as well as a physical one.

He appears unexpectedly at the back door on Saturday night, and since he's a member of the gambling group the butler lets him in with no reservation. He immediately shoots everyone in the room and snatches up the money, to replace that which he has previously hidden in the local policeman's backyard, in order to frame him for the crime. To his horror, Trent is not in the gambling room as expected. All his perfectly-laid plans begin to unravel. He had intended to catch the next train to Brighton, but he lingers in London, wondering what to do. Naturally, he can't go home, so he takes lodging in some nondescript hole on the edge of town. He doesn't know if the money hidden under the birdbath has been discovered yet, and, with this turn of events, he hopes not. Even if the policeman has been arrested, he must take the chance to kill Mr. Godwin. There is no other way to collect on the tontine."

Tibbles had begun to walk as he assembled the facts. When he reached the corpse's feet, he made a smart about-face and headed back toward the attaché case. "As fate would have it, on Sunday an early-evening fog sets in. Attwater certainly knows Mr. Godwin's penchant for staring out the parlor window at that time. He takes himself to Green Street, advances in the fog, and fires. Mr. Godwin falls so quickly that he must assume he's succeeded in the assassination. Miss Godwin happens by in a cab and is later able to describe his clothing, hat, and limp. Acting by revised plan, he hurries to Victoria Station and catches the next train to Brighton, to establish his alibi. But, on the way, he realizes the mushrooming problems. He may have recognized Miss Godwin in the cab and guessed that she recognized him. The birdbath idea might have just been too clever, failing to be discovered. The guilt may not have been focused on the policeman. Worst of all, he had not returned to Brighton on Saturday. Therefore, his bed was not slept in. He has no alibi, as he had once so carefully planned. Perhaps remorse sets in. Certainly he feels a mortal dread of being cast into prison with the scum of London. The nearest place from Brighton Station where he can be sure to be alone is his warehouse. He comes over here, jots down his confession—"

"We still haven't found the rest of that paper," John pointed out. Tibbles regarded him with a mixture of annoyance and disdain. "Perhaps he had used the top of it for something else earlier in the day. I'll admit it is slightly vexing, but with all the rest we have, I think we can let it go. At any rate, he locks himself inside here, needing to pull the padlock in to do so. He drops the key on the floor, takes a few steps back, and blows his brains out. Stood facing the center of the warehouse, since the spray of blood and brains are over there." He pointed above Attwater's head. "Made a quarter turn as he fell, appropriate to the position of the body. Gun no doubt leapt from his loosening grip. It hit the floor there." He picked up the revolver and cracked open the six-chambered cylinder. "Two empty casings: one shot at Trent last night; one at himself."

Tibbles turned his palms up, inviting Le Brun to contradict him. John shrugged. "What was the caliber of the slugs from the gamblin' room?"

"Eleven millimeter. Same as this one," said Tibbles.

"Shouldn't you have picked up that weapon with a pen or somethin' and had it dusted for fingerprints?"

Tibbles laughed. "Every policeman around the world is obsessed with fingerprints since Galton proposed them for identification. I hardly think we need go through that trouble inside a locked warehouse, with the gun right beside the man. I'm assuming you read about our Scotland Yard inspector teaching American law officers the method last year at the St. Louis World's Fair."

"No. I read about the method years ago, long before your Mr. Galton and Sir Edward Henry became famous. An Argentinian lawman named Juan Vucetich used fingerprints to discover a children's murderer way back in 1891."

"Really?" Tibbles said, clearly not believing the American.

"Yes. Really. I would have had that gun *and* the letter dusted before puttin' my paws on them, but you know best. Did you dust the gamblin' room at the Sceptred Isle Club?"

Tibbles' eyes narrowed and his chin elevated. "We did. The drawer and the empty billfold. We found the butler's prints on the drawer and Mr. Wilbye's on the billfold. No others. We suspected the killer wore gloves. Mr. Attwater here didn't need to, though. He would have known that Wilbye wrapped his billfold in his handkerchief. He certainly could have drawn that out first, then wrapped the cloth around his hand and opened the drawer. I fear you're assuming we're the bumbling morons at Scotland Yard that Conan Doyle needs us to be for his stories, Mr. Le Brun. In point of fact, I would have been on the same train this morning as you two, working with fewer facts than you had, had Sir Arthur not detained me for more than twenty minutes on the telephone arguing that Mr. Trent is the real murderer."

"The ruddy bastard!" Trent exclaimed. "I shall have a word with him when next I see him."

Tibbles stared at Le Brun as he pocketed the revolver and note. "So, we didn't need the help of our American cousin after all."

"I never doubted you did," John replied. "I stuck my oar in because I was literally around the corner from the murders and was directly asked to help. I fully intended to write up tonight what I had found and continue my vacation."

"Two days only. So you said in my office," Tibbles remembered. He walked over to Le Brun and gave him a patronizing pat on the back. "If you'd like, we could wire a report to your hometown, praising you for your part in the case. Puff it up a bit for your sake."

"Thanks, but that won't be necessary. You may have recalled the two days promised, but you forgot I'm retired."

Tibbles removed his hand. "It's time to fetch the coroner and my counterpart in Brighton. Will you two stand guard over the body until I return?"

Trent glanced at his watch. "I really would like to get to my office."

"I have nothin' special to do," John volunteered. "There's no reason for more than one of us to stay here. You can both attend to business."

"Thanks ever so much, John," said Godwin.

John nodded. "I'll take the rest of the afternoon sight-seein', and see you at your house tonight."

"Very good indeed." He did not look or sound as positive as his words. Ever since laying eyes on his former gambling companion, Godwin had become as pale as the local chalk cliffs. For the past several minutes, he had been sitting on the steps next to Attwater's case, staring blindly out at the world beyond the warehouse. The look in his eyes was similar to that John had seen on many of the men in the Civil War, after facing prolonged cannon fire and lines of blazing muskets. John was sure that if Conan Doyle had been able to look at the lawyer at this moment, the author would no longer suspect Trent.

"If you can manage it, you should contact Mr. Attwater's house and his daughters," John suggested to Trent. He turned to Tibbles. "I have a physician friend at University College Hospital. If we can have the body delivered there, I can promise delicate treatment."

Tibbles shrugged. "One hospital is as good as another to me. Certainly, *he* won't complain." He turned and strode purposefully out of the warehouse, gesturing for the policeman to accompany him.

Trent rose on wobbly legs. He used the railing to work his way down the steps. "So, it was him after all. I shall never trust a friend so innocently again. I'll be off then."

"Take care," John wished.

"I wouldn't have believed it unless I saw it with my own eyes," Trent said, before he took one last glance at Attwater. He shook his head slightly and followed after the two officers.

John waited until the three men were out of sight. "I still don't believe it," he said, to the corpse. He knelt and put his hand to the corpse's neck, feeling its temperature. He lifted the closed eyelids, studying the degree of wetness of the eyeballs. He lifted the left hand, again felt its temperature, then tugged on the fingers, noting the degree of rigor mortis. He worked the head to the right, observing the exit wound. He noted with distaste the numerous rodent bites taken out of the corpse's face. He moved around to the right hand, lifted it and sniffed in vain for powder residue. He likewise found no stains of blood on the right hand or shirt sleeve.

"Good thing Robert Louis Stevenson wasn't a detective," he muttered to himself. "Dead men *do* tell tales."

Le Brun reclosed the corpse's eyelids. He bent and sniffed around the clothing. He examined the shoes and how the laces were tied. Then he felt inside the man's jacket pocket and withdrew his billfold. He counted the money. He found two ten-pound notes. It was not enough for a man of Attwater's means to be carrying. He replaced the billfold. In the rest of the pockets he found the hotel room key, a handkerchief, his personal keys, and a few coins. He had hoped to find some evidence of either weekend trip to London better than a marked-up schedule, but he hoped in vain.

The sound of a rat scurrying across the floor above caught John's attention. He ascended the steps to the main part of the warehouse. It had been well cleaned out, in anticipation of sale. Several pallets and empty packing crates stood in one corner. He worked his way back to the cold storage section. He investigated the chute, finding the pair of pins that held the door in place so that it could not be lifted from the outside. He put his hand to the door, then let it drift down along the metal loading surface. It was damp and cold. Not far from the chute lay a good-sized galvanized horse trough. It looked spanking new. He felt this as well. It, too, was wet, as was the planking beneath and around it. Just beyond it lay a ladder leading to a loft area. John ascended. Among several rusty ice hooks and a box of rusted hinges, he also found an ice pick. Unlike the hooks and hinges, however, the pick looked as if it had been purchased the day before. The pick lay on a rubberized tarp, neatly folded. He unfolded the material and ran his hands over it. The tarp appeared just as fresh as the trough and pick had. The three items stood out in the dusty and well-worn warehouse like modern bathroom fixtures in a Lambeth shanty. He flicked his fingers above his head and let the drops of the water fall onto the crown of his head.

"Well, hallelujah!" John exalted as he slicked back his hair. "Now it's rainin' clues!"

John nosed around the rest of the building, but with greater and greater speed. When he had covered the last cranny, he rushed outside and rounded the corner to the metal refuse drum. He snatched the empty ink bottle out of the trash and trotted back inside the building. His search had informed him of the nearest spigot. He unstopped the ink bottle and ran water into it until it was clean of all but the most stubborn residue. Then he hurried to the corpse and, using an old paint stirrer he had hunted up, scooped much of the blood that had not dried into the bottle. He shoved the rubber stopper back into its neck and returned to the spigot to wash off the stirrer. He had just laid it down where he found it when Tibbles returned with five men in tow.

"He didn't attempt to flee from justice?" Tibbles said to John, smiling at his own attempt at humor.

John slipped the ink bottle slowly into his back pocket. "No. He's been a model corpse." John's reply made two of the men behind Tibbles laugh out loud. The chief inspector turned to deliver a baleful look. As he did, he spotted several gawkers who had followed the group to the warehouse. "Sergeant, see that those people disperse!" When he saw that the officer was moving, he looked again at John.

"We'll take it from here, Mr. Le Brun. Thanks for your good offices, and enjoy Brighton, won't you?"

"Thank you, Chief Inspector Tibbles," John said. "Oh, which of you is the coroner?"

"I am," said the ridiculously happy-looking man with the bright red cravat.

"The family would like the body sent up to University College Hospital in London when you're through with it."

"Have them remit the transport costs to this address, and we'll be pleased to," replied the man, handing John a card.

Satisfied, John walked into the afternoon. He saw that the men had arrived in two motorized trucks. One had a large black compartment in the back, looking like a cross between a lock-up wagon and a hearse. He caught up with the sergeant, who was having a rough time shooing the several onlookers. John recognized them as the sort of ne'er-do-wells that preyed upon resort towns, begging, pickpocketing, and running street scams on the unsuspecting.

"Hey, I saw what you did to that lady!" John accused, walking toward the crowd and focusing on no one in particular. Their leader quickly led his pack away.

"What do you see 'em do, sir?" the sergeant asked.

"Nothing. But every mother's son of them is guilty of somethin.'"

The sergeant nodded and gave his savior a congratulatory thumbs-up.

"Can you direct me to the nearest icehouse?" John asked.

"My pleasure, sir. This way's north. Three blocks north and two west."

"Obliged."

SEEING THE SIGN for Seaforth's Ice House, John patted his pocket. If he had been Tibbles and sure the case had been solved, the first thing he would have done would have been to relieve the American of his Scotland Yard letter. John figured the inspector was so excited about solving the crime of the decade that he wouldn't think of it for days. Days was more than John needed. He revised his schedule and determined he would be done with the case by late afternoon on the morrow. That timetable, however, required full steam ahead.

Le Brun entered the icehouse with a casual stride, watching burly men using large ice tongs to transfer fifty-pound blocks to waiting wagons. Behind them, inside a two-story insulated room, lay the dwindling remains of hundreds of hours of sawing in the frozen ponds and rivers of the previous winter. The place smelled of sawdust and rotting wood.

"Can I help you?" a wrinkled old man asked, approaching with a slow, rolling gait.

"I'd like to speak with the owner," said John.

"I'm him. Sam Seaforth."

John produced his letter and unfolded it.

"I don't have my spectacles," Mr. Seaforth said, staring at the paper. John suspected he was not a skilled reader and was cowed by the several single-spaced, typed paragraphs.

"It says that I am deputized by Scotland Yard to investigate the murders committed at the Sceptred Isle Club up in London."

The man whistled. "You don't say."

John pointed to the embossed seal at the top of the page. "This is Scotland Yard's official seal."

Seaforth turned toward the main part of the icehouse. "Hey, Simon!" he bellowed. "C'mere!"

In a few moments, a younger version of the owner appeared. He was not more than five-foot-seven, and at that two inches taller than his father, but he was built like a barrel on stilts, with massive arms starting from his great chest. As he walked with a gait similar to his father and his long arms swinging, it produced a simian effect. His slack-jawed expression did nothing to mitigate the look. The phrase *Simple Simon* popped into John's head.

"This here's my son, Simon," Seaforth said needlessly. "Show him your letter."

Simon apparently had less skill at reading than his father. He merely stared at the seal.

"This fellow's helping investigate those club murders up in London."

"G'won!" said Simon. "So why are ya down in Brighton?"

"The scent leads here," John said, giving his voice a suspenseful sound and folding up his letter. "I'm sure you know the warehouse down on the sidin' tracks, the old brown brick one that was just sold."

"I should say so," Simon exclaimed. "I just took 'em a test delivery."

"Who is 'them?' " John asked.

Simon chuckled. "Don't actually know but one. We got a letter from London about a week ago. Let me fetch it." When he returned, he held a folded and dirt-stained piece of quality stationery with a small bill-spike hole through the middle. He handed it over.

John examined the paper. It looked like it had come from Nahum Attwater's attaché case; the shade of white and the embossed font appeared identical. With his habitual thoroughness, however, John held the paper up to the light and looked at the watermark. He blinked in surprise. The watermark was different. He knew that that alone was conclusive of nothing. A man who conducted the volume of business that Attwater no doubt did must have run through a ream of letterhead in short order. The fact that this paper was sent only a few days earlier and didn't match the one in the supposed suicide's hand, however, was suspicious.

John read. This piece had been typed on. It indicated that Mr. Nahum Attwater would take possession of the specific warehouse on Friday afternoon and that he wished a test load of four hundred pounds of ice to be delivered on Saturday afternoon, no earlier than 3:00 P.M. There would be an employee of Attwater's there, it went on, to supervise. This employee would pay the charge.

"And did you make the delivery as ordered?" John asked.

"Three on the dot," Simon attested. "And the fellow was standing right there on the platform, waiting for me."

"What did he look like?"

Simon's eyes narrowed as he focused on the past. "Tall. Maybe six foot. Thin. I'd guess eleven stone. Late twenties? Certainly not much older than thirty. Curly red-brown hair, starting to thin. Good looking. Irish."

"Irish from Ireland?" John asked.

"No, a Southie."

"From the south side of the Thames," the father interpreted.

"Lambeth or Southwark," John expanded.

"You live in London?" asked the father.

"No. Just visitin'."

"You know a good bit for a foreigner," the old man observed, his chill tone warming. "Care for a spot of tea? I've got some brewing."

"That would be nice," John allowed. They walked the short distance into Seaforth's office, where a teapot whistled atop the Franklin-style stove. The office was crowded with papers and dusty around the edges, but the desk was neat in the middle, and a small vase held a fresh rosebud.

"How do you know the difference between an Irishman from Ireland and one born in London?" John asked as he sat.

"Accent and sayings," Simon supplied. "We get tons of them here in Brighton during the high season, doing the donkey work. They migrate down and then drift back."

"One lump or two?" the firm's patriarch asked.

"Two, thanks." John noted the lack of milk or cream and resigned himself to just sugar. He returned his attention to the son.

"Any tattoos?"

"None as I could see."

"How was he dressed?"

"Right proper for his job. Suit. Not high class, mind you, but better than the normal boyos." Simon slapped at the side of his head. "How could I forget? He had a scar. Big as life on the left side of his forehead. An old scar. T'was white."

"Like a knife wound?" John suggested.

"No. Thicker. Like a big U. Starting just under his hairline." He traced the shape on his own forehead.

Sam Seaforth stopped pouring his own tea. He looked at his son with disgust. "Ya idiot! From a block."

Simon snapped his fingers. "O' course. A ship's block. Some of 'em even have iron rims."

Sam held his hand up for his son's silence and magnified Simon's comments. "You see, thousands of 'em Lambeth and Southwark lads work on the river. As lightermen, transferring the cargoes to smaller boats; as dockers; and, if they're dependable and get experience, as stevedores, loading the big ships. He's lucky he wasn't killed. Dozens of 'em are every year. They fall into the holds and break their necks; they get caught in nets and strangle; loads shift and crush 'em. And plenty get hit in the heads by blocks and tackles. I'll bet he was promoted to Inside Warehouse to keep him from pressing charges."

John sipped on the tea, the blend of which he failed to recognize and didn't like. He smiled blandly, saluting their health with the teacup and regarded the son. "So, he met you alone on Saturday, at three in the afternoon."

"That's right."

"He was on the platform waitin'."

"Right again. I personally sent the eight blocks of ice down the chute. Then, since it was a test, I asked if I could go inside and see how the thing had worked."

"And he wasn't keen on that," John said.

"You're right. He told me that if the chute hadn't worked well, there was nothing I could do. I argued that I'd had plenty of experience and could suggest improvements. You know, thought to add value so as to get a long-term contract. But he wasn't having none of it. Paid me and wanted me gone."

"What could all this possibly have to do with murders up in London?" the father asked.

"Much more than you'd believe," John replied.

"Try me."

"I'm afraid I can't."

"You done?" Sam asked, taking the teacup from John without waiting for an answer.

"Yes, thank you." John had set the typed letter down on the desk when he sat. The elder Seaforth snatched it up and made to return it to the bill spike. John touched his hand before he did. "One moment, sir." He turned to the son. "I wonder, Mr. Seaforth, if you'd mind dictating the main points of what you've just told me so I can jot them down on the back of that paper."

"Hold on," said the father. "That's one of our records. And we've given you enough free time, Mister."

John understood. He reached into his other jacket pocket for his billfold. He pulled out a five-pound note. He knew he had made the right move when both men's eyes bulged. "I believe this will more than compensate you for your record and time."

"Find him a pencil, Dad," Simon Seaforth said.

BY THE TIME JOHN arrived at the Attwater warehouse in East Ham, it was past five-thirty. His hometown, Brunswick, was a seaport as well as resort, and he was used to ships and wharves, but there was a grittiness, a hustle-bustle, and an air of desperation to the docks and warehouses of East Ham that he never saw at home. Men moved about their business with grim, head-lowered determination. The roads were congested with all manner of vehicles picking up and delivering goods, and their drivers cursed at each other as they attempted to maneuver. In the advancing evening chill, the roadbeds smoked from the piles of dropped horse manure. As John stepped from the closed carriage and came to the curb, a boy with a dustpan and broom darted from the side of a nearby building. The moment John stepped into the street to cross, the boy was in front of him, scooping the manure out of the way. This was clearly the boy's livelihood. John dug into his pocket and came out with two shillings. He had watched other business-suited men drop small copper coins on the ground for such lads, but he handed his coins over directly. The boy was effusive in his thanks.

When John stood in the shadow of the Attwater warehouse, it looked to him like a prison. A twelve-foot-high brick wall, jagged up with broken bottles cemented into its top, surrounded the dark, looming edifice. Two guards stood at the entrance. Trent Godwin had passed a remark on the ride down to Brighton about another negative aspect of owning warehouses: theft was rife. In some places, men were routinely stripped on the way out, to prevent them from hiding items down their pants legs, under their jackets in the small of their backs, and in more unmentionable places. A high wall all around and guards were the least an owner could do to keep from being pilfered out of existence. This worked to John's advantage, as he expected few if any workers made it into Attwater's warehouse without coming under their watchful eyes.

"How'd'ye do?" John said, imitating greetings he had heard over the past few days. "What time do your workers knock off?"

"Main body works eight to six," the older man answered. "We have shifts late as midnight, dependin' on when a ship arrives. You waitin' for someone?"

"Lookin' for someone, sir." John affixed his most affable smile. "An Irish lad. About six foot tall. Eleven stone. Thin.

Curly hair with some red in it, goin' thin. Good-looking young man."

The guards looked at each and shrugged. The one who did the talking said, "We've had hundreds of Irish lads workin' here. I can think of several fit that description."

"This one has an old scar on his forehead. Like so." John traced a large U on his own forehead with his forefinger.

Both men shook their heads.

"Not in my memory," said the older guard.

"And not in the warehouse up in the City neither," the younger volunteered. "I worked there two years afore comin' down 'ere." "Sorry," said the older. "You got the wrong place."

Le Brun was celebrated throughout lowland Georgia for the accuracy of his intuition. Few times in his fifteen years as sheriff had he been wrong about the nature of someone he directly questioned. He was almost certain these two men told the truth. Despite that, he said, "The sign says 'Attwater.' That's where he should be." He fished into his pocket for his precious Scotland Yard letter, opened it, and dangled it in front of the guards' noses. "I need to see the boss."

The older man shied back from the words as if they exuded poison. "Coo! Straight ahead. Up the stairs."

A TYPEWRITER GIRL USHERED Le Brun into a small office with a large desk and a Persian rug beneath it. The windows in the back of the office looked down on the warehouse courtyard. A young man in a three-piece suit sat behind the desk, his head buried in a pile of paperwork. His right hand almost touched an ashtray with the remains of more than half a dozen cigarettes. When he looked up, John saw a much-younger, animated version of Nahum Attwater's face. It was not without early evidence of hard living and hard drinking, but it was also not as dissipated as Trent had led him to expect. He looked more harried than hungover.

"Yes, sir?" the businessman asked.

"Mr. Attwater, my name is John Le Brun. I've been engaged by the Sceptred Isle Club to conduct inquiries about the murders of Saturday past."

"You're American." His statement still sounded like a question.

"I am. But I happen to be in London on vacation. I have an extensive police background."

"I see. Doesn't sound like much of a vacation."

"I'm not complainin' . . . yet." John's eyes fixed unblinkingly on the man he suspected of masterminding all the mayhem. "You were neither at your own home nor at your father's home this weekend. I believe you were in Brighton."

Lionel Attwater's brows furrowed for a second, and a question came into his eyes. "I certainly was not. I was on the opposite end of London at the time of the shootings. I can confirm that."

"You were not in Brighton any part of the weekend, to help your father conclude the purchase of another warehouse?"

Now the young man's expression turned firm. He leaned forward onto the desk and looked directly into John's eyes. "I just said 'No.'" Against his fondest wish, John's intuition was not telling him this man was lying. He felt his stomach knot. He might not after all have the case solved by Tuesday. "If you're investigating murders in London, why are you inquiring about Brighton?" Lionel Attwater asked.

If the man was not lying about his presence in Brighton, the mention of the place at least had had an effect. "Have you recently heard from Mr. Godwin?" John asked.

"Not directly, but I have," Lionel admitted, now clearly wary of his visitor.

"I was in Brighton this mornin' with him," John admitted. "We had taken the train down from London to ask your father questions concernin' the murders."

Attwater eased back into his tufted leather chair. His hand gestured in the direction of the lone chair on the opposite side of the desk. "Please close the door and take a seat." John did as asked. "I heard indirectly of my father's death, less than an hour ago. The news was telephoned by Mr. Godwin to one of my sisters," he said. "But I'd greatly appreciate hearing what happened from your lips."

John related the story detail for detail, including Chief Inspector Tibble's speculations concerning Attwater's need for money. He included Trent's suspicions on the same matter without naming the father's old friend. He related up to the point when he was left alone with Nahum Attwater's corpse and stopped there. Several times during the narration, the son shook his head vigorously.

"This is absurd. My father was a ruthless man in many ways, but he was also incapable of killing anyone. As far as his being desperate for money, that's ridiculous. It's true he had spent quite a bit in the past three or four years but never more than he could afford."

"Would you be willin' to open the business books and prove that?" John asked.

"I would. But I can't act alone. My mother would have to agree."

Le Brun's jaw came up abruptly, as if Attwater's last sentence were a sucker punch. "Your mother?"

"Certainly. She inherits the bulk of my father's estate. Why does that seem so strange to you?"

"Well, the people I've been talkin' with mention that your *sisters* were to get almost everythin' and you almost nothin'. They never spoke of your mother, so I assumed she was dead."

"These 'people' must include Mr. Godwin, my father's lawyer. So much for professional confidentiality. If my mother were dead, my sisters *would* get almost everything. However, my mother does not view me in the same dim light as did my father. There's a marked difference between mother love and father love, as you probably know. Did Trent also tell you of my father's mistress?"

John struggled to master the fusillades of shocking information coming at him. "No."

Lionel shrugged. "So, he tosses the dirt only on me. I might have known. I thought that if he talked about another woman, it might have further encouraged you to assume my mother was dead."

"No. Rest assured that he and others I've met who might have known about that were discreet."

"Almost everyone else who might have known was recently murdered," Lionel pointed out. "There's nothing like death to improve one's discretion."

Lionel's last words fetched up the memory of John's self-directed comment about dead men telling no tales, but he was not about to share any of that with the man he interviewed. Instead, he said, "When we telephoned your father's house, the servants also made no mention of your mother."

Lionel nodded. "That's because whenever he travels, she goes home to Devon, to be with my grandmother. When he's home, he demands that she be at his beck and call. Tell me what else my father's club friends have said about Nahum Attwater's black sheep son."

John's facile mind weighed the advantages and disadvantages of responding, in the same manner as he would an opponent's movement into the center of a chess board. He decided the telling would work as a goad in his favor. He repeated the supposed facts of Lionel overspending his allowance, not finishing college, habituating pubs, getting a barkeep's daughter pregnant, not showing up often to work and, when he did, coming in hung over, farming out their child, and spending huge amounts of his life dragging from one tavern to the next.

As he listened, Lionel Attwater ran his hand over his hair and around his face several times. When John had finished, he folded his hands on top of the desk with a concentrated effort.

"And yet here I sit, managing his substantial businesses," he defended.

"But lookin' like someone who'd spent the weekend paintin' the town," John observed, wanting to see where keeping the young man on the defensive would get him.

Lionel ran his tongue over his upper teeth, as if tasting the residue of a lost weekend. "Trent Godwin and I have never gotten along. For some reason, we're like oil and water. He's always expected the worst from me and ever ready to expand on any negative remark my father passed when frustrated about me. That's not to say he's lying and that I'm an angel. I do drink. And I drink too much. As far as enjoying life, I also favor the more common man. He knows better how to hold an honest conversation, tell a good joke, and punch a man who offends him in the face rather than stabbing him in the back. My father and his colleagues vociferously disapproved of my companions. Do you know why I went to university? Because my father had grand plans for me. I was to become a lawyer. Perhaps that's why Godwin dislikes me so. I despise lawyers and have never been shy about saying so. From lawyer, I was to become a politician. And from there a statesman. Another Disraeli." Lionel laughed and dipped his head in a mock apology. "My father would have chosen a different name; Disraeli was just a Jew. Do you know how much pressure those sorts of expectations place upon someone with only average scholarly assets?"

"I think I can imagine," John replied.

"I don't think you can. For a time, being a loving son, you try your damnedest to achieve. But there are already students besting you in school. You're taken to task for every shortcoming, alternately encouraged and scolded. In the end, there is only one thing you can absolutely control: failure. It took me until my third year of university to realize that. That was the only way to get him off my back. But do you know the real irony, Mr. Le Brun?"

"What's that?"

"I couldn't be what he wasn't and longed to be, but I *could* be and *am* much better at doing what he did. I'm a crackerjack warehouseman. *I* was the one . . . at eighteen . . . who badgered and argued him into consolidating in London and extending into Cambridge and Swindon. He used my successful model to continue into Northampton and Brighton. I've also been the one to tell him he'd get the same amount of work out of the men if he cut them back from sixty hours to fifty-five at the same pay. If he didn't make more, he didn't see the point in it. I *know* we'd have much more loyalty and less sick time from critical workers if we paid something towards health care. Oh, did we fight about that! He wanted to know how he was supposed to keep a wife and three ungrateful children in finery if he gave away the profits to the workers. I replied that he had forgotten the mistress."

"And every time he won, you punished him by goin' on drinkin' binges," John followed.

"That's right."

"What did he do that caused you to marry the publican's daughter?"

The muscles of Lionel's jaw started out. "He insisted I marry for wealth. But Sally and I love each other. I'm not such a fool I'd saddle myself with a poor woman just out of spite. Not if I didn't love her. I admit she's not a good mother. That's why I pay her mum to watch our baby much of the time. I'm amazed you didn't hear about the stolen jewelry."

"I did."

"I assure you, it was the new maid."

"So, I can assume there was not much love lost between you and your father," John said.

"I loved him as much as he deserved," Lionel answered. "I always respected him. But he wasn't an easy man. And certainly not a fair one. You're wondering why I didn't drop everything when I got the telephone call and run out of here."

"Not after what you've just told me."

"The living need my attention much more. These workers need the warehouses to continue running smoothly; my family needs the income to flow smoothly. Care for a cigarette? They're American. Machine rolled."

"No, thanks."

The warehouseman pressed open a silver case and withdrew a cigarette. He found a match in his top drawer, struck it, put it to the cigarette, and needfully drew in the flame.

John took the moment to find and hand over the card the coroner had given him. "You have to square expenses with the coroner's office in Brighton before they'll release the body. I took the liberty of directin' them to send it to University College Hospital. I have a friend there who is a chief of surgery. Dr. Thomas Saye. I've written his name and telephone numbers on the back of the card. He'll see that your father is treated with respect. I've already spoken with him."

"Thank you." Attwater placed the card carefully into his billfold. Then he stared hard at Le Brun. "You, too, don't believe my father committed suicide."

"That's right."

"But you didn't know him, did you?"

"No. I never met him alive."

"So, what causes your doubt?"

John smiled. "Several things. All of them require that the killer be down there longer than merely to catch your father unaware, pull the trigger, and drop the gun by his side. Scotland Yard is satisfied with a suicide, but I have already begun a search for a busy young man."

"If I also retain you as investigator, will you be more specific?"

"No. To work for more than the Sceptred Isle Club would

be unethical."

"You suspect me. That's why you asked me about Brighton."

"Do you know of the tontine your father participated in years ago?"

"Yes."

"Did you know that you are your father's primary beneficiary if he was the last survivor?"

"I can't remember. Perhaps I once did."

"Do you know how much was originally put into the tontine?"

"No."

For the first time, John was sure that Lionel was lying. He would not, however, assume that these two lies made false everything he previously said.

"Since Trent Godwin survives your father, that would end your motive. Do you follow?"

"I do."

"But now, with your news of your mother and her less harsh attitude about you, you're right back on the list. I'd say, gettin' rid of the possibility of bein' cut out of your father's will is a strong motive for his death . . . wouldn't you?"

"Enough to murder a roomful of men?" Lionel scoffed.

"Perhaps. Perhaps the pea soup that descends upon your streets isn't the only London fog."

"If you mean hiding one crime amongst many, I wouldn't do it."

"Does your mother have a will?"

"Not yet. She's afraid that if she ever writes one, that will guarantee her death. But now she'll have to."

"And will *she* leave you with little?"

"I can continue to keep father's empire afloat for her. She knows it. She won't alienate me." Attwater ran his tongue around his teeth again. "If I heard correctly, you only suspect me if my whereabouts conform with a certain 'busy young man' who spent some time this weekend in Brighton."

"That would be a correct assumption."

"And you haven't gone to the police with this?"

"I already told you that the police are satisfied with pinnin' the Sceptred Isle Club murders on your father's lapel. I would need to bring them the 'busy young man' in order to change their minds."

Lionel glanced at an ornate desk clock and stood. "If you won't accept my financial help, there's nothing more I can do for you than repeat you're wasting your time with me."

John also stood. "Then we shall leave it at that. If somethin' that might have a bearin' on the case should occur to you, or if you are contacted by a 'busy young man,' you can reach me at my hotel. I'm stayin' at the Westminster Palace."

"I know the place. Let me walk you down to the front gate," Attwater suggested. "Unlike my father, I like to mix with our employees. They're about to knock off for the day."

"That's very kind of you. I was goin' to ask you to walk me out and reorient me toward the East Ham electric tram route."

The young man led the way with long strides, forcing John to hurry to keep up and obviating the possibility of more conversation. True to his word, young Attwater put himself by the gate just as the quitting-time whistle shrilled. He had a pleasant exchange with the guards while he waited for the workers to file out. Then he greeted each man and woman by first name, inquiring of a few about their personal lives. John noted that this was not some spur-of-the-moment ruse he had invented for his visitor's benefit, because the workers chatted back at him in a manner indicating long habit. He saw that this was not a boss's son who was despised. As they passed, John kept a sharp eye open for the young Irishman with the U-shaped scar. He did not expect to find him among the crowd, and he was not proven wrong.

"Thank you for your time, Mr. Attwater," John said, after the last worker had straggled out. He offered his hand, which was taken. "I am truly sorry for your loss."

"Thank you. You walk up this street and two more blocks, then turn west and follow the signs. And Mr. Le Brun: When you find your 'busy young man,' come to me again. You will find me substantially grateful."

John walked slowly along the pavement, trying to rein in his self anger. He was not a man to use oaths casually, but now he uttered a string of them under his breath that would have rivaled the repertoire of the roughest London dock worker.

The boy with the pan and brush had vanished. John threaded his way across the street, around new manure and crushed cabbage leaves. He looked back when he had walked about a hundred steps beyond the Attwater warehouse gates. Lionel Attwater stood watching him. He returned the stare, while out of the corner of his eye he assured himself that the carriage he had arrived in and which had turned in the street while he interviewed Attwater was still there. Sighing at the prospect of at least one more day of investigation, he plodded toward the East Ham electric tram.

JOHN VISITED THE Sceptred Isle Club and reported to Mr. Roundsville, the club manager. It seemed that the club was already abuzz with word of Nahum Attwater's suicide and suicide note. Trent Godwin's busy schedule had not precluded several minutes on the telephone breaking the news. John was certain that Godwin had not stopped with merely one call.

"The club is in an uproar," Roundsville confided. "Mr. Godwin says that the evidence is all but irrefutable, but most of us still cannot believe Mr. Attwater capable of such villainy."

John carefully cultivated his lowland Georgian vocabulary, but he privately doffed his hat at the manager's vivid turns of speech. In the man's apartment, he had enjoyed the use of the word "callipygian", but he particularly respected Roundsville's correct use of "perused." Most people thought the word meant "give a quick and superficial glance," when in point of fact it meant precisely the opposite. He tried not to smile at the manager's latest words. "You tell everyone that the last 't' has not been crossed, nor the last 'i' dotted in this case, Mr. Roundsville. While I do not think it will do much good, you should expostulate to the members to hold their speculations for a few more days."

"Expostulate? Yes, yes I shall, Mr. Le Brun."

John had read the word only a few weeks previous and looked up its meaning. He had been itching to use it in context, and he found himself quite pleased to have found the opportunity in the presence of such a wordsmith as the club manager.

"The press has been hounding me," Roundsville confided. "I have declined comment on anything to do with the murders."

"As you should. Merely use the opportunity they afford you to promote the club. In America, we have a sayin' for the press: 'Write anythin' you want about me, but please spell my name right.'" The beleaguered manager managed a wan smile. "Have you dined yet?" he invited. "We would be honored to have you eat with us . . . at club expense, of course."

"I have already eaten, sir," John lied, "but I will be sure to take you up on your most kind invitation in the near future. If anyone should ask, I have moved my residence to the Westminster Palace Hotel."

"Let me write that down," Roundsville said.

John lowered his voice. "I came up from Brighton and didn't have the chance to retrieve your photographs. I promise to return them next time I visit."

"No hurry," the manager said, in an equally subdued tone.

"Very good. And might I have a cab called?"

WHEN JOHN RETURNED to the Godwin home, he found the cook and her husband there. They told him that the family had gone off to pay their collective respects to the newly-widowed Mrs. Homer. John was pleased with the circumstance; it made leaving the house so much easier. He explained to Mr. and Mrs. Comfort his ill ease at being a house guest during such turbulent times. It was not only the many deaths, he went on, but the impending charity ball which was consuming Maeve Godwin's time. He had returned merely to collect his belongings and would move directly to the Westminster Palace Hotel. He asked Alice to arrange for a cab to pick him up in twenty minutes.

Having finished his recitation, John hurried upstairs, to clean himself out of the house before the Godwins returned. When he had finished packing, he sat and composed an effusive thank-you note to Maeve and Trent. When he had finished that, he began a second one, to Veronica. It read:

Miss Veronica-

While I do not dare assume that you may be so inclined, I would be greatly pleased if you would visit me at the Westminster Palace Hotel. I will make sure to be in my room from nine o'clock on.

If you cannot visit tonight, leave a message indicating another time.

Your ardent admirer,
John Le Brun

John folded the note, placed it in an envelope, sealed it, and left it in Veronica's room, prominently displayed atop her chest of drawers. He was embarrassed, upon leaving her room, to find Alice's husband waiting in the upper hallway to help him down with his suitcases.

The hired carriage stood ready outside the Godwin home. It took him scenically south, along the eastern verge of St. James

Park, into Hyde Park and past Buckingham Palace. Despite all the beauty, John registered very little of it. His mind worked diligently on the increasingly complex puzzle of the murders. He was let off at the large hotel's front entrance and ushered in with style by the doorman and a bellhop.

"We've been expecting you, Mr. Le Brun," the registration clerk greeted brightly. "Your reservation was made by Dr. Thomas Saye. He has also paid for this evening's lodging."

"That was right nice of him."

"Yes, sir. Your room is four-fourteen. It has an excellent view." The clerk handed over the old-fashioned key.

"I'd like my suitcases brought up but not opened," John said to the hovering bellhop. He handed the man a coin and turned immediately back to the reservation clerk. "Where might I find a public telephone?"

"We have several cabinets just on the other side of the lobby, sir."

John hunted up the hotel's main restaurant and was led to a small table, where he dined on a salad, a roll, and soup, so that he might not have to wait long for his meal. As he ate, he noted that the hotel had indeed lost cachet with age. When he called Dr. Saye from Brighton and laid out his plan, Saye had suggested the hotel for its location but warned that it was now more than forty years old and had lost some of its luster. For all of its three hundred guest rooms, for example, it had been designed with only fourteen bathrooms. The guests were not swells but ordinary men and women, like himself. He felt at ease and glad to be away for a time from the elite of London.

When he had finished eating, John crossed the lobby toward the telephone cabinets. He consulted his pocket watch, then reached for his billfold and dug out Thomas Saye's business card as he walked. He closed himself in one of the tiny rooms and had an operator ring the number. The physician was quick in answering.

"I must thank you for your kindness in payin' for the hotel

room," John said directly after announcing himself, leaning in to the wall-mounted mouthpiece.

"My pleasure."

"Were you able to follow young Mr. Attwater when he left the warehouse?" John asked.

"Absolutely. Your notion of bringing him to the front gate worked to perfection. He returned to the warehouse for almost half an hour. I was about to give up when he re-emerged. He left on foot. We let him get about a block ahead of us before I had the cabman follow. When it seemed he was heading for the electric tram stop, I had the cab get in front of him, and I went into a shop with a large front window. I then followed him onto the tram. He took it to the tube and caught a train to King's Cross. He went back to his own home. I made a few inquiries to be sure it was his. He lives a little more than a mile from my home."

"Was anyone waitin' for him?"

"No. Nor did anyone arrive in the time I lingered there. I just got home five minutes ago. Did he seem guilty when you interviewed him?"

"It was difficult to determine," John replied. "The man is a boilin' cauldron of emotions. He did not like his father. And, it turns out, his mother is alive."

"Does that change the issue of his inheritance?"

"Accordin' to him it does. He actually presented me with a motive I had not even suspected. I am a donkey's hind end for makin' the assumption the mother was dead."

"Were you purposely led to think that?"

John sighed. "I don't believe so. It was an amateur mistake I would bless out my deputies for makin'."

"But you know it now, and that's what's important."

"Perhaps. All things bein' equal, Nahum Attwater's body should arrive at your hospital tomorrow afternoon. I'd be obliged if you gave it the attention we discussed as soon as you could."

"Of course."

"And a report on that bottle of blood."

"I've stored it in my icebox. I'll have it analyzed by our hematologist in the morning."

"That's excellent. Can you tell me somethin' else: If the Westminster Palace is no longer one of the elite hotels, why would someone want to host a high-society charity ball here?"

"Oh, that's easy. The guest rooms are antiquated, but the ballroom remains quite magnificent. One of the best rooms in London for events. And their special affairs staff is top shelf, I understand."

"That must explain it."

"What does that have to do with the murders?"

"Nothing whatsoever. Just my idle curiosity about an upcomin' ball Mrs. Godwin is chairin'. I appreciate the time you're givin' me," John said.

"And I appreciate my freedom. I am at your service, Sheriff Le Brun."

"It's a long shot, but your work at the hospital in Lambeth might just help uncover an Irish lad with the right scar. Have you had the chance yet—"

"Yes. I made calls the moment you and I hung up this afternoon. By tomorrow, I expect that no fewer than thirty Irish men and women who owe me their lives will be extending a net over all of Lambeth and Southwark."

"That's truly excellent. Did you tell them where I'm stayin', so there's no time wasted in relayin' information through you?"

"I did indeed."

"Wonderful. That's all we can do for now. Good night, Doctor."

"And a good night to you."

JOHN WAS INSIDE his hotel room well before nine o'clock. He busied himself by putting away his belongings. When everything was in its place, he opened a notebook and recorded the day's events, jotting questions and points to ponder in the margins.

At nine precisely, a knock sounded at the door. John's heart leapt.

"Maid service," a female voice called out. "Do you want your bed turned down?"

It did not sound like Veronica's voice, but John wondered if she had altered it to surprise him.

"Yes, I do. One moment." John opened the door. He found himself staring at a short, plump woman of no fewer than fifty years. She had affixed a smile, but when she saw John's grin fade, her bright expression slipped as well. She went about her business with speed. John offered her a coin on her way out, along with thanks.

After he closed the door, John secured the safety chain. It was just as well he had retired from law enforcement, he told himself. He was slipping badly. First, he had let a succession of comments convince him that Nahum Attwater's wife was dead. Now, he had let himself become so besotted by Veronica Godwin that he just threw open his door without caution. He had told half of London he was staying at the Westminster Palace Hotel precisely so someone would pass the information on to the Irishman with the scar. He had figured that the man could not get the news this quickly and also that he would probably follow John out of the hotel in the morning and try to kill him in a less risky place. Nevertheless, the man might have been alerted right away. Lionel Attwater might have telephoned him when he returned to his office, for example. And if John could get the room number of Nahum Attwater's room this morning, a determined killer could do the same to him. Put a gun to a maid's head and get her to call out about turning down the bed. Then, as soon as the door was opened, blast both John and the hapless maid. It was what he would have done in a killer's place.

"Ya damned old fool!" John muttered, as he threw himself on the bed.

By nine-forty, John's eyelids were drooping. He badly needed sleep. He determined that if Veronica came to him, she would have to rouse him from a nap. To be sure, his last experience with her had proved that she could bring him to life quite quickly.

Le Brun slipped out of his jacket and shoes, extinguished the room light, and flopped back on the bed with his trousers still on. As he lay in the dark, he realized that the flashing in his right eye had returned. His vision, especially for reading, had for years been far from perfect, but he dreaded to the point of near-panic the prospect of blindness. He determined to visit a vision specialist on the morrow. He knew one already: a celebrated author who lived in the country. With that thought, he drifted into an uninterrupted sleep.

EIGHT

Tuesday, October 24, 1905

JOHN AWOKE WITH LONDON still dark. His first thought was of Veronica. He turned on the light and looked at his watch. The night had all but passed without her visit. He was disappointed but not surprised. She had probably had some gay young socialite appointment after the visit to the widow. He pictured her at the theater and then a smart, smoky dance hall. Even if she hadn't gone out on the town, she might not have been able to get out of the house. Most probably, she had no desire to see him. When he stayed in the Godwin home, the danger of making love to him with her mother and stepfather on the other side of the wall was highly attractive. He was simply the object necessary for the daring act. Now that he had moved to a hotel, he was back to being just an old man, a forgotten toy. It was just as well, he told himself, unhappily.

John used the early hour to compose a long memo on hotel stationery. He stuffed it into an envelope and sealed it. After addressing it as best he could, he placed it in his jacket pocket. He then went down to breakfast. Since he had eaten little the day before, he indulged in poached eggs and ham, fried potatoes, and most of a pot of coffee. He took a leisurely read of two London newspapers he had purchased, glancing every few minutes at his watch.

On the night of the club murders, Arthur Conan Doyle had asked John to stay in close touch and make use of Doyle's deductive skills, pressing a card with his address and telephone number into Le Brun's hand while he spoke. As the days passed, John felt increasingly guilty for not following through. Now, with his eye problem, he had a double impetus to visit the author.

As soon as he deemed respectful, John telephoned the number on Doyle's card. Sir Arthur answered personally and greeted him with enthusiasm. John announced that he had spent the day with Trent Godwin in Brighton and had learned a great deal about Nahum Attwater. When Conan Doyle failed to jump at the bait, John knew he was still unaware of the man's death. Conan Doyle made emphatic his wish that John visit as soon as possible. He had, he said, several errands to run in Haslemere, and he would be waiting at the Haslemere train station when the southbound 11:08 arrived.

John purchased postage stamps to cover the weight of his letter, affixed them, and handed it to the concierge to post. He left the hotel and headed for Victoria Station, which was within view. While he had not traveled much, he recognized that the Westminster Palace Hotel had been built by the railroad company to capture clients leaving the terminus. As he stepped onto the pavement, he had his right hand inside his trouser pocket, fingers wrapped around his derringer. At his fingertips he felt the spare two bullets he had also packed. The weapon was quite inaccurate at more than twenty feet, but in this most civilized of countries which so abhorred the private carrying of guns, he had felt that anything larger would have constituted an insult. Because London was so huge, his hope was to entice the young man with the scar to him. Even after telling his location to Lionel Attwater, the manager of the Sceptred Isle Club (and, by extension, all its members), the Godwins, and Thomas Saye (and, by extension, hundreds of Irish), the odds of success were very long. Nevertheless, John maintained a wary eye, turning often as he walked, steering clear of alley openings, watching the windows of passing carriages and motorized vehicles.

Late April a year earlier, in Brunswick, Georgia, a man who knew Le Brun's reputation for solving cases decided to eliminate the sheriff before John could link him to a murder. He used the Confederate Memorial Day parade, with its milling crowds, brass bands, and other distractions. His intent had been to get behind Le Brun and slip a stiletto knife between the sheriff's ribs into his heart, to withdraw the knife, catch John as he collapsed, cry out to the crowd that the man had had a heart attack, and vanish during the ensuing confusion. Four circumstances had worked against him: the crowd was too tight for him to give the knife a full push; John had been wearing a shoulder holster with a wide leather strap running across his back; the knife had penetrated the leather just enough to drive the tip into John's skin, causing him to cry out; and John's deputy, Bobby Lee Randolph, had been patrolling the sidewalk only a few yards away. The greatest frustration of John's current investigation was the lack of deputies to command, those extra legs to speed and widen the search, and those vigilant eyes to watch his back.

John caught the local train to Wandsworth and took a window seat. He watched again the passing of the city into suburbs, saw the evidence of villages that had been swallowed whole by the encroachment of London. At Wandsworth he changed trains for one that headed to Portsmouth. Not long after, they were out in the rolling countryside, and John admired the lush foliage going to color in the crisp autumn air. Before he expected, the conductor was announcing that Haslemere was the next stop.

Haslemere was a delight from the moment John exited the train. It was precisely the size and vintage of English town he wanted to nose around in. He had seen from the train that it was nestled between two lines of hills, surrounded by heath and conifers. He hoped that Conan Doyle would have some trouble finding him, so that he could at least amble up and down the town's main street. His wish was in vain. The blare of an electric horn turned him around, so that he faced a shiny, black motorcar parked on the opposite side of the street. Sir Arthur was leaning out the right side, waving at him.

"Delighted to see you, old fellow," Conan Doyle greeted. He gave John a handshake that was painful in its vigor. "Hop in."

"You're an adopter of modern contraptions, are you?" John asked.

"Absolutely. This is, in fact, my *second* horseless carriage. My first was a ten-horsepower Wolseley. This one has twice the power."

"I'm even more impressed that you drive it yourself."

"Not often. My coachman, Holden, usually handles this and our horses, but every now and then I like to do the honors."

"And it's not dangerous?"

"Life itself is dangerous, old chap. Climb in."

Immediately, Doyle made a U-turn whose centrifugal force threw John against his door.

"Got a ticket for speeding last month," Doyle remarked. "Idiotic police. I was the only one on the road. Couldn't have killed anyone but myself. And yet they fined me. When we get outside of town, keep a sharp eye open for the constabulary. I want to show you what this machine can do."

"I don't have sharp eyes," John said, becoming alarmed.

"Then I'll watch for both of us. How do you like Haslemere?" Doyle asked.

"Right fine. I wouldn't mind seein' more of it. Perhaps you'd take a slow turn through the streets for me."

"Glad to. This is where Lord Tennyson died, you know. And the chap who founded your state of Georgia, General James Edward Oglethorpe, was from here. Great place to soak up history."

Doyle rattled on about the town even after he had driven out of it. He steadily picked up speed until John thought they would lift off the ground. The wind came over the top of the windscreen with so much force that John turned his head to the side to avoid the dust and bugs. The passing countryside became a blur over his left shoulder. Once, Doyle wandered off the dirt road into high grasses and cursed as he fought the steering wheel to correct his course. John's grip became painful on his seat, but he held tight nonetheless.

Doyle finally slowed as they passed into the village of Hindhead. From train station to estate, the trip lasted only about seven minutes. He introduced his place as "Undershaw." "Shaw means woods or copse in Anglo-Saxon," he explained, gesturing at the thicket of trees that climbed the hill behind the property. "It's nice not only to look at, but they also protect us from the wind." In contrast to his open-road driving, he drove cautiously through the front gate. John saw that the property was large but not a manor. Conan proudly showed him the tennis court, the stable, and then the garage, which housed a motorbike as well as the automobile.

"Just before I left Georgia, I read about a couple of Ohio brothers who built a flyin' machine," John said. "Will you buy one of them, too?"

"Perhaps," Conan Doyle replied. "If I'm convinced it can work."

They wandered around the outside of the massive house, which to John seemed like three residences stuck together. It was grand in a country house style, of redbrick with a tiled roof and four chimneys. The windows were so many and so large that

John wondered if the outer walls could still be sturdy. Light came into the third-story rooms through dormer windows.

As John admired aloud, a young teenage boy and a small girl came bounding up, calling out for their poppa. As he hugged the two, Doyle introduced them as Kingsley and Mary. The boy held a .22 rifle. When they had disappeared into the house, John said, "I thought the owning of private weapons is discouraged in England."

"It is, and that's a grave disservice to the nation. A war with the Kaiser is inevitable, and boys Kingsley's age should be practicing already. Six weeks of training won't keep them alive. You should have seen the marksmanship of those Boer farmers we went up against. Lethal, in a word. I'm on a personal quest to set up as many shooting clubs as I can. I've built a miniature range down on the opposite side of the road for the citizens of the region. We call it the Undershaw Rifle Club. I pay for the weapons and ammunition myself. Twice a week, members meet. We're damned good. The Kaiser would think again about war if he visited during a match."

"You are a man of convictions, I am learnin'," John remarked.

"That's true. I believe I know what's right and fair, and I pursue and support these things with a vengeance. Come inside, won't you?"

As with every room, the hallway was massive. A stained-glass window showed the Doyle family coat of arms.

"We have our own generator for electricity, since it's so unpredictable out here in the country," Sir Arthur bragged, as they walked out of the huge billiard room and into the dining room that could seat thirty. John was introduced to three servants in the kitchen. They moved on to the wood-paneled drawing room. A wooden shelf ran completely around the room above the height of the doors. On it sat walrus tusks, stuffed birds, antique weapons, and the multitude of awards and memorabilia the author, adventurer, and athlete had collected.

They went upstairs, so that John might meet Doyle's wife, Louise. They found her bolstered up in bed. She had a book in front of her, but she had not been reading when they entered. Although quite pale and sickly looking, she offered John a warm smile and words of welcome. She had kind eyes as well, but John doubted that she had ever been a handsome woman. There was something puggish and manly about her, despite carefully coiffured curly hair and a cameo choker around her neck. She struggled valiantly not to cough during their brief acquaintance. As John left the room, he noted that European lever handles were on the door in place of doorknobs.

Conan Doyle followed John's eyes. When they were out in the hall and walking back downstairs, he said, "The handles are necessary because Louise has such terrible arthritis."

"That's what confines her?" John asked.

"That and her tuberculosis. She's only forty-eight, but she's had it for thirteen years." Doyle uttered a rueful little laugh. "Her doctor diagnosed it as galloping consumption. Crawling consumption is more like it. It's been a curse upon us both. Some days she rallies, but they're increasingly few. She lives in a sick room, but we're both confined to it."

Knowing what he did about Doyle's girlfriend in London, John tried not to read too much callousness into his host's words.

"And now, let's retire to my study," Doyle said. "Would you care for coffee?"

"Do you ever make iced tea?"

"We can do that, I'm sure." Doyle called for the cook and ordered the tea as well as cakes. Then he opened the door to his sanctum sanctorum.

John took his time looking around the room. He especially admired the many filled bookcases. One held nothing but books and magazines containing Conan Doyle's work.

"I had no idea you wrote so much," John observed.

"I'm a prisoner to the success of Sherlock Holmes, but detective fiction isn't my main passion. I prefer historical fiction and horror, actually."

"Horror?"

"Yes, indeed. Bram Stoker is one of my closest friends. I've even tried my hand at domestic novels. But the arrogant detective and his faithful doctor pay the bills."

The study had its own hearth, with a nine-point buck's head mounted over it. A Bengal tiger rug graced the hardwood floor. Two curve-backed chairs faced the large desk. Conan Doyle pulled these up facing each other and invited John to sit.

"If I mailed a letter this mornin' from the Westminster Palace Hotel, how long until I could expect it to arrive at Scotland Yard?" John asked, as he sat.

"This afternoon's delivery, if you're lucky. Tomorrow morning's, first thing, if you're not. They have a priority on all deliveries."

John nodded at the information.

"What did you mail?" Doyle wanted to know.

"Information I picked up yesterday."

"I spoke with Chief Inspector Tibbles yesterday morning," said Sir Arthur. "I'm sure he'll be glad to receive anything you've discovered."

"Not him," said John. "I mailed to Inspector Cooper . . . the one we dealt with the night of the murders."

"And why not Tibbles? He's the ranking officer in this investigation."

"Because I don't like him."

"Not to put too fine a point on it," Doyle marveled.

"I believe in gettin' to the point and whittlin' it sharp," John said. "Speaking' of gettin' to the point, I must confess I have a second reason for visitin' you today. I've been experiencin' periodic flashes of light in my right eye. The problem is that sometimes there's no light to make the flash."

"You see it in complete darkness then."

"That's right."

Conan Doyle's face scrunched up into an expression of empathetic pain that frightened Le Brun. "Hmmm!" he said.

"What is it?"

"I take it you've heard that I was a doctor of ophthalmology."

"That's correct."

Doyle repeated his distressed look. "The truth is that I had intended to improve my position as a physician by specializing in the area. I even went to Vienna in 1891 with my wife, planning to spend a full year learning. I had no idea that the German would be too specialized. I simply couldn't follow the lectures."

"So, you practiced as an eye doctor with no study?" John asked, trying not to sound alarmed.

"Oh, I did stop in Paris for a time and work with a man named Edmund Landolt. He's one of the foremost scientists on diseases of the eye. At any rate, if your problem is what I suspect, I may have enough knowledge to pronounce on it." Doyle leapt up and crossed to a closet. "It's been some time since I've practiced, you understand." He emerged with his black physician's bag. He drew his chair close to John's. That done, he reached into the bag and pulled out a head strap with a magnifying lens and reflecting mirror attached to it. He took his lamp from the desk and tilted it so that the bulb filament shone directly into John's eye. He drew the eyepiece down.

"Look up!" Doyle commanded, leaning in close. "Now down. Now left. Now right. Up again. And down once more. Right." He replaced the lamp on the desk.

"What is it?" John asked, in a small voice.

Doyle removed his eyepiece. "I was hoping it was something harmless, called a 'floater.' However, it doesn't appear so. This could become quite serious. As we grow older, the clear jelly inside our eyes, which we call the vitreous humor, begins to dry out and shrink. The jelly is a holdover from evolution . . .

probably when our ancestors were in the oceans. It does no good; you can lose it and still see. But it can cause damage. Sometimes, as it shrinks, it pulls away part of the back wall of the inner eye. If it pulls on the retina, the retina can become detached. You'll go blind in that eye."

John felt his stomach lurch. "What can be done?"

"Nothing, I'm afraid."

"How long does this shrinkin' process go on?"

"Sometimes for years. As far as we know, it doesn't matter if you're active or in a coma during the process. Whether or not it tears the retina is pure fate."

"That's not heartenin' to learn."

"I'm sorry. You should have it checked by a fully-qualified ophthalmologist when you can." Doyle lifted the strap from his head and returned it to his bag. He stood to return the bag to the closet. "It's another grim reminder that none of our gifts lasts forever. I believe it actually helps us to enjoy them that much more while we have them."

"I'll try holdin' on to that," John said, suppressing other, more colorful phrases that screamed inside his head. He looked again around the room, wondering how much longer he would enjoy binocular vision. Memories filled his mind, of his neighbor on Jekyl Island who had lost his eyesight and of a regiment mate barely out of his teens blinded by a bullet during the Civil War. They had lost all vision. At least, he counseled himself, he would still have one good eye if the worst happened. Perhaps Doyle's counsel rang not so hollow after all.

"You should feel luckier than most men, in fact," Doyle added, returning to his chair. "You have extraordinary *insight.* You also possess the gift of observing human behavior and being able to divine how they will act in a given situation. We both do. That's why it's a pleasure working on this case with you. Have you read through all the depositions from the Sceptred Isle Club?"

"I have not," John admitted. He was frankly convinced the interviews he had made were all he needed, but Conan Doyle's expectations had him feeling slightly defensive.

Doyle said, "I went over Godwin's interview yesterday at Scotland Yard with Inspector Cooper. Saturday was Trafalgar Day."

"Yes, I know. The hundredth anniversary. Geoffrey put me right in the middle of it."

"I should have been there. That glorious victory paved the way for the British Empire," Doyle remarked. "It deserved to be well celebrated."

Remembering the scent on Doyle's suit Saturday evening, Le Brun thought he knew what had ranked higher. "Did Mr. Godwin celebrate it?"

"No. Curiously. Anyone in London who couldn't earn a farthing from the occasion had the day off. The office staff of Godwin, Penfield, and Bushnell usually work the morning on Saturdays, but they had a full holiday. According to Trent Godwin, he was the only one in the office . . . from mid-morning until late afternoon. But no one can corroborate. Perhaps he was busy with other plans."

"I take it he's still your prime candidate," John said.

"Indeed. In spite of the supposed murder attempt on him Sunday night."

"You've deduced that an accomplice was needed for the gamblin' room murders."

"Yes. However, before I rattle on, tell me about your trip down to Brighton with him yesterday. Perhaps you'll relate something that will blow my theory out of the water, and I'll save myself the embarrassment and you the boredom of my solution."

John related from his point of view the Sunday-night incident of the attack on Godwin from out of the fog. Doyle sat wide-eyed, nodding every so often, and grunting affably, drinking in John's methodical unveiling of every minute detail with no show of impatience. John then shifted to midnight and Trent's sudden recollection of the tontine.

Sir Arthur clapped his hands together in delight, as if he were a child receiving a long-awaited present. He refrained from remark until John had completed the segment, then leaned back in his chair and folded his arms across his chest. "Isn't that *amazing*? The man can't think of a motive for mass murder until more than twenty- four hours later. Tens of thousands of pounds in this tontine, and it doesn't ring a bell right away."

"Well, two of the four killed weren't in the tontine," John pointed out. "And two members of it were still alive after the attack."

"Nevertheless," Sir Arthur scoffed. His waggled his forefinger from its resting place on his chest. "Are you saying you *don't believe* Trent . . . ? Never mind. Now speak to me about your trip with him to Brighton, and give me the vicarious pleasure of whatever your senses recorded."

Again, John plodded through the smallest details of the day. He had expected that the news of Attwater's supposed suicide would rattle Conan Doyle for a time, but the man took it all in stride. John plowed on. Unlike the truncated tale he told Lionel Attwater, he included those minutes he spent alone in and around the warehouse after Chief Inspector Tibbles and Godwin left together.

"Astonishing!" Conan Doyle exclaimed. "You've done magnificent work. This startling turn of events only serves to confirm my theory. May I use you as an expert sounding board?"

"Be my guest."

"Let me begin before the murders in the Sceptred Isle Club. I have access to highly placed sources in the financial world. I'm not at liberty to reveal their identities, but suffice to say their credentials are impeccable. It seems that Godwin has lost several big clients over the past two years. What's worse, he's failed to replace them. He's been under pressure from his partners to pull his weight, and a monetary accommodation was made to reduce his share of the profits until he turned his portfolio around. At the same time, his wife and stepdaughter are profligate spenders. He had little outlay in those years after his first wife's death, and he laid a considerable sum of money aside in investments and securities. Ever since he purchased their residence on Green Street, gutted it, and refurbished it, the money has been flowing out faster than he can replace it. And they throw parties."

"I attended one," John broke in. "It wasn't very lavish."

"But they do it fortnightly, I understand. Over the months and years, it adds up. Finally, Maeve Godwin has been buying her way into the lower echelons of elite society by organizing and supporting charity functions. She buys seats at fund-raisers to the tune of one hundred pounds per seat! In short, Trent could really use the . . . how much is in this tontine?"

"About thirty-five thousand pounds."

"You see? I knew there had to be financial gain for him! Does Scotland Yard know about the tontine?"

"Trent told Inspector Tibbles about it yesterday, around noon."

"In Brighton. That's why I wasn't told. Here's how it went:" Conan Doyle capitalized on his athleticism and apparently boundless energy by leaping again from his chair and racing around to the far side of his desk. As he reseated himself, he grabbed a pack of heavyweight note cards neatly positioned on the center of the desk top. Each of his points had been recorded on one card, so that he could shuffle or discard them as he refined his theory. As he spoke, he dropped cards onto the desk.

"As you agree, Godwin couldn't bring off the entire plot himself. Somewhere in his daily life, he happened upon an accomplice." Doyle grabbed a pen and scribbled notes on the top card. "You have revealed this person as a 'young Irishman with a U-shaped scar.' What we don't know is why Godwin could trust this man literally with his future. Perhaps it was a law case he took pro bono and won, where the young man owes him greatly. No point in wasting time speculating further; we'll find out when he's caught. At any rate, Godwin needs money badly. When three men of the tontine he had subscribed to died, he devised a plan to get rid of the other three. He learns that Nahum Attwater will be gone from London to Brighton to conduct business. This news allows him to pin the murders on Attwater, since Brighton is close enough to allow quick rail travel." He took another card and wrote furiously on it. "*Now* I see why you were interested where Godwin was on Trafalgar Day morning and afternoon! His office is empty, so no one can contradict his alibi.

"In preparation for the gory part of the plot, he hides the approximate amount of a night's gambling funds under the birdbath of the Uniform bobby who patrols clubland on Saturday night. This is the first feint, made to satisfy Scotland Yard long enough to prevent them from pursuing their investigation. Since this is a clever man we are dealing with, he might have hidden the money days earlier. After all, who would bother lifting a common man's yard ornament in search of treasure . . . unless that man were suspected of a capital crime?"

"Not I," John chimed in, doing his part to keep Doyle's steam up.

"Nor I. Next, he kills Nahum Attwater, to prevent the scapegoat from returning to London early and ruining his plan. I thank you again for your excellent sleuthing in uncovering the delivery of ice, the pick, and the long trough." Doyle pulled out one of the desk drawers and produced a dozen or so blank versions of the note cards. He scribbled on one of them and placed it on the desk atop those already laid down. "In spite of having recruited the young Irishman, it is vital that Godwin go down to Brighton himself. He cannot envision a stranger being able to get Attwater alone inside his warehouse. Trent, however, could pretend to have sudden business in the town." His eyes became brighter. "Or perhaps he had even been asked by Attwater to be present for the signing of the contract."

"No," John replied. "The realty agent told us he signed—"

"Right. Right." Doyle scribbled on another blank card. "Sorry. You said Attwater signed the contract on Friday afternoon. I'm getting too fancy. Habits of a fiction author. So, Godwin just shows up, offers a plausible excuse, and asks Attwater to show him the warehouse.

"They go together to the place. While Attwater is talking, Godwin quickly pulls the gun from his greatcoat, aims it close to Attwater's temple, and fires. This is why you report no blood specks on Attwater's sleeve or his hand. No powder marks either." Another card was plucked from the blanks. "Before you arrived, I *did* expect Attwater would be dead and that it would be made to look like a suicide. I also expected that it would be done with the same revolver used at the Sceptred Isle Club and, because of this, that it would most likely be done in the deserted warehouse. Ah, but with this tontine information . . . So neat, so neat!" The card, now filled with notes, went onto the pile.

"Godwin is not a young man anymore," Conan Doyle continued. "You say that Mr. Attwater wasn't very heavy, but he *was* dead weight. I suspect that the Irishman was not far away during the killing. If I planned this, I'd have had him outside, to keep any errant person away from the warehouse when the gun was fired. At the sound, he enters the place and carries the body up to the cold storage area.

"Godwin is no longer needed. His job is to get back to London as soon as he can, to establish the best possible alibis. You can be certain that he pays at least a cursory visit to his office, to sign papers and move them onto other desks, proving his presence. Probably the Irishman takes the correct key off Attwater's ring, locks the chain, and pulls the lock inside. The key is dropped where Attwater ostensibly would have dropped it. Any holes in my version so far?"

"Not that I can think of," Le Brun conceded.

"Excellent. The Irishman waits around for the delivery of ice. He will not let the helpful iceman into the warehouse for obvious reasons. When the iceman leaves, he half fills the trough with five or six ice blocks, then lays down the rubberized tarp. He seals Attwater inside it, careful not to leave any opening where melting ice might seep inside. He uses the ice pick and surrounds the wrapped body with chips from the remaining ice. Attwater should have also had the key to the office door entrance on him, shouldn't he?"

"He had keys on him. I didn't think to look for that specific one," John said.

Conan Doyle smiled, a subtle but palpable rebuke. "I'm willing to bet that key was taken off Attwater's key ring. There's a chance the Irish lad didn't return it to Attwater's pocket ultimately, which would further prove the case. The lad leaves by the business door, locks it, and catches a train to London in plenty of time to participate in the club murders.

"Godwin arrives for cards just as he always does. The appointed time comes. Godwin leaves the game, bounding up the stairs and passing remarks to be noticed. He descends the other set of stairs and into the lavatory. He locks the door, exits via the window, and gets the revolver from the Irishman, who waits in the side alley and who has rented a carriage and tied it up on St. James Street. Godwin runs around to the back door, is let in by the butler, and shoots his fish in a barrel, as you so aptly put it. He collects the money, to replace that which he laid out to frame the bobby, and he is out of the room perhaps fifteen seconds before you break in. He rounds the corner, hands the money and revolver over to his accomplice, and crawls back into the lavatory. Then he sprinkles some water on his crotch—"

"The spot he showed was made by urine," John told his host. "I had a chance to smell his trousers later that night and took it."

"You did?" Conan Doyle absorbed the unusual image for a moment, then waved John's pronouncement away with his hand.

"We must keep reminding ourselves that this is a very clever man. Since it was clearly part of his plan, then he made sure to urinate on them. If he'd let a few drops fall in moderation at an earlier time and let them dry, the odor wouldn't have carried . . . especially in a room filled with cigar and cigarette smoke. All that was necessary when he crawled back into the lavatory was to sprinkle some water on the area. Precious seconds saved." Doyle cocked one eyebrow. "How did you find an opportunity to sniff his trousers, if it's not too indelicate to ask?"

"He left them on a clothes butler out in the upstairs hall. So would I have if I'd wet myself."

Conan Doyle tidied up the cards he had laid down to that point. "Or if you wanted the celebrated Sheriff John Le Brun to smell them and be satisfied. You know the fact that truly proves the man is clever and ruthless?"

"That he invited a lawman into his home at the very time he was plannin' to commit a crime."

"Exactly! Who but a fool would do such a thing? A fool . . . or a genius."

"You make him sound like Professor Moriarty's brother," John quipped, speaking of Sherlock Holmes's criminal genius rival, about whom John had never read but had heard much from friends who were fans. He thought about observing aloud that Conan Doyle was exercising his author's prerogative too much and adding elements the facts did not support. Instead, he asked, "Have you ever worried that your stories might give criminal types ideas?"

"My stories are too famous," Doyle answered confidently. "Police all around the world read me. The Paris police actually use my tales as casebooks. A copycat would be caught in a trice." The author took in a deep breath. "So, the accomplice now has the weapon and the money . . . explaining why neither we nor the police could find either. He walks casually out of the alley, across the pavement, and into the carriage. You arrived on the same spot half a minute later, in time to see him rounding the corner. Everything still agree with the evidence?"

"Nothin' contradicts it," John said.

"I'll take that as a positive statement. We now skip ahead to Sunday. Where was Godwin during the day?"

"He said he had much work to do for his two dead clients. He claimed to work with their wives throughout the afternoon in his office."

"I don't doubt that in the least. This man is far too smart to tell a lie that could easily be exposed. However, the accomplice is perfectly free to travel back down to Brighton. Let us stick with your assumption that he's a dock worker."

"Actually, it was the guess of the icehouse owner," John corrected.

"And a damned fine observation, don't you agree?"

"Since so many London Irishmen work the docks, it *is* a logical guess," John granted.

"Beyond logic," Conan Doyle countered. "Rather, a mathematical likelihood. So, this lad returns to Brighton. He uses the office entrance key he's removed from Attwater's ring to gain entrance to the warehouse. He's a dock worker, used to lifting great weights. He takes the corpse down to the lower floor and unwraps it. He positions the body precisely where it originally fell. He lets the revolver drop from shoulder height, probably taking off the safety only after it has fallen, to prevent accidental discharge."

Conan Doyle rubbed his hands together. "Now, to the suicide apology. Your description indicates that you are dubious of its originality."

"That's not exactly true," John replied. "It *was* his handwritin'. I could tell Trent recognized it. I'm sure at any rate that Scotland Yard will make a comparison, to be certain. I question why the so-called suicide apology was written on only the bottom third of the paper."

"You believe the words might have served a different purpose and been saved for the convenience of a double meaning."

"That's right."

"Good for you!" said Conan Doyle. "I've already told you that the Godwins hosted some two dozen parties a year. Undoubtedly, Attwater was invited to several of them. Equally undoubtedly, he either had a conflict or simply didn't want to return for the same boring fare. He wrote an apology. Godwin saw the words that could help him cement the image of a suicide. He neatly tore off the part that didn't apply and saved the rest. Such props don't land in one's lap on the day before a murder. This would suggest Godwin had been planning this infamy for weeks or months." He looked suddenly toward the door. "How long does it take to boil tea and ice it down?" he asked the door. Not waiting for it to answer, he sprang up and headed for the kitchen. "Excuse me, John."

John waited until the noise of Doyle's movements had faded, then reached across the desk for his cards and examined them. He found no surprises, set them down, and contented himself to examining instead various photos and placards on the walls. One of the frames held a thank-you note from Joseph Caillaux, the French Minister for Foreign Affairs, for not only deigning to meet with the dignitaries visiting England to celebrate the signing of the Entente Cordiale but for also entertaining them royally at his home. His host had pictures taken with the highest ranks of royalty. He also associated with the likes of H. G. Wells and Arthur Balfour. John decided that Arthur Conan Doyle was a complex creature, fiercely proud of his intellect and accomplishments, always believing himself right, not easily swayed and not lightly contradicted but also humble and self-effacing when he chose to be.

Minutes piled up, until a quarter hour had elapsed. John was about to rise to search for his host when Conan Doyle returned, carrying a tray with ice-filled glasses, a pitcher of tea, and glazed tea cakes. "Now, where were we?" he asked, setting the fare down in front of John. "Right. The corpse is rearranged in his original death position. The accomplice puts the piece of stationery in the left hand. I just telephoned Scotland Yard and had the Brighton coroner's report read to me. The coroner estimated that Attwater had been dead six to twelve hours. He used rigor mortis and temperature as his main determinates. Goes to show you how easy it is to fool that branch of medical science."

"It's still more like an art," Le Brun said. "There are simply too many variables. Body weight, how athletic the person was, how vigorously he'd been using his muscles just before death. Temperature, humidity. If the body's been moved, forget it."

"Especially if it's been moved into a tub of ice, eh?" Doyle said, saluting John with his glass of iced tea. "Using the warehouse's built-in capability was a stroke of genius. Godwin is truly a formidable adversary. Attwater was shot on Saturday, no later than three in the afternoon. When would you say he was put back where you found him?"

John finished chewing the cake that filled his mouth. "As late on Sunday as possible would be the prudent plan. Perhaps half an hour before the last train back to London. If—"

"Have a care!" Doyle crowed with delight. "You've forgotten about the farce played out on Green Street. The reason you couldn't find the weapon again was because Godwin didn't fire the bullet through his own window; his accomplice did it. Moreover, the Irishman took the trouble . . . no doubt under Godwin's direction . . . to disguise himself as Attwater. Same style suit, same hat, same limp. Godwin might even have guessed correctly that his stepdaughter would arrive home soon and got for his trouble her accurate description of the fleeing man. Therefore, the accomplice had to have arrived back from Brighton considerably earlier."

John waited patiently to see if the excited author had finished. When he was sure, he said, "I was goin' to say, 'If the accomplice is indeed a dock worker, then he gets his jobs when he shows up for a roust. Nobody is countin' on him bein' someplace day after day, if it's like our docks in Brunswick. So he could have taken a late train.' The original plan was probably as late as possible. Your explanation of movin' the body early on Sunday would need for Godwin and the accomplice to know that a maskin' fog would be rollin' in."

Conan Doyle's smile slipped slightly, but then he caught himself. "I often can predict London fogs, given the day's weather and the time of year. Godwin may well have also. It was certainly worth trying. After all, the ruse got you off his trail. Didn't it?"

"I shifted my focus after that," John conceded.

The smile that resurrected on Conan Doyle's face was far wider than before. "Not to belittle his esteem for your reputation, John, but I do believe the ruse was meant to throw *me* off the scent. It was *I*, after all, who boldly indicated my suspicion of him at the club. Deservedly or not, my opinion carries weight at Scotland Yard. Godwin had to prove that he had only survived the slaughter at the Sceptred Isle Club by the chance of a full bladder. Moreover, a clear attempt on his life Sunday gave him the perfect opportunity to remember the tontine and get you to travel down to Brighton with him to find the penitent suicide. Note, however, that he did not recall the tontine when the police were in his house interrogating him. He waited until it was no longer possible to get to Brighton that night. His timetable had to be adhered to.

"Godwin comes to your room at midnight to pretend to remember the tontine. He knows full well that the trains have stopped running to Brighton. The earliest you'll get to the warehouse is mid-morning. The body will have warmed up and appeared as if it had only lain there twelve hours or so. You have been manipulated since the moment you walked into his house."

"But he left me alone in the warehouse," John argued, "to find the tools of the ruse. Why would he do that?"

"Because he underestimated you." Conan Doyle sat on the corner of the desk and looked down on John. "The man is very smart. But in the end, anyone who commits murder by definition is not thinking rationally. His ego refused to let him worry that you would continue your investigation with so much evidence in front of you."

"Before you cement in your theory," John said, "I'd better tell you about my visit to Lionel Attwater, the dead man's son."

Conan Doyle's self-satisfied expression became somewhat wary. He stood up, walked around the desk, and placed himself down on his high-back chair. "By all means."

Omitting the presence of Dr. Saye, John began at the Attwater warehouse front gate and ended at the same place. He put particular emphasis on the facts of Mrs. Attwater's existence, that she had not yet made out a will, and that Lionel Attwater was Nahum's beneficiary for the tontine. His dissertation had a patently sobering effect on Conan Doyle.

"Very interesting indeed. Yet, I still say Trent Godwin is the inside favorite," Sir Arthur proclaimed. "Regardless, the definitive solution would seem to rest upon the capture of the 'busy young man' as you call him. He is necessary in either case."

John took a sip of the tea. It was as delicious as the iceman's tea had been repulsive. "In *every* case, I would say. And he should not be captured but simply found and followed, until he leads us to one of our suspects. If swiftly arrested, he could very well say he'd been hired by Attwater the older to get ice for his new warehouse and refuse to be linked to the crimes. So far, the ice pick, tarpaulin, and trough are circumstantial. Even if the police are able to make him an accomplice to murder, he might not reveal who hired him."

"You're right, of course," said Doyle. "He must be found but not arrested. I believe I'll move up to London for the next night or two. I can easily get extra help for Louise; I do it all the time. I'll stay in a room I often take at the Reform Club."

"You said you had membership in several clubs."

"The Athenaeum, Reform, Author's, and Turf. If you lived in London,you'd understand the need to join as many as you can reasonably afford." Doyle's eyes lit up. "Which reminds me: Last year, I was made a member of the Crimes Club. Several highly placed law officers as well as detective authors are members." He neatened up his stack of cards. "I should run all of our thoughts by them and see what they have to contribute. They might also know of this scar-faced Irishman."

"I suppose it couldn't hurt," John said, even while thinking the idea was all but useless. "What we really need is a force of men in plain clothes coverin' the waterfronts, watchin' for the man. That's what I wrote to Inspector Cooper. I didn't want him comin' after me for withholdin' evidence either."

"That's wise. And you emphasized the need to not alarm the man when found?"

"I did."

Conan Doyle leaned back in his chair. "Have another tea cake, why don't you?"

"Don't mind if I do."

"If it turns out that Trent is the man we ultimately seek, I hope I can count on you to give me credit for suspecting him from the first."

John bit down on the tasty treat, at the same time noting the earnest look on Sir Arthur's face. His plunge into the Boer War at an advanced age, his throwing himself into the political arena, his joining of many clubs, all attested to the fact that he felt his fame as a crime author was not enough. This day, he badly wanted public credit for the solution of a real crime.

"That's fine with me, Arthur," John allowed.

"Terrific!"

"Will you come back on the train with me?"

"Sorry. I've got several things to tend to before I can leave." John imagined him furiously amending his notes and adding all that John had just told him, then writing it out longhand for Scotland Yard. Doyle glanced at his watch. "The next train is in twenty-three minutes. I'll just accompany you up to the station, dash back here, and catch a later train."

John washed down the rest of his second cake with a large gulp of tea. "I believe we should meet this evenin' to coordinate our activities. I'm supposed to join Geoffrey Moore at the Sceptred Isle Club for dinner at eight and then go on to a lecture."

"I'll meet you there." Doyle sprang up from his chair. "Let's be on the way."

AS DOYLE LED LE BRUN toward his garage, he advised, "You're becoming too well known in relation to this case. You should affect some sort of disguise when you look for the Irishman. Perhaps shave off your mustache."

"Think of somethin' else," John replied.

"A goatee, then. A little spirit gum, some false hair, and *voilà!* A military uniform would be nice as well. You're of French ancestry. A French sea captain would fit right in on the docks. And you wouldn't be arrested for impersonating a British officer."

"Where would I get such a goatee and uniform?"

"Nothing is easier." Conan Doyle extracted a small notepad from his jacket pocket, found a pen, and scribbled several lines. "This is the name and address of London's best-equipped theatrical costumers. They also excel in wigs and beards. Just show them my card and say you're a personal friend, and they'll treat you like royalty. I depend on them as a resource for my detective mysteries. In fact, tell them why you need the costume, and they'll probably offer its loan gratis."

John accepted the paper. "I'll consider it seriously."

Holden, the chauffeur, was buffing the automobile when

they entered the garage. He raced around the car and opened a back door with sprightly movements.

Doyle gestured for John to enter first. "It's not just the greater speed that's so wonderful about motorcars," he remarked. "They require far less care. You don't have to curry them or rub them with liniment or feed them whether you ride them or not. But the greatest advantage is that they don't piss and poop all over the streets. London is a misery throughout the year and hell in the heat of summer. Each horse produces between three and four *tons* of manure a year, if you can believe it. Flies and other vermin live on it, and they spread typhoid, diarrhea, and dysentery. I was reading just the other day that there were almost a quarter million horses within the city of London in 1900. What was it . . . eighty thousand pulling trams and omnibuses and one hundred and ten thousand cart and van horses. The rest pulled two- and four-wheeled cabs, and then there were the private carriages. Just five years later, that number is down forty percent! Another five years, and they'll have all but disappeared."

"The world is changin' at an incredible speed," John agreed.

"Well, the stablemen can turn their places of business into parking lots. But woe to the buggy whip maker and the blacksmith. Pretty soon, horseshoes will be used only for sport."

The car lurched into first gear, disguising John's reaction as he sat bolt upright in his seat. He looked to see if Conan Doyle had caught his shock, but the man had busied himself observing that the car's right fender safely cleared the garage frame.

"I wonder if I might ask you a personal question?" John said.

"Ask away," Doyle invited. "You know, we're so proper and stuffy in England that we won't even speak to someone we're sitting next to unless we've been introduced. It's always a joy to me to meet an American, because you're so friendly and direct. I made a whirlwind tour of your country in 1894. Didn't get to see many sites, but I was feted by many gracious folk."

"You didn't travel through the South."

"No, unfortunately. Just the North and Midwest."

The reply was no surprise to John. Conan Doyle had formed his opinion from people who were frank. The people John lived among were rarely direct; a stranger seldom knew if an effusive invitation to visit again was genuine or not. He figured that someone as perceptive as Arthur Conan Doyle would have caught that and, consequently, not have made a remark about directness to a Southerner.

"Geoffrey said you once ran for parliament."

"I did. I was only defeated because of a last-minute scare campaign launched by an Evangelical fanatic. Posters by the hundreds pretended that I was attempting to hide my Irish background. They called me a Papist conspirator."

"Are you sure it wasn't because you supported Home Rule?"

Doyle looked at Le Brun askance. "Supported? What gave you that idea? I vigorously reject Home Rule."

"You do?"

"Absolutely."

"In spite of your birth and your Irish Catholic background?"

"I had no control over those circumstances. I consider myself *British*," Conan Doyle declared with obvious pride. "A citizen of the British Empire."

"But, bein' of Irish ancestry," John persisted, "don't you feel at least ambivalent about the centuries of English oppression? The land stealin', and even allowin' the Irish to starve durin' the potato famines?"

"I don't condone the cruelties and abuses of past governments," Doyle answered, in a calm and even voice. "However, these do not argue sufficiently that Ireland should not have been annexed. For one thing, British rule stopped the constant clan warfare. As part of the greatest empire in the world, they benefit immensely from being able to export their linen and crystal around the world. To import from dozens of countries. If Ireland weren't part of the Empire, they wouldn't have thousands of men at work building British ships. Are you an opponent of Imperialism, Mr. Le Brun?"

"I believe there are better ways to run the world."

"Really? Well, you live in a land that has practiced imperialism since the Monroe Doctrine. Your country effectively controls the entire New World. In fact, I have read of your politicians referring to Central and South America as 'Our backyard.' Not to mention your control over Hawaii and the Philippines."

Le Brun smiled. "I was not consulted on any of those matters."

"My fondest wish, Mr. Le Brun," Doyle said, "is that one day the United States and the British Empire might join in an English-speaking confederation and benevolently rule the world for its own good. We are natural allies, and the world hates and envies our supremacy."

John knew that a large part of the world had certainly come to hate England for its war with the Boers over the control of South African gold and diamonds. In their frustration over Boer guerrilla tactics, the British army had come to burn farms and crops, kill livestock, rape and loot, and pack Boer women and children into concentration camps, where typhoid and measles killed them in appalling numbers. He registered that Conan Doyle's volunteering for that war at forty spoke volumes on his confidence in imperialism and that such reminders why England was hated would not be well received. John would not pursue the general subject, but he could not let drop the Irish Question.

"World issues, aside," John said, "in Ireland, the British badly botched the potato famine. They made it even worse when they took over lands that were vacated by a million deaths and two million emigrants. They would burn down cottages, to make sure families didn't squat in them. I got firsthand reports from Irishmen servin' beside me durin' the War of Northern Aggression."

"It's all true. Those same men returned with plenty of experience and were intent on using it to free their homeland. The British began to be afraid, especially after they were forced to put down an uprising in 1867. Ever since, there have been Irish and English parliamentarians believing the troubles won't end until Ireland has its own self rule. In 1893, it passed in the House of Commons but was defeated by the Lords. It was reintroduced in 1900 and came even closer. Ever closer, but not yet passed."

"And how close is it to passing today?"

"Close indeed, unfortunately. The Liberals have made great gains in elections. If they win enough districts, next year might actually see Home Rule pass. And that's all I can tell you, for here we are in Haslemere."

To John's great relief, Holden had driven the vehicle at a safe speed all the way. The drive had been so smooth and uneventful that he had been able to concentrate on Doyle's words without distraction.

"One last, quick question," John said. "Are Exeter and Devon close to each other?"

"Exeter is a town. It's the county seat of Devonshire, which people call 'Devon' for short."

"I see."

"Why do you ask?"

"Just somethin' that two people said which confused me." John hopped out of the car and shut the door, leaving Doyle wearing a quizzical expression. "See you tonight at the Sceptred Isle Club!"

SIR ARTHUR CONAN DOYLE had told John a great deal more than he could have imagined on the ride from his home to the train station. His words were enough to set Le Brun's mind churning for the entire return trip to Waterloo Station.

From there, John took a motorized cab across the Thames to Harrods department store. He tried on his new formal togs, found them to his satisfaction, and paid the price. He asked directions to the Westminster Palace Hotel, learned that it lay only a mile to the east, and decided to walk. He had still not finished working out his thoughts, and the day begged exercise. He threaded his way through the fashionable streets and parks of Belgravia, where Geoffrey Moore had his home. Every time he saw a man mounted on horseback, he stopped and stared. As many times, he was disappointed.

When John checked with the hotel desk for messages, he found one waiting. It was inside a light pink envelope and was fragrant with the smell of Veronica Godwin. He waited until he was up in his room to open it. It read:

Dearest John—

I received your note and am sorry that you felt you could not stay longer with us. I was unable to get away last night as you requested. I came by today at noon but found you gone. I will come again tomorrow at noon, so that we may, as the French say, explore a matinee. If you cannot be here at that hour telephone the house, or if you are ill at ease doing that, leave me a message at the front desk.

Yours,
Veronica

John smiled and set the note on the dressing table. He opened the box with his formal wear and laid it out for the evening. He had half-expected another note from Inspector Bob Cooper, but evidently his morning posting had not yet arrived at Scotland Yard. He glanced at his watch and saw that the time was nearing five. He hurried back down to the hotel's main desk.

The Office of Events, it turned out, was on the second floor, close by the Westminster Palace's grand ballroom. After learning this, John trudged up the wide staircase and pictured the parade of peacocks ascending in exactly this place to Mrs. Godwin's Mayfair Mothers for Cleanliness Ball three nights hence. He located the booking office, knocked, and entered.

"Mr. Pierre Dancourt?" John asked, of the petite man seated behind an equally petite French baroque desk.

"That is I," said the man. He wore pince nez glasses, had his hair heavily brilliantined, and sported a tiny mustache such as John knew to be the fashion in Paris. He pronounced his "th" as a "z." Whether it was for real or effect, John could not have cared less.

"I am John Le Brun," he said, softening the "j". "I'm currently a guest of your fine hotel."

The man set down his gold nib pen and swiftly blotted the sentence he had just written. "Yes, sir?"

John reached into his inside pocket for his old business card. He handed it to the man. "I'm in London on holiday, but I'm also explorin' the possibility of hostin' the International Law Enforcement Symposium here." While the agent looked over his card, he added, "I am on the symposium committee, you see. We come from forty-seven countries around the world and would have approximately three hundred representatives stayin' for five days." He paused, so the man could let the numbers sink in.

"And when would this be?"

"Twenty-one months from now. Third week in July, 1907," John embroidered. "I was wonderin' about group rates for, say, two hundred rooms and the cost of rentin' the grand ballroom and meetin' rooms."

"We can certainly work up competitive figures for you, Monsieur Le Brun. May I ask what other hotels you are considering?"

"Oh, I suppose some of the newer ones toward the center of the city. But right now you're my first choice. You see, I'm a friend of the Godwins."

Dancourt smiled broadly. "Mrs. Maeve Godwin?"

"Yes. Exactly. She says you're doin' a smashin' job with her Mayfair Mothers for Cleanliness event."

Dancourt dipped his head in a humble gesture. "We are doing our best."

"Although I hear the flowers have been somethin' of a disaster."

"But that has nothing to do with us," the agent was quick to reply.

"She was here most of Saturday afternoon, was she not?"

"Yes, indeed. And most of Sunday as well. We have supplied her and her committee with a room next door, from which they coordinate everything."

"Did you personally work with her on Saturday and Sunday?"

"Yes, I did. Mrs. Godwin is one of my favorite ladies. This will be the third year we have hosted the ball for her."

"That's a recommendation in itself."

The man swung around on his revolving chair, to grab a large ledger book on the cabinet behind him. John noted that he wore white spats over his patent leather shoes. "Shall we discuss specifics?"

Having gotten the information he needed, John resigned himself to working his lie through to its conclusion. When they had finished, he rose and said, "I'm stayin' in Room four-fourteen. You can leave the estimate with the desk."

"Yes, of course. My pleasure." The little man held out his equally small hand, with its thin, long fingers.

As John gave the hand a firm shake, he said, "If you would, don't mention our conversation with Mrs. Godwin. I don't want her feelin ' upset if my committee should decide to book another hotel . . . if you know what I mean." John himself didn't know what he meant, but the agent nodded firmly.

"Of course. We are the soul of discretion at the Westminster Palace."

"And the heart of service," John added, wincing internally.

The agent beamed.

BEFORE LEAVING FOR the Sceptred Isle Club, John took himself to one of the hotel's telephone cabinets and dialed Thomas Saye's residence. A woman with a low yet feminine voice answered. When John identified himself, she recognized his name and called out to her husband. Several moments later, Dr. Saye picked up.

"Hello, John," he said, somewhat out of breath. "Not a bit of news from Lambeth or Southwark. I asked my scouts to pay special attention to the docks, but—"

"I don't believe the man we're lookin' for will be found on the river," John interrupted.

"What about his scar?"

"I no longer believe it was made by a ship's block."

"Really? Then by what?"

"A horseshoe."

"Yes, that would make a U-shaped scar as well. But why abandon the search on the waterfront?"

"Because I'm fairly sure I know who involved him."

"Who?"

"I won't say until I'm certain." John switched the earpiece to his other ear. "Don't call off your scouts, just in case I'm wrong."

"Very well."

"Have you examined Attwater's body yet?" John asked.

"No. I called the Brighton coroner's office mid-afternoon, but they still hadn't released him. The money wasn't wired."

"Now, that's strange," John said. The figure of Lionel Attwater came into his mind fleetingly, but he shoved it back into memory. Other suspects were far higher on his list. "Was the blood sample analyzed?"

"Yes."

"I'm speculatin', but I say it's either cow or pig blood."

"Wrong. It's human. Moreover, its blood group is 'O.' I'll have Attwater's blood typed when he arrives."

"Please do."

"Let me guess: You thought that when the body was put back in the same place where it was slain, they went through the trouble of bringing in fresh blood, in order to make the murder seem more recent."

"I did. I still think it . . . except now I believe Mr. Attwater's own blood was bottled, frozen, and thawed, purely for the same reason."

Saye made a low whistling sound. "And I thought I was meticulous in executing Erastus Springer."

"You were. But this goes beyond meticulous," John judged. "I would call it extravagant in the details of its execution. There was no way this crime could have been simple, but it's unnecessarily complicated."

"And do you know why?"

"I believe I do. Please see that your calendar is cleared for the next three nights."

"I . . . " There was a substantial silence on the other end of the line. Then, in an unhappy voice, Thomas Saye said, "Can you at least let me know by five o'clock if you won't need me?"

"You have a considerable debt to repay, Dr. Russell," John reminded, purposely using Saye's former name.

"I'm sorry."

"I will endeavor to let you know by five o'clock. And I will call you tomorrow mornin'. Where shall I try you?"

"At University College Hospital."

"Thank you, Doctor. And wish your dear wife a pleasant evening for me, won't you?"

THE SCEPTRED ISLE CLUB was not the morgue that Mr. Roundsville had predicted it would be. In fact, the manager made a point to rush up and tell John so the moment he saw him enter the club.

"We haven't had this many members in on a Tuesday evening in years," he gushed. "I was able to corner two of them and force them to pay their back dues."

"That's nice," John said, removing his topcoat.

"And we've had seven new applications for membership in the past three days," Roundsville went on. "It turns out that you and Inspector Cooper were right; the murders have given the club notoriety without making it notorious."

"Well said, Mr. Roundsville," John praised. He wished the man were a member, so he could have dined with him and enjoyed his mastery of the language. At the same time, he was dismayed at the manager's seemingly callous glee. *If Trent had died also,* John thought, *he could have had ten new applications.*

"Let's step into the coatroom together," John suggested. "I have a package for you."

Roundsville accepted the dozen pornographic photographs, which John had wrapped in brown paper, and acknowledged his thanks with a sharp nod. "I'm still wagering that Mr. Attwater is innocent," he imparted, dropping his voice to a half whisper. "Have I a chance of winning?"

"Bettin' is a bad habit," John replied.

"You won't say more."

"And neither will you. *If*... and I do emphasize 'if,' there is more to this crime, only bad will come of discussin' it. A word to the wise."

"Mum's the other word, then. I knew I was clever to hire you. Give me your coat and hat then. Mr. Moore's in the coffee room."

John entered the dining room. He saw Geoffrey leaning over one of the tables, chattering away as two other members listened. John watched his friend's animation, his hands flying and his eyebrows working up and down. The listeners nodded slowly, as if their heads were filled with helium and caught in a gentle breeze.

Geoffrey spotted his American friend and excused himself. Hurrying up to Le Brun, he gestured at a vacant table. "Good evening, John. Is that your new suit? You look splendid. I've reserved this for us."

"You know who will also be arrivin' soon is—"

"Sir Arthur. Yes, I know. He contacted me. Not being a member himself, he telephoned and asked if I'd add him to our reservation. I'm sorry that we shan't have some time alone," Geoffrey pouted.

"We'll talk before the lecture. I have been preoccupied . . . on *your* club's business," John reminded him.

"Yes, I know. We're still in a mild tizzy over Nahum Attwater. I didn't know him all that well; he favored the club more for the gambling than the historical pursuits. And he was, in several ways, a negative fellow. If the choice of villain were between him and Trent, I'd certainly choose him."

"I understand. I've been meanin' to ask you somethin', Geoffrey. You tried to impart some fact about Miss Veronica at their party that sounded rather salacious. What was that?"

Geoffrey struggled in vain to read his friend's mindset from his eyes. "Oh, she has a reputation for liking older men."

"As old as me?"

"Nearly."

"Nearly? That word indicates you know the age of at least one older man she's been linked to."

"It's not fair to her to spread a rumor."

But innuendo is evidently in bounds, John thought. "Is it a rumor?" he countered. "I thought you always got to the truth."

"I really shouldn't—"

"Just answer yes or no to this: He has been a Godwin party guest in the past six months but was not at the party I attended."

Geoffrey hesitated.

"We were recently speakin' of him," John encouraged. "You know that I know. Just say 'yes' so that your conscience remains clear."

"Yes."

"Thank you."

As surreptitiously as possible, John had kept his eye on the entrance to the coffee room while he spoke with Moore. It was of paramount import for him to get to Conan Doyle as early as possible, in order not to thwart the conclusion of the investigation.

"Arthur said you went down to Haslemere, to visit him," Geoffrey prompted.

"Yes. I've been havin' eye problems and wanted his professional opinion."

"Nothing serious, I hope."

"I hope also. Nothin' that can be done short of prayer." John stole another glance into the hallway. "It may clear up all by itself."

"Good. Was Arthur crushed that his suspicion of Trent was wrong?"

"He wasn't crushed at all," John evaded.

"Really?" The wrinkle in Geoffrey's cerebellum that controlled gossip kicked into high gear. "Arthur's a complex character. He hates to be wrong, y'know."

"I've observed."

"Very obstinate in his opinions. But, at the same time, he has so many positive virtues. He's generous to a fault. Humble and self-depracating when it comes to his writing talents. Supports much of his family."

"Really?"

"Bought at least one a house. And thinks he can master almost anything. I hope you didn't drive with him."

"I did."

"Oh, my. In his old car, he once approached a horse-drawn

cart so quickly from behind that the frightened animal reared up and dumped its turnips into the car's interior, burying Arthur and his mother. Not long afterward, he lost control of the machine coming through the gate to his home. The car ran up a steep incline and toppled over, throwing his brother clear but pinning Arthur. For a few moments, he was saved by the car's steering wheel and column. Otherwise, he'd have been instantly crushed. Then the steering wheel broke off, and he was pinned across his back and shoulders. Luckily, the loud noise of the accident had attracted a crowd, which joined together to save him."

During Moore's last sentence, Trent Godwin appeared in the coffee room archway. He spotted the duo and crossed to them.

"How are you, Trent?" Geoffrey inquired.

"Still wading through the morass of these murders," he replied. "Had the Ravenscroft and Wilbye funerals today, back to back."

"Oh, yes. Should have gone. But I've had the most dreadful business and domestic problems. We're having Sir Arthur to dinner," Geoffrey told Trent, as John consulted his watch. It read two minutes past eight.

"Will you both excuse me?" John asked, rising. "I forgot somethin' in my topcoat."

As John stepped into the club's main hallway, Arthur Conan Doyle came through the front door. John hurried to him.

"Something wrong, John?" Conan Doyle asked.

"Yes. Geoffrey Moore *and* Trent Godwin are here. If we want to bring this investigation to its proper conclusion, neither they nor anyone else in this club must believe that it is ongoin'. *Especially* Trent Godwin."

"I agree," Conan Doyle said, shrugging out of his topcoat. "When I spoke with Geoffrey this afternoon, I said nothing. We must present a charade for them."

"We must," John echoed.

"But we must also coordinate activities for finding your 'busy young man.' How should we do that?"

John knew that Doyle would be pleased to have control over the districts with the most Irish workers. He, on the other hand, had no intention of working near the river. "I'll take north of the Thames; you take south."

"I can enlist three persons to work with me. Can you rally any help?"

"One other," John answered disingenuously. He was not about to ask Dr. Saye to roam the docks looking for the man with the scar, although the man was certainly helping.

"Better than none, I suppose. That was simple enough. Let's dine."

"Lead the way," John invited.

Walking in Conan Doyle's wake, John detected the telltale trace of expensive perfume. The afternoon had not been a single-minded pursuit of the club murders for the author.

"Gentlemen," Sir Arthur greeted.

Trent Godwin glowered at Doyle. "Am I supposed to dine with you, after you tried to pin these wicked crimes on me?" he asked.

"And why not?" Doyle replied, nonchalantly pulling out an unoccupied chair and sitting. "After all, you've triumphed and made me out the fool."

"It's like besting Sherlock Holmes himself," Moore the perennial peacemaker suggested.

Godwin did not seem mollified. He looked at John. "I understand you two spent the morning together. Can I assume Sir Arthur knows about the tontine?"

"He does," John admitted.

"Is there any other motive you can think of for my murdering half my friends, sir?" Trent asked Conan Doyle.

"More than thirty thousand pounds seemed quite enough motive for me," Conan Doyle replied.

Trent snapped his linen napkin sharply above the table and laid it on his lap. "Then let me put your mind completely at rest about my innocence: It is my intention to donate the entire sum to charity."

Only the motion of sitting disguised John's startled reaction to the news. Geoffrey Moore's quick exclamation of praise further distracted his dinner companions.

"Have you discussed your decision with your wife?" John asked.

"I *informed* her," said Godwin. "There was nothing to discuss. I might hold back my initial investment of four thousand pounds, but I couldn't under any circumstances keep the rest. It's become blood money."

"A noble decision, Trent," Geoffrey said again.

"Will you make the donation at the charity ball this Friday?" John asked, laboring to keep the alarm out of his voice.

"No. I won't get a check for about a month. I suppose I could make a pledge that night, but that's Maeve's charity, not mine. I'm still thinking about a fitting use for it. Perhaps to Hugh, Ralph, and Eddie's favorite causes."

John looked at Conan Doyle, who was studying Trent Godwin with new eyes. Godwin, in turn, regarded the author with a forward-thrust chin, his eyes blinking furiously. Geoffrey's eyes darted back and forth between the two. No one said anything.

"What's good on the menu?" John asked, brightly.

IT WAS AFTER DINNER, when Trent and Geoffrey were taken into another room by club members curious about the latest news, that Conan Doyle said to Le Brun, "I must admit, Godwin's statements about the tontine money set me aback."

"Me as well," John said, with a completely different meaning than his companion.

"You read of murderers who get away with crimes for lack of evidence pledging not to rest until the real culprits are found. The minute they walk out of the courtroom, their pledge is forgotten. I believe he's blowing smoke at us, trying to become the hero of the day in everyone's eyes. You mark my word: He'd think and think about which charities to send the money to, but it will never happen. Next thing you knew, if anyone should have the temerity to ask, he'll be compelled to borrow against the money for some disaster. But he'll replace it, he'll say. Time will pass. Everyone will forget." Doyle threw himself restlessly against the back of his seat. "But, of course, we'll see that his little plan doesn't have a chance to work. He'll have to sign over that check from his jail cell."

"Did you have a chance to stop by Scotland Yard this afternoon?" John asked, wondering if Doyle had turned in his modified solution to Trent's exquisitely planned crime.

"I did. Everyone assigned to the case was out. I did leave my report for Chief Inspector Tibbles. I'm sure he'll be at the Reform Club's front door tomorrow early to see me."

"I'm sure. He won't like what he reads. By then, he's certain to have gotten his name in the newspapers as the triumphant detective."

"Has your letter produced any reaction?"

"None that I know of."

"I meant to ask you: Have you secured a disguise yet?"

"Not yet."

Conan Doyle gave out a soft snort. "What's that line from *Hamlet*? 'That one may smile and smile and still be a villain.' If that doesn't describe Trent Godwin. He is one cold bastard."

"It is amazin' how nice some villains can smile," John agreed, grimly.

NINE

Wednesday, October 25, 1905

AFTER HE REQUESTED THAT his room be changed, John ate a light breakfast of a raspberry muffin with black coffee. It was the day after his second solemn promise to himself to quit the Sceptred Isle Club investigation and get on with his vacation. As far as he was concerned, he had actually solved the crime under his self-imposed deadline of Tuesday afternoon. How long it would take to bring it to a satisfactory conclusion, however, was beyond his knowing. If he could gain some control over the matter, his new timetable to having the entire affair behind him would be Saturday morning. Control depended on those in authority lending their authority to him.

On the way into the Westminster Palace Hotel's main dining room, he chanced to see a pair of opera glasses in the window of the jewelry shop that operated just off the lobby. Using Southern charm and the persuasion of a one-pound tip, he was able to have the shop opened early to purchase the glasses. He learned that they only magnified his view two-and-half times, but he figured that would be all he needed. For his purpose and for the place where he expected to use them, military binoculars would have been out of place and apt to draw attention.

John hailed a hansom cab and directed the driver to Mayfair. He had secured a city directory of services that listed two riding academies in that section of town. There was also one in the Lancaster Gate/Paddington area and three in Kensington/Knightsbridge. Unless others existed which were unlisted, a total of six academies around the rectangle of Kensington Gardens and Hyde Park was not a daunting proposition for John to cover. Mayfair was the most likely, however. He walked a short block to the first academy and, without any disguise, ventured several steps inside. A young Irishman working the docks or warehouses might have been warned of Le Brun's interest in him and even had a description; a young Irish stable hand or riding instructor would not. The man with the U-shaped scar was not there. John did the same in the second stable and had similar results. He was not discouraged; the hour was quite early. In all probability, he reckoned, the stable hands and riding instructors came and went in shifts.

Hyde Park abutted the Mayfair district. He had been told by Geoffrey Moore that Rotten Row was the path on which the elite of the city paraded most often on horseback. He hiked to the park and walked halfway down the road's nearly-one-mile length. Because it was the middle of the week, the equestrian traffic was relatively light. However, single or paired horseback riders passed him every half-minute or so. Geoffrey had also informed him that during the three months of May through July (which he had learned from Veronica was the London Season) there was a daily parade in Hyde Park. It took place on the Knightsbridge side of the park between noon and two o'clock, with carriages converging on the southeast corner of Rotten Row in overabundance. The point was to be seen. Young women in carriages could pause and converse with dashing young men on sleek mounts. Mounted guards kept a careful eye on the barouches and landaus and limited the number of circuits, so that other private conveyances could take their turn. Clockwise they would roll, down Rotten Row and back via the Carriage Road. Both roads were extremely wide, separated from the gravel walkways by iron posts and rails. Farther back stood magnificent old trees, limbs spread wide as if in beneficence. John would have liked to have witnessed the parade. He imagined there was something stirring and elegant about it and, at the same time, vapid and silly.

John put himself down on a bench every few minutes, took out his opera glasses, and pretended to be bird watching. Instead, he focused on every young man riding past. None had a scar on his forehead. When nearly two hours had passed, he left the park and hunted down the academies in the Kensington/Knightsbridge area. His quarry was again not to be found.

Footsore, John caught a pair of trams back to the hotel. He made a telephone call to Dr. Saye. The doctor was not available, but when his secretary heard John's name, she passed along the information that Nahum Attwater's body was on its way up from Brighton. Dr. Saye expected to have the second autopsy performed by the University College Hospital's chief pathologist and under his own watchful eye by the end of the afternoon.

When he checked in at the front desk, John learned that he had a message. Inspector Bob Cooper had come by the hotel around ten o'clock and been extremely disappointed not to find him. His note said that he would return at one o'clock, and if John got the message and could not wait in the hotel, he must inform the desk where he would be. Under no circumstances was he to leave the city. John tore the note into unreadable pieces and handed it over to the clerk. He had no intention of going anywhere. His one problem would be to prepare Veronica for Inspector Cooper's appearance. He handed over his opera glasses and asked the clerk to store them in his letter cubicle.

John positioned himself in the lobby where he could watch virtually every entrance. Two minutes before noon, Veronica Godwin strode long-legged into the hotel, wearing high-button shoes, a long-skirted tailored suit, a blouse with *jabot*, and, on her head, a toque with a short veil thrown back. All of this was under a duster that she had left unbuttoned. She was the perfect image of the society damsel set to motor.

"Bon jour!" Veronica exclaimed, as John stood. She offered her gloved hand for him to kiss.

Her buff yellow suit and ecru dustcoat blended beautifully with the huge floral decoration of chrysanthemums directly behind her. He wished that photography had advanced enough to capture color. He would have paid a small fortune for such a miracle of science just to capture this moment. "I admire your outfit very much," he said.

Veronica leaned in to his ear. "But there's hardly a stitch under it. Not enough to stuff into a snuff box."

"What a pity that I won't be able to admire that as well," John replied, whispering back.

Veronica blinked in surprise. "Why not?"

John put on a dismayed face as he helped her out of her dustcoat. "They're changing my room. Something about a group having engaged the entire fourth floor. I won't get my new room until after three."

"My God! Should we nip off to another hotel, or just rut in their back alley?" Veronica's eyes were merry.

"I would never hear of either. It may surprise you to learn this, but I would be just as delighted if you would spend an hour or so conversin' with me and havin' lunch."

Veronica took a step back and surveyed John as if with new eyes. "Now I know why I've taken such a fancy to you. You really do like me for more than my body."

"You are among a handful of the most interestin' women I have known in my life," he replied.

Peeling off her gloves, she replied, "Then how can I be disappointed *or* refuse your new invitation? And you're right that I am a handful."

They strolled into the dining room with Veronica's arm inside the crook of John's elbow.

"The last time I saw you was from under your bed," Veronica announced, loudly enough to scandalize the matrons standing next to them who were also waiting for a table. Fortunately for them, they were led away at that moment.

"True enough."

"A great deal has happened since."

"A great deal," John echoed. "Surely Trent has told you."

"He told Mother and me about the two of you finding Nahum Attwater inside the locked warehouse and of Chief Inspector Tibbles showing up shortly after. The evidence of his guilt and suicide was abundant."

"Indeed. I expect by now that they have proven the gun next to his body was the same gun used in the gamblin' room."

The maître d' approached with a spring in his step and a sly smile on his lips. "Two for luncheon?" he asked.

"Since the hotel won't let us do anything else," Veronica declared, crushing the man's smile.

"Yes. Two for luncheon," John confirmed.

They were led to a table for two located by an exterior window. After they received their menus, Veronica said, "I'm only slightly surprised that Nahum Attwater was the culprit. A charming man when first you met him, but a snake underneath." She stared at John. "However, you must not be surprised but dubious; you're still investigating."

"What makes you think that?" John evaded.

"Trent said you went down to Arthur Conan Doyle's house yesterday. He and you began working together last Saturday night."

"I did visit him," John admitted, "but in his capacity as eye doctor." He told her about the problem with his right vitreous humor and received effusive sympathy and a promise to kiss it and make it better.

The waiter arrived, announced the specials, and took their drink order. Veronica asked for mineral water, and John allowed that that would be fine with him as well.

"Actually, I *was* investigatin' after returnin' from Brighton," John shared.

"Really? What?"

"Before we found the body, your stepfather had put forth the theory that Lionel Attwater was behind both the killin's and the attack on your father at your house. He knew that Lionel was the beneficiary if Nahum Attwater was the last survivor of the tontine. I visited the Attwater warehouse in East Ham, found the young Mr. Attwater there, and confronted him."

Veronica's violet-blue eyes widened with interest. "Did you? I've never met him. Trent says he's a worse cad than his old man."

"He's not as terrible as your stepfather paints. However, I did learn from his own lips that he was cut out of his father's will. The interestin' part is that his mother still lives, has no will, and does not share the father's and Trent's low opinion of him."

The young woman screwed up her mouth. "Hmm! So, he as much as gave himself a motive for murdering his father."

"He did."

"Could he have done it?"

"There's the question. Yesterday morning I posted a letter to Scotland Yard, telling them what I'd learned. It's up to them to determine if there's a possibility Nahum Attwater didn't actually kill himself."

"But you saw the evidence."

The waiter returned with the mineral water, suspending the conversation. John and Veronica took the opportunity to order. Veronica's soup was Consommé à l'Andalouse, which had a garnishing of timbales, cucumber crescents, and small quenelles. John asked for Consommé Balzac, with timbales, chicken, shrimp, green peas, and turnip balls. For their main course, both ordered Grenadins of Tenderloin Marcus Aurelius, with side orders of cucumbers fried and breaded "in the English style." Their wine was a *cru classe* Bordeaux.

The moment the waiter had left, John said, "The desk clerk tells me that Inspector Cooper will be visitin' me here at about one o'clock. That's the other reason we must limit our sensory pleasures to food."

"Did any evidence suggest that Lionel might have set his father up and murdered him?" Veronica persisted.

"Nothin' I saw around the body," John evaded.

"He may have been very careful and thorough. Did he offer alibis for his presence on Saturday and Sunday nights?" Veronica asked.

"He said he could produce witnesses."

"A dozen drinking cronies, no doubt."

John was not amazed that Veronica should know such a detail about a supposed stranger's life. He made no comment on the fact and rather answered, "Again, I've left all that footwork up to the police."

"Good for you! You are, after all, on holiday."

"And I am so dreadfully behind in the things I've wanted to do," John said. "Added to that is your kind offer to chaperone me. I declined that horseback ride Sunday and am now desolate for havin' done so. Perhaps you'll give me another chance."

"Certainly." Veronica patted John's hand.

"Where do you ride?"

"Various places, both in the city and the country."

"Where in the city?"

"Hyde Park mostly. Also Regent and Richmond Parks."

"And do you have your own horse?"

"I did, but it died last winter. I rent one now."

"Different ones for different parks."

"Exactly. The variety of mounts is something of a challenge."

"Which you adore. And are you takin' motorin' lessons?"

"I am. But well outside the city, where I can't do much damage. I'm taking a lesson this afternoon, in fact. As if you couldn't tell. Do you motor?"

"No indeed. It's not my idea of sport." John looked at the passing crowd on the other side of the window. "I also want to go to Albert Hall. I don't care what I see there. And I must attend a Gilbert and Sullivan operetta done by the D'Oyly Carte company."

"Yes, at the Savoy."

"May I take you to one of them tonight?"

"I doubt that you could get tickets on such short notice," Veronica said. "And I do have another engagement."

"Some handsome young man, no doubt."

Veronica momentarily shifted her gaze to the center of the room. When she looked back, she said, "Don't tell me you're the jealous type."

"Of youth in any form I am," John replied.

Veronica's look took on a wicked aspect. "Have you noticed all the stares we're getting?"

"Yes. They're tryin' to figure out if I'm your uncle and they should be ashamed of themselves or if I'm your sugar-daddy and they're justified in their righteous disapproval."

Veronica giggled, and John heard the distinctive tinkling of garden bells.

"Tell me about your three older lovers," John invited.

"Absolutely not. I don't kiss and tell."

John straightened his utensils. "One of them wasn't Geoffrey Moore, was it?"

Veronica put two fingers in her water glass and sprayed John. "Certainly not! But he would love it. I believe he learned of my predilection from one of my former paramours who *does* kiss and tell. What about your *indoor* sports?" she asked and then brought her hands together in front of her mouth. "Why, John, that's the swiftest blush I ever saw on a man. I meant chess."

"That's a game, not a sport."

"Sex is a game *and* a sport. I believe I know how to beat you at chess now. This time if I lose, you can do anything you want to me."

These words were not so unexpected. John merely smiled back. "You know, my hometown of Brunswick is a resort. Naturally, you can get all kinds of entertainment there. A lady of easy virtue moved into town and didn't know I was sheriff. She sashayed up to me and said, 'If you pay me twenty dollars, I will do whatever you ask, as long as you express it in only three words.' I wanted to say, 'Paint my house,' but instead I flashed my badge and said, 'Leave town now.' "

"You wouldn't have said that if it were I, would you?" Veronica asked. Not waiting for an answer, she added, "Now that our plans were ruined today, we'll have to wait until this weekend to play. Mother's charity ball has me tied up right through Friday night. Get tickets for something on Saturday afternoon or evening. I can guarantee I won't be up before noon after the ball. It doesn't end until two."

"How can the men stay up so late after a long week of work?" John asked.

Veronica shook her head. "You must remember that these are wealthy men, John. They're the bosses. They come home in the early afternoon Friday and nap until six. I promise you Trent will. Not that he needs to; he rarely stays 'til the end of a party or function. Sometimes not even the final act of a play or opera."

"So I heard from him and Geoffrey."

"Why don't you come to the ball?" she suggested.

"I can't afford a ticket."

"Don't let that stop you. I'll sneak you in. You can be my date."

"That makes it enticin'. But I wouldn't fit in. I'd be ill at ease."

"I understand. And there might be a free-for-all anyway."

"What do you mean?"

"There's always the danger of two persons showing up in the same costume. In order to prevent that, Mum asks the attendees to return with their meal preference a card listing their characters on it. Only about half do. This year's theme is Nineteenth Century Americans. Last Friday, she got her second George Custer. She's contacted both, but each refuses to defer to the other."

"What an unmitigated disaster," John said in a mocking tone. "And over a Yankee general who graduated last in his class at West Point and who willfully led his troops to slaughter. If I was one of them, I'd change my character to Sittin' Bull, walk in with a tomahawk, and scalp the blond wig off the other."

"What a good idea! I'll pass your suggestion along to Maeve." She shrugged. "The problem is that nobody but me seems to want to portray a red Indian."

"Who are you?"

"Sacagawea. The Shoshone Indian maiden who led Lewis and Clark over the Northwest Passage."

"Good choice. I doubt, however, that many in the crowd will ever have heard of her."

"All the better. I shall make her my ice-breaker and reason to speak with everyone. I intend to campaign actively to win the best female costume."

"Is there a formal competition?"

"Absolutely. It's one of the highlights of the evening. For the best male and female costumes. Some man is missing the golden opportunity to win. I imagine a handsomely beaded buckskin outfit with war bonnet and paint would carry off the prize. But, then again, the winners aren't always those best costumed. After all the expenses, we only clear five pounds per person. The real profit comes from voting for best costumes at one pound per vote."

"I take it one can vote as many times as one likes."

"Right. So the ballot box gets stuffed. It's good for the charity, of course. Last year, a hundred and fifty-odd attendees cast more than a thousand votes. Say, why don't you come as a Southern sheriff, complete with genuine drawl?"

"Because there wasn't enough room in my suitcase for the penguin suits y'all wear *and* my sheriff's rig."

"Well, if you change your mind . . ."

"Who's your mother goin' as?"

"Lizzie Borden."

All John could say was, "Oh, my."

Their soups arrived, pausing the conversation. When they continued, John deftly steered around Veronica's innuendoes and overtures and forced her to talk about herself.

"Tell me about when you were very young," he invited.

"Have you ever been to Belfast?"

"No."

"It's a boring city. A work city. Not cultural like London. And it's just like other parts of Ireland; it looks ancient. That's because the commerce is so much slower. Buildings are never torn down for progress." She went on to describe her education at St. George's Episcopal School, her girlhood friends, and her early male admirers.

"How did your father die?" John asked.

Veronica cast her eyes downward. "He was an alcoholic. We lived in a two-story house. One night, he fell down the stairs and broke his neck."

"Horrible. Was he good to you?"

"When he was sober, which wasn't often. Here comes the main course."

Veronica changed the subject to plays and books. She talked almost without pause. Her depth regarding Irish drama and literature was impressive to John. While she spoke, John marveled at her captivating nature. Part of it she did with calculation she had clearly perfected over the years. What he liked, however, was that she was completely aboveboard about using it. Not for her the pseudo-subtle wiles of dropping handkerchiefs, sighing languidly, or swaying her hips as she passed. But she exuded a totally natural attraction as well, one which she undoubtedly had evidence that she possessed but which she would have been powerless to control. When his turn came to speak, she listened with rapt attention, without letting her mind jump ahead to what she wanted to say in reply. And while she spoke seriously about Oscar Wilde, she dipped the corner of her napkin into her water glass, reached across the table, and daubed a bit of sauce from the corner of John's mouth with no ceremony or calling to attention. All this, combined with the rest of what he knew about her, had him heartsick.

"I also know great Irish poetry," she said brightly. "There was a young lady of Gloucester/Whose friends they thought they had lost her/Till they found on the grass/The marks of her ass/And the knees of the man who had tossed her." When John had finished laughing, she said, "Tell me about some of the crimes you've solved."

John's stories took them through the main course and through the hour. After he paid and they left the room, John spotted Inspector Cooper waiting beside the huge floral arrangement.

Bob Cooper's eyes lit up as he focused on John's companion. "Good day, Miss Godwin! Mr. Le Brun!" he greeted.

"Good afternoon, Inspector Cooper," Veronica returned warmly. "Any more news about the club murders?"

"Well, that's what I'm here to speak to Mr. Le Brun about."

"He's told me; the business with Lionel Attwater."

Cooper shot a quick glance at Le Brun. "Yes. He's told you, has he?"

Veronica slipped her arm under and around John's. "Indeed. We have no secrets."

"How nice. However, I'm afraid this is official police business between the Sceptred Isle Club's consulting detective and Scotland Yard. You'll have to excuse us."

"How bureaucratic of you, Inspector," Veronica complained, sticking out her lower lips and pouting theatrically. She pivoted gracefully to face her would-be lover full on. "You'll let me know about Saturday, John."

"I will indeed."

Her merry expression blossomed. "You didn't think I'd forget about your eye, did you? Here's something to make it better." She took John's head lightly in her hands and kissed his right eyelid. Then she moved her lips to his ear. "And something extra, in case you get a toothache." She planted a quick kiss on his lips. "Thanks for lunch. Ta-ta, gentlemen! Keep London safe for us helpless females, won't you?"

Veronica moved toward the front doors with purpose, her dustcoat over her arm.

"You lucky sod," Bob Cooper said. "Now *that* is the face of an angel."

"An angel of death," John Le Brun replied softly.

Cooper's head reared back. "What? Surely you're joking."

"I wish I was."

"Are you telling me you think *she's* the Sceptred Isle Club murderer?"

"She's one of them."

"One? How many are there?"

"Two or three, dependin' on how many pulled triggers."

Cooper looked at the passing hotel clients, several of whom were staring at his excited face. "One moment. I'll have the manager find us a quiet place to talk."

Three minutes later, Le Brun and the inspector were closed inside a small office behind the front desk. A memory of Trent Godwin's office three nights previous swept over him as he smelled the odor of Cooper's cherry pipe tobacco. Cooper took out John's letter to him and shook it in front of John's nose. "Just yesterday, you posted this letter referencing evidence that Nahum Attwater did not commit suicide. You further suggested that perhaps his son, Lionel, was the engineer of all this mischief."

John purposely crossed one leg over the other. He deemed a façade of casual confidence important for controlling the moment. "That's true. Have you dispatched investigators to Brighton to look at the evidence I observed?"

"Not yet." Cooper's face was slightly flushed. "Your letter arrived in the afternoon mail yesterday, but no one was in the office to open it. We were exchanging shifts."

"I see. You're now on the daytime shift."

"Nominally." Cooper looked as if smoke should be rising from his ears. "Why the devil didn't you voice your suspicion directly to Chief Inspector Tibbles while he was with you on Monday?"

"First of all, I didn't find the ice pick, tarp, and trough until after he'd left. Secondly, your chief inspector was so damned pleased with himself for solvin' the crimes that he probably would have brushed me aside even if I had."

Cooper tried too late to suppress an involuntary laugh.

"You're older than him by years," John observed. "And probably more experienced. How is it that he's your superior?"

"Oh, come now, Mr. Le Brun. Are you saying that you never came up against politics and connections in your tenure as sheriff?"

"All too often. Then you wouldn't be opposed to bringin' Tibbles down off his high horse."

Cooper lost his look of amusement. "You draw whatever conclusions you wish. I won't be caught responding to a question like that. Now, what makes you believe Miss Godwin has a role in these murders?"

"The same busy young Irishman with the U-shaped scar I described to you in the letter."

"You've found this man?"

"Not yet."

Cooper drummed his fingers against his knees. "Then why should a nebulous character suddenly lead you away from Lionel Attwater and to Veronica Godwin?"

"Because the scar could just as easily have been made by a horseshoe as by a ship's block."

"I suppose it could. Probably an iron shoe would leave an even cleaner impression. But why would you suddenly think of that, and how can you be so sure it's one over the other?"

"First, because I know that Veronica goes horseback ridin' in London, usin' several academies and stables. Second, because I know that she and her mother are liars."

"Do you?" Cooper pulled a notepad and pencil from his jacket pocket, the sure sign to Le Brun that his doubt was vanishing. "How so?"

"Because I found a Bible hidden away in the Godwin guest room. It was a Roman Catholic Bible, with Maeve Godwin's family tree in it. But she tells the world she's always been Episcopalian. Furthermore, her daughter tells the world she's twenty-one, and the Bible says she's twenty-two."

Cooper shrugged. "That's merely a white lie."

"Perhaps not 'merely'."

"Why not?"

John flicked a blade of grass off the toe of his shoe. "I'll tell you why in a couple days. I have an inquiry to make first. In the meantime, you really must get someone down to Brighton to look at the back end of the warehouse. And to interview those icehouse men."

"I want that piece of paper you have with their testimony about the Irishman," said Cooper.

"No problem. I'll bring it down from my room after we finish talkin'. I want you to do somethin' else right away: Have the major newspapers throughout Ireland researched for the last week of September, 1900. That's when her first husband,

Graeme Meany, died. Here, give me your pencil and pad, and I'll write it all down for you. Accordin' to Veronica, he was an alcoholic, fell down the stairs in their home, and broke his neck. Every day of every year, Inspector, people are gettin' away scot-free with murder because they keep it simple. Wives push their husbands down stairs. Husbands get their wives drunk, run them a bath, and, when the wife is in it, reach down and pull them under by the ankles. I'm sure Maeve wanted to keep this business just as simple, but she had too many goals all at once. I think you'll find that Maeve Godwin was indeed Catholic until 1901. A little legwork may also reveal that her first husband was not an alcoholic. Five to one he had money or at least a good-size insurance policy. And I wouldn't be surprised if they lived someplace other than Belfast, which is where she claims they lived."

Cooper took back his notepad and pencil. "The business of Trent Godwin being shot at in his home was because of one of her goals?"

"Absolutely. But the shootin' that night wasn't part of the original plan."

Cooper exhaled forcefully in exasperation.

"Let me begin at the beginnin'," John said. "First, years ago Trent mentioned to Maeve that he was part of a tontine that involves a tremendous sum of money. She admitted this in front of me late Sunday night. This was stowed away in her bank vault of a mind. She couldn't kill him to get it because others in the tontine were alive, so there was no point even thinkin' about it. Next, picture the Godwin home. You've been inside it. You were preoccupied with the shootin', but surely you noticed some of the paintin's, the vases, the lamps, and that one-of-a-kind chandelier."

"It's an amateur museum," Cooper agreed.

"Thousands of pounds' worth of possessions, sure to impress their many party guests. The entire house was bought and renovated since Trent married Maeve. Trent spends on his clothin', his gamblin', and his clubs. They've traveled on the continent. They throw their parties every other week. Maeve is buyin' her way into Society. This all takes serious money. More money than the Godwins have. I have no way of checkin', but I also hear from Sir Arthur Conan Doyle that Trent has lost important clients in the past few years."

"Doyle told me that as well," said Cooper. "All of this is why he's fixed his suspicions on Trent."

"He wasn't too wide of the mark. But Trent is the victim in their house, not the perpetrator," Le Brun said with emphasis. "He was supposed to die on Saturday night, along with his friends. I am guessin' that perhaps three months back, Trent and Maeve had a heart-to-heart discussion. Trent informed her that she would have to cut back on every aspect of their lives. He may have said she might have to do this for years to come. Now, Maeve is still a fetchin' woman and one with a personality that could nab another wealthy husband. But she knows she won't be able to do that for much longer. Like her first husband, Trent must die an early death. *This* is probably the shove that gets the whole thing rollin'. Weeks ago, they threw one of their parties, to which Nahum Attwater was invited. For whatever reason, he declines. Naturally, he sends his letter of apology to the hostess . . . not to Trent. She sees the fortuitous wordin' on the bottom third and saves the apology for a suicide note."

"This speculation, albeit with Trent, is very much as Tibbles and Conan Doyle have stated," said Cooper.

"Stolen from me. But if Maeve is such a smart woman . . . and she is . . . why would she contrive such a complicated murder of her husband?" John asked, rising from his chair.

"Because the mass murder and all the money in the room would hide her narrow motive," Cooper declared.

John rocked back and forth on his heels. "As well as kill two Tory M.P.s."

Cooper dropped his pencil. "My God!"

"Is there not an impendin' election?"

"There is."

"And are the seats of Mr. Hugh Wilbye and Ralph Homer not bein' contested by two Liberals?"

"They are."

"Is not Maeve Godwin Irish?"

"She is."

"And are the liberals not determined this time to give the Irish Home Rule?"

Cooper did not speak for several seconds. "That's how the young Irishman comes to be involved."

"And why he can be trusted by Maeve. I believe Veronica met him at one of the ridin' academies, and eventually they began talkin' about Irish politics. If we are lucky, we will learn if he recruited her or vice versa. I have heard from Veronica's own lips that her mother is a frustrated politician. Veronica complained to me about the lack of power women have to effect change in government. But her mother and she were not willin' to accept that."

"Are you *certain* the mother couldn't have pulled this off without the daughter?" Cooper asked, almost a plea.

"I am, and I understand your question. I, too, would love to keep Veronica innocent of all this, for I believe that she has always been little more than her mother's pawn. However, it's not possible, and this is the proof: Trent mentions durin' breakfast one mornin' that Nahum Attwater is goin' down to Brighton to buy a warehouse. He probably speaks about the fact that it has a cold storage section. Very much to Maeve's favor, this weekend also holds Trafalgar Day. It is also the one just before the charity ball that she heads. People will be comin' and goin' madly. An excellent time to commit mass murder. She secures . . . undoubtedly through the Irishman . . . a pair of identical revolvers. She expects that there will be five men in the Sceptred Isle Club's gamblin' room, and six bullets simply aren't enough."

"We've discussed this already."

"You understand, but Tibbles couldn't figure it out by himself. The man should be a beat cop," John proclaimed. "Here's the part about Veronica. Now, unexpectedly invited into their home by Trent comes a small-town sheriff from a former colony. He's supposed to have solved a complex set of murders in Georgia years ago, but he doesn't seem very formidable. Maeve decides to continue the plan. What better way to show the world you're an honest citizen than to offer lodgin' to a former policeman?"

"Cheeky, but to great potential effect," agreed Cooper.

"Except that the dopey-lookin' sheriff is dogged. But Maeve isn't satisfied to use me as a mere cigar store Indian. She sets me up for alibis. Geoffrey Moore tells her at her party Friday night that he and I will be down by the Nelson monument late Saturday mornin'. Doesn't she just show up with her entire troupe of charity ball ladies, ostensibly to witness the event but also to meet me? Rather strange for someone who professed not to have a spare moment, due to mishaps concernin' the ball."

"Good observation," praised Cooper, scratching away on his pad. Le Brun leaned back against the door. "If she isn't in Brighton, Veronica must be. One of them must show up at Attwater's hotel and profess great interest in his new warehouse. Now, I happen to have learned from his own son that Nahum Attwater had a mistress. How interested would he have been in Veronica's attentions if she turned on the charm?"

"Extremely."

From Veronica, Lionel, and Geoffrey, John had assembled enough isolated remarks to prove that Attwater had been one of Veronica's old paramours. He guessed from Veronica's bitter words that the rich man, whose wife went often to Exeter in Devon, had lost Veronica's attentions by somehow disappointing her. Their split was probably the reason he chose to decline attendance at a recent Godwin party. The affair gone wrong, the apology, and Veronica's sudden appearance in Brighton and renewed attention, John thought, might have sealed his doom. Every bit of it, however, was speculation on his part, and he deemed mention unnecessary to win his case. He kept his surmise back, just as he held back a guess about another of her older men.

"So," John went on, "she convinces him to take her to the warehouse. The young Irish accomplice will definitely be there in the late afternoon, to move the body, receive the delivery of ice, and put the body in cold storage. Most likely he is in the area already, to insure that no one chances near enough to hear the pistol crack.

"While Attwater is expoundin' on his most recent acquisition, Veronica removes the gun from her bag, points it at his head, and fires. She has been well rehearsed by her mother what to do and to note. She has done her part and hurries back to London. The Irishman moves the body to the rear of the warehouse. Spilled blood is collected into a vessel, so that it may be chilled along with Attwater . . ."

"How gruesome!" exclaimed Cooper.

". . . and redeposited later when he is returned to his place of death. A surgeon friend has confirmed that the relatively fresh blood was human. He will shortly be performin' other tests to verify my theories. This careful act with the blood, more than any other, speaks of the woman's touch."

Cooper nodded forcefully. "I understand that he had to be killed, to prevent him from showing up at the game and removing himself as a suspect."

"Exactly right. I have forgotten to mention the money under the policeman's birdbath. Certainly, even if Maeve didn't have the ability to withdraw the huge amount from a bank account, such a woman would have been saltin' away money over the months and years in a private place. She used this money and the poor bobby as a means of freezin' the investigation, so that police were not visitin' Nahum Attwater's Brighton hotel room on Sunday mornin'. The tontine is involved not for her to claim it but to provide an excuse for Nahum Attwater to kill three other members of it. When his body is finally discovered, certainly a fourth of the money found under the birdbath will be returned to the Godwins. But eventually, one-third of the tontine money will go to widow Godwin as well."

"Because, as a murderer, Attwater or his beneficiary could not make claim as last survivor," Cooper followed.

John was pleased to be working with the pleasant, open-minded, and patient inspector instead of with the hard-edged, take-charge, and rushed Chief Inspector Tibbles. He nodded and sat again. "Now, Sir Arthur and I believe we know the order in which the men died. From where he sat, Trent would have been shot last. But I doubt our learned speculation would hold up in a court of law. The tontine money would have been divided among the beneficiaries of the three tontine members in that room."

Cooper waggled the pencil. "So, the women come out several thousand pounds ahead, in spite of planting the birdbath money and only recouping part of that."

"An added benefit. Of course, Trent's insurance, his house, and the value of his partnership in the law firm are what they're really after. That and killin' the two M.P.s."

"You've proven that Veronica could have killed Nahum Attwater to my satisfaction," said Cooper. "Let's turn the table. Why can't she and the Irishman have done the whole thing without Maeve?"

"Because Veronica was at the theater with several girlfriends durin' the massacre," John enlightened. "I had it verified that same night by a giddy but pretty young thing borrowin' a wrap after droppin' Veronica off. Maeve and Veronica were quite diligent in seein' that I witnessed this. If someone should suggest Maeve for killin' Attwater or shootin' at Trent in his window, I could vouch as to the impossibility. If someone then focused on Veronica, I could point the law to girlfriends who could prove her whereabouts Saturday night. And who would believe that they both were in on such infamy?"

"What about the business with Trent being shot at?" Cooper asked.

"Improvisation. Maeve knocked on the door to the gamblin' room, was recognized by the butler and let in. Right behind her came the Irishman. She surely placed the first three shots. Sir Arthur can confirm that they happened within seconds. But she must have been astonished that her husband wasn't there. So she had to get more complicated. If she had only used the bobby for establishin' motive and opportunity, she wouldn't have been able to go after Trent again. But because she had made Attwater the main scapegoat, she had the excuse of him comin' after Trent to close the tontine. I have modified my earlier conjecture about when the Irishman returned from replacin' the body and cleanin' up in Brighton. I now believe it to be fairly early Sunday afternoon. Maeve enlisted Veronica and him to attempt one final murder and accomplish all their goals. The fog was a perfect accomplice. They dressed the Irishman up in an outfit that looked like Attwater's. He came up to the Godwin's window and fired. He barely missed. Perhaps his hand was shakin'. Perhaps he doesn't have the cold blood that mother and daughter do."

"And he had a much greater distance and the fog to contend with," Cooper added.

"Just so. He thought he had hit Trent, so he dashed off into the fog. Up the street, Veronica is holdin' the reins of the carriage the lad had probably borrowed from his stable . . . perhaps even the same one he used on Saturday night to get himself and Maeve away with the money and the revolvers we couldn't find. He quickly exchanges a derby for a top hat and pulls on a muffler and topcoat. Veronica gets in as passenger. While I'm outside stupidly ruttin' around lookin' for the gun that broke the window, she pulls up. I don't pay the cabman much mind, except to see that his hat is low and his scarf high. Veronica is in a tight outfit that would have prevented her from runnin', so I can't suspect her. She invents her story of a Nahum Attwater-like figure limpin' away from the scene of the crime. She conveniently leaves her bag behind in the foyer for me to make certain there's no gun. However, once I prove that Attwater was dead on Saturday mornin', her description throws suspicions right back on her. Not that I thought of it then." John's eyes narrowed.

"What is it?" Cooper asked, as involved in the story as a child with a bedside tale.

"That was a calculated but prudent risk Veronica took, but Maeve dropped her façade completely for a moment, directly in front of me. She was livid over the shootin' of her prized chandelier. She spit out somethin' to Veronica about 'Look what the stupid creature has done.' I was a bit sad on Mr. Godwin's part that he was bleedin' from several cuts and his wife was more concerned with a material possession. But I should have observed not only the peculiar wordin' of her outburst but also the play between mother and daughter. Veronica was quick to recognize her mother's improper words in front of me and guided her right back to solicitation for Trent."

"You have developed a prodigious and detailed memory, Mr. Le Brun," Cooper exclaimed.

"A gift of nature, I assure you." John chose not to tell the inspector the several lapses he had had during the investigation. Far worse than not finding out if Mrs. Attwater was still alive was falling under Veronica's spell and letting her blind him to the possibility of her guilt.

"And she is still leading you around by the nose, I see," Cooper commented, continuing on the subject of the young woman. "She pumped you for information this very hour, did she not?"

"She did. And I did my best to allay her fears that I was anywhere near bein' on to her."

"This is very compelling conjecture," Cooper said, "and it all seems to hang together. But we ultimately need the young Irishman to prove it. The Irishman will be the key to any solution, in fact."

"Absolutely correct," John replied. "But you can't simply mobilize the entire London police force to find him. He must be found in a way that doesn't alert him, so that he can be observed until he connects with Maeve or Veronica."

At last the inspector seemed lost. "Why would he do that, now that the crimes have been committed? I should think their plan would be for him to stay as far away from them as possible."

John leaned toward Cooper. "Except that Trent Godwin still isn't dead."

"Oh, come now, Mr. Le Brun," Cooper exclaimed. "With Mr. Attwater gone, there is no more bogeyman to shoot at Mr. Godwin. Suspicion would fall right back on his wife. Surely, if she wants to kill him, she must wait at least a year. And now, with all that tontine money added to their bank account, she can easily bide her time."

"That's what I would have thought," John answered, "except that last night Godwin announced to Sir Arthur, Geoffrey Moore, and me that he would give away all the tontine money as soon as he gets the check. You think Maeve Godwin will allow thirty-five thousand pounds to slip through her fingers?"

"But how can she escape suspicion?"

"She's the hostess for a fancy dress charity ball Friday night. If she and Veronica are there, they can't very well be murderin' Trent, can they?"

"But won't he be there also?"

"He'll leave before it's over. It's his habit. I envision one of two scenarios, both requirin' the lad with the scar. The first would somehow bring Trent and Lionel together. Lionel would be set up as exactin' revenge for Trent pointin' the blame on him. Remember that that young man has flimsy alibis *and* a motive for havin' killed his father. I just put the flea in Veronica's ear, to try to focus their choice this way. I'm sure the young Mr. Attwater can be worked with. He is most eager to prove his father innocent. Both this and the next plan would work best inside the Godwin home, while the ball's in full swing. The alternative would be for them to stage a burglary, wherein Trent surprises the intruder and is shot dead. One of the newspapers reportin' the Sceptred Isle Club murders spent an entire paragraph on how Trent escaped and how he lives in a big, beautiful townhouse in Mayfair. Also mentioned his wife's upcomin' ball. Just the sort of information second-story men comb papers for. With either scenario, you see that we must find this Irishman immediately and then never let him out of our sight."

"Provided he hasn't left the city," Cooper pointed out. "They could have felt better with him gone."

"I'm hopin' the Godwin women are confident enough in the success of their stratagems that they allowed him to remain. I'm sure he doesn't want to lose a perfectly good job over a couple of dead M.P.s. There are only a dozen or so stables that the likes of the Godwins would use. How soon can you deploy several plainclothesmen?"

Cooper threw up his hands. "I'm only an inspector. And they're not a faucet I can turn on and off at will. I'll return straight away to the Yard, present the case, and petition for the men." Cooper stood. "You're lucky it isn't Tibbles's shift. You'd make such a fool of him, he'd sit on this right proper."

"Even so, it sounds like you won't get men into the field before tomorrow mornin'," John worried.

"I think you can safely assume that."

"Which only allows us a day to find the man and hope he meets with either of the women."

"If time gets short when he's found, we'll bring him in. That will prevent Mr. Godwin from being murdered. Then we'll sweat it out of the lad."

"And how well do you ordinarily sweat Irish fanatics?" John asked, knowing the answer. Cooper's silence was his confirmation.

AFTER JOHN BROUGHT the icemen's testimony down to Inspector Cooper, he went outdoors once more and visited the academies and stables in the Kensington and Knightsbridge sections of the city. He found no one remotely resembling the icehouse son's description. Yet again, he railed privately at his inability to muster forces. Being a one-man police force was hard on the ego and the feet. He returned to the hotel and made a call to Thomas Saye's office in University College Hospital. The secretary said that he would locate the doctor and asked for John's telephone number.

Within five minutes, the telephone rang. When John answered, Saye was on the line.

"He had orange slices and cherry crêpe in his stomach," Saye reported. "Well chewed but hardly digested. He was killed within an hour of eating."

"Excellent!" John crowed. "That sets his death before noon on Saturday."

"His blood is also type 'O.' You're undoubtedly right about them stowing some of it away. What a ghoulish group."

"Please have a signed and notarized copy of your findin's sent to Inspector Robert Cooper at Scotland Yard right away," John asked. "And include a separate note to Cooper askin' him to verify the breakfast menu at the Metropole Hotel on the mornin' of . . . what was it . . . October twenty-first."

"It will be done."

"And as far as your duty tonight, you can assume that you're off the hook," John allowed.

"Thank you. But I had planned to be home already, so I'll be there if you need me. Can I assume you've had no luck finding the man with the scar?"

"You can. But I'm on it," John asserted. "I'll be in touch."

John took the time to change socks and shoes and went out again, opera glasses in hand. The weather had clouded up, although rain did not seem imminent to him. He decided to try Rotten Row a second time. The expected long shadows of afternoon had disappeared into diffuse light. A chill was coming into the air. He had the pavement practically to himself. He walked briskly along, heading toward Mayfair.

As he went, John thought about his Voyage of Discovery. He had accounted well for himself in his own estimation. At the Godwin party, his opinion on the politics and social issues of the day were soberly received by accomplished and influential men. He had heard from the world-famous Arthur Conan Doyle's lips and seen from the man's body language that he was impressed with John. He had also won the respect of the clever and well-read manager of the Sceptred Isle Club. The citizens of "the most civilized city in the most civilized nation on earth," on the other had, were not uniformly of a higher caliber. His boon companion, Geoffrey, had let slip out his interest in persons based on their fame. He had also revealed his manifest disinterest in family life. Veronica, who professed such passion for the rights of all people, did not scruple to murder some of them for her beliefs. Maeve and Daphne Moore, who despised

Maeve, were fundamentally of the same order of social climbers and materialists. Inspector Tibbles was willing to bungle a case for the sake of expedience. And Arthur Conan Doyle, Nahum Attwater, and at least one other among the men John had met had no problem betraying their women in another's caresses. It was a good thing Londoners used big words and pronounced everything so well, he decided, wryly; it did put a shine on the tarnish. If John decided to quit Brunswick, it would be for the institutions such as theaters, museums, and libraries that a large city afforded. People truly were the same the world over.

The sounds of approaching horses carried well in the damp atmosphere. He heard the clip-clopping of a pair of steeds before he heard the voices of the riders. When he turned, he saw a young woman in a black riding jacket with brown suede patches and a beige skirt riding sidesaddle. She had an enormous white bow against one cheek, and gauzy white cloth fluttered from her top hat. She seemed at ease on her horse and chatted comfortably with her companion, who was equally well dressed. The companion was a good-looking man who sat very straight in his saddle. John walked on the pavement to their right, heading in the same direction they did. The woman, closer to John, rode slightly in the lead of the man, so that it was difficult for John to see his forehead. But there appeared for an instant the opportunity to glimpse a curve of white against tan as the man rode past.

John looked down the length of Rotten Row. It continued a good fifth of a mile until it emptied into Park Lane, which ran north by northwest along the western edge of Mayfair. In all, at least a mile lay between where John walked and the nearer of the Mayfair equestrian academies. He gulped down several large breaths and began to trot after the riders. Within five minutes, despite his valiant effort to dog after them, they had ridden out of sight of his opera glasses, behind the verdant fullness of the towering trees. For all he knew, they might be circling Hyde Park and riding to the Lancaster academy. John redoubled his speed for two hundred paces, until he was gasping for air and his heart felt like it would burst through the base of his throat. Cursing his age, he slowed to a walk. His knees throbbed. When he could, he began his trot again. He thought about taking his watch from his vest pocket but decided knowing how many minutes had passed would only torture him.

He was certain that not ten minutes had elapsed before he entered the Mayfair district, perspiring profusely and feeling all the more clammy in the damp chill. He crossed the southbound side of Park Lane with burning, overlong strides and headed directly for the nearer stable. As he reached it, he saw with joy the woman who had ridden sidesaddle exit the building and climb into a carriage. John hobbled across the street, dropped his posterior on a granite stoop, and mopped away what he could of his sweat with his handkerchief.

When the man on the horse emerged from the academy, he had changed outfits. No more was he the dashing instructor in the crisp riding habit. Now he wore a tweed cap, plaid cotton shirt, rough vest, and baggy woolen pants. The U-shaped scar was prominent enough to read from the opposite side of the street. He gave John not so much as a glance. Whistling brightly, he started north. John groaned, sidled off the stoop, and followed.

A tram stop existed at Marble Arch, which lay about a third of a mile from the academy. The Irishman walked up to it and stopped. It was an open, exposed place, and John was compelled to approach it and stand right beside him. They were the only two waiting. A moment after John arrived, several drops of rain fell upon them. The young man turned to John with an infectious smile.

"Wouldn'tcha know it? And neither of us with brollies." His "Southie" accent was unmistakable.

It was bad enough that John had forgone Conan Doyle's suggestion of a disguise; to have spoken with his accent would have given him away in a heartbeat. He was sure that Veronica had mentioned the Southern sheriff to the man. He prayed she had not described him. Mustering his courage, John spoke in his best approximation of the accent he had heard in the clubs.

"As if we didn't know this is London," he said.

The young man shot him a surprised look. Adrenaline flamed through John's chest.

"Sorry," the young man apologized. "I thought you were from out of town. French."

Between his sarcastic reply and his phony accent, John had managed to pull off his charade. "Quite all right," he forgave, turning away to stare intently at nothing.

They stood together for the next two minutes, exchanging no other remarks, John out of fear, the Irishman to obey the unwritten British law of not speaking to an Englishman unless introduced. The rain was light but persistent.

"At last," the man with the scar said.

An electric tram came rumbling onto Oxford Street, heading east. It stopped, and the Irishman gestured for John to get on first. John made sure to move to the last empty seat in the back. He watched the riding instructor pick an empty seat next to a young woman, flashing her his smile as he sat.

The tram stopped and started several times, letting passengers off and on. The Irishman did not bother to look up from his conversation with the woman. Evidently, he chanced an opening line with everyone and continued if social mores allowed. Or, perhaps, his looks made him bolder with the women. John expected that he lived a great distance from his place of work and that he would change trams for something that ran across the river into Lambeth or Southwark. But suddenly, as if from internal signal created by long practice, the Irishman stood. He handed the woman a business card, gave her a grin and wink, and dashed toward the front of the tram.

As he passed, John plucked the business card out of the

woman's hand. The Irishman was already off the tram, unable to hear her cry of complaint.

"One moment, please," John cried out to the driver, still using his phony accent. He hurried along the aisle and down the steps onto the street.

The Irishman was intent on not getting any wetter than he had to. He jogged across the intersection of Oxford Street and Tottenham Court Road, weaving between conveyances. John held back until the traffic spread out. By the time he had crossed, his quarry was a hundred paces ahead. John glanced down at the card in his hand. It gave the name of the riding academy, its hours of operation, and its location, but there was no name at the bottom. John swore under his breath; he had risked exposure to learn the man's name and gotten nothing. Handling the card by its edges, he dropped it into his left-hand jacket pocket and walked on.

Now the Irishman was nearly a full block ahead of John, with four pedestrians between them. This was what the ex-sheriff wanted. He reached into his side pocket and wrapped his hand around his opera glasses. After three short blocks, the man turned left and disappeared into a small street. John went into a trot to close the distance. When he arrived at the turn, he saw his quarry enter a wide courtyard. He could not follow until the Irishman had crossed the open area. He rushed forward a dozen paces and pressed himself against the wall of the nearest building, behind the partial concealment of a rain downspout. They were now in a section of solid and depressed tenements, with no reason for a stranger to be wandering through. This was especially true of a stranger with a high-class accent who had boarded a tram at Marble Arch. One glimpse of John behind him, and the Irishman would be gone like smoke up a chimney.

John peeked out from his hiding place. The man had vanished. Le Brun wondered if he had realized he was being followed and had lured his pursuer into a street where tailing was difficult. *Now comes the gutsy part of the game*, John thought. He could stop where he was, report what he knew to the police, and hope that the man was not leading him through a neighborhood far from his own. Or he could press on, learn more, and risk total exposure.

Le Brun took the chance, not only stepping into the street but angling to the other side, so that he could look to the limits of his perspective. An intersection lay ahead some five tenements beyond the far side of the courtyard. He raised his opera glasses to view the continuation of the street beyond the intersection. No one walked there. He returned the glasses to his pocket. As he ventured forward, he saw that a narrower street ran off to the right. He was fairly sure he would have caught the movement of his quarry if the man had gone that way. There was also a street to his left. He came to the intersection, was confronted by a toothless old woman carrying a bundle of rags, tipped his hat at her and smiled. She regarded him with momentary distrust but decided he was no threat to her. She rolled arthritically past like a boat in a gale.

The street to the left was a dead end alley. It contained two old tenements on either side and the back of another building at its extreme. John walked to the far building, saw by its signage and the piles of beer and ale crates that it was the rear of a pub, and tried to open the door. It was locked. Unless the riding instructor had broken into a full run when he crossed the large courtyard, or unless the pub's door had stood open and the Irishman locked it after him, he had to be in one of the four tenements facing Le Brun.

John opted for immediate retreat. Daring any other plan would be pure folly. Before he could act, someone exited from the door directly across from him. Le Brun's heart nearly stopped. As the figure stepped from shadow, it was revealed to be a pimply-faced, skinny fellow with oily black hair, similar to the Irishman only in height. He gave the stranger on his block the briefest glance, then hurried on his way.

John collapsed against the wall behind him. His muscles trembled from the tension. He sucked in a quick breath. Then he heard a familiar laugh. It was like the tinkling of garden bells. It came through the window just to his left. He lowered his head and moved to the building's entrance. He memorized the number painted on the keystone above the entry arch. Then he labored to memorize the six names that were written on various pieces of paper and affixed to the line of mail slots. Finn, O'Shaughnessy, Coughlin, Devlin, Burke, and Shea.

As he hurriedly retraced his steps, John repeated the names over and over like a short prayer. When he came out onto Tottenham Court Road, he tried to orient himself. He vaguely recollected that he had walked down this street before. He thought he saw the illuminated side of the British Museum down the length of two side blocks. If he was right, Dr. Saye's house was not far distant, and Saye was at home. Moreover, according to Saye, Lionel Attwater lived somewhere nearby. But they might as well have lived on Mars for John's ability to find them. He needed a bobby or a telephone.

The raindrops became larger and more frequent. Too much more time on the street would have John soaked to the skin. He ducked into one shop after the next, inquiring if they had a telephone. If they did, they were not about to admit it, and no public phones were in evidence. The rain, moreover, had sent all patrolling policeman plunging into those magic holes they knew about when weather turned inclement. John himself had been guilty of the act in his early days as sheriff. He understood the practice, but at the moment he could not forgive it. He pulled out his watch. Precious minutes were draining away.

At last, John spotted a motorized police van, parked on Tottenham Court Road on the opposite side of Oxford Street. He went to it, put his head into the open-sided vehicle, and found no one there. In desperation, he began tootling the horn.

It took more than a minute for a ruddy-faced bobby to appear. He did not look pleased.

"Here now, get away from the van!" he shouted. "What's the matter with you?"

Rather than reply, John climbed into the van's passenger seat. The bobby stuck his head in and was about to follow with both hands when John said, "Be patient, Officer. I'm on business for Scotland Yard." He reached into his inside jacket pocket and took out his precious letter from Chief Inspector Tibbles. "Please climb in. I mustn't get this letter wet."

John's words shifted the policeman's anger to curiosity. The man entered the van, wiped his wet hands on his trouser legs, and reached out for the letter. He read it carefully with his lips moving and, when he had finished, began to read it again.

"Time is flyin', Officer," John urged. "I have tracked one of the suspects to his apartment, and I need to get in touch with Scotland Yard immediately."

"Very well, Mr. Le Brun." The officer handed back the letter. "I'm Officer Hennings." He reached under his seat and took out a hand crank, which he gave to Le Brun. "Might you dash out and turn over the engine for me?"

"Can't we find a telephone and call Scotland Yard from here?" John pleaded.

"Much better to go to the station, sir. Only a few blocks."

John sighed and clambered out of the van.

THE CHIEF OFFICER on duty in the Soho station Wednesday evening was Captain Fletcher Moon. He was a bright-eyed civil servant who prided himself on efficiency and following the letter of the law. He moved with clockwork precision and a strong suggestion that he had fulfilled considerable military service. He came around the corner into the station lobby as if on parade, pivoted in front of the seated Le Brun, and brought his trailing leg smartly even with the planted one. His large hand thrust out as he introduced himself.

John stood and took the hand in his. "A pleasure, Cap'n."

"Likewise, sir," Moon said in a resonating voice. "Officer Hennings has given me your general story. May I read your note from Scotland Yard?"

"By all means."

Moon's eyes scanned the document with speed. As he handed it back, he said, "This is indeed the Yard's case. I must coordinate with them before I make a move."

"But if we hurry back there right away, we can catch two of the people involved," John argued urgently. "It's no good delayin' and missin' the woman who's visitin'. Tyin' up the case depends on findin' them in the same place at the same time."

"If you say so, sir," said Moon, looking genuinely sympathetic. "We'll move as swiftly as possible. Step into my office, and we'll ring up the detective on duty."

Captain Moon had already pivoted again, missing the baleful rolling of Le Brun's eyes. With the shifts changed, Chief Inspector Tibbles was the case's detective on duty. John hoped against hope that the man was out of his office.

As Moon promised, he connected rapidly with Scotland Yard. Just as quickly, Tibbles was on the other end.

"I have with me Mr. Le Brun," Moon said after the requisite pleasantries. "He's got exciting news, I believe. Here he is."

John accepted the telephone without enthusiasm. "Inspector Tibbles, I hope you're—"

"Bob Cooper's informed me of your latest theory, concerning the implication of Mrs. Godwin and her daughter," Tibbles interrupted. "This is based on your guess that the accomplice's scar was made by a horseshoe instead of a ship's block?"

John counseled himself to keep his voice neutral. "As well

as the fact that Veronica rides in the city *and* the information in their Catholic Bible *and* the remark Mrs. Godwin passed when her chandelier was damaged."

"Anything more substantive?"

"No."

"And you've seen Miss Godwin in this man's neighborhood."

"Not face to face. But take my word for it; you want to come up here," John said.

"We'll be there, Mr. Le Brun. However, it's probably for naught. Your initial conjecture has worked wonders already. A group of detectives spent the day covering the waterfront. In mid-afternoon, we found an Irishman with a U-shaped scar on his forehead. We followed him back to his flat in Lambeth and entered on suspicion of murder. Found almost two hundred pounds and a considerable stash of opium. Also found a Webley and Scott Mark IV revolver."

"What caliber is that?"

Tibbles's voice had lost all pretense of cordiality. He knew exactly what point John was trying to make. "All of the Mark series are four hundred fifty-five caliber. The Sceptred Isle killers didn't have to use identical weapons, you know. Nor was more than one needed. The Galand revolver found with Attwater held six bullets."

John shook his head all the while Tibbles spoke. "I assume your suspect is claimin' innocence."

"Of course. As you can imagine, he has no telephone. Anyone who wants to get ahold of him has to come to his door. We've left a pair of men in his flat."

"The money and gun probably have to do with his drug business," John said. "I'd wager one out of every ten dock workers does somethin' illegal. In my hometown—"

"And how many have the scar the icehouse man reported?" Tibbles broke in again. Before John could reply that the father and son had speculated many men had similar wounds, Tibbles added, "And speaking of that, I am quite vexed with you, Mr. Le Brun. You're conspicuously slow to turn over information in this investigation. Why didn't you find me that afternoon and present what you'd found in the back of Attwater's warehouse?"

On a less vital occasion, Le Brun might have allowed himself to grin. Instead, he said soberly into the mouthpiece, "It was only an ice pick, a rubber tarpaulin, and a horse trough at that point. I didn't go lookin' for the iceman until after you'd left with the body and I couldn't find you. I sent a letter the next mornin'."

"To Inspector Cooper. You thought he'd be more open-minded."

"Frankly, yes."

There was a pause at the other end of the line. "Did you follow your suspect right to his home?"

"No. I couldn't shadow him that closely. It's in a back alley."

"So, you don't know his exact flat?"

"I do from Veronica's laugh."

"And how did you come to hear her laugh?"

"Through a window."

"Through a window. You didn't see her?"

"No."

"One laugh."

"It was enough."

"And you've known this woman for how long?"

John yanked out his watch and glanced at it. "That's not the point. I know her laugh."

"Let's hope it wasn't wishful thinking. Tell Captain Moon that we'll handle this ourselves. Give me the street name."

John offered precise directions.

"We'll be there directly," said Tibbles, not sounding at all enthusiastic.

"And how soon is 'directly'?" John prodded.

"I have to gather men. And I haven't talked with this other suspect personally yet. I hope within the hour."

"Please hurry."

"Mr. Le Brun, thank you for your stout service to this city. However, we will handle it from here. Go back to your hotel. We'll contact you in the morning."

Rather than answer, John hung up. He looked at Captain Moon and offered a wan smile. "Nothin' for you to do. But Chief Inspector Tibbles would like me to be dropped off where Officer Hennings picked me up. I wonder if I could make a telephone call first? I'm gonna miss a dinner appointment I had."

"Certainly," Moon granted.

John dipped his head apologetically. "A special engagement with a member of the opposite sex."

Moon's head started forward from his neck. "Ah. Right. I'll just wait outside while you call." Moon closed his office door after him.

John had Thomas Saye on the line within the next minute. "I'm afraid I must ask for your help after all, Doctor," he said in a soft voice.

"Happy to give it."

"It shouldn't inconvenience you for too long. Do you know where Bedford Street meets Tottenham Court Road?"

"Yes. It's not far from me. Just above Great Russell."

"Can you be there in twenty minutes?"

"Or less. Need I bring anything?"

"Think of an excuse to knock on some back-street tenement doors."

"I have just the thing."

THOMAS SAYE ARRIVED carrying a doorman's umbrella large enough to ferry a Sunday school class through a monsoon. Rain ran off it in sheets like bits of cellophane. Saye was dressed in a suit and had over it a raincoat which was unbuttoned and had the collar turned under.

"You are a man of your word," John greeted. "I should have thought to ask you if you own a pistol."

"I do not. Difficult as it will be for you to believe," said Saye, "I abhor violence. But I did bring something that will let me knock on the doors of the poor without raising any suspicion."

"And that is?" John asked, stepping into Tottenham Court Road and gesturing for Saye and his umbrella to follow.

"A badge identifying myself as a health inspector for the London County Council. You remember I said I voluntarily perform that function once a month, to try to prevent disease outbreaks?"

"You did. I benefit from your wages of virtue." John had been about to fix the physician's collar but decided the effect would work well for his portrayal. "I can't go into the house with you. If the woman is in there and saw me, they might escape and never be found together again."

"I understand. Give me their descriptions," Saye said.

They walked together down the narrower street and into the large open courtyard as John provided visual images that would make identification absolute. The neighborhood was deserted. It was the dinner hour for most residents, a time when the streets would have been naturally less traveled even in good weather. Faint, yellow lights poured from windows into the evening gloom and lingered atop puddles.

John came to a halt, grabbing Saye's coat to stop him as well. "I can't go no further. Down at that intersection, there's a blind alley on your left. It's the second house on the left, front apartment on your right as you enter. Look for the names Shea, Burke, Coughlin, and Devlin on the postal slots."

"I'm simply going to knock on the door, identify myself, and ask several questions about pests," Saye said. "If the woman's not in ready evidence, I'll say that I'm obliged to come inside and inspect all rooms."

"Don't be too pushy," John coached. "She'll smell a setup

a mile away. If you do find them both, visit at least one other flat and ask your questions. I want them to hear you knockin' on other doors before you come back out."

"I shall."

"I'll wait out at the intersection. If either one of them looks skittish, don't go into the flat. Get yourself out of the buildin' and come for me."

"You have that little cannon in your pocket?" Saye asked.

"You can be assured. Both barrels are loaded."

Saye gave a sharp nod and tried to pass the umbrella to Le Brun.

"You keep it. What kind of London County Council agent would go out on a night like this without his bumbershoot?"

"Of course. Wish me luck, then."

"Luck."

Saye strode down to the intersection and turned left. John followed at a shambling pace. The rain had become a steady, soaking nuisance. When he came underneath a particularly bright window, John hoisted his watch from its pocket and studied it. He made an unhappy sound in his throat. Tibbles's promised hour would not arrive for another thirty-five minutes.

The physician appeared around the corner. As he approached, he was shaking his head.

"Tophet!" John exclaimed, whirling about and pounding the nearest wall with his fist.

"I put my ear to the door first and heard nothing," Saye reported. "Then I knocked, waited half a minute, and knocked again. No one answered. That's not quite true; the woman from the flat across stuck her head out."

"Let's go back together," John said.

"And what happens when the woman sticks her head out again?"

"I say to her," John answered, putting on his best Mayfair accent, " 'Good evenin', Mum. We're from the London County

Council.' How's that for the king's English?"

"That's not half bad," Saye judged. "But not half good either. The king doesn't drop his final 'g's. I'll do all the talking, if you please."

"Fair enough."

As they walked to the alley, a horse and driver came up the street from the opposite direction with a manure cart. Saye began speaking. His words were loud enough for the cart driver to hear. "I'm telling you, the whole place should come down," he said. "It's a blight on London. A holdover from two centuries past. A horror out of Dickens."

The driver kept his head low, under a broad-brimmed hat that dripped rain. He flipped his reins so that the horse would turn left, and soon enough he was gone.

"You have a knack for this," John said.

"Best defense is a good offense," Thomas returned. "Make them too afraid of you to look."

They went into the ancient row house together. The building stank of cabbage and echoed with the wails of squalling babies. Saye rapped confidently on the first story's left-hand door. The woman who answered had an abundance of brown hair and cool blue eyes. She looked to be in her late thirties, not more than five feet tall and quite broad of hip. In her left hand was a dirty dishrag.

"Brought a friend back, eh? He ain't home," she said.

"It's you we wish to speak with, Madam," Thomas Saye said.

The woman blinked at the news and the high-class accent in which it was delivered. Saye flashed his badge.

"London County Council. Health Service."

John saw a look of fear flash through the woman's eyes.

"Your name, Madam?" John asked, a clear demand.

"Nora Shea."

"How many live in this flat, Mrs. Shea?"

"Me, me t'ree kids, and the fadder . . . whenever he can find his way home."

"We're here to assess the conditions concerning pests. Rats, mice, spiders, cockroaches."

"Wadderbugs. Yeah, yeah. I understand. Sometoimes we get moice from the pub behind us. But there's two cats in the buildin'. Never any trouble for long. This place is foin."

"Glad to hear it. Do they own a cat across the way?" Saye asked, pointing over his shoulder.

"Tim Burke?" Nora Shea laughed. "*Tim's* the cat. The tom of this here alley."

"Just him living there?"

"Let's just say he alone pays the rent, but most of the toime it's two. A regular parade o' women over the years. Except of late. Past two months it's just this . . . grand duchess."

"A woman of royalty?" Saye asked, feigning shock.

"Nah! A young t'ing. Must have some money. She carries herself like the queen of Sheba. I'd love ta be dere when her fadder catches her slummin'. Some foireworks I'm bettin'!"

"Well, that's none of our business, is it Reginald?"

John wriggled up his nose and shook his head.

"Thanks, Mrs. Shea."

"T'anks to you gentlemen fer doin' us the sorvice." Punctuating her reply with a broad smile, the woman eased her door closed.

John gestured for Dr. Saye to continue his charade on the next floor. He took the lock-picking tools out of his pocket and worked on Timothy Burke's door, with the creak of the wooden steps and the babies screaming more than enough to cover the sounds of his efforts. He was inside within a minute.

Giving the flat a cursory once-over, John figured that Burke had to have more than good looks to attract women to his rooms. The place consisted of a tiny bathroom with a shower that wet the entire space when turned on, an efficiency kitchen that opened onto a dining area, and a good-sized bedroom. It was clean and neat if not fashionable. Sparse furniture prevented it from seeming as cramped as it was. On the walls around the dining area were pious prints of Saints Brigid and Patrick. Over the bed hung a wooden crucifix.

John began with the bathroom. He noted the missing toiletries. The kitchen sink had two dirty teacups in it; the kettle was still slightly warm. There was precious little food in the icebox. The rough cabinet that held the plates, cups, saucers, and serving dishes was well stocked, as if Burke entertained.

In the bedroom, there was a bed, a dresser with a mirror over it, a night stand, and a coat tree. On top of the dresser sat a comb and a shiny, new tin whistle. Slid under the frame of the dressing mirror was a picture of Burke astride a beautiful mare. He looked quite dashing in his tailored riding clothes. It would be a good image to copy for the police of London, John thought. The top dresser drawer hung open. About half its contents appeared to be missing. It was the same with the lower drawer. The wall between dining area and bedroom had had a closet built in. John noted immediately that the shapes of two suitcases were formed on the floor where a fine layer of dust had not settled. More than half of the hangers had nothing on them. John investigated the shelf above the clothes rod. It contained a few innocuous magazines. When he flipped through one, out fell three identical inflammatory tracts on the plight of the Irish and their mistreatment by the English. The dresser and bedside stand as well held nothing but common items. Everywhere, however, belongings were clearly gone.

The bedclothes were disheveled, as if more than they had recently been tossed. They had the faint odors of sweat and worse on them. While not a dainty man, the image of Veronica under that blanket and top sheet had him loathe to touch them. He thought of Veronica's limerick at lunch. Then he remembered how sloppy he had been during this investigation, and he determined to leave nothing more, figuratively or literally, unturned. He flipped back the covers. The bottom sheet was dark in several places from moisture but was otherwise the only thing, except for two pillows, on the mattress. John lifted the first pillow and dropped it at the foot of the bed. Then he lifted the second.

"Hello," he said, using his best English accent. "What have we here?"

It was a simple pad of white paper, lifted from the Monarch Hotel. John riffled through it, found no writing, and was about to toss it onto the bed when he spotted indentations on the top sheet. He carried the pad into the kitchen, sat at the table, and twisted and turned the pad under the light. He found a pencil atop the cabinet that held the plates, cups, and saucers and used it to rub lightly over the top sheet of paper. What he exposed was architectural in nature, straight lines and right angles. He recognized what it was with no difficulty. He placed the pad in the center of the table, where the detectives were sure to see it, and returned the pencil to the cabinet.

The ex-sheriff spent another few minutes prying at floorboards with his jackknife and rapping on the walls, vainly trying to find a hidden compartment. When he was fully satisfied, he exited the hallway and whistled up the staircase for his companion.

Once outside and around the corner, Saye asked, "Did you find anything?"

"He's cleared out. Looks like they filled two valises with his belongin's."

"Do you think he spotted you following him?"

"No. Veronica was waitin' for him. They took the time to have tea. If I did anythin' to arouse suspicion, I must have done it when I had lunch with her today. But perhaps not. Early on she mentioned that she had an 'engagement' this evenin'. When I suggested that it was a man, her eyes drifted the way women's do when that subject is broached."

"Then don't beat yourself up. He was going before you ever saw him." Saye lowered the umbrella around them as the rain began to come down at an angle. "Now what?"

"I wait for Chief Inspector Tibbles to show."

"I'll wait with you."

"You've done everythin' I needed and more," John said. "Why don't you go home to your family?"

"I'll just stay a few more minutes."

John didn't object this time. He had a question that had itched the inside of his skull for years, and now he shared an umbrella with precisely the man who could answer it.

"You know," John began, "I really did think you had died out there in those marshes. How did you manage to escape?"

"The Negroes," the former Dr. Russell replied.

"Ah."

It all made sense to John now. In Baltimore, Thomas Russell had been the surgeon of the Negro charity wards that Johns Hopkins himself had insisted must be maintained if his money was to go toward building the medical college. Russell had, in Baltimore, saved the life of the brother of one of the black workers at the Jekyl Island Club. During his seasonal residency at the club, he had sneaked off from time to time to minister to the Negroes without remuneration. The harsh rules of the club and the callous treatment of servants by its members and guests guaranteed an animosity on the workers' parts. Probably many of their number wished calamity would befall some of the more hateful rich. The native Negroes were never spoken to except in command. They were, in fact, all but invisible to the membership. Therefore, there was no risk in giving Dr. Russell detailed instructions on how to navigate the marshes of Glynn to regain the mainland even if they did suspect he was the murderer.

"Friday Cain supplied me with a map," Saye went on. "It

directed me to a black family that lived on the edge of the marshes. They took me in until you had given up your search. Then they hid me in a wagon and drove me to another family north of Brunswick."

"A white Underground Railway," John mused aloud.

"Kindness repaid."

"Indeed." John drew in a large breath. "On second thought, it would be a bad idea for you and me to be seen together. Just in case there's an old poster of you lyin' around in Scotland Yard, you understand."

"I do. Take my umbrella. I'll be back home in ten minutes. Who knows how long until they arrive."

"Thank you kindly." John accepted the umbrella. "This may be the last time you and I communicate. Fare you well, Thomas Saye."

"And you also, good sir."

The two men stood staring at each other in silence for several moments. Then Saye patted Le Brun's shoulder, turned, and trotted down the street.

John watched the man disappear into the darkness, marveling at how he could be happy a murderer had outwitted and escaped him. *It's a strange world indeed,* he told himself, *especially if you live long enough.*

The shoulder that Dr. Saye had patted was the same one that had been pierced by a bullet in the Civil War. It had felt so good over the past six months, but now, in the pelting rain, it began to ache anew. John backed into a corner formed of two walls, making himself as waterproof and inconspicuous as possible. He thought about the times he had been compelled to weather rain as a lawman. One was to solve the Jekyl Island Club mystery. Another was in trying to extricate a man who had barricaded himself inside Brunswick's only remote office for a New York Stock Exchange firm. The year was 1893, and John had served as sheriff a little more than two years. It was also a period of financial panic, with a serious depression setting in. At the suggestion of the firm's brokers, a town patriarch named Barrows had invested heavily in companies with new inventions. In the face of a growing bear market, such companies' stocks had plummeted. Mr. Barrows had been seen walking into the brokers' office carrying a gun. John was summoned and arrived just in time to hear two shots ring out. Barrows spotted the sheriff as he opened the front door and fired a wild shot at him. The rest of that afternoon and into the early evening, in the midst of a record low barometer and what Brunswickers called "pour down rain," John had patiently crouched behind an advertising kiosk and shouted out all the reasons Barrows should surrender peaceably. At ten o'clock, Deputy Bobby Lee Randolph broke through a second-story window as John emptied his revolver into the building's front door to cover the noise. A minute later Barrows lay dead, beside the two men he had earlier killed. What John remembered most vividly of that day was not the blood but the rain.

Almost precisely an hour after speaking with Inspector Tibbles, two black motorcars, one longer than the other, drove past John and the courtyard and into the intersection beyond. John watched as two men emerged from the second car and jogged toward the alley. Satisfied that the Yard had once again been pointed in the right direction, John headed toward Tottenham Court Road. When he neared the thoroughfare, a man dressed in a rubberized pancho with a hood stepped out from the corner of the building and confronted him. The man held a revolver in one hand and a badge in the other.

"One moment, sir!" the man called out. "Scotland Yard. You can't leave the area."

"I'm John Le Brun."

"I don't care if you're Henry VIII. I have my orders. Please keep both hands on your umbrella, turn around, and walk that way."

By the time John crossed the courtyard again, a solitary dark figure had emerged from the second car and was elevating an umbrella. From the street beyond, a man came running up to him. John was certain it was one of the detectives who had gotten out of the first car, returned to report Timothy Burke's flat was empty. Another few steps made it possible for John to recognize Chief Inspector Tibbles as the man from the second vehicle. He turned and looked at Le Brun.

"Why am I not surprised to find you here?"

"I was just tryin' to leave the place to you," John said, "but your officer prevented me."

"As you see, we're treating your alarm seriously."

"What about the man in your custody?"

"He's a criminal, but he's not related to the Sceptred Isle Club murders. For one thing, his scar was on the wrong side of his head. For another, he's ten years older and two stone heavier than the description we and you received from the icehouse men."

John merely pursed his lips, nodded his head, and rocked back and forth on his heels as he received the unsurprising news.

"I'm told that the door to the flat you sent us to was open. You've been using your tools again."

"I'm not in the habit of unlawful entry," John replied.

"Your habits are of no concern to me, Mr. Le Brun. Why don't you and I go into the flat together and look around?"

JOHN WATCHED THE inspector's investigatory techniques with interest. Unlike in the warehouse, Tibbles was thorough to a fault. He dropped into his jacket side-pocket one of the inflammatory pamphlets. He found a long, wavy brown hair stuck to the bottom of one of the kitchen chair legs and, under the sink behind where the garbage can was stored, a felt plug which had been drawn through a gun barrel to clean out residue powder. Both items he placed in brown paper bags which he had in his outside coat pocket. He walked around the table with his hands clasped firmly behind his back, staring at the white pad with the pencil rubbing all the while, but he neither picked it up nor said anything about it.

One of Tibbles's underlings appeared at the flat doorway. "The lady next door says that two men were here earlier, ostensibly from the LCC," he announced.

Tibbles looked at Le Brun. "*Two* men, eh? I won't even ask." He refocused on the officer. "Send her over."

Mrs. Shea appeared, wide-eyed, at the open doorway. She spotted John and glowered.

Tibbles introduced himself. "And who might you be?"

"Mrs. Shea." She looked back to John. "I *knowed* you weren't English!"

"This is Sheriff Le Brun," Tibbles told her. "He's working with us. We'd be obliged if you described Mr. Burke's current girlfriend."

"Beautiful, tall girl. Hardly more than twenty. Brown, wavy hair, dark blue eyes. Skin like ivory. Never did a lick o' work in her life."

"And where have they gone?"

"Gone?" Mrs. Shea shrugged. "Maybe out for a bite ta eat."

"You didn't see them walking out with suitcases?"

The woman looked genuinely surprised. "Not at all. I been cookin' . . . moindin' me own business."

"Thank you," Tibbles said. "That's all for now."

When they were alone again, Tibbles said to Le Brun, "The lads who were guarding the flat in Lambeth should be up here within the hour. Do you think there's a possibility Burke will come back?"

"I doubt it. I might have said somethin' that warned Veronica."

Tibbles moved into the bedroom, expecting Le Brun to follow. "Not necessarily. If they're indeed planning on murdering Mr.

Godwin, as you posited to Bob Cooper, this move may have been precautionary," Tibbles replied. "You've proven that Mrs. Godwin and her daughter are meticulous in their planning. Let's say they intend to murder Mr. Burke, to tie up every loose end. They may have wanted him to pull up stakes two days early so that his disappearance wouldn't be linked to the murder of Mr. Godwin. I'm going out on a limb here, but if I were one of these two women, I'd have Burke kill Godwin while they're at the ball, then have him hop directly on a train to Birmingham. A week later, under the guise of bringing him his share of the gains, I'd have the irresistible Veronica visit him, lay several thousand pounds on the table, get him good and drunk, slit his throat, reclaim the money, and light out. An unknown corpse is found more than a hundred miles from London, drunk, with his wallet missing. They figure to get away with everything and share nothing."

"It's quite possible," John allowed.

"It's more than that. I'm assuming that the pad you found, rubbed, and laid so neatly on the table for me is a sketch of the Godwin house first floor."

"It is." John was discovering with some surprise that the man could do his job with flair when he put his mind to it.

"What will you do to protect Mr. Godwin?" John asked.

Tibbles plucked the photograph of Timothy Burke from the dressing mirror and deposited it in his inside jacket pocket. "I should think that he'd be fairly safe until he leaves the ball. Just to be thorough, though, I'll have him watched and protected as best we can without alerting him. We can't depend on him to keep a poker face at home if he's told his wife and stepdaughter are planning to kill him."

John had ambivalent feelings about alerting the lawyer, but he held his tongue. Instead, he said. "Maeve and Veronica may have intended to eliminate Burke all along. For all we know, he may be dead before the night is over. They may simply have decided to let the tontine money go."

"You know them better than I. Do you truly believe these two would let thirty-five thousand pounds slip through their fingers?"

John looked up at the ceiling. He had posed the identical question to Inspector Cooper earlier in the day, certain in his mind that the answer would be no. Now, with the Irish accomplice gone, he wasn't so sure. His silence became protracted, and when he thought any more of it would be rude, he said, "I honestly don't know, Chief Inspector. This is your case."

"I beg to differ with you, Sheriff Le Brun," Tibbles said. "It's yours. You have told more persons than me that you only intended to spend two days on it. You've also made it clear that you're retired. The case appeared to have been solved Monday morning. A chief inspector of Scotland Yard was satisfied as such. And yet you persisted. Have you asked yourself if your true motivation has been a need for personal glory?"

John did not consider the question unreasonable, addressed from a chief of the world's greatest police force to a small-town Southern sheriff. But he also knew that if he had needed this case to boost his self worth, he would have sat down with the rude reporter on Sunday and gotten his name in a London newspaper instead of sending him packing. He would have gotten his name in the Brunswick newspaper every month during his career. And he certainly would have told Geoffrey Moore about discovering J. P. Morgan's connection to the sinking of the *Maine* during the Jekyl Island Club case. In fact, he had never shared that information with anyone. He might have doubted his worth as an intellectual and an educated man before his Voyage of Discovery, but regarding the art and science of criminal investigation, John Le Brun had no self doubts.

"No, sir," he said simply.

"You're just a relentless crime-solving machine, then?"

"I suppose I am."

Both in his voice and his physical bearing, Tibbles's hard

edge evaporated. "Well, I for one am glad you are. You must admit that you've had considerable advantages over me. First, you were in the club during the murders. Then you were in Godwin's house when he was attacked *and* when he remembered the tontine. You've had Sir Arthur Conan Doyle working with you, and clearly another friend who was able to pose convincingly as an LCC agent. But none of these detract from the fact that you, a foreign visitor on holiday, have forged on while I was twice satisfied it was solved."

"I've been lucky." Confronted with what from Tibbles must have amounted to an abject apology, John was feeling magnanimous.

Tibbles closed the bedroom door. "You're too modest. As you no doubt have surmised, I've risen early to my position through political connections. However, once one stands out from the crowd, he's made himself a target. Opposing political factions are eager to see me fall on my face. I'm still learning, but I've accounted reasonably well for myself this past year. Then come these Sceptred Isle Club murders . . . with two M.P.s dead. An incredible amount of pressure was placed on me to provide an early solution. I got anxious and sloppy and had no inkling of the kind of Byzantine planning I was up against."

"I understand. I've had politicians try to rush me as well." What John graciously declined to say was that no one, even when he was just beginning his career, had ever rushed him in a criminal investigation.

Tibbles raised his eyebrows and hands at the same time, gestures of concession. "What I mean to say is that if it hadn't been for you, I'd have cocked this whole investigation up royally. I'd like it if we were truly playing on the same side."

"I'd like that, too." John stuck out his hand, which Tibbles accepted. Tibbles then opened the bedroom door and gestured for Le Brun to lead him out.

As they headed toward the longer automobile under Tibbles's

umbrella, John observed, "You're nearsighted."

"Is my squint that pronounced?"

"It is to me. But even if it wasn't, I noticed the indentations on the bridge of your nose when Veronica and I visited you at Scotland Yard. Why aren't you wearin' your specs?"

"It's raining."

"Why weren't you wearin' 'em when you were in Brighton?"

"You truly are dogged. Because almost none of the Yard's inspectors wear them. Physical sign of weakness."

"With the piles of reports y'all read and write, I *know* most of you must need them." John made a tsking noise with his tongue. "Headaches followed by bad tempers. And they say women are foolish about their appearances."

"You wear spectacles, too," Tibbles said.

"How do you know?"

"All the piles of reports you must have read and written."

"You're right. But I only wear them when I'm alone. Physical sign of weakness, y'know." John winked, causing Tibbles to laugh. "What's your first name, Chief Inspector?"

"John."

"John. Now that's a right nice name."

TEN

Thursday, October 26, 1905

AFTER WHAT PROVED A remarkably good night's sleep, John went down to the Westminster Palace Hotel's lobby with a leisurely breakfast and old-fashioned touring as his plan. He was prepared to truly begin his vacation and to leave the rest of the case to Scotland Yard, with only a scheduled check-in at five from either Chief Inspector Tibbles or Inspector Cooper. On the way back to his hotel the previous night, John had discussed with Tibbles his concern that he had focused Veronica on Lionel Attwater by talking to her about the man's double motives for wanting his father dead. Rather than seeming annoyed by the extra work implied, Tibbles congratulated Le Brun on suggesting a potential plan of action for the Godwin women in laying the blame squarely on the younger Attwater's doorstep. Attwater and Godwin both would be shadowed and finally contacted a few hours before the ball, to prepare and protect them. Tibbles and Le Brun agreed down the line on the plan of action, which removed a great burden from the American's mind.

John's carefree day was almost immediately reburdened, however, when he was told at the front desk that he had a message. It was from Conan Doyle, requesting that John lunch with him at one o'clock at the Reform Club. Doyle had taken a room there for the remainder of the week, it went on, and he was anxious to compare notes with Le Brun. John penned an affirmative reply and paid for a runner to deliver it immediately. That done, he arranged through the concierge to purchase a ticket for *The Mikado,* the Gilbert and Sullivan operetta playing that night at the Savoy Theatre. Directly after, he took a cab up to Regent's Park and wandered through a soggy Queen Mary's Gardens. A short stroll south over puddle-dappled paths brought him to Madame Tussaud's Waxworks, where he viewed the noble and the maudlin from England's history. On the ride down to Pall Mall, he passed 221 Baker Street, where the peerless if fictional Sherlock Holmes had his residence.

The day was damp and chill, in keeping with John's mood. The day's diversions failed to beguile him from aspects of the case. Even though he and Tibbles had agreed on the plan of action, he was still not in charge. Consequently, he could not stop worrying. He had not one but two formidable foes. He had a gnawing apprehension that perhaps the team of Veronica and her mentor mother could best him in the larger chess game. At worst, Trent Godwin would be added to the five victims of the crime, and Veronica and Maeve would elude conviction; at best, the two women would be trapped and convicted, but the shadow of their crimes would darken all of Solicitor Godwin's remaining days. At the same time, John's heart was heavy from mourning. The extraordinary creature that Veronica might have become if raised by parents with scruples had been lost years earlier.

The moment he entered the Reform Club, John felt ill attired. This to him was true elegance. The building had an enormous, two-story center court supported by Ionian columns. The floor was tiled in classic Greek and Celtic designs. Above the second story, spacious windows allowed cloud-filtered sunlight to bathe the space. While his eyes were being delighted, the hearty aromas of food came to his nostrils.

As John stood gawking, Arthur Conan Doyle appeared out of one of the rooms and greeted him with his knuckle-breaking handshake.

"Now *this* is my idea of a club," John admired.

"Quite grand," Doyle agreed. "The design is based on the Farnese Palace in Rome. Service is equal to the architecture. Newspapers are pressed, coins are boiled, and the kitchens are a marvel of science. The only problem is, so much steam is used that it carries the smell of the cooking throughout the building. If you aren't hungry when you come in, you are shortly thereafter."

Before dining, Conan Doyle showed Le Brun the library. The ceiling stretched twenty feet above them, with florid coffering and a great multi-bulbed chandelier reflected to infinity in opposing mirrors. The bookcases lining the walls held more than thirty thousand volumes.

"There are a few thousand more books in the smoking room. We have a billiard room as well. Comradeship, intellectual pursuit, and fun are the watchwords here, and very little politics."

"Sounds like my idea of heaven," John remarked. He suspected he might fit in such a place, where members seemed to be left alone if that was their desire but where a good smoke or a challenging game of chess or billiards could be pursued amidst the most attentive service. He had to give Geoffrey Moore his due: The unadulterated concept of the men's club was not a bad one. Ultimately, it was the membership that degraded it.

"Shall we dine?" Doyle suggested.

The "coffee room" was crowded. Unlike Geoffrey Moore, Conan Doyle did not parade John about. He had gotten them a quiet corner table. John ordered a caviar appetizer, breaded lamb cutlets, mushrooms sautéed with thickened butter, and blanched spinach boiled in salt water.

The moment the waiter had gone, John said, "A second autopsy I arranged confirmed that Nahum Attwater was murdered on Saturday mornin'. He had his breakfast undigested in his stomach."

Doyle nodded his large head slowly. "That's good. When did you learn this?"

"Yesterday afternoon."

Doyle folded his hands on the edge of the table and fixed his eyes on John. "And when exactly did you get the idea that the mysterious Irishman might work in a riding stable?" he asked.

John was not surprised by the question. Clearly, the author had been receiving periodic updates from Scotland Yard. He believed Conan Doyle was man enough to weather his answer. "On the trip back from your estate. You put the idea in my head when you talked about motorcars replacin' horses in London. But I had no more support for it than we did for the dock worker."

"Let's be brutally honest, John," said Doyle, "because that's the kind of men we really are. When you were at my home, you felt that I was trying to wrest the credit for solving the Sceptred Isle Club murders from your hands."

"I did feel you were bein' proprietary about it," John admitted.

"To tell you the truth . . . I was. At least when I was still convinced Trent Godwin was guilty. After all, only minutes after the crime I thought of the means for Trent to get back into that gambling room and out. But you *will* recall I openly invited you to blow my theory out of the water."

"I remember those very words."

"Good. However, once you told me about your visit to Lionel Attwater and the reasons he had for killing his father, my dog-in-the-manger attitude vanished. You may not have noticed, but it did. That was when I said I would come up to London and work with you and Scotland Yard on all the theories."

"Your scribblin' all my thoughts on your cards still seemed proprietary to me," John confessed.

"I understand. Let me explain. I'm a very successful author, but I'm also a frustrated one. Do you know how many people think that Arthur Conan Doyle is merely the literary agent for Sherlock Holmes? It sounds stupid to you, doesn't it?"

"Frankly, yes."

"But believe me when I say I'm constantly receiving mail from people asking me to get his autograph for them. I've worked on real mysteries. You heard a few: That man who withdrew his money and fled to Edinburgh. The Marquess' missing jewels. However, this is something else altogether. First of all, it's murder. Even more spectacularly, it was mass murder. Beyond that, it was done in one of London's most elite clubs. Not only were these elements enough to rivet England's attention, but the complexity of their planning and goals when revealed will make them famous for decades to come."

"You wanted the world to see Arthur Conan Doyle solvin' a real crime."

"Exactly. If I could do that, then maybe the dolts would understand that Sherlock Holmes is simply a figment of a first-class mind. Credit where credit is due. And then perhaps they'd begin to read my historical, supernatural, and domestic novels . . . the ones with my real talent and life's blood in them."

"I'm sorry I ruined your plan."

Doyle's hand waved through the air as if he were shooing a fly instead of a desire. "Don't be. *I* was the source of my own undoing here. My solution of Trent climbing out the lavatory window was so attractive that I fell in love with it to the exclusion of other possibilities. That's the difference between solving crimes in fiction and in fact. As I told you when we first met, I begin with the motives and clever executions and work backward. I've created enough thunder in my life; I'm not interested in stealing yours."

"And all I'm interested in is seein' justice done," Le Brun rejoined.

Doyle tapped the top of Le Brun's hand. "Which is one of the things that makes you so successful. As I'm in London for a few more days, we should work more closely. I don't mind serving in support."

"I won't think of you that way, and neither should you. You know, you aren't the only one who's let his desires cloud his thinkin'," John graciously revealed. "I allowed Veronica Godwin to mesmerize me utterly."

"I really must meet this siren," said Doyle, laughing lightly. "She's your Irene Adler, then." The lack of recognition in John's eyes told Conan Doyle that the American was not as familiar with Sherlock Holmes's exploits as he might have suggested. "She's a femme fatale from my short story, 'A Scandal in Bohemia.' She's the only woman who's outwitted Holmes . . . and the only one who's revealed him to be something more than a scientific automaton."

"I'd like to read that one," John said.

"Then you shall."

"Veronica has so many strong points. I keep hopin' for her sake there might be an even more bizarre twist, provin' me wrong entirely," John said. "However, whatever the correct solution is, I'm sure it involves the lad with the scar."

"I concur one hundred percent," Doyle rejoined. "He can't be a red herring dragged across the hounds' path. The proof is that *you* hunted down the icemen, not the other way round. There was no way the murderers could have known you would deduce your way to that icehouse. Tibbles understands this as well. He's having young Mr. Seaforth brought up to London tomorrow, in the hopes that Timothy Burke will be caught."

"Is he? You must have set up your own office in the Yard," John marveled.

"Ah, but I haven't heard about Burke and last night's exploits from the master's mouth," coaxed the author.

John told Doyle about his adventures and concluded by declaring that the rest was in the hands of Scotland Yard. "At best, they'd let you and me watch the Godwin house with them on Friday night."

"I can see to that," Doyle said, as he smoothed down his walrus mustache. "Oh, and to prove that I have continuing value in this investigation, I've expanded my sources on Trent Godwin. I was right that he lost two large accounts in the past two years. But now I know the reason. In both cases, it was over Mrs. Godwin and her pushy ways. Whether it was the clients themselves or their wives I don't know, but this *nouveau riche* Irishwoman, her fortnightly soirees, her liberal views, and her self-invented charity ball have rubbed more than a few established London families the wrong way."

"Like me marryin' a black woman in my town and expectin' to keep my office," John said.

"Precisely."

"Shame on them! I defy any man to explain why the Irish should be treated so shabbily. I despise prejudice of any form," John revealed.

Conan Doyle smiled wryly. "In this case, it was warranted."

"Those English families who dropped Trent didn't know what we know. They paint Maeve, Veronica, and every other Irishman with the same black brush. What about the election that was stolen from you with those dirty posters? You, too, Mr. Doyle, have suffered from prejudice against the Irish. I would think you'd be quite indignant over this news."

Doyle's smile faded. "Well, I am. But Trent Godwin is no babe in the woods. He knew the common antipathy toward the Irish when he married Maeve. Let's give him a high mark for courage on that. But afterward, he must have understood the sort of trouble her pushy antics would cause him, Irish or not. And yet he allowed them."

"You can't blame some of her pushin'," John countered. "She was just workin' for rights she believes she's due. I can't help thinkin' that at least four of the dead men would be alive today if the world were different. If women had the right to vote in every election, Maeve Godwin might not have felt the need for such drastic measures to affect an election. In fact, if every educated citizen had the right to vote, Home Rule might no longer be an issue."

"That's going a bit far. I note you managed to omit Veronica from culpability. She is a grown woman."

"I don't know about you, Arthur, but I still didn't have my own mind when I was twenty-two. I *thought* I did, but they were borrowed thoughts and opinions. Until you're away from your parents' influence, you're still paintin' your pictures with the palette they hand you. She's guilty, but I doubt very much that she's as guilty as her mother."

"Maybe so. However, even if Maeve had the right to vote, she'd still have murdered another husband and pinned the blame on someone else. And her daughter would no doubt do nothing to save him."

"But the two M.P.s and Mr. Ravenscroft would be alive tonight," John insisted. "And so would the poor butler. It's unfair, but I feel worse about him than the others."

"A birdbath, a tontine, M.P.s, Home Rule," Conan Doyle said, shaking his large head and rolling his eyes in wonderment.

"This case *is* like a Chinese puzzle box," John agreed.

The waiter had returned, to deliver a salad to Conan Doyle and John's caviar with crackers. "I agree," Doyle replied. "I only wish we knew if there are more hidden boxes to be discovered."

John did not have to wish.

WHEN JOHN RETURNED to his hotel from *The Mikado*, softly whistling the tune to "I've Got a Little List," he was handed his second message of the day. This one was inside a thick envelope with the embossed address and insignia of Scotland Yard on the front and a seal of red wax on the back. He waited until he was inside his room before opening it. It read:

Dear Mr. Le Brun—

Today was Nahum Attwater's funeral. Unfortunately, your revelation of the young Irishman arrived too late to prevent the besmirching of Mr. Attwater's name. There were far fewer people at the funeral than a man of his import should merit. This made it that much more difficult for us to have an inconspicuous presence. His daughters eulogized by the graveside. Lionel did not, but he wept alongside his sisters. He has been occupied all day with the funeral and subsequent activities.

We intercepted Lionel's mail and determined that no letter suggested he meet with Trent Godwin. We have secured permission to listen in on telephone conversations to his office and home and are in the process of so doing.

Concerning Maeve and Veronica Godwin, as per your suggestion, we have left them completely alone, except to monitor their home telephone as well.

Timothy Burke did not come to work today. We had the Uniform officer on that beat casually ask of his whereabouts. He was told that a letter was found under the academy's front door this morning when it opened for business. It said that Burke's father was dying and that he had to travel to Ireland for an indefinite period.

Regarding your request to have the death of Maeve Godwin's first husband investigated: Graeme Meany did indeed die of a broken neck. There was no evidence of foul play. However, Meany was not known to be a drunk. Furthermore, he and his wife and child did not live in Belfast but rather in Dublin. At the very least, the ladies of the Godwin household are liars. Well done!

Could you make yourself available tomorrow at noon in my office? If not, please drop by no later than two o'clock.

Yours respectfully,
Chief Inspector John Tibbles

John refolded the note and returned it carefully to its envelope. "Now, this must go in my collection along with that apology on J. P. Morgan's stationery," he said aloud to himself. He resumed whistling the tunes from *The Mikado*, right up to extinguishing his room's lights. His lips unpuckered when he again saw the dreaded flash of nonexistent light.

ELEVEN

Friday, October 27, 1905

LE BRUN WAS LONG awake by quarter to nine. Since he expected the day to continue into the early hours of the morning, however, he elected to stay in his room and read the previous day's newspapers. He also felt the beginning of a head cold coming on. He was sure the reason was from having spent so many hours out in the chill damp two days before. He decided to coddle himself all morning. Trent Godwin found him in his room, wrapped in a blanket, dressed in shirt and trousers but without shoes or tie.

When John opened the door and saw Godwin, a flash memory of the man standing at his own guest bedroom door, with Veronica under the bed swept through his mind. This time, however, there was no excitement in Trent's eyes or voice.

"Hello, John," Trent said. He looked like he badly needed rest. "I'm glad you weren't sleeping."

"I'm wide awake," John replied. "Come in. How are you?"

Godwin went directly to the room's stuffed chair. "Not well. I'll come straight to the point. Some of the members of the Sceptred Isle Club said they saw you draw a small gun the night of the murders."

"That's right. It's called a derringer."

"After I was shot at Sunday night, I had planned to buy a gun, but then the next day the crime seemed to have been solved. Now . . . I wonder if I might borrow yours until I can purchase my own."

John sat on the corner of the bed nearest the lawyer. "What's the matter?"

Godwin sighed. "I thought this nightmare had ended, but yesterday I was followed."

"How do you know?"

"Because the same man was standing outside my firm in the morning, across the street from where I lunched, and then again outside my firm in the afternoon."

"Have you told Maeve or Veronica about this?"

"No. I couldn't upset them on the night before the charity ball."

John breathed an inward sigh of relief at the news. Godwin's women would know in a trice who was following him and why. John wrestled with his next words. He had determined to let Scotland Yard handle the case the moment he had reached accord with Inspector Tibbles. But Tibbles had also said it was John's case. He would not have gone to Trent Godwin, but now the man had planted himself on John's doorstep and was asking for help. John found himself wincing when he determined the best but most painful course. Trent had to find out sooner or later at any rate.

"Trent," he began softly, "you know that Geoffrey Moore has been rather hyperbolic in praisin' my powers of deduction."

"Not as hyperbolic as I had thought before I met you," Godwin complimented, although he was clearly confused by Le Brun's redirection of the conversation.

"I'm glad you have confidence in me. That way, you'll know I'm not guessin'."

"About what?"

"About you havin' had sexual relations with Veronica five years ago."

Godwin's eyes grew enormously round. When he had recovered his breath, he asked, "How could you *possibly* know?"

"Because you told the world that you would never marry again, and yet you did . . . precipitously. Because Maeve Godwin is a brilliant and handsome woman but clearly not your soul mate. Because Veronica gleefully told me that you have always lived your life by the rules and have longed to be wild and adventurous. But mostly because Veronica lies about her age."

Godwin straightened up. It took him several seconds to glean the meaning behind Le Brun's last words. And then he had it.

"You were set up," John said. "Veronica is one year older than she says. I saw it in her family Bible. She was actually of the age of consent when she had relations with you."

"My God!"

"Did she convince you she was a virgin as well?"

"Yes. Of course."

"A pinch of alum can work wonders in restorin' a young woman's virginity."

Trent's eyes unfocused into memory. "I *was* set up! I was dating Maeve for about three months. Then she said she had to return to Belfast for a week over some real estate business."

"And she left Veronica in your keepin'."

"She did. You know Veronica's charms. I was helpless."

"She provoked you into the forbidden adventure about which older men like you and me only fantasize. Ever since you married her mother, the two of them have been keepin' you in line with ongoin' guilt. You believed you were the cause of her fascination with older men."

"Yes, precisely."

"And every time she or her mother want another extravagance, they find a way to remind you of your sin."

Trent's face was turning rapidly crimson. His eyelids batted up and down. "They do."

"Even when you knew that your business was sufferin' from the bad opinion of clients regardin' your women, you did nothin'."

"You're right yet again."

John felt a sneeze coming on. He dug into his trouser pocket for his handkerchief and just got it to his nose before erupting.

"Bless you. You sound a bit nasal this morning," Trent observed. "Are you under the weather?"

"Just a little head cold," John replied, tucking the handkerchief away. "Of course, with this nose, it's like a giraffe havin' a sore throat or an elephant a bellyache."

In spite of his emotional turmoil, Trent managed a small smile.

"You haven't gone to bed with Veronica since you married, have you?" John asked.

"No! Of course not."

"I'm gonna caution you to take a few deep breaths now, Trent," John said. "This is just the beginnin'."

Parceling out the bad news as delicately as he could, Le Brun first offered the news that Maeve had most likely not returned to Belfast, as she had lived in Dublin previous to her emigration to London. He revealed Maeve and Veronica to be Roman Catholic. He next spoke of the dead husband and his suspicious broken neck. At that point, John hauled out his hip flask of whiskey and allowed Trent to half drain the remains.

"A little calmer?" John asked.

"Not really." Trent yanked at his collar, undid it, and popped off the stay. "What does this have to do with the man following me?"

"There are at least two men. Both from Scotland Yard. They're tryin' to protect you."

"From Maeve and Veronica?" Trent asked.

"From the murderers of your friends at the club, includin' Nahum Attwater. They happen to be one and the same."

Not a muscle on Trent moved, but the blood drained from his face until he had taken on the shade of raw wax.

"You'd better switch places with me and lie down," John prescribed.

"No. I'll be all right," Trent insisted. He lifted his chin, swept back his hair, and took what John considered a characteristic British "stiff upper lip" attitude. "What a blind fool I've been."

"Don't blame yourself," John said, rising to pace the room. "I was only a guest in your house for two days, and I was made blind *and* deaf. They are a deceivingly formidable pair. When I met them, I said to myself, 'My! Those women have strong wills.' But I also assumed a lot of it was bluster and thwarted desire. I was wrong. The lengths to which they are willin' to go is beyond imagination."

"This Monday, Nahum was the murderer. What has happened to change that?" Godwin asked.

John told him about the Irishman at the warehouse, of finding him, following him to his home and hearing Veronica's voice. "You must have laid down the law about domestic economies some weeks back," he said when he had finished.

"Yes. Months ago, actually. I told them that after this Christmas our spending would have to be cut back radically until I could secure other significant clients. They would murder me over that?"

"Not that alone." John went on, explaining about the deliberate murder of the two M.P.s. "When was Nahum last invited to one of Maeve's soirees that he didn't attend?"

Trent thought. "Five or six weeks ago."

"And you had your money discussion before that."

"Yes. What does one have to do with the other?"

John told him about Nahum's apology on his stationery and how Maeve had used it. "He inadvertantly encouraged his own death with that note, providin' a nice detail to prove his suicide."

"It is all true, then," Godwin said.

"I'm afraid so."

"What now?"

"You want another swig from my flask?" John asked, halting his pacing.

"No. Thanks."

"Then I shall finish it." And he did. John decided a towel was too far away and wiped his lips with the back of his hand. His room was, after all, his territory and good form be damned. "Do you have a busy day today?"

"It could be. But I was going to quit work at two, go home, and take a nap in preparation for the ball."

"You should plan on meetin' me at Scotland Yard at noon."

"If you wish."

"It's what they wish also. The inspectors and I are very afraid that there's a plan to kill you tonight, on account of that tontine money." John explained how Godwin might otherwise have been safe for several months but that the £35,000 he had pledged to give away had probably assured his precipitous death.

"This is appalling! I am ruined even if I survive," Trent lamented. "I wish you had more whiskey."

THE NIGHT FOG on Green Street was not a London "pea soup." It was more akin to the mist on a moor. It hovered knee-high above the street and swirled easily whenever a carriage passed. It did nothing to conceal the motorcar parked within the darkest stretch of the street.

Tim Burke did not like the presence of the automobile.

Such expensive machines were invariably off the streets at night, inside stables, or at least on driveways. It was, however, only ten o'clock. Most probably, someone of wealth was visiting at one of the lighted houses. Just to make sure, Burke walked up to the car and looked inside. It was empty. He felt the bonnet. The engine was cold. It had been sitting there for some time.

In keeping with the upscale neighborhood, Burke was dressed well. He wore his dark "Nahum Attwater" suit with vest. Tucked up between his shirt and jacket was a small khaki-colored duffel bag. Stuck between the back hem of his shirt and his belt was a small revolver. In his right hand, pressed hard against his body, he held a crowbar with a "cat's paw" at one end. He crossed the street, moving resolutely toward the Godwin house. It lay dark, except for a lone light glowing in the middle of the downstairs level.

As Burke neared the Godwin driveway, he glanced over his shoulder, to be sure no one could observe him. It would have been difficult; the street lamps were not bright on Green Street, and the moon was new, with no borrowed light to bathe the old city. Satisfied, he darted down the drive and into the back garden. He paused and listened, heard nothing suspicious, and bent to find the key under the stone Veronica had told him about. The plan was to open the back door with the key, lock himself inside, and wait. Almost certainly, Trent Godwin would take a cab home and enter through the front door. If for some reason he came around back, however, it would not do to have that door jimmied and broken, warning him. Burke had been coached to mangle the door on the way out. After he had killed Godwin.

He fitted the key into the lock. The door opened with no difficulty. He returned the key to its hiding place, again to have nothing amiss when the lawyer came home. Burke locked the door from the inside. The only light sources were an electric wall sconce in the hallway and a trace of illumination drifting through the back kitchen window from the lamp above the stable door. Veronica had drawn him a map of the lower floor, but she had made him throw it away on the trip to his temporary digs. He struggled to recall all the details she had sketched, as well as the elements of the house she had spoken of but not drawn. At the moment he stood in the pantry, which held the back door and the door to the cellar at opposite ends and an unbroken line of cabinets along its outside wall. A wide archway led into the kitchen. He waited for his eyes to adjust to the increased dimness, shifting uncomfortably from one foot to the other.

Veronica had said that once her stepfather was dead, once the money had been transferred and the property sold, she and her mother were moving back to Ireland. Tim, she promised, would go with them and share in the fortune. Looking around at the grandeur, even dimly lit, he wondered if they would truly leave.

Timothy Burke had never robbed a house before. In fact, until he had met Veronica Godwin, the worst physical act he had ever committed was knocking the helmet off a bobby's head with a large rock. His worst unlawful behavior was inciting violent demonstrations in the streets of London on behalf of Home Rule. But then Veronica had come into the stables where he worked. Six months later, lying in his bed beside her, he was convinced of murdering for the good of Ireland. Not that he had had to kill Nahum Attwater; Veronica had calmly put a bullet through the man's skull. Nor had he been compelled to kill a single man in the Sceptred Isle Club; the even more cold-blooded mother had slaughtered all four with only six bullets. Standing guard outside the warehouse for Veronica, he had not had to view Attwater's execution. But inside the gambling room, the squirting blood, the screaming in abject terror, the scrambling to stay alive, had so appalled him that he felt afterward that he would not have been able to use the revolver in his hand to finish Maeve Godwin's work. By the time the plan to shoot Trent Godwin through his front window was improvised, Burke had become a bit more accepting of pulling a trigger. After all, this was the man who had seduced Veronica when she was only sixteen and taken her virginity. Nonetheless, his hand had shaken, causing him to miss his target. Tonight, there was no more avoiding the issue; Godwin must be murdered. The gun tucked against the small of his back felt cold and heavy.

If the gun felt cold, the crowbar in Burke's grip was like an icicle. He thought to put it down next to the back door but remembered its need in the study. He wiped the sweat from his brow, running his fingers over his old horseshoe scar. He took a pair of calfskin gloves from his trouser pocket and tugged them on. As he sidled across the kitchen, he pulled the duffel bag from under his armpit. The plan was to make it look as if Godwin had interrupted a robbery and been killed for it. Toward this end, the Irishman's instructions were to make off with the family's good silver, the small collection of ancient British coins Trent had locked in one of his study desk drawers, and the three vases that stood on the living room mantlepiece. The fictional robber was not to have had time to rummage through the upstairs; Maeve would not abide losing any of her jewelry.

After banging into the corner of the butcher block and swearing loudly, Burke got himself into the dining room and located the drawer with the silverware case. He opened it and found, as he expected, a soft apron of cloth with pockets for each type of utensil. It had stout ribbons to tie the cloth into a bundle. He bound the lot up and pushed it into the bottom of his bag. There were supposed to be many place mats in the same sideboard, but he couldn't find them. These he was supposed to use to carefully wrap up Maeve Godwin's precious vases. Veronica had warned him over and over that no damage had better come to them. He retraced his path into the kitchen and blindly opened several drawers, feeling in vain for dishtowels. He decided to postpone that part of the job and ransack Trent's study first.

The study lay in the middle of the house, with only a small window facing a narrow alley. Burke yanked down its shade and drew its curtains before turning on the banker's lamp that sat on the desk. He first inspected the half closet that was located under the house's upper staircase. He opened Trent's attaché case and dumped the papers on the floor. He found the cash box Veronica had told him was there, stuffed into one of his pockets the eighty pounds he had found, and tossed the box aside. He scattered piles of note cards and other stored items. Then he went to the desk and used his crowbar on the drawers. He located the cigar box that held almost two dozen old coins, each respectfully secured in its own cardboard sleeve. He dumped the coins unceremoniously into the bag. For effect, he left the desk drawers hanging open.

Burke moved into the living room for his third assignment. By the faint light filtering in through the two front windows he saw the shapes of the vases. One by one, he took them down and set them carefully on the floor next to the duffel bag. He stood for a moment in front of them, thinking of how he could best protect them. Then he decided there had to be a closet or piece of furniture upstairs where fleecy, thick bath towels were stored. Still holding onto the crowbar, he picked his way back through the room, into the foyer, and up the black staircase. When he reached the top step, he thought he heard a noise in the rear of the house. He froze in place and withdrew the revolver from his belt.

Another noise sounded from downstairs. This time, it was from almost directly below him. He cursed under his breath. Veronica had predicted that Trent Godwin would not be home earlier than midnight. He could not just wait for the man to come upstairs and shoot him as he turned the corner; Godwin would probably discover the bag on the living room floor and run out of the house. And yet, if Timothy rattled down the dangerously dark stairs, the man would also be alerted. Burke's dilemma was solved when the foyer light came on and a voice called out.

"Timothy Burke! This is Chief Inspector John Tibbles of Scotland Yard. Give yourself up. This house is surrounded."

The Irishman was no Oxford scholar, but he had more than enough intelligence when it came to self preservation. Not wasting a moment, he continued onto the second floor and sought out the room that lay above the back entrance to the house. A rather substantial gabled roof overhung the back door, more than enough to drop down onto and thence jump to the ground and flee over the back garden wall. Burke entered the bathroom and found the window he needed. He set his crowbar down on a wicker clothes hamper. It promptly slipped off the back side and rang loudly as it struck the tile floor. Burke returned his gun to the small of his back and lifted the window. As he clambered out, he heard heavy footsteps pounding up the stairs. He wriggled around so that his elbows alone supported him on the window sill. Then he dropped. The cant of the roof was such that his feet landed at different instants. He pitched sideways and tumbled headlong onto a sizable hedge. The branches gave way, spilling him onto smaller plants. He righted himself and stood, snatching the weapon from under his belt.

A dark figure came running into view from the driveway. Burke thrust his gun out wildly and fired. The figure grunted and spun around as if it had been punched. It disappeared back beyond the corner of the house. Burke oriented himself and limped toward the high wall that backed the property.

"Halt! Halt!" a voice yelled from the back doorway as the Irishman reached the wall.

An instant later, two shots rang out. The second one tore through the center of Timothy Burke's chest. He pitched forward awkwardly and struck his head hard on the stone figure of an angel. The world went away.

SO MUCH FOR the best-laid plans," John Le Brun said, staring down at the body of the would-be killer. Beside him, Arthur Conan Doyle held another of his toys, a carbon-battery-powered lantern which he called a torch. On the other side of the corpse stood Inspectors Tibbles and Cooper.

The plan had been simply to trap Timothy Burke inside the Godwin house and force him to give himself up. His presence was enough to link him to Veronica and Maeve. Once he was positively identified by the younger iceman, he would have little choice but to confess to at least being an accomplice to the greater crimes. When the women arrived home from the ball, they, too, would have been arrested on suspicion of murder. The case would be solved without spilling another drop of blood.

"All he had to do was stop. I'd like to kick the ruddy bastard," Tibbles lamented. "Now this will drag on forever. The iceman's son is somewhat slow-witted. Mrs. Shea is what one would charitably call shanty Irish. Our chief witnesses are not exactly shining stars."

"It doesn't have to drag on. We can create unimpeachable witnesses tonight," John said, before a solution other than his own could be suggested. "Let's get him inside the house."

Two plainclothesmen stood beside Inspector Cooper. Their heads turned as one toward Tibbles, waiting to see if he concurred.

"I'd like to hear your plan before doing anything," Tibbles said.

John nodded in the direction of a next-door home. The silhouettes of two figures peered out of windows on the first and second floors. "I, on the other hand, believe we should take this all indoors as quickly as we can. It was a mercy your bobby was only wounded and we didn't need an ambulance to take him away. As it is, I believe you'd better send someone over to the adjoinin' houses and see that they stay inside and away from their windows. Otherwise, you can bet the Godwin women will smell a trap."

"All right," Tibbles relented. He gestured to the body. "Get him inside."

"Only as far as the kitchen," John instructed.

"And then go to the neighbors as Mr. Le Brun suggests."

"If he'd only run out the front, I'd have winged him in the leg," Conan Doyle said, brandishing his Colt Army revolver.

"Put that away, Sir Arthur!" Tibbles commanded. "I remind you that you are here as an observer only and to stay well out of harm's way."

"Yes, yes," said Doyle, in a voice that showed he was not in the slightest cowed. He handed his weapon to Le Brun butt first. "I picked it up during my lecture tour in your country. The 'Peacemaker,'" he said with reverence. "The gun that tamed the Wild West."

John spun the well-balanced weapon around his forefinger several times and returned it to its owner. "I own one myself. Reliable weapon."

The two junior detectives, whom Tibbles had failed to introduce, had just carried the dead man through the back door.

"Let's get in out of the damp," Bob Cooper suggested.

"I would very much appreciate that," said Le Brun, suffering from the pressure of his clogged sinuses.

When they entered the kitchen, Timothy Burke had been laid out on his back, with his arms over his head.

"Not a convincin' position for a fallen burglar," John judged. "What happened to his gun?"

"I have it," Cooper said. He produced the weapon and handed it to Le Brun. John examined it briefly, then yanked back the cylinder latch, disengaged the hinged lever on the right hand side of the frame, swung the cylinder out to the right, and looked at the bottoms of the shells.

"Curious design. What kind of gun is this, Chief Inspector?" John asked.

"It's French. A Lebel. Eight millimeter. The French are even oblique in their gun manufacture."

"Thank you." He handed the gun over to Tibbles. "Excuse me for a few moments, gentlemen," he said. John walked down the hall to the study. He had barely entered the room when he came back out and returned to the kitchen, blowing his nose into his handkerchief as he moved.

"Here's the drama I propose," John said. "We have Mr. Godwin's promise that he will arrive home not later than half past twelve. The hostess must stay until the evenin's end, which is two o'clock. They should be back here by no later than a quarter to three. That gives us a safe hour and a half to decorate the stage."

John glanced up at the dark rooms over the stable, where the husband and wife team of servants lived. "This is Mrs. Godwin's third charity ball, so habits have been established that we may rely upon. Due to her age, Mrs. Comfort retires at midnight to the suite in the hotel that's provided to the Godwin ladies for their last-minute preparations. Mr. Comfort naps there from eight until midnight, to be fresh to serve the ladies for the remainder of the night. Veronica and Maeve are also relyin' on these habits in order to kill Mr. Godwin.

"The women are driven back by Mr. Comfort after the ball ends. Trent says that their habit is not to be dropped off at the front door but rather to let him drive onto the property. They leave the vehicle. While he garages it, they enter by the back door. Trent also told us that there are inevitably a number of items left over from the ball . . . floral arrangements, the money collected for the costume votin' and such . . . that must be brought in. It would help very much with the police if Mr. Comfort could testify that he came into the house only seconds behind the ladies and found Mr. Godwin dead at the same time they did. So they wait for their chauffeur in the kitchen, usin' some excuse or other not to move to the front of the house. Once Mr. Comfort is inside, they all find Mr. Godwin lyin' in the foyer or the livin' room."

John put his back against one of the countertops. “What I propose is that we arrange Mr. Burke here with his gun in his hand . . . much as he must have done with poor Mr. Attwater. At the other end of the lighted hallway, we have Mr. Godwin lyin’ on the floor, ostensibly badly wounded and unconscious but not dead.”

“Go on,” bade Tibbles.

“The two women will find Burke without Mr. Comfort by their sides. They will wonder how he came to be shot. There is no evidence of a struggle. He has his gun by his side. Then Maeve will remember that on Monday mornin’, after havin’ been shot at through his front window, Trent remarked that he thought he should purchase a gun. Of course, after the supposed solution to the crime with us findin’ Attwater dead, he reconsidered. But as she witnesses the dead Irishman here, then looks down the hall and sees another weapon in Trent’s hand, she will assume that her husband reversed his decision again and got a gun. They will rush to see if he is dead. He will still be breathin’. At that point, the women will have to use Burke’s gun to finish Trent off.”

“How can they?” Cooper asked. “The chauffeur is about to enter the house.”

“We will give them the excuse to get Mr. Comfort back out of the house after he has taken a brief look at the carnage. An ambulance must be called for Mr. Godwin. The study has been fairly wrecked by our robber. I am sure that this was done at the command of Maeve. She will have little cause to be suspicious when the telephone cord is found to be pulled out of the wall.”

“But *is* the cord pulled out of the wall?” asked Conan Doyle.

“No.”

“Then why should she believe that Burke extemporized and pulled it out?”

“He may have tripped over it in the dark,” replied Le Brun. “Or he wanted the phone to stop ringin’. She will not have much time to worry about the reason, and since it suits her needs, human nature says she will accept it."

"But one way or the other, the chauffeur must be briefly gotten out of the house," Cooper said.

"That's correct," John answered. "He'll probably run to the nearest home that has a telephone. In that short amount of time, Maeve and Veronica will attempt to finish off Mr. Godwin. They can't club him. They can't strangle him. They'll have to do it with a gun, because that'll be the wound and the scene the chauffeur saw."

"And how do we manage to witness the attempt at this heinous act?" Tibbles asked.

"You position Mr. Godwin in a direct line with the foyer closet and leave the door open a crack. I'd volunteer to stay there, but I won't be around for the trial."

"You and Sir Arthur must be well out of the way," affirmed Tibbles.

"Accepted. You should also put someone inside the cellar stairs, with his ear to the door, in case they talk in the kitchen." He jerked his thumb over his shoulder. "Finally, you'll note that they have a speakin' tube here runnin' up into the ceilin'. There's a tube in the upstairs hallway. We can test, but I'm sure they're connected. Unless Maeve and Veronica whisper, I believe someone with his ear to that upstairs tube might could also hear them."

"All this hinges upon Godwin's cooperation," Doyle reminded the group.

"It's not really dangerous if we empty the chambers of Burke's gun," suggested Cooper.

John shook his head gravely. "I wouldn't do that. These are very cautious women. What if she should crack it open and inspect it? However, we should have the time to replace the remainin' unfired shells with ones without powder or primer."

"Yes!" said Tibbles with enthusiasm. He snapped his fingers at Cooper. "Call the Yard! Grenville is in tonight." He looked at Le Brun. "He's our ballistics man. He can make up five eight millimeter dummies in a trice."

"I can improve the authenticity of the scene," Conan Doyle said. "I wrote a play for Sir Henry Irving several years ago."

"I saw it!" piped up Cooper, who had begun toward the study but paused. "*A Story of Waterloo.* Smashing piece of theater."

"Thanks," Doyle accepted with a smile. "At any rate, I visited him and his business manager, Bram Stoker, today."

"The same Stoker who wrote *Dracula*?" asked Cooper.

"Will you place that call, Bob?" Tibbles asked, peevishly.

Cooper nodded but backed slowly into the hallway, still listening to the exchange.

"The same," said Doyle. "I told them how my boy loves to play wounded soldier, so they found me a bottle of stage blood. Very convincing stuff. It's in the boot of my auto."

"I like the idea," John said. "Anythin' that aids the drama. Speakin' of that, we should work on a way to keep this corpse warm for the next two hours. Don't want them touchin' him and realizin' he's too cold for a twelve-thirty gunfight."

Tibbles shook his head gravely. "God help us if you should ever turn to crime, Mr. Le Brun."

THE CAR WILL SMELL like a funeral parlor for a few days, I expect," Maeve Godwin pronounced, as the Godwin automobile rolled smoothly up Park Lane toward the Mayfair district. Two enormous bouquets of fall flowers filled the space between the front and rear seats.

"I don't mind the smell at all," Hugh Comfort remarked from his place behind the steering wheel. "And they're too beautiful to throw away."

"True, true," Maeve said. "I want to thank you for staying up so late for us, Hugh."

"My duty and my pleasure, ma'am. I overheard a few of the people as they were leaving. They sounded as if they had a super time."

"It did go well, if I say so myself."

"And how much money did you clear, if you don't mind my asking?"

"Well, we might have a few unseen expenses, but I can tell you that the costume votes alone garnered one thousand, three hundred forty-seven pounds!"

"Oh, excellent. And so lovely that you won for your Pocahontas costume, Miss Veronica."

"Sacagawea, Hugh," Veronica corrected, in a soft voice. She held her black wig with the feather-festooned braids in her lap, but she still wore her buckskin outfit and tuscan makeup.

"You sound tired, Miss."

"I am."

The chauffeur eased off the accelerator and turned the steering wheel slowly. "We'll be home in another minute."

Veronica looked at her mother, who also remained in costume. Maeve returned her daughter's apprehensive look with a calm stare and an affirming pat on her hand.

The fog had thickened somewhat, although it still hung low to the ground. The blackness of the night, the silence of the hour, and the lack of any movement but theirs made the city seem surreal.

"Here we are," Hugh announced, pulling into Green Street, "safe and sound. Another ten minutes and you'll be warm in your beds."

The car made a wide swing to negotiate the turn into the Godwin's narrow driveway. The house's foyer light was on, faintly illuminating the living room. The upstairs was black as pitch.

The chauffeur brought the car to a halt five feet in front of the closed stable doors. He left the motor running, set the brake, and, for a man of his age, hopped lightly from his seat and opened Maeve's door with a flourish.

"The flowers and money must be carried in immediately," Maeve ordered. "The rest you can take care of tomorrow."

"Right, ma'am."

Maeve got slowly out of the vehicle. Comfort waited in place to offer Veronica his hand. Both women had their coats draped over their costumes.

"I'll just be a moment," Hugh promised, striding forward to open the stable doors.

Maeve led the way to the house's rear entrance. Several paces from the steps she took a hitch in her stride. She reached out to stop Veronica.

"Something's wrong. Look at the door."

"What about it?"

"It's not broken. Could that imbecile have forgotten?"

"Perhaps he was so upset after—"

"No time for speculation," Maeve cut in. "Let's see."

The women moved swiftly up the steps. Maeve already had her key out. Before pushing it into the lock, she tried the doorknob and found the door open. She shot her daughter a fierce-eyed look.

"Be on your guard, girl. Take your lead from me."

Maeve moved through the pantry into the kitchen. She gasped as she found Timothy Burke lying on the floor. He lay face down, head to the back of the house, very close to one of the cabinets. Blood spread in irregular pools to his left and right and between his legs. The Lebel revolver was clutched in his right hand. A few feet away lay the khaki duffel bag, bulky with its swag.

"Mother of God," Maeve exhaled.

"Tim!" Veronica exclaimed, from behind her. Her coat slipped from her shoulders to the floor.

Maeve whirled and thrust her open hand against her daughter's mouth. She took a few more steps and looked down the hallway. What she saw made her smile grimly.

Veronica had knelt by the body, put her hand to the head, and knew the truth by the coolness of the flesh. "He's dead. Can we let Hugh in?" she asked, in a whisper.

"We must," Maeve hissed back. "Trent's lying in the foyer. Stand up and wait beside me."

Hugh Comfort's feet sounded on the back steps. He pushed back the door with his shoulder and set a bouquet and the carpetbag filled with pound notes on the floor.

"Hugh," Maeve exclaimed in a loud but breathy voice, "there's a man dead in our kitchen!"

"What?"

"Look for yourself. He's been shot. But by whom?" Maeve circled the body as she spoke. Then she half-turned and looked over her shoulder down the hallway. "Oh, my God!" she wailed. "There's Trent!" She threw herself headlong down the hallway and into the foyer, finally kneeling beside her husband. He, too, lay face down. He still wore his long, black frock coat. His stovepipe hat had rolled off into the living room. An Abraham Lincoln beard hung off one ear. Blood was under his neck and on his right hand. A foot from the bloody hand lay a single-shot Smith and Wesson, Model 1891, its long silver body glistening in the foyer light, its carved bone grip covered with blood.

"Trent!" Maeve called to the unmoving man.

Hugh strode into the foyer. "Go sit on the step there, ma'am," he directed in a manly tone. "I'll tend to him." He forcibly lifted the woman and gently deposited her. Then he knelt by his employer and felt his neck for a pulse.

"Grace of God! He's still alive," Hugh announced. "He has a good pulse."

"Don't move him!" Maeve said.

"I'll call for an ambulance," Veronica said, from the hallway.

Maeve ran the back of her hand across her mouth. Her eyes darted back and forth in thought. "Yes. Right."

"Hadn't I better turn him over, to see if we can stop the bleeding?" Hugh asked Maeve.

"No! You might cause more damage. He's managed to stay alive for more than an hour in that position. Leave him."

"Perhaps you're right," Comfort granted.

Veronica appeared from the study doorway. "The telephone wire's disconnected!"

"Oh, how horrible!" Maeve wailed. "Hugh . . . there's a police phone box just at the corner of the next street, isn't there?" She leapt up and crossed to the front door.

"Yes, ma'am."

"Don't bother with the car. Run like the wind and summon them and the ambulance together." Maeve threw open the door, let the chauffeur pass through, and closed it again. She put her back against the door. Her nostrils flared as she drew in a big breath. Holding the breath, her eyes grew extraordinarily wide. Then they darted left, right, and up the stairs.

"Oh, my poor Trent!" she said, crossing to the still form of her husband and kneeling. "Please don't die." As she spoke, one hand patted his back lightly; the other went to the floor, as if to steady her. Two of her fingers touched blood. She stood.

"Veronica!"

"Yes, Mother?"

Maeve's sharp eyes swept the living room as she began to move. They fixed directly on the mantlepiece. "Are you sure we can't reconnect the telephone?"

"I don't think so."

"Show me!"

"Yes, ma'am."

Maeve herded her daughter into the study. As she did, she put her forefinger into her mouth and tasted the blood. The moment she had, she pushed Veronica against the wall, leaned in, and whispered, "We're in great danger. Everything's gone wrong, and the police are inside this house. Steal very quietly into the pantry. The cellar door may be open a crack. Whether it is or not, grab the doorknob when I cry out and be ready to push anyone behind it down the stairs."

"Should I get Tim's gun?"

"It won't be worth a thing. But do grab the bag next to him. And mind you treat it gently. My vases are in there. And get the bag with the charity money as well. Go now!"

As the women exited the study, Maeve said loudly, "Hugh was probably right about treating him. Go into the pantry and fetch me some towels!"

Maeve went back to Trent's prone form. "Don't die, my love," she said, gently, as she reached into the umbrella stand. The moment she had the makeshift weapon in her grip, she twisted like a cobra, grabbed the foyer closet doorknob with her free hand, threw the door fully open, and stabbed the metal tip of the umbrella directly into Bob Cooper's groin.

The surprised inspector groaned in agony from the attack. As he doubled over, Maeve struck again. This time her attack was leveled at his right hand. She smashed the end of the umbrella into it, causing him to drop the revolver he held. With her free hand, she sent her best uppercut into Cooper's eye, bringing him erect once more. She dropped the umbrella and snatched up the fallen gun.

"Now!" Maeve screamed, as she grabbed Cooper by his ear. When she came even with Trent, who had risen on one elbow to view the commotion, she delivered a sharp kick to his ribs.

"Don't rise on my account," she growled. Without looking back to assess her last attack, Maeve marched the bent-double Cooper across the foyer and down the hallway. To further cow him, she pushed the barrel of his own revolver against his temple.

Maeve heard the slamming of the cellar door and the resounding clatter and outcry of a man tumbling down the stairs as she moved along the back end of the hallway. She also heard heavy footsteps descending from the second story.

"Move!" Maeve screamed, yanking Cooper through the kitchen and then the pantry. The back door lay open. The spare car key was missing from its hook. Veronica had already run outside. She pushed Cooper ahead of her into the night. "If you slow me down, I'll shoot you dead," she told him.

SINCE THE GODWINS had given up their horses, the part of their stable unnecessary for the automobile had become a handy storage area. A file cabinet, Trent's favorite easy chair before his second marriage, the summer lawn furniture, sporting equipment, and half a dozen large boxes had been deposited there. John had dusted off the easy chair and put himself on it. He had also wrapped himself within a horse blanket he had found while he waited for the arrival of Maeve and Veronica. Two steps from his place lay the stable's side door.

John had been assigned the job with the least likely results but also the second highest level of safety. He had been positioned in the stable in the remote likelihood that Maeve and Veronica might be left in it alone and share words that would prove their guilt. Only Conan Doyle was farther removed from the action, hunkered down in his car on Green Street. His task would be to follow the women if one or both should happen to escape the house.

As many times as he had reviewed the trap he had devised, John set his mind to work picking it apart once more. Just as the meticulous Godwin women had erred in letting a new ice pick, tarpaulin, and horse trough be used in the old warehouse, John knew that he was fallible. Probably Timothy Burke had purchased the items just before or after Nahum Attwater was killed. Purchase in Brighton made sense, since the transportation of old materials from London would have been a great nuisance. Further, Burke might have planned to dispose of the items Sunday afternoon except that Trent had eluded death the previous night. Therefore, Burke had to hotfoot back to London to try to shoot him through his front window. Instead of the original plan, he had dispersed the pick, tarp, and trough inside the warehouse and hoped no one would associate them. But for the help of fate, John might never have solved the case. So it could be tonight with one slip warning the cunning Irishwomen; John had to rely once again on men who had not been trained by him, who did not think as he did, and whom he could not command. Three of them were inside the house now, doing who knew what to alert the Godwin women.

Lemme think. What have I missed? Le Brun asked himself over and over. He approached the puzzle from the angle of man, of room, of what would be called in a theatrical play a prop. If there was something, it had eluded him. He briefly switched on Conan Doyle's electric torch lamp and examined his watch. The time was 2:38.

John turned off the light and wrapped himself again in the old horse blanket. He covered himself with it for extra warmth, protection against his head cold becoming worse. *I wonder what my suit will smell like when my nose works again,* he thought. His head jerked up. He threw off the blanket and pushed out of the chair.

The sound of an automobile engine came through the stable doors. Growling at the bad timing, John went around the stuffed chair and crouched down. Half a minute later, the stable doors opened. Twenty seconds after that, the large car eased in. When the engine died, he heard Hugh Comfort exiting the driver's seat and opening one of the rear doors. This door he left open when he quit the stable.

John was certain that Comfort would not return soon. Faintly, he heard the outcry of Maeve Godwin and her calling of Trent's name. He came forward, to the edge of the stable door nearest the house's back door. The fog was thin enough to view the house fairly clearly, but he had no hope of seeing down the driveway as far as the street. At best, he might hear the chauffeur's footsteps as he ran for help. He waited and waited. He told himself the plan would work. The one detail he had missed because of his nose would not matter. Any moment now, Bob Cooper or John Tibbles would appear at the back door and call for him to come inside. But it did not happen.

The first noise John heard from the house was the slamming of a door. Then he heard footsteps clicking down the back steps and over the lawn's stepping-stones at high speed. Veronica ran past him into the stable, unaware of his presence. She threw open the driver's door and leaned in, carefully placing the duffel bag and the carpetbag on the front passenger's seat.

John drew the derringer from his pocket and silently advanced on the young woman. When he was three steps distant, she whirled around with the engine crank handle in her hand. Her expression proved that she had not heard him approach, but by dumb luck her position was perfect for striking John in his right hand. He winced from the pain and dropped the gun. Before she could bring her arm back, he hurled himself upon her, driving her into the open door and pinioning her arms to her sides with a great bear hug.

"Let her go!" Maeve called from the stable entrance.

John turned his head. The woman pointed a police service revolver at him. She had a much-distressed Inspector Cooper in an armlock with her other hand.

Cooper used Maeve's divided attention to move on the offense. He twisted his right arm backward and up, causing her to lose her balance. As she lost the lock, he reached around for her right wrist.

Deftly, Maeve raised her gun arm out of the detective's grasp, continued the counterclockwise circle, and struck him a good blow under his left ear. He staggered backward and fell clumsily on his bottom.

Maeve reaimed the revolver at Le Brun's head and took two more steps toward him. "I said 'Let her go,'" she said in a businesslike tone.

John released his hold and took several steps backward.

Maeve tossed to Veronica Cooper's handcuffs. "I was going to take the inspector hostage, but I think an American visitor would be a much better choice," she declared, loudly enough so Cooper could hear. "What horrible publicity for the Yard if a tourist helping them were killed because they wouldn't let us go. Secure his hands behind his back."

John assessed his chances of pulling Veronica in as a shield, then darting out the stable's side door. He decided he would be killed if Maeve were a truly good shot and ruthless enough to endanger her daughter. If he had a little luck, he'd only be wounded. If he had great luck, he'd make it out the stable's side door without a scratch. But then Maeve would simply recapture Bob Cooper. He allowed himself to be cuffed.

"Push him in the back of the car!" Maeve commanded.

Veronica obeyed with vigor. Not for nothing did she have height and an athletic build. John found himself sprawling atop several boxes and an ax. His feet were kicked into the car and his door slammed shut.

"Pick up his gun, Veronica! Start the car!" Maeve shouted into the stable. "Stand up, Inspector!" she shouted into the night.

John heard Veronica fit the key into the ignition and turn it. A few moments later, he heard her cranking the flywheel. The engine sputtered to life and caught. Outside, Maeve was saying something else to Cooper, but he could no longer make out the words.

Veronica jumped into the driver's seat and threw the car into reverse. She backed it out of the stable and steered right, so that it drove onto the lawn. Then she put the car into first and got its nose pointed down the driveway. While she was negotiating the turn, John rolled over and wriggled up onto the backseat.

Maeve's back appeared through the left window. She was retreating slowly toward the car, pulling Cooper along with her. She had his left arm again pinned high against his back and pressed his revolver to his right ear.

John watched Veronica lean across the car and open the front passenger door. She transferred the duffel bag and carpetbag to the floor just behind. Maeve eased herself onto the seat.

"When I say so, you drive out of here fast," Maeve directed. "Now!"

She shoved Cooper roughly forward and delivered a kick to his posterior, sending him sprawling onto the lawn. Deftly, she pivoted into the car and slammed her door. Veronica already had her foot on the accelerator, so that the door narrowly missed the side of the house in closing.

Maeve stuck the revolver out her window and steadied her right arm by grabbing it at the wrist with her left hand. Just as the car cleared the house, a shot rang out from the pavement. The bullet flew through the open front passenger compartment, just in front of the women's noses, and hummed down the street. Maeve fired once in return.

"That made him drop!" Maeve crowed.

During the exchange, John had turned his head and watched out the rear window. He saw Bob Cooper rounding the corner of the house in a game but slow hobble.

The car bounced onto Green Street and veered sharply right, coming up momentarily on its two left tires.

"Damnit, Veronica!" yelled Maeve. "I said 'fast,' not insane. You'll kill us before they do."

"Sorry," Veronica said. "I've never driven quickly."

John kept his attention riveted on the sights beyond the rear window. The man who had fired from the pavement was John Tibbles. He had leapt up and darted into the street and was wildly gesturing to Conan Doyle's car, which had come to life and was moving down Green Street in the same direction as the Godwin car. It slowed just enough as it came even with Tibbles that he could run around to its left side and hop onto its running board. A moment later, the policeman had the door open and was slipping inside.

"Turn on your headlamps, girl!" Maeve commanded. "Oh, I'll do it."

"Which way?" Veronica asked, as they came to the end of the block.

"Right, dolt! Do you want to drive us into the middle of London?"

Maeve turned and stared at John. She was about to say something, when her attention was diverted to the rear window. John looked behind and saw what she saw: Conan Doyle had also turned on his headlights and was bearing down on the Godwin vehicle with speed.

"They're chasing us in an automobile," Maeve reported. "Get out onto Oxford Street. Then look for the first opportunity to cut across the road and head north."

"You'll have plenty of chance, Veronica," John commented, doing his best to sound relaxed. "It's three o'clock in the mornin'. Only drunks, robbers, and whores are out. Present company excluded."

"And all the lorries, vans, and wagons that supply the city," Maeve said. "Be mindful, girl." She stared at Le Brun with burning eyes. He noted that her real hair was covered by a blond wig with the hair parted in the middle. She wore a high-collared lace blouse. Between the two, she was virtually the double of a famous photograph of the good-looking American Lizzie Borden, who many believed had used an ax to give *"her father forty whacks/ and when she saw what she had done/she gave her mother forty-one."* Now John knew the reason for the long-handled ax lying on the floor in front of him.

"Just think," John said to Maeve, returning her wild look with his most courageous smile. "Next year at the Mayfair Mothers for Cleanliness Charity Ball, the theme can be famous English murderers, and somebody can dress up as you."

"Where's his gun?" Maeve asked.

"Right here," said Veronica, patting the derringer that had rested in her lap. "You're not going to shoot him, are you?"

"No, your mother won't shoot me," John assured her and Maeve together. "First, because there's no need. Second, because the bullet might go through to the upholstery. Your bank accounts will surely be closed tomorrow. You need every shillin' you can lay your hands on. This car is very handsome. It will fetch a princely sum . . . provided it's not filled with bullet holes and blood."

"He's right. I'm turning," Veronica warned. The car executed a smart left onto Marylebone High Street, with only the faintest noise of tire squeal.

"What gave us away?" Maeve asked John.

"The ice pick, tarpaulin, and water trough in the warehouse."

Maeve turned on Veronica with furious energy. "Didn't you tell him to dispose of them?"

"Of course I did."

Maeve redirected her wrath at John. "Were they in a pile?"

"Oh, no. They were carefully scattered around the back of the warehouse. They just stood out. I asked myself why the seller wouldn't take such good hardware with him, and my answer was: He would."

"*You* found them?"

"That's right."

"And Trent play-acted with us since Monday afternoon?" Maeve asked.

"Why would you think that?"

"Because . . ." Maeve's eyebrows knit in confusion. "You found the items and brought them to Inspector Tibbles. Trent was right there. You or Tibbles must have told him to keep quiet about them."

In spite of his disgust over the woman's amorality and ruthlessness, John still respected her criminal mind. He could not prevent himself from earning her mutual respect for his detective's mind.

"You're mistaken. Tibbles was perfectly happy to accept the picture presented to him. He and your husband left the warehouse convinced that Nahum Attwater had killed everyone in the club gamin' room, had shot at Trent, and had committed suicide on Sunday night. The bottom third of that apology to you for missin' one of your soirees just didn't look right to me."

"You see?" Veronica said. "I *told* you it was too much."

"And how else would Tibbles have decided he committed suicide so quickly?" Maeve shot back. "Could I know that Trent would wake up Sunday night and remember the tontine? That's what ultimately fostered your trip the next morning to Brighton, wasn't it?" she asked John.

"It was."

She made a thankful gesture to John for supporting her. "We had assumed that, being the money-grubber Nahum was, he'd have a crew ready to start working on the warehouse Monday morning and that they'd discover the body. We never intended that *you* would go down there."

"Mother was nervous all day Monday, until Trent came home with the news that Mr. Attwater's suicide had been accepted," Veronica volunteered.

A large pothole loomed in the road ahead. Veronica oversteered to avoid it and began fishtailing back and forth in wild attempts to wrestle the machine back under control.

"Watch the road!" Maeve yelled.

"Easy for you to say; it's covered with fog!" Veronica yelled back.

John had more than once wondered if he would have the courage to affect gallows humor if he were ever in such a situation as this. Now he knew. Fresh from that triumph, he encouraged the exchange of information. He was hatching a plan to save his life and perhaps theirs. After cheating Maeve out of a fortune and sending her on the run, he was sure she would put a bullet into his head in retribution. Before that, however, Veronica's driving was likely to kill them all if the chase went on much longer. Something had to be done before either; something he could do with his hands secured behind his back.

"This is all my fault," he apologized, adding a theatrical sigh. "I shoulda warned y'all I'm the worst house guest."

With the car resettled on all four wheels, Maeve turned again. "And, bad penny that you are, you turned up at our house again tonight. Since the detectives allowed you on our property, I'm assuming you were the one who came up with the trap."

"*C'est moi.* Which you so masterfully wriggled out of," he complimented. "Was it Cooper's cherry tobacco that tipped you off?"

Maeve narrowed her eyes. "If you must know, the first thing was the back door. It was supposed to be chewed up as if it had been broken in."

John winced. "But we didn't find a crowbar or any such tool."

Maeve stared past John through the rear window. "He's still with us. Continue north. Go around Regent's Park, and if you lose him by Prince Albert Road, turn east." She looked again at John. "The imbecile may have forgotten it. Then it was indeed the cherry tobacco and the slightly open closet door."

"I have a head cold," John excused himself. "Otherwise, I'd have caught it."

Maeve smiled wickedly and pointed the revolver between his eyes. "I can always open your sinuses for you."

"I can't see," Veronica said. "Is he still behind us?"

"Closer than ever. You must make some unexpected turns."

"And risk getting us in a blind alley?" Veronica countered. "I don't know this part of London."

"I don't think you'll lose him anyway," John said. "That's Arthur Conan Doyle behind the wheel. He drove me to and from his home. His skill with an automobile is somethin' indescribable."

"Don't let him demoralize you, Veronica," Maeve advised.

"What you don't know is that you two don't need to be fleein'," John said in a loud and clear voice. He was ready to deploy his major pieces in a life-or-death chess game.

"Oh, right!" Maeve said. "We should just let them hang us."

"I am opposed to capital punishment myself," John said, truthfully. "As a law officer of the State of Georgia, I made it my business to keep up on the capital punishment practices of civilized countries. England has hanged only one woman in the past five years."

"I'll bet she didn't kill five men," Veronica chimed in.

"She also didn't have a ruthless, blackmailin' Irishman pushin' her until she became desperate."

"What's that?" Maeve asked. Before John could reply, her attention redirected past him. "Drive faster, girl!" she ordered. "They're nearly upon us!"

John struggled around and saw that Conan Doyle had brought his car within only three cars lengths. John Tibbles was leaning out of the vehicle, sighting his revolver.

Maeve flung the top half of her body out of the car and pointed her weapon.

"Don't do that!" John yelled.

Maeve ignored him and squeezed the trigger. Doyle's Wolseley veered hard to the right, out of her line of sight.

"If you hit either of them, you'll end a good chance of savin' yourselves!" John exclaimed.

The report of Tibbles's gun sounded through the fog. A bullet ricocheted off the Godwin's rear bumper with the next report.

"But he's shooting at us!" Maeve cried out in great indignation. "Doesn't he care if he hits you?"

"He's probably aimin' for your tires," John said.

"Hand me that toy gun, and then let me know when you're turning left," Maeve told Veronica. She took the derringer and cocked it. "Two can play at this," she muttered. "I'll aim low and hit his radiator or his tires."

"Get ahead of him, Miss Veronica," John said with urgency. "I need time to talk with you."

"Oh, my God!" Veronica cried out. "Hold on!"

A lumbering, horse-drawn wagon was entering the intersection just ahead of them. John knew that Veronica would never be able to stop in time. He expected the shriek of the brakes and the roar of impact, but instead she merely took her foot off the accelerator and steered up a break in the pavement, hurtled between a telephone pole and the corner building, and bounced back down into the street.

Behind them, the shrill complaint of Conan Doyle's tires filled the night.

"How's that for getting ahead?" Veronica asked proudly.

"It'll do," John replied, hoping he would not have a heart attack. "I need to tell you both that I know Timothy Burke was blackmailin' you."

Maeve stared at him for a second. "How?"

"Because this whole affair is really about killin' M.P.s. He knew about your first husband and Dublin. I don't know how *he* found out, but I came across your family Bible when I stayed in your guest room. You were Catholic, not Episcopalian. You lived in Dublin and were the wife and daughter of Graeme Meany."

"You are amazing, Mr. Le Brun," Maeve said, for the first time lowering the revolver onto the back of her seat.

"Yes, I am. He knew that members of the Dublin police suspected you killed your husband, and he threatened to ruin you in London society and Trent's business by association with you."

"Go on."

"Now, I'm guessin' here, but I believe Mr. Meany did unspeakable things to Veronica. That's why she has an unnatural attraction for older men. She makes no secret of it . . . do you, Miss Veronica?"

"No, I don't."

"This would further suggest a reason for your wantin' your husband dead," John said, feeling his way through the half-truths and half-fictions with increasing assurance. "I don't think anyone will ever be able to tell what happened to Mr. Meany. Any judgment is up to God now. But the point is that accusation and exposure of the two of you as Catholic and lyin' about your backgrounds was enough to ruin you and Trent."

"Very perceptive, Mr. Le Brun," Maeve said.

"We found several fanatical tracts in Mr. Burke's flat. I'm convinced, in time, that some good, old-fashioned legwork around London will show him to be a violent radical on behalf of Irish separatism. He met Veronica as a ridin' instructor. I'm sure he was very curious how two women with Irish backgrounds got so high up in British society. He was a handsome man and, I understand, had kissed the Blarney Stone." John looked out the back window. As they had motored away from the Thames and to higher ground, the fog had thinned until it was almost nonexistent. John could see a pair of headlamps turning the corner Veronica had so boldly negotiated, a good quarter of a mile behind them. He would have time to complete his gambit before Doyle and Tibbles threatened the women again.

"Burke learned all he could from a smitten Miss Veronica. Then he set about diggin' up the dirt. Once he had it, he knew he could blackmail you. You told him that Trent is a member of the Sceptred Isle Club, didn't you, Miss Veronica?"

"Yes, John. I did."

"And, bein' a fanatic, he knew the political tendencies of the membership. It wouldn't take him long to find out that several members were Tory M.P.s. Did you tell him that two of these M.P.s played cards every Saturday night with Trent, Miss?"

"No," Maeve broke in with energy. "He already knew it."

John smiled. "Hmmph! So, he devises a plan to kill them, in order to affect the outcome of the next election and possibly allow Home Rule to pass. He wants to conceal this, however, so he murders them among several other men, in a gamblin' room of all places, so no one will suspect his real motive. But one of these men is Trent. He tells you that your choice is your ruin and your husband's, or else you can allow Trent to be sacrificed. Burke will pull the trigger; Maeve is needed only to get the butler to open the door. Burke also killed Attwater down in Brighton. Since Maeve was with her lady friends at the Trafalgar Day celebration, I know that he used Veronica as the bait to get Mr. Attwater to take her into his warehouse. As soon as they were inside, Burke appeared from around the corner, ran in, and shot him dead. I knew all along that you two had a hand in the details of the scheme. You've been sayin' so yourself the past few minutes. But I also know that once you allowed yourselves to be blackmailed, you had to be sure the scheme came off. Repulsed as you were, you created the beautiful details, includin' the money under the birdbath. Otherwise, you knew you'd be sucked down with Burke. He had nothin' more than an evil will and low cunnin'. He was, after all, only a ridin' instructor."

"You are astounding," Maeve said.

"I'm even more astoundin' than you think," John went on. "Some people will say that you were the brains behind this, Mrs. Godwin, because a follow-up attempt was made on Trent's life. But I *know* that was Burke. Miss Veronica was wearin' a dress she could hardly move in that night. She could not have fled down the street. But Burke was drivin' that carriage you arrived in . . . wasn't he?"

"Yes, he was."

"You held the horse's reins while he calmly walked up to your front window and tried to assassinate your stepfather."

"Yes, she did," Maeve interjected.

"And tonight, he insisted on finally killin' Trent. Why? Because he was greedy. He knew he had Veronica's love and both your fear. He wanted you two to inherit Trent's money and then marry Veronica and live in the lap of luxury. Now, he should have waited to kill Trent, run him over with a carriage a couple months from now, but he wouldn't wait. Therefore, I suspected he knew about the tontine money and Trent's pledge to give it away."

"He did, through his connection inside the Sceptred Isle Club," Maeve replied. "The same one who told him about the M.P.s in the Saturday night card group."

"And who is that?"

"He never told us."

"I see. Well, that's why he made the original crime so complicated: so you two would inherit a third of the pot. Then, by sheer luck, Trent ends up the last survivor. *Now* the pot is up to thirty-five thousand pounds. He cannot let it go. This is what finally convinced me that Burke was behind it. I *know* you and Veronica would be too smart to go after that money if you were the truly guilty ones. You'd have to be desperate or crazy to go after more money . . . knowin' you'd be suspected . . . when you stand to inherit, what, one hundred thousand pounds or more?"

"He's catching up again," Veronica reported, looking into the mirror outside her door.

"But after you killed Timothy—" Maeve began.

"We had to. He shot at the police like a mad dog. Wounded one of 'em," John broke in.

"But then you set a trap for us," Maeve finished.

John shrugged. "Chief Inspector Tibbles insisted on it. I haven't been able to convince him Burke was the mastermind and you two his pawns. He demanded to create what you saw and badgered Trent into it to prove me wrong. I helped him make it as convincin' as possible just to show him absolutely that you two are innocent."

"He will be proven wrong," Maeve said with force. "We tried to save Trent. The phone line was pulled out. We immediately sent our chauffeur for the police and the ambulance. I just panicked when I smelled the tobacco and knew a man was inside the closet. I knew, with Tim dead and unable to confess, that we would hang for his crimes." She shrugged sheepishly. "I did kick Trent on the way out, but only because he was low enough to participate in a scheme to prove his own wife's guilt."

"You won't hang," John assured her.

"You're damned right we won't," Veronica said, ramming her foot all the way to the floor and coaxing the last bit of speed from the car. "We won't be caught. John doesn't know what he's talking about; he's a foreigner. If a chief inspector of the Yard is out to hang us, he'll have his way. We have money and the car to sell, Mother."

"Money?" Maeve said. She laughed. "We have one thousand three hundred forty-seven pounds and Trent's coin collection. If you call that money, you'd better keep your outfit and plan to live in a teepee."

Veronica glanced to her right. John followed her line of vision. The road they were on paralleled a set of train tracks. An overburdened engine was pulling ten freight cars along in the same direction they were fleeing, slightly behind them.

"We can make a new start," Veronica responded. "When we tell the right people that we killed two Tory M.P.s—"

"*Timothy Burke* killed two Tory M.P.s!" Maeve insisted in a shrill voice. "Stop the car!"

Veronica's jaw was rigidly set. She glanced at the train. "We'll buy forged papers and move to America or Australia."

Maeve looked ahead and gasped. John sat up and saw what she saw. The road crossed the track just ahead. A guard had lowered crossing gates on either side of the tracks and was gesturing wildly for Veronica to stop. Veronica kept her foot mashed against the accelerator.

"Stop the car!" Maeve shouted. When Veronica persisted, she reached to the ignition and turned the key.

The engine died.

"My God!" Veronica wailed. She stomped on the brake, but the momentum of the automobile was too great. With tires howling, it burst through the first crossing gate, bumped over the tracks, and hit the second gate. The far barricade held. The wood's slight elasticity allowed it to bow outward and then snap back, trapping the car on the tracks.

The locomotive's steam whistle shrilled out an alarm. The great mass of fire, water, and metal was hurtling forward less than five hundred feet from the car.

"Get the bags!" Maeve screamed as she threw open her door and swung out. When she turned, she saw that Veronica had already left the driver's seat. Both her daughter's hands were empty. Maeve glanced beyond to the oncoming train. It had locked its brakes so that every wheel was throwing off a miniature fireworks display. In spite of the brakes and the vented steam pouring from every available valve, it was obvious that the locomotive could not stop in time. She threw open the left rear door. John, who had put himself tightly against it, tumbled out. Maeve gave one last look at the bags, then bent and helped her enemy to his feet. Together, they fled the tracks.

Three seconds later, the locomotive hit the car at a marathon runner's pace. For a moment, it looked as if its abbreviated cow-catcher would merely brush the machine out of its way. Then the car's running board caught, and the machine dipped and overturned. It slid noisily along the rails for a few moments on its side, and then the car split in two. The backside disappeared from their view, but the front bounced up and down as it detached from the front of the locomotive. Its vital fluids sprayed the monstrous machine, the liquids shimmering in the light of a thousand sparks.

Then the petrol caught fire. A whoosh of flame was swift-followed by a flowering explosion.

Veronica shielded her eyes.

Maeve continued to stare. “My vases!” she wailed.

Above the conflagration, pound notes fluttered gracefully in the air. The locomotive continued on, drawing its freight cars from the fire that threatened their wooden exteriors.

Maeve slapped her daughter hard across the face. “Why didn’t you steer left?”

Veronica took a step backward and clutched her cheek. “I had enough power to crash through both gates until you turned off the motor! Why would you want the car to stop? Don’t you realize that John was lying to us?”

Le Brun stood in the roadway, gulping air.

“Of course I realize,” said Maeve. “But he also lied for us. At least for you.”

John started walking toward the tail end of the train, so he wouldn’t have to look at the women. A few seconds later, Tibbles and Doyle appeared, their guns drawn. Doyle moved forward cautiously, to take his long-desired gawk at the storied Veronica Godwin.

“They could have escaped us,” Tibbles said to Le Brun. “What happened?”

“They had a fallin’ out,” John said. “I told them a story, which Maeve believed could save us all.”

“What story?” Tibbles asked.

“I’ll explain it to you on the way back. You’ll be able to tear it apart in court, unless your lawyers are stupid. However, I do want you to know that one thing is true: Maeve didn’t have to pull me out of that car, but she did.”

“Now *this*,” Doyle proclaimed, tearing his eyes from Veronica and looking around the smoking landscape, “is what I call an ending.”

Standing not ten feet from him and staring at the same scene, John Le Brun said nothing. Half his world had gone suddenly and permanently dark.

TWELVE

Thursday, April 20, 1906

JOHN LE BRUN SAT in a wicker rocking chair under the broad veranda of Brunswick's Oglethorpe Hotel. Next to him on a table sat an iced tea with a sprig of mint in it. The chair had not been rocked, the tea not sampled. Le Brun sat like a statue, taking in the world in front of the hotel. His right eye saw nothing, but from nearly sixty years of practice it still moved in tandem with the other. Few town folk knew about his affliction, and that was how he wanted it.

Brunswick, Georgia, was quiet and would grow quieter now that the high vacation season was coming to a close. John might not find a new chess opponent for months. That truth was enough to turn him peevish without all the other unhappy thoughts he had let take him captive.

Into John's view came Warfield Tidewell, holding a rolled newspaper in his hand. Warfield had been John's chief deputy since early in 1899 and had been warmly recommended by the ex-sheriff for his position when he retired. Tidewell was the son of the former town judge, Princeton University educated, a former lawyer, and a conscientious law officer. But when it came to investigations, he was no John Le Brun.

Warfield waved as he strode up the hotel's curving walk. John merely nodded. With an athletic grace, the young, good-looking sheriff took the front steps two at a time. Having registered John's dour greeting, he knew better than to offer his hand. Instead, he pulled another rocking chair close by his old friend and mentor.

"Where were you this past week, John?" he began.

"Up to Atlanta. Took in some big-city entertainment and restocked my library."

"That sounds like time well spent."

Le Brun merely nodded. "Had to do somethin'. Garden's planted. Ever since that budget shortfall, the library's stopped buyin' books. How's Aurelia?"

"Just fine." Warfield had married John's niece.

Warfield unrolled the newspaper. It was the *Brunswick Call.* He flattened it as best he could on the edge of the table and placed it on John's lap.

"Yesterday's paper. You seen it?"

John nodded.

"Did you read the article about the missing women's clothing?" He pointed to the headline that read UNMENTIONABLE CRIMES.

"I did."

Warfield ignored the terse responses and treated John as if the man had not been restless and moody for the past few months. "Since this article came out, two more women dropped into the office, and two others called up to complain."

"That's nineteen in all with ladies' garments plucked out of their backyards."

"Correct."

"So, have you solved it?"

"No. That's why I'm sitting here."

"I'm not sheriff anymore."

"Maybe you should be."

"Nope. I'm retired."

"But your brain's not retired."

"Oh, come on, War," John said. "Stop playin' with me. You know what this is. You just want me to solve it to lift my spirits."

"I swear I don't. I was thinking it was a couple of teenage boys, but . . ."

"Why teenage boys?"

"You know the trouble we have with them . . . even the good ones. They're changin' from children to men, getting large bodies they don't know what to do with. Their hormones are playing havoc with their heads. They look for outlets for all that energy. Couple that with their confusion over having hated females up to that point and now becoming obsessed with them, and they must find some physical expression."

"You took a psychology course up at Princeton, didn't you?"

"You know I did."

"A little knowledge is a dangerous thing."

Warfield swallowed the dry rebuke, as he had a hundred like it over the past seven years. "Well, it can't be another female." His finger swept across the article. "Look who was stolen from: Linda Edwards, Becky Cook, Betsy Kiser, Wendy White. They're all different sizes and shapes. And anyway, a woman from the town wouldn't dare wear another's clothing in public. She'd have her head snatched bald when the dress was recognized."

"True enough."

"Every name is from the white side of town. It can't be any of the black boys. They wouldn't dare roam through white neighborhoods in the daytime."

"Not to mention that this time of year there's plenty of work to keep them busy."

"Anyway, I put Red and Burt out patrolling those areas."

"The first robbery was reported when?" John asked.

"April fourth."

"A Tuesday. Any of these robberies reported on a Friday?"

Warfield was nonplussed by the question. "Uh . . ."

"Check it out. I think you'll find there were none."

"Why?"

John gave his former deputy a stern look. "The thief or thieves were otherwise occupied. What opens up the first Friday of every April and runs every Friday until November?"

Tidewell closed his eyes and squinted in concentration. He could not disappoint his old friend. His eyes snapped open. "The open-air market in Darien!"

"That's right," John said, smiling slightly. "Good secondhand clothes sell well there . . . especially women's clothes. Tomorrow, pull Red and Burt from their stakeouts and have them ride up to Darien with a detailed list of the missin' items. I believe they'll find some of them hangin' on display in one of the stalls."

"Damn, you're good!" said Warfield.

"I might could be wrong."

"And Christmas might come next week, too."

"Why don't you take my drink? You been eyein' it since you set down."

"Believe I will." As Warfield raised the glass, he spotted a familiar figure emerging from a carriage at the side of the hotel. "You may be better at solving crimes, but I'm better at making predictions. I predict that you will be engaging in a spirited game of chess before the afternoon is over."

John turned and saw Geoffrey Moore approaching.

"I'll see that his things are taken care of," Tidewell said, rising with the drink in his hand. "You two must have a great deal to talk about."

"You know, Linda Edwards is about Aurelia's size," John said. "And she buys her undergarments from Charleston. You might see that—"

"You're bad, John." Warfield laughed and walked out to greet Moore.

"Bad," John repeated when he was alone. "That's what I am."

When the Englishman finally ascended the hotel steps and walked up to his old friend, he carried a carpetbag. John rose slowly to greet him, and the two shook hands for longer than usual.

"You look wonderful, John," Moore enthused.

"You look like ten miles of hard road. Iced tea, or somethin' more fortifyin'?"

"Iced tea will do fine." While John snapped his fingers for a waiter and delivered the order, Moore collapsed into the rocking chair the new sheriff had moved.

"This is an unexpected pleasure," said John.

"I really shouldn't stop back in Brunswick after having been here only six months ago, but I was importuned to bring you several personal deliveries."

"I feel like Napoleon in exile," John remarked. "Who is sendin' me things?"

"Your admirers." Geoffrey opened the bag and took out an engraved plaque and read, " 'To the peerless John Le Brun in gratitude for his indefatigable work on behalf of The Sceptred Isle Club. Be it known to all that he has a permanent membership in the same for nonpareil service in preserving its esteemed name. Attested this twenty-third day of January, 1906.' "

"Mr. Roundsville, the club manager, wrote the words," John remarked.

"Dash it all! How did you know that?"

"He has a wonderful control of the language. I miss talkin' with him."

"I'll tell him."

"And tell everyone in the club that it shall have a prominent place of honor in my parlor."

"I also have the princely sum of sixty pounds in my billfold from the club. Payment for services rendered. You left without collecting it."

"I'll dine out for months on that," John said, ignoring Moore's last words.

Next, Moore withdrew a white envelope. As he handed it over, he said, "It's a thank-you note from the Attwater family, along with a cashier's check for one thousand dollars! It's drawn against the First National Bank in New York City."

John lowered his chin and gave Geoffrey a reproachful stare. He took the envelope, examined its seal, held it up to the light, and determined that neither the contents of the note nor the printing on the check could be discerned. "I should never have told you that one can freeze an envelope, break the frozen glue, and reseal it without any telltale marks."

Moore blushed.

John ripped open the envelope, read the note, and examined the check. "I do declare! If I'd have known how lucrative detective work is in London, I'd have moved there when I was thirty."

"There's still time."

"No, thanks. How long will you stay in Brunswick?"

"Two days."

"Good. I'll compose a note of thanks which you can return. I'll seal it with wax."

"I shall be your winged Mercury. A message from Chief Inspector Tibbles: The ice pick, tarpaulin, and horse trough are being displayed in Scotland Yard's Black Museum, with a legend prominently mentioning you. He voiced his deep regret that he did not have the opportunity to thank you as he wanted. In fact, a great many people were crushed that you fled to Brighton after the capture of the Godwin women. You could have been feted for days."

"Which is why I chose to move on," said Le Brun. "It was not a happy conclusion for me."

"Yes, I understand." Moore dug again into his bag and came out with a book. "Finally . . . an autographed copy of *Adventures of Sherlock Holmes.* Sir Arthur said he had promised this to you."

"You might as well tell me if there's an inscription," John said archly.

Moore scowled. "I'll let you read it. I *will* tell you that you now have two town criers expounding on your deeds. I dare say, Arthur Conan Doyle's approbations are much more readily received than mine." He took a fortifying sip of tea. "I have a stack of newspapers in my steamer trunk for your leisurely reading. The trial ended just a few days before I left. Spectacular as it was in England, I don't suppose it made too many headlines over here?"

"No," John said, simply. The truth, however, was that some of the New York newspapers had daily articles on it during its two-week duration and conclusion. John had asked his former collaborator on the solution of the Jekyl Island Club crimes, Joseph Pulitzer, to provide him with copies of the *World, Journal,* and *Herald.* Unasked, Pulitzer had also sent over from Jekyl Island the word-for-word transcripts of the trial, obtained through the *London Times.* Although he was retired, John's cachet had not faded in some circles.

"The most far-reaching result is that it's killed the possibility of a Home Rule vote passing for years to come. Exactly the opposite of what those three scoundrels wanted. Sir Arthur said to tell you the following: 'The Union Jack still flies over all Britannia's empire. And long may it wave, for it's brought civilization to every benighted corner of the globe.'"

"You remind Sir Arthur that the ancient Romans created an empire far greater in its day than England's will ever be. They, too, brought civilization. They taught barbarian armies by example how best to wage war. They created straight, fast highways that allowed those armies to rush right into Rome itself. Tell him that if the English are revolted by the Irish—their racial cousins—how will they feel when London becomes equally crowded with Chinese from Hong Kong, blacks from South Africa, natives from Guiana and Honduras, aborigines from Australia, and Indians? Ask if it isn't their right as British subjects. Ask how you'll hold onto your empire when it learns to copy England's mills and her army's British square. Will you ask all that for me?"

"I don't think so."

"You should never have invited the cat to look at the king."

"The cat made quite an impression. He should come back soon and ask his own questions. Perhaps he'll really meet the king."

John stared into infinity without responding.

Moore coughed uncomfortably. "It's amazing what can be done to your name when you're no longer alive to defend it. Timothy Burke was made out to be the Devil in green, blackmailing women of his own race to help him accomplish his unholy deeds. I know you warned Inspector Tibbles that you had given Maeve a plausible excuse about her part in the crimes. Despite that, His Majesty's best barristers were confounded. No hanging for them. I attended some of the sessions. Maeve was brilliant in her own defense. But Veronica? Exquisite Veronica was something to behold. She's a natural actress, y'know. I knew precisely what they had done and who was to blame, and I found myself dewy-eyed at her performance. She'll be out of prison in ten years with good behavior. She should definitely think of going on the stage when she gets out."

"And how is Trent holdin' up?"

"Remarkably well. You know, we all thought his career would be ruined by the scandal. Nothing could be farther from the truth. One of the newspapers took the angle that Maeve was a seductress and had put Trent in her spell. Then they all picked up the theme. He became a symbol of the fair-minded Englishman being taken advantage of by the ungrateful Irish. He had half a dozen new clients before the trial was over."

"Good for him."

Geoffrey leaned in and lowered his voice, even though no one was remotely within earshot. "And do you want to know the supreme irony of that? He was the one who paid for Maeve and Veronica's defense. Got them the best attorneys money could buy. I'm sure he did it for Veronica, not Maeve."

"I can understand that," John said softly. He would not share with Moore his secret about Trent. An irony far beyond Geoffrey's was that the women who were supposedly blackmailed had, in fact, been the blackmailers all along. His personal irony was that just as he successfully shed himself of ambivalent feelings over Dr. Thomas Saye's escape from Jekyl Island, he had picked up another dilemma. In order to preserve Trent Godwin's good name, he could not let the world know that the man had believed himself a seducer of an underage woman. Yet, the release of that very information would have damned both Maeve and Veronica and vaporized any hope they had of painting themselves as victims. Night after night, John told himself that he had withheld the information for Trent, even as he feared he had done it for Veronica.

"Not to say that he was the only one who helped their case," Moore declared, presenting John with raised eyebrows. "I was there the day they read your affidavit. While every fact about the case was true, the way you worded it allowed the women's lawyers to argue blackmail quite effectively. You did that on purpose, didn't you, John?"

"And that is the real reason you contrived this detour, isn't it, Geoffrey?"

"Well. . . partially."

"In that case, if I deny it, you won't believe it anyway."

"But *do you* deny it?"

"No."

"She really got to you, didn't she?"

John pursed his lips for several seconds before he spoke. "Despite all her sophistication and education, she's very young. She was a saplin' bent by an unrelentin' and evil wind."

"And you would keep the mother from swinging to protect the daughter."

"How many years did Maeve get, and how old is she?"

Geoffrey saw the point and declined to reply. During his silence, John opened Conan Doyle's book. The inscription read:

To John Le Brun—
Sherlock Holmes' American cousin.
With admiration,
Arthur Conan Doyle

John consulted the table of contents, then turned to "A Scandal in Bohemia," the short story Doyle had once cited. He read the first line, which the author had underlined: "To Sherlock Holmes she is always the woman."

"How's his wife?" John asked.

"She's taken a turn for the worst. Won't last the summer."

John sighed.

"What about a game of chess?" Geoffrey asked. "I've learned a new opening that doesn't require a thorough development. Beaten five different players in a row with it."

"Do tell," John said.

An hour later, Geoffrey's impressive string of wins was broken.

ABOUT THE SCEPTRED ISLE CLUB

Due to the needs of the book, the club was fictionalized. However, the information on the other English gentlemen's clubs was as accurate as research could make it. Democratization and changing lifestyles have resulted in the demise of most of the clubs that flourished at the turn of the twentieth century. A number of the great ones live on, however, and most are located on or around St. James and Pall Mall Streets in London.

ABOUT THE AUTHOR

BRENT MONAHAN was born in Fukuoka, Kyushu, Japan, in 1948, as a World War II occupation baby. He received his Bachelor of Arts degree from Rutgers University in music. He received his Doctor of Musical Arts degree from Indiana University, Bloomington. He has performed, stage directed, and taught music and writing professionally. He has written thirteen published novels and a number of short stories. Two of his novels have been made into motion pictures. *The St. Sceptred Isle Club* is the fourth in a series of John Le Brun novels. The series started with *The Jekyl Island Club*, which was first published in hardback in 2000. Brent lives in Yardley, Pennsylvania, with his wife, Bonnie.

CPSIA information can be obtained at www.ICGtesting.com
Printed in the USA
BVOW02s2159250216

438005BV00004B/6/P